CHUNKY
GOES TO CAMP
YAY
HUDI

KATHERINE TEGEN BOOKS
Imprints of HarperCollins Publishers

Dedicated to Pepe and Lonnie

Katherine Tegen Books is an imprint of HarperCollins Publishers.
HarperAlley is an imprint of HarperCollins Publishers.

Chunky Goes to Camp
Copyright © 2022 by SuperMercado Comics, Inc.
All rights reserved. Manufactured in Italy.
No part of this book may be used or reproduced in any manner
whatsoever without written permission except in the case of brief
quotations embodied in critical articles and reviews. For information
address HarperCollins Children's Books, a division of HarperCollins
Publishers, 195 Broadway, New York, NY 10007.
www.harperalley.com

Library of Congress Control Number: 2021953134
ISBN 978-0-06-297282-8 – ISBN 978-0-06-297281-1 (pbk.)

The artist used Adobe Photoshop to create the digital illustrations
for this book.
Typography by Yehudi Mercado and Laura Mock
22 23 24 25 26   RTLO   10 9 8 7 6 5 4 3 2 1
❖
First Edition

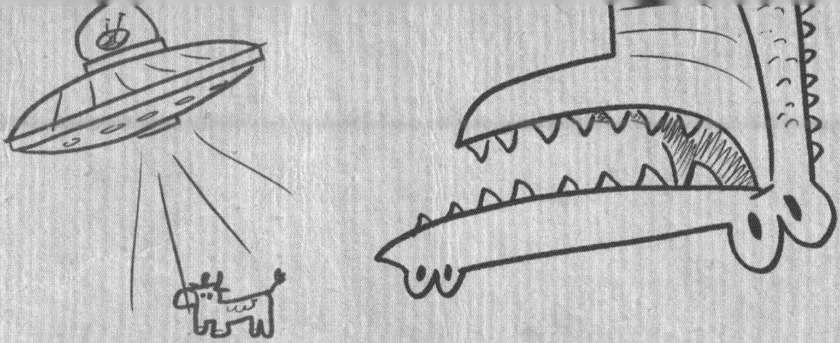

CHAPTER ONE

DETENTION

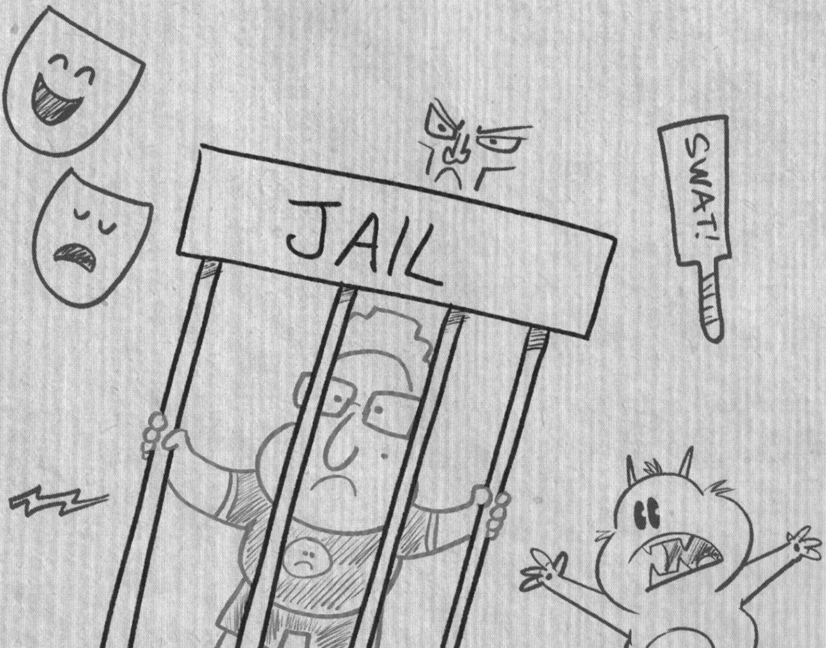
JAIL
SWAT!

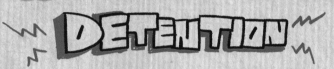

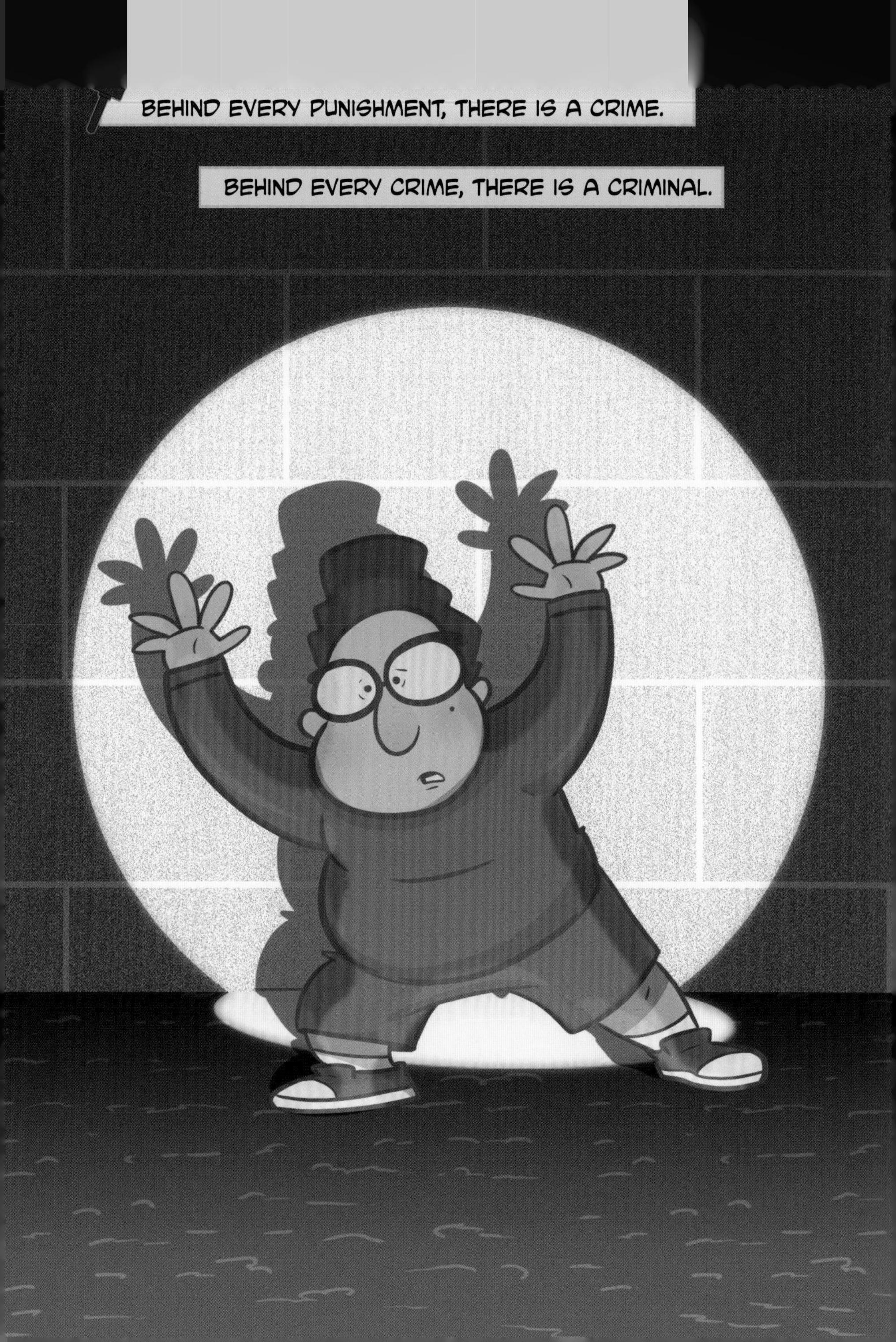
BEHIND EVERY PUNISHMENT, THERE IS A CRIME.
BEHIND EVERY CRIME, THERE IS A CRIMINAL.

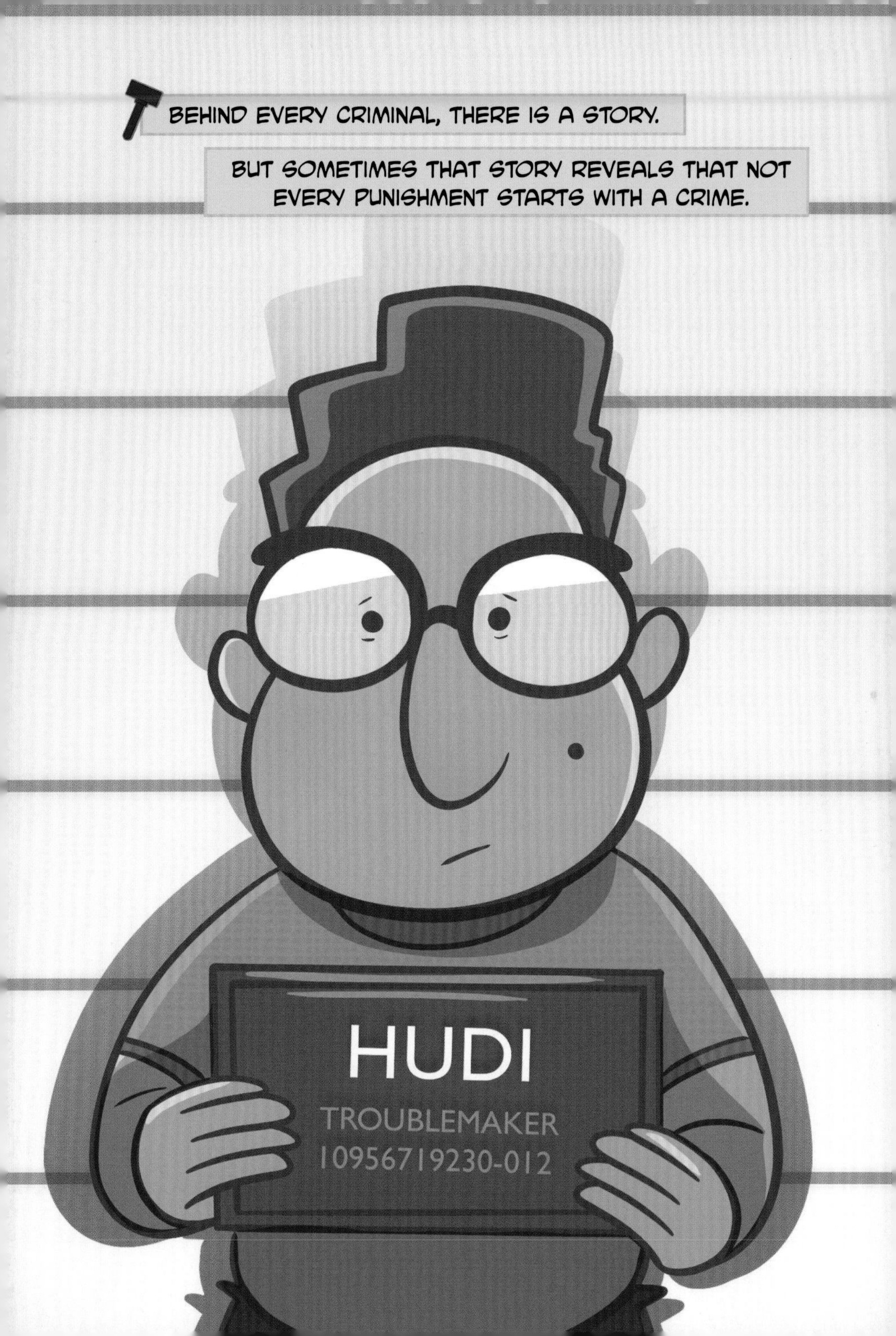
BEHIND EVERY CRIMINAL, THERE IS A STORY.
BUT SOMETIMES THAT STORY REVEALS THAT NOT EVERY PUNISHMENT STARTS WITH A CRIME.
HUDI
TROUBLEMAKER
10956719230-012

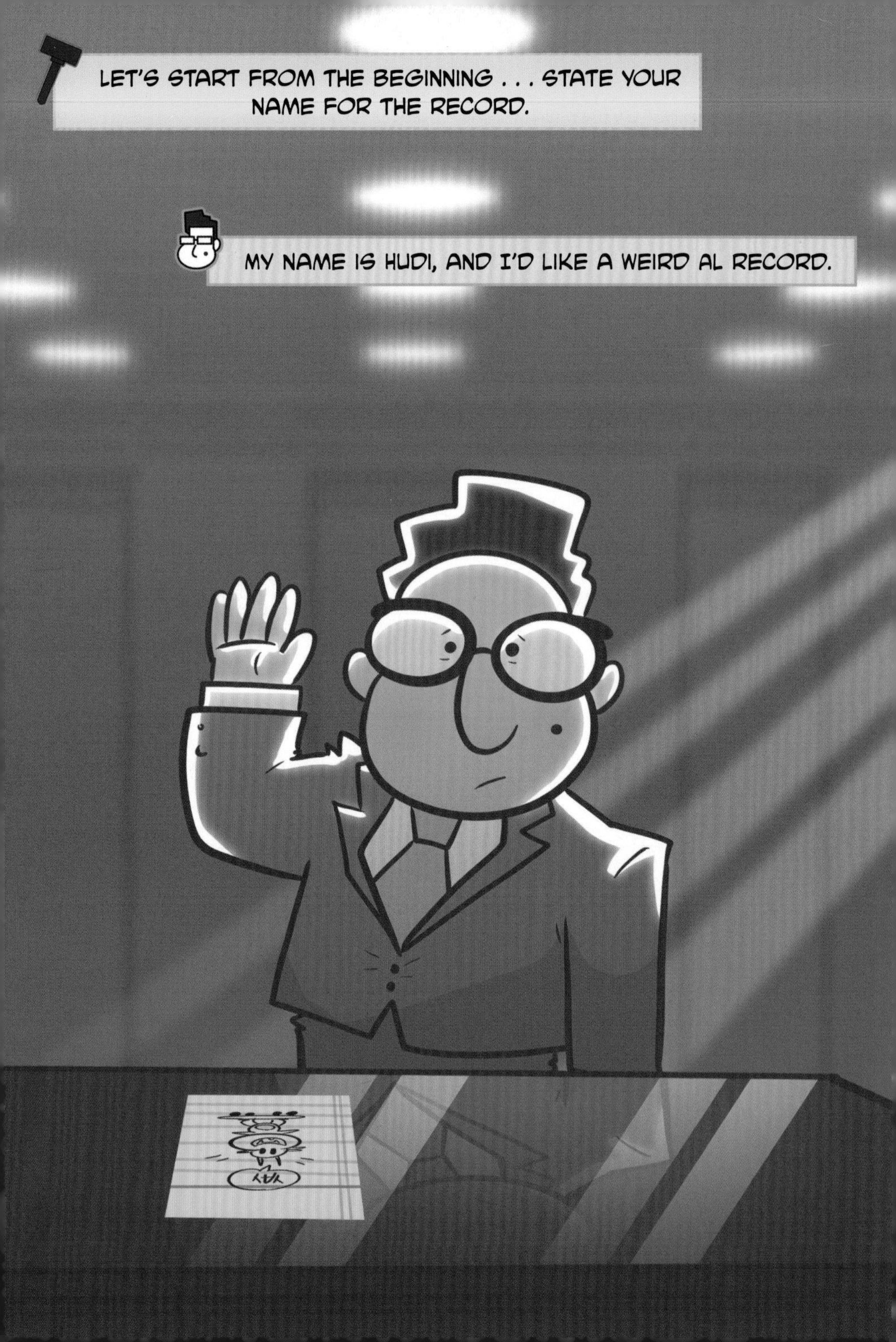

LET'S START FROM THE BEGINNING . . . STATE YOUR NAME FOR THE RECORD.
MY NAME IS HUDI, AND I'D LIKE A WEIRD AL RECORD.

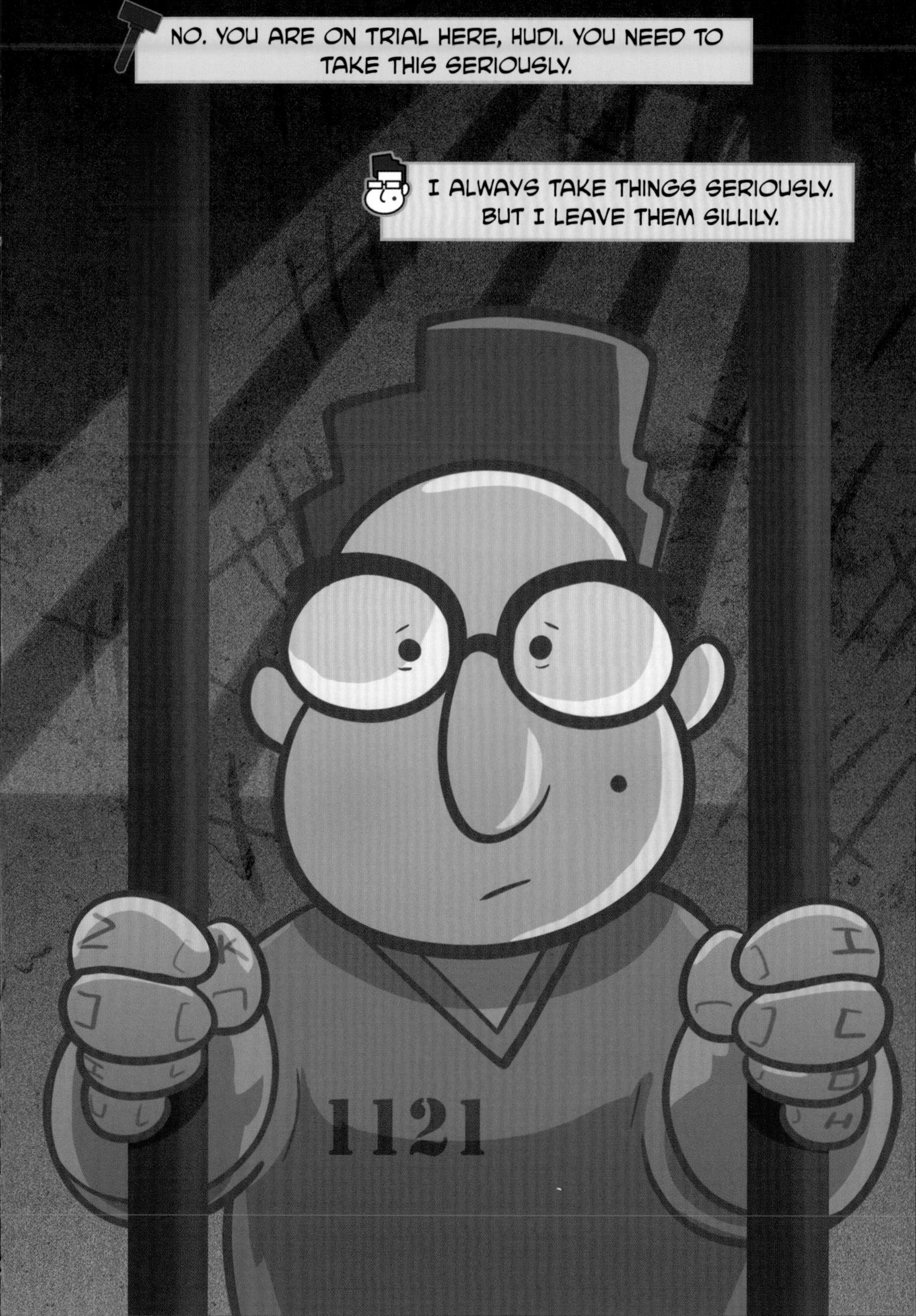
NO. YOU ARE ON TRIAL HERE, HUDI. YOU NEED TO TAKE THIS SERIOUSLY.
I ALWAYS TAKE THINGS SERIOUSLY. BUT I LEAVE THEM SILLILY.
1121

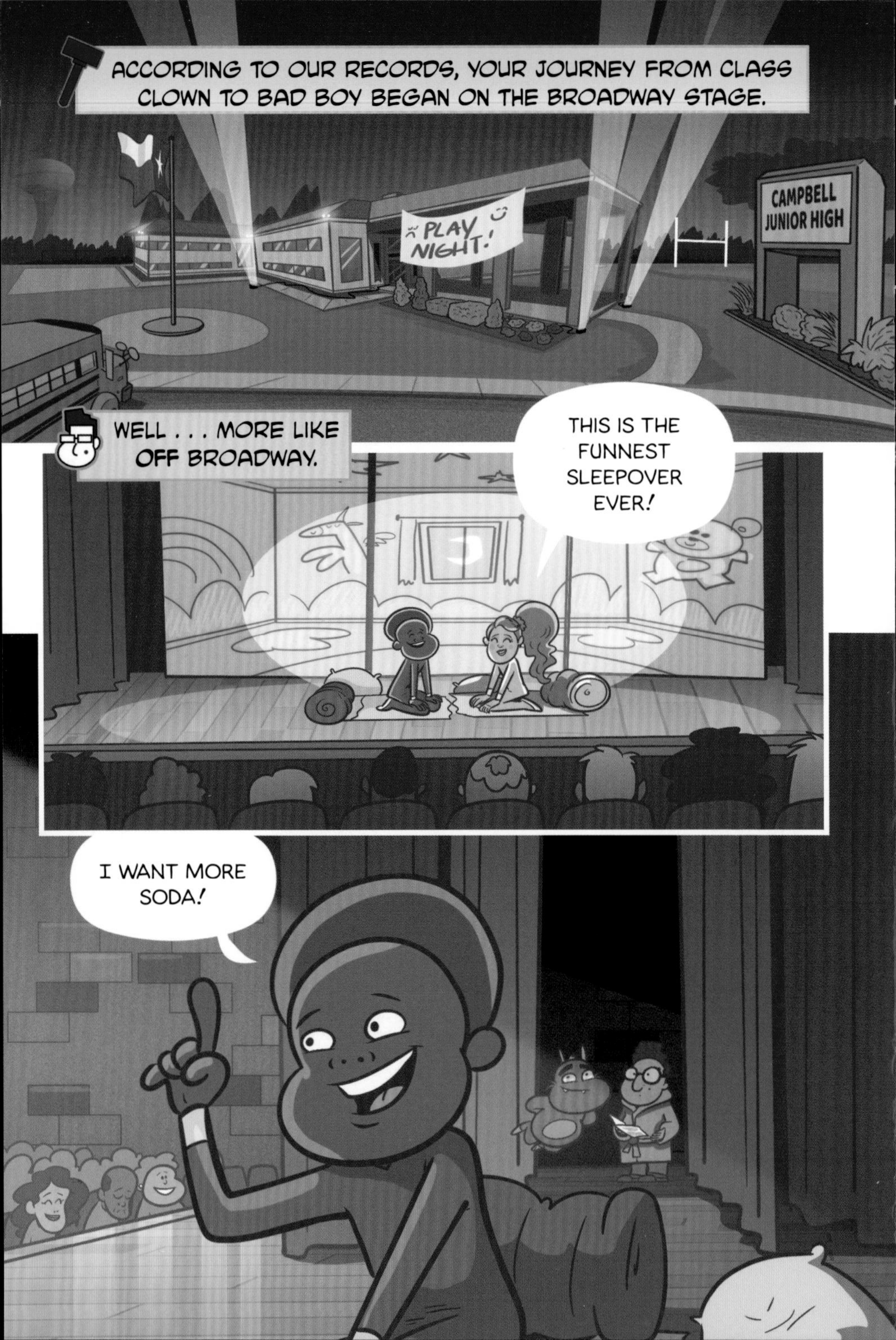
ACCORDING TO OUR RECORDS, YOUR JOURNEY FROM CLASS CLOWN TO BAD BOY BEGAN ON THE BROADWAY STAGE.
PLAY NIGHT!
CAMPBELL JUNIOR HIGH
WELL . . . MORE LIKE OFF BROADWAY.
THIS IS THE FUNNEST SLEEPOVER EVER!
I WANT MORE SODA!

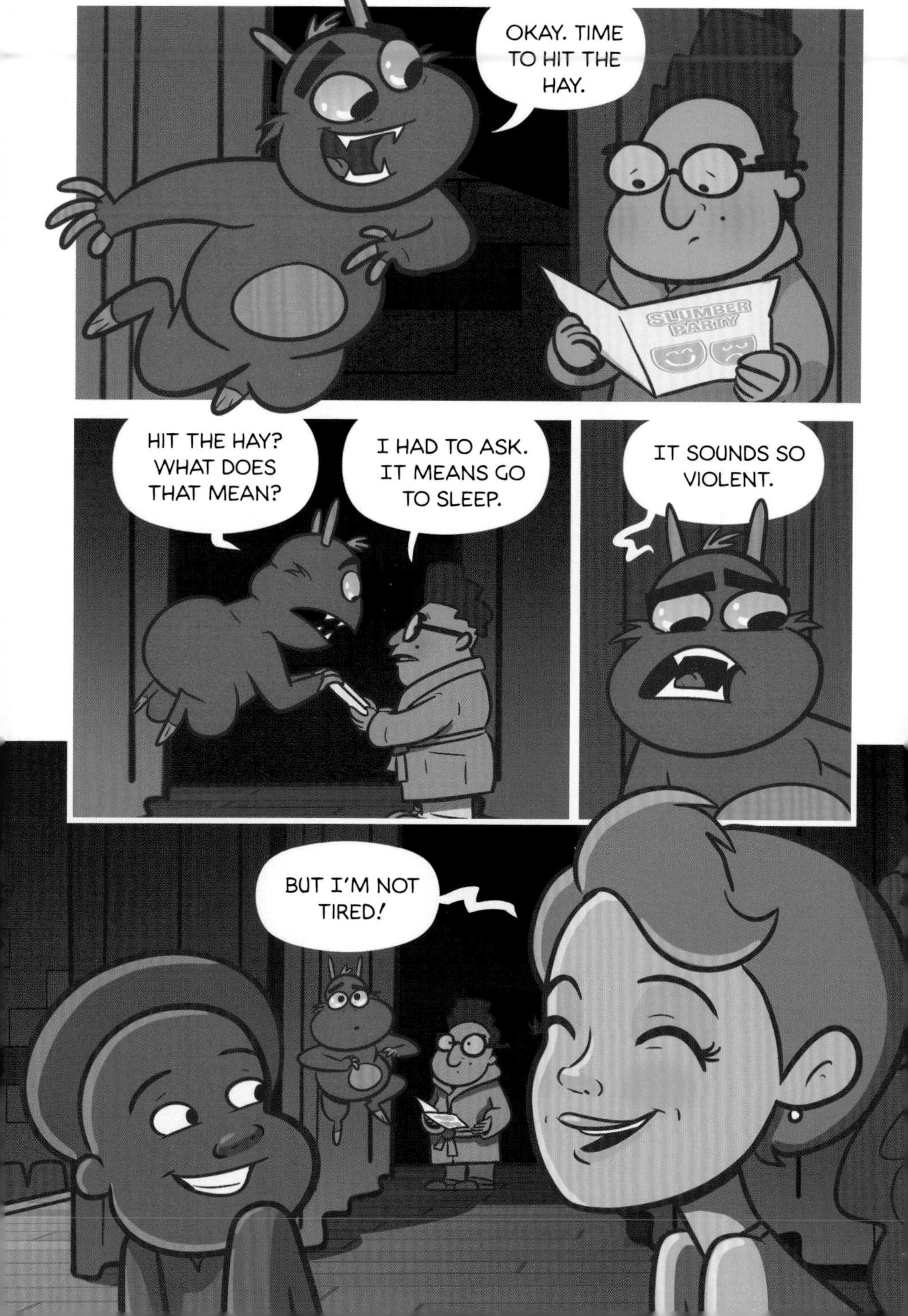
OKAY. TIME TO HIT THE HAY.
SLUMBER PARTY
HIT THE HAY? WHAT DOES THAT MEAN?
I HAD TO ASK. IT MEANS GO TO SLEEP.
IT SOUNDS SO VIOLENT.
BUT I'M NOT TIRED!

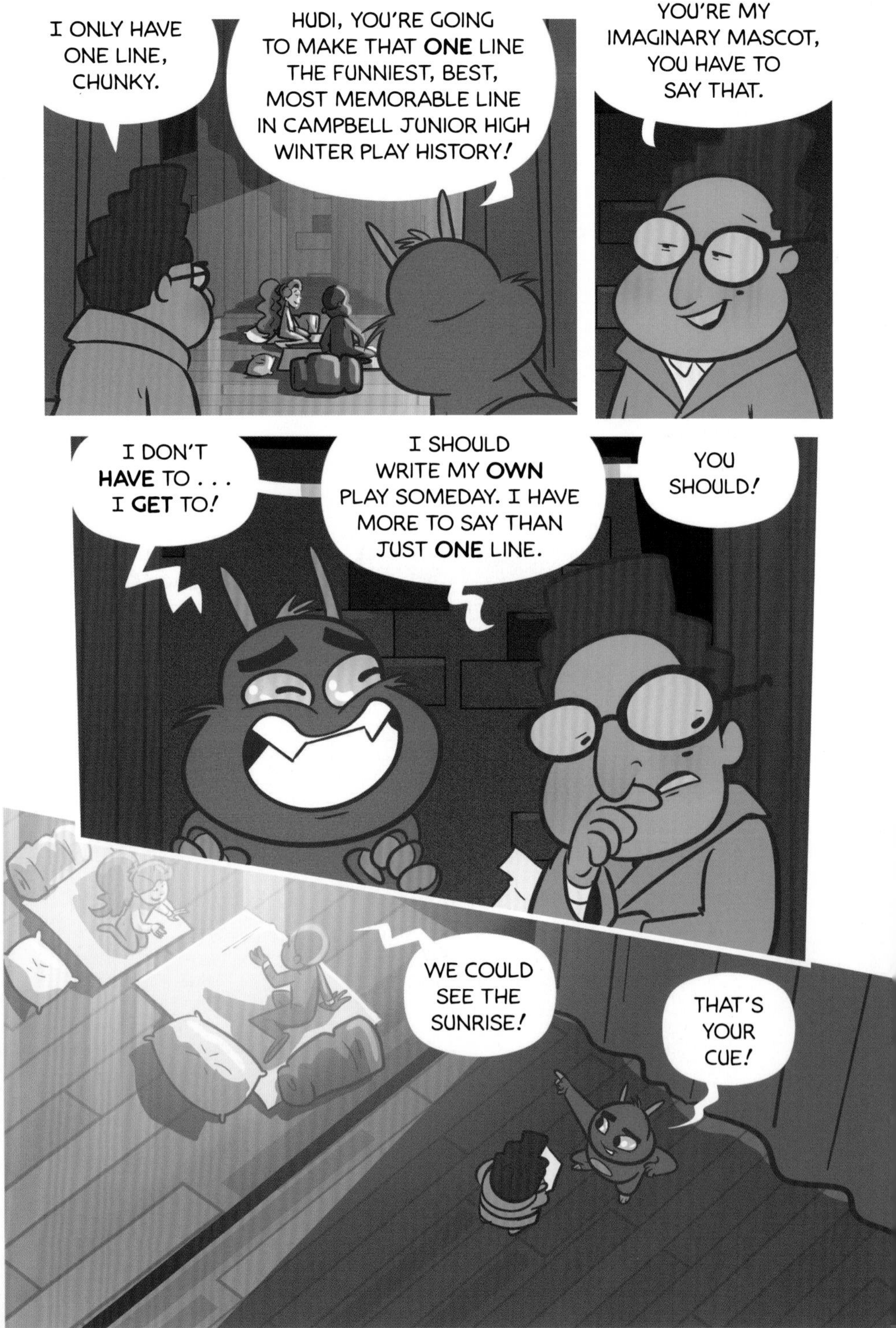
I ONLY HAVE ONE LINE, CHUNKY.
HUDI, YOU'RE GOING TO MAKE THAT ONE LINE THE FUNNIEST, BEST, MOST MEMORABLE LINE IN CAMPBELL JUNIOR HIGH WINTER PLAY HISTORY!
YOU'RE MY IMAGINARY MASCOT, YOU HAVE TO SAY THAT.
I DON'T HAVE TO . . . I GET TO!
I SHOULD WRITE MY OWN PLAY SOMEDAY. I HAVE MORE TO SAY THAN JUST ONE LINE.
YOU SHOULD!
WE COULD SEE THE SUNRISE!
THAT'S YOUR CUE!

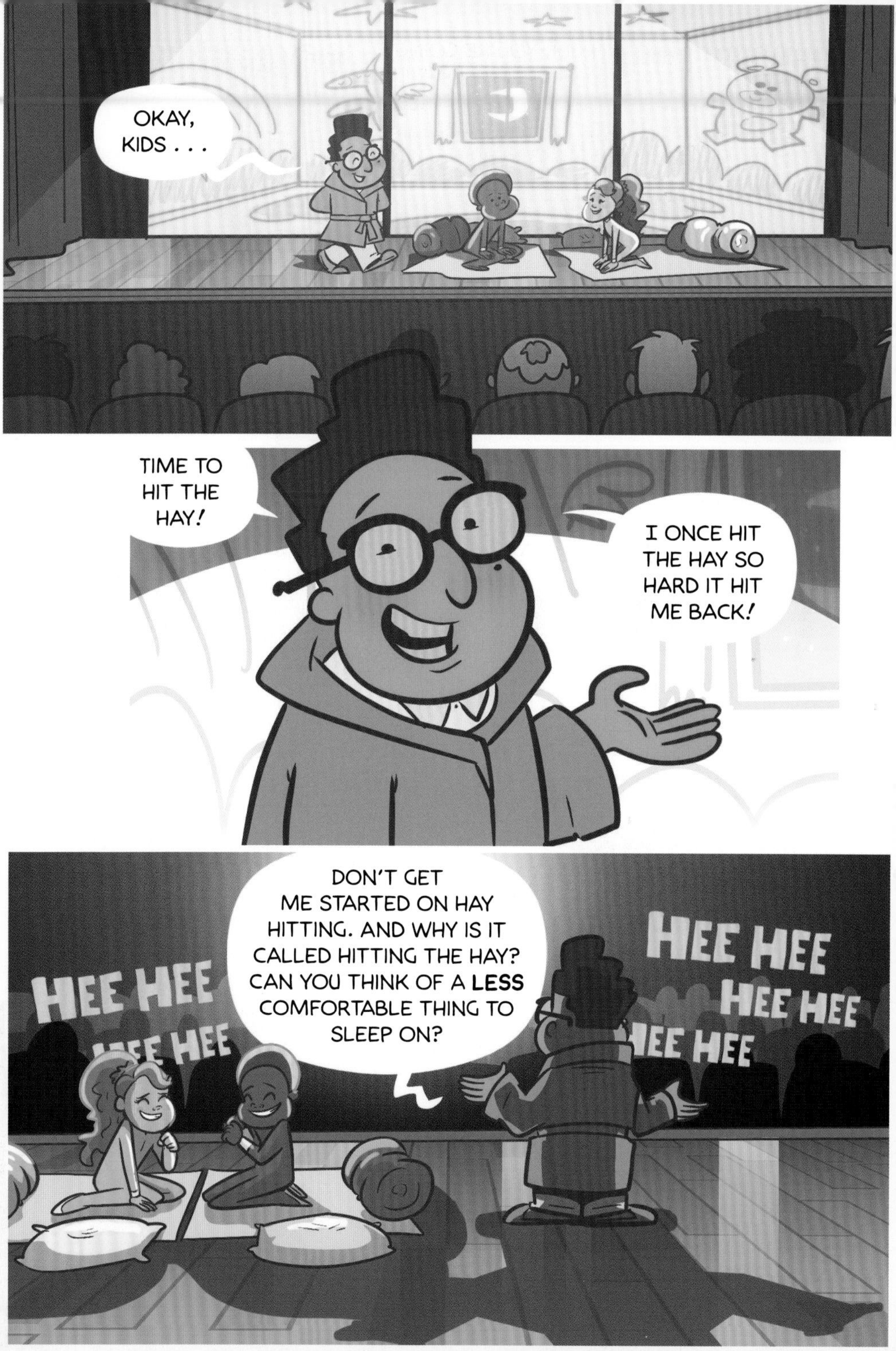
OKAY, KIDS . . .
TIME TO HIT THE HAY!
I ONCE HIT THE HAY SO HARD IT HIT ME BACK!
DON'T GET ME STARTED ON HAY HITTING. AND WHY IS IT CALLED HITTING THE HAY? CAN YOU THINK OF A **LESS** COMFORTABLE THING TO SLEEP ON?
HEE HEE
HEE HEE
HEE HEE
HEE HEE
HEE HEE

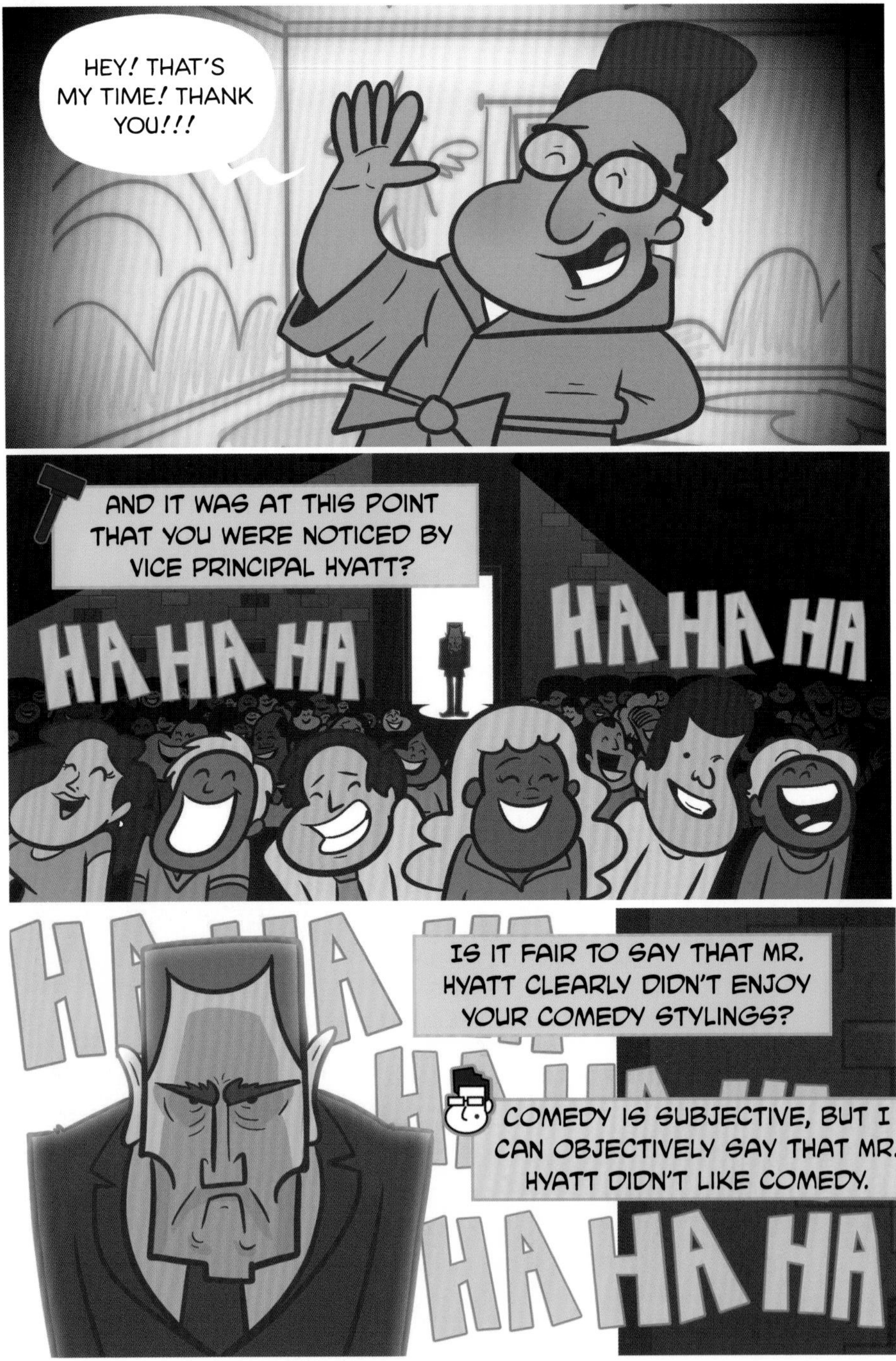
HEY! THAT'S MY TIME! THANK YOU!!!
AND IT WAS AT THIS POINT THAT YOU WERE NOTICED BY VICE PRINCIPAL HYATT?
HA HA HA
HA HA HA
IS IT FAIR TO SAY THAT MR. HYATT CLEARLY DIDN'T ENJOY YOUR COMEDY STYLINGS?
COMEDY IS SUBJECTIVE, BUT I CAN OBJECTIVELY SAY THAT MR. HYATT DIDN'T LIKE COMEDY.
HA HA HA

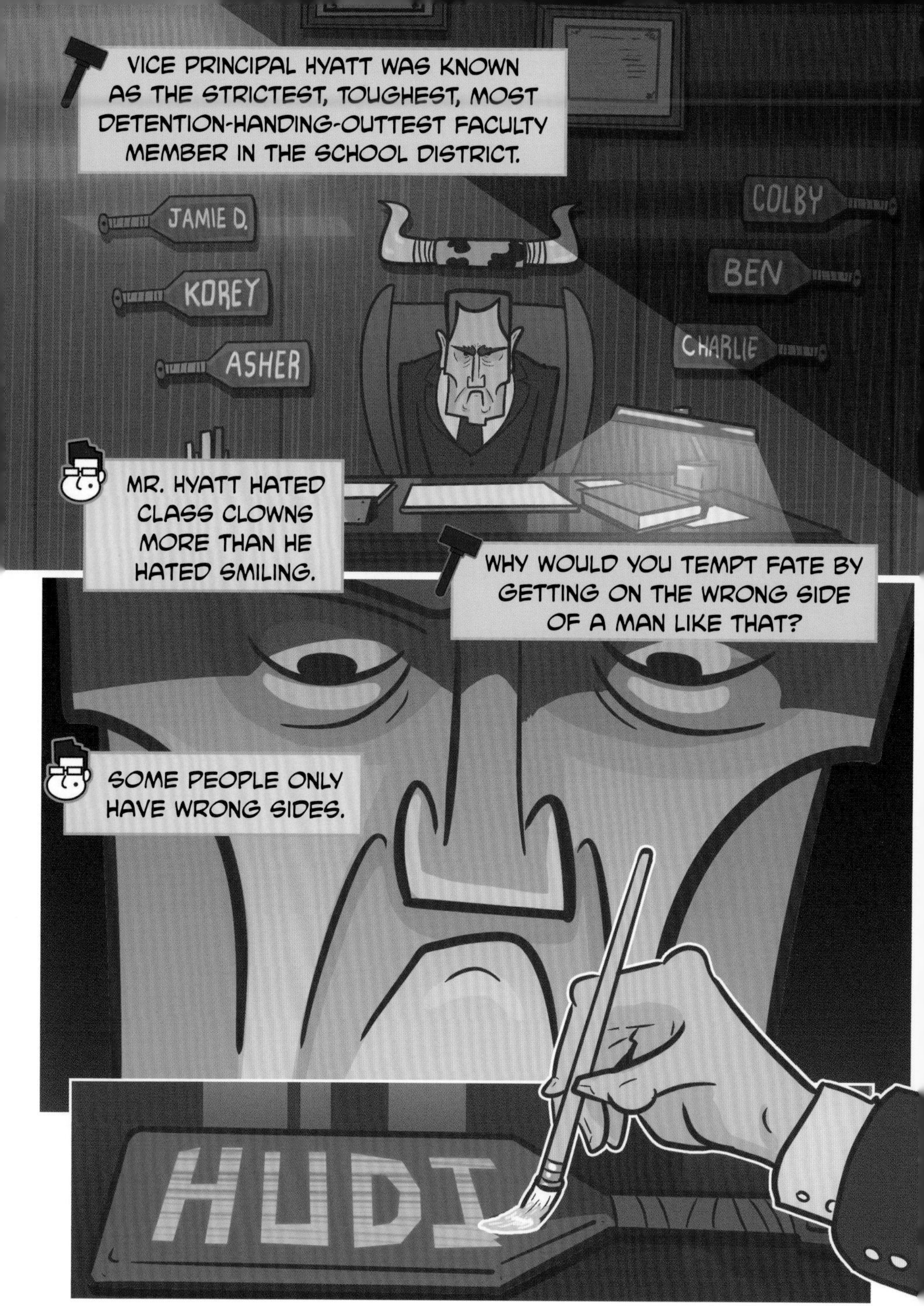
VICE PRINCIPAL HYATT WAS KNOWN AS THE STRICTEST, TOUGHEST, MOST DETENTION-HANDING-OUTTEST FACULTY MEMBER IN THE SCHOOL DISTRICT.
JAMIE D.
KOREY
ASHER
COLBY
BEN
CHARLIE
MR. HYATT HATED CLASS CLOWNS MORE THAN HE HATED SMILING.
WHY WOULD YOU TEMPT FATE BY GETTING ON THE WRONG SIDE OF A MAN LIKE THAT?
SOME PEOPLE ONLY HAVE WRONG SIDES.
HUDI

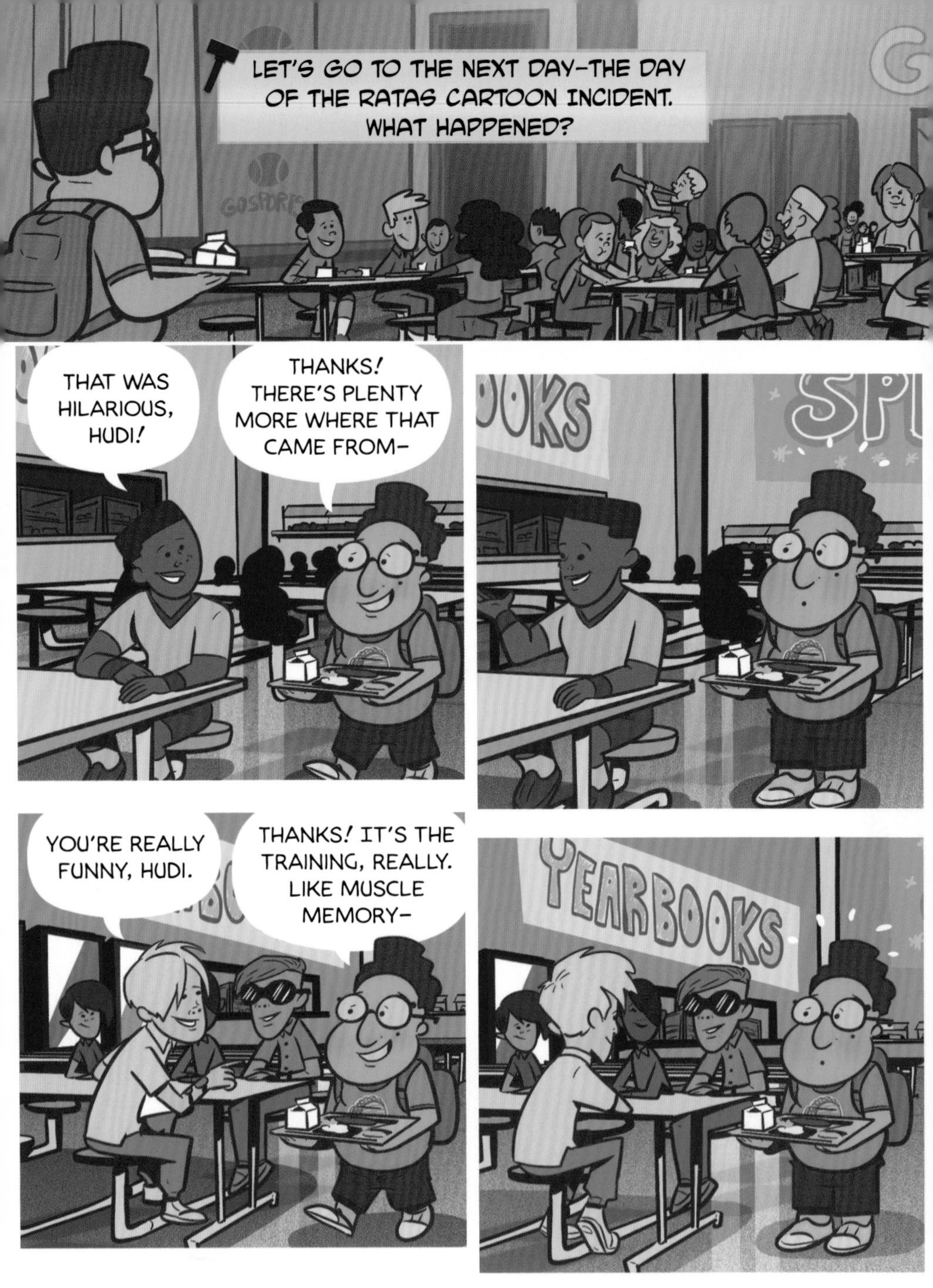
LET'S GO TO THE NEXT DAY—THE DAY OF THE RATAS CARTOON INCIDENT. WHAT HAPPENED?
GOSFORD
THAT WAS HILARIOUS, HUDI!
THANKS! THERE'S PLENTY MORE WHERE THAT CAME FROM—
YOU'RE REALLY FUNNY, HUDI.
THANKS! IT'S THE TRAINING, REALLY. LIKE MUSCLE MEMORY—
YEARBOOKS

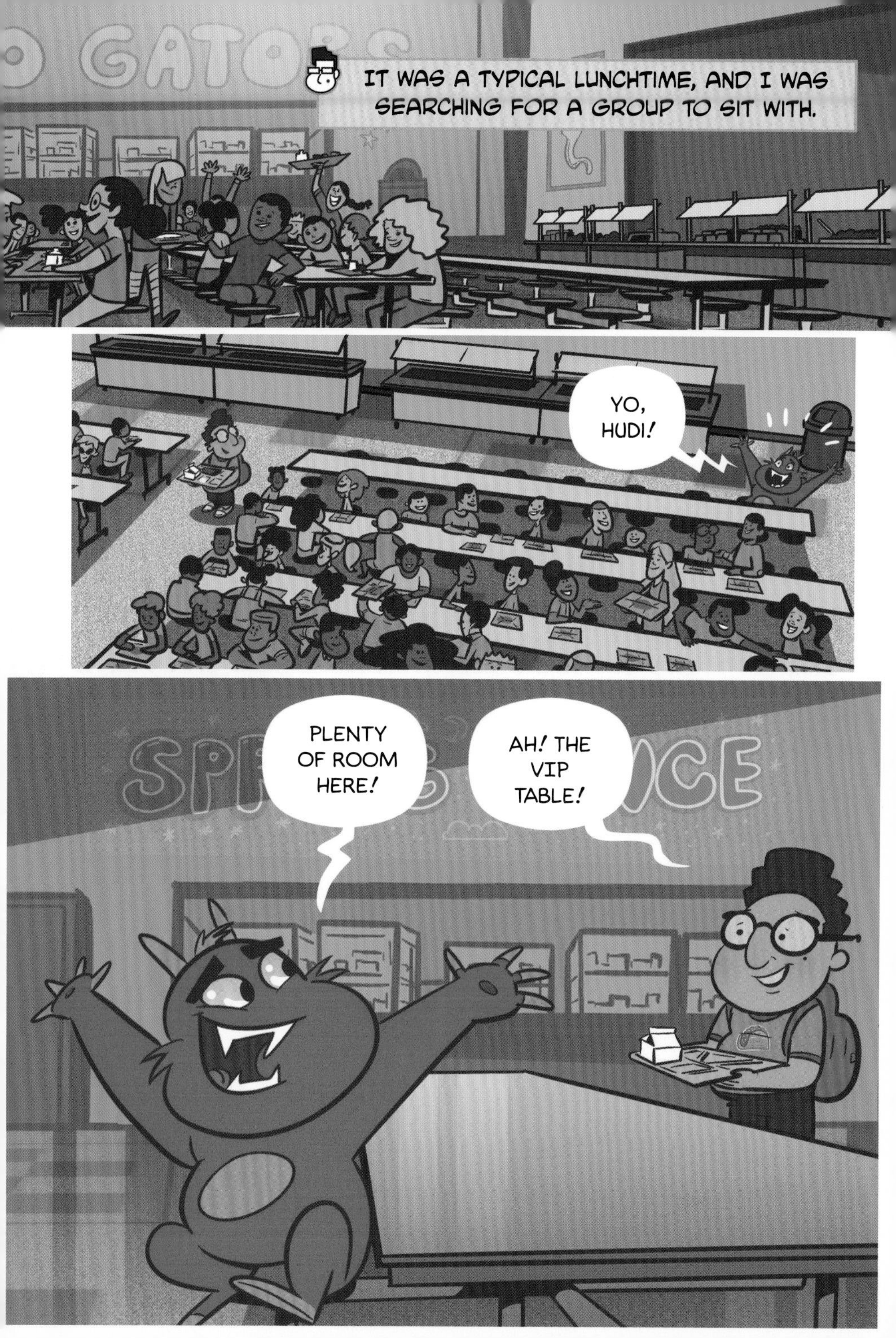
IT WAS A TYPICAL LUNCHTIME, AND I WAS SEARCHING FOR A GROUP TO SIT WITH.
YO, HUDI!
PLENTY OF ROOM HERE!
AH! THE VIP TABLE!

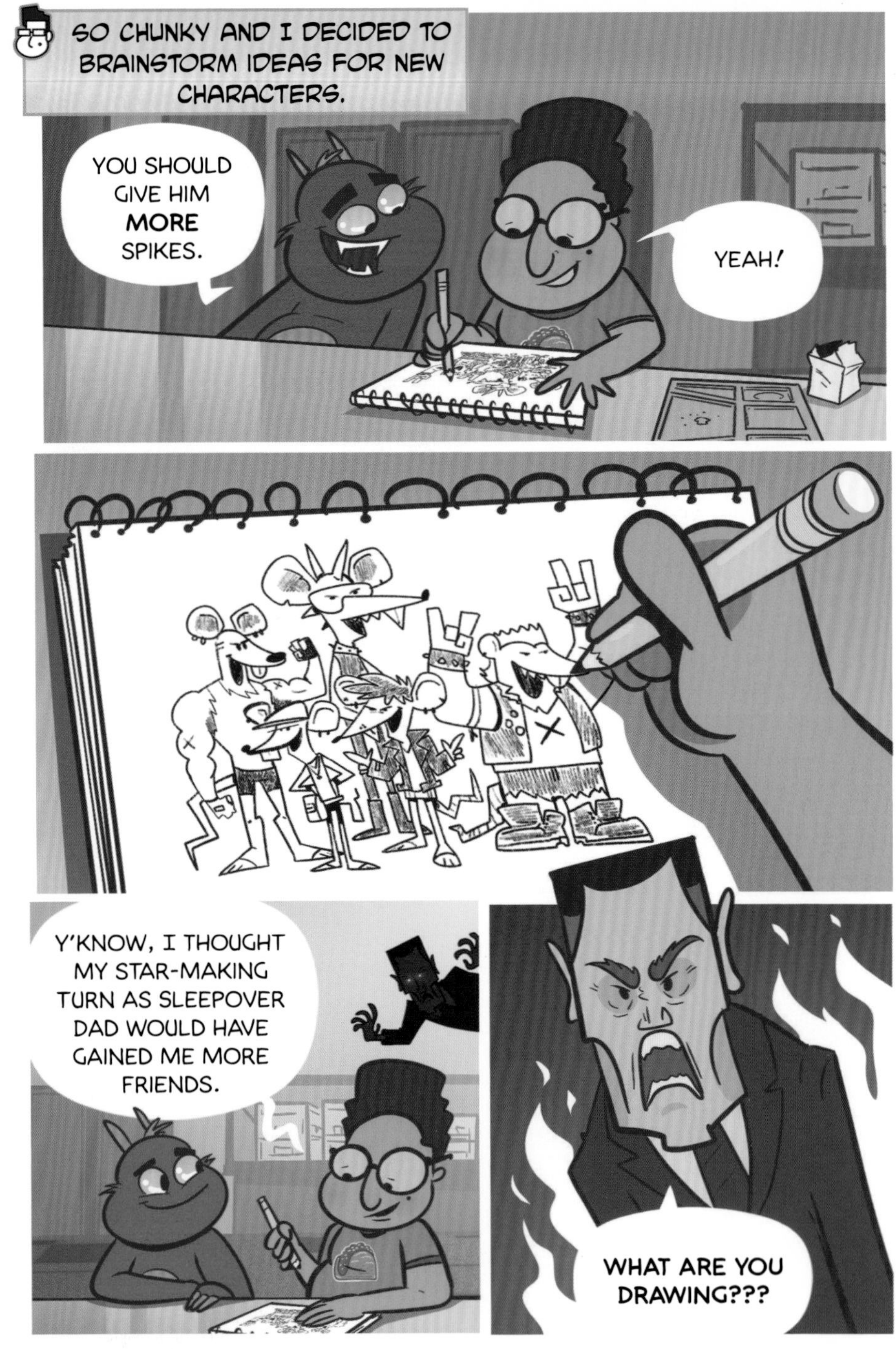
SO CHUNKY AND I DECIDED TO BRAINSTORM IDEAS FOR NEW CHARACTERS.
YOU SHOULD GIVE HIM **MORE** SPIKES.
YEAH!
Y'KNOW, I THOUGHT MY STAR-MAKING TURN AS SLEEPOVER DAD WOULD HAVE GAINED ME MORE FRIENDS.
WHAT ARE YOU DRAWING???

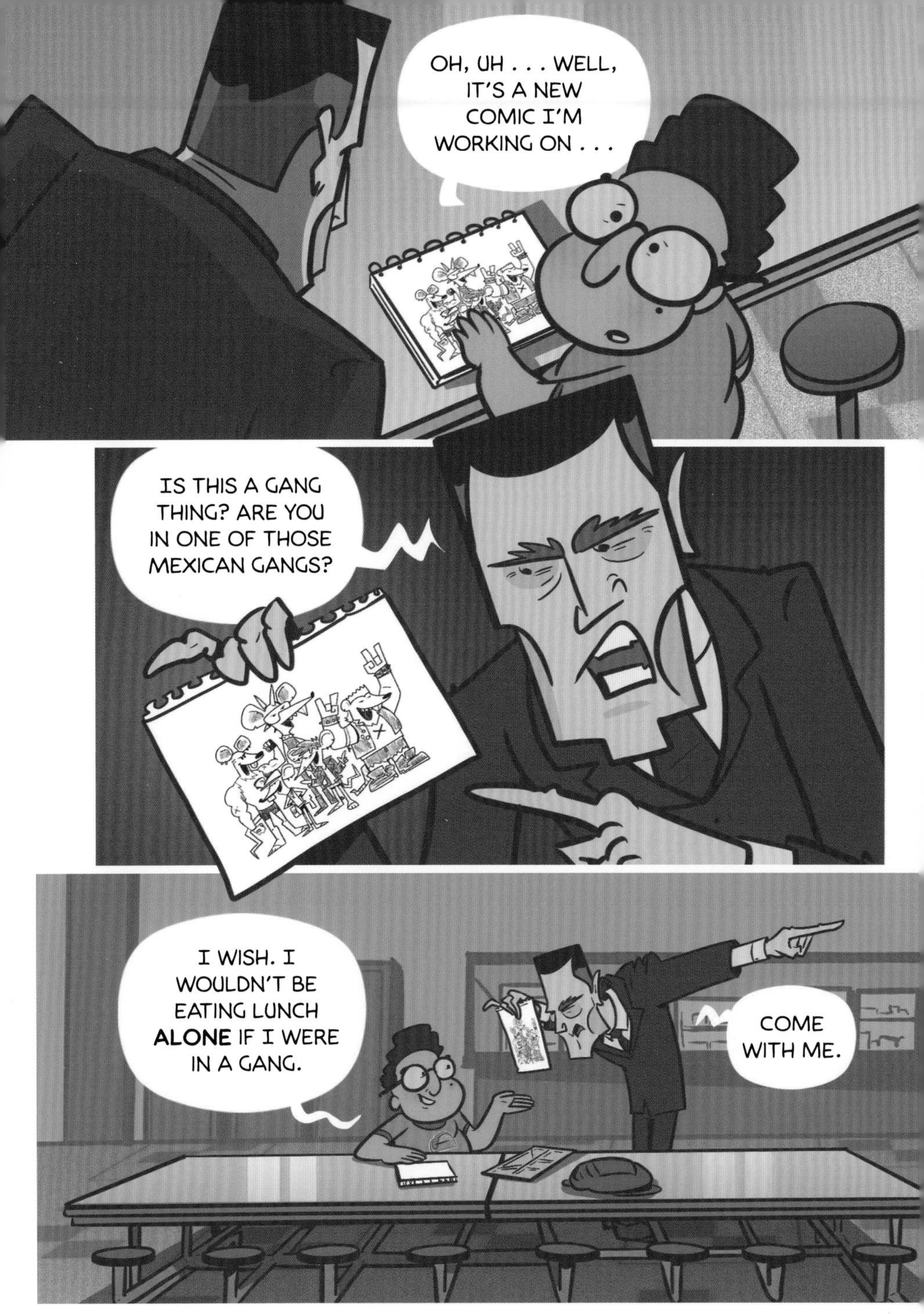
OH, UH . . . WELL, IT'S A NEW COMIC I'M WORKING ON . . .
IS THIS A GANG THING? ARE YOU IN ONE OF THOSE MEXICAN GANGS?
I WISH. I WOULDN'T BE EATING LUNCH **ALONE** IF I WERE IN A GANG.
COME WITH ME.

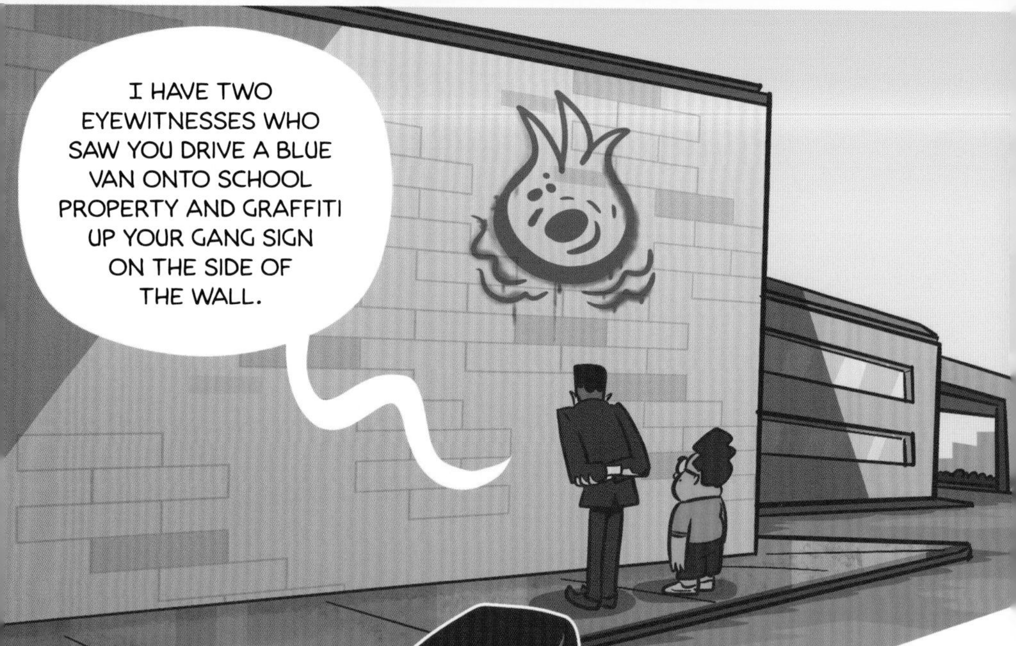
I HAVE TWO EYEWITNESSES WHO SAW YOU DRIVE A BLUE VAN ONTO SCHOOL PROPERTY AND GRAFFITI UP YOUR GANG SIGN ON THE SIDE OF THE WALL.

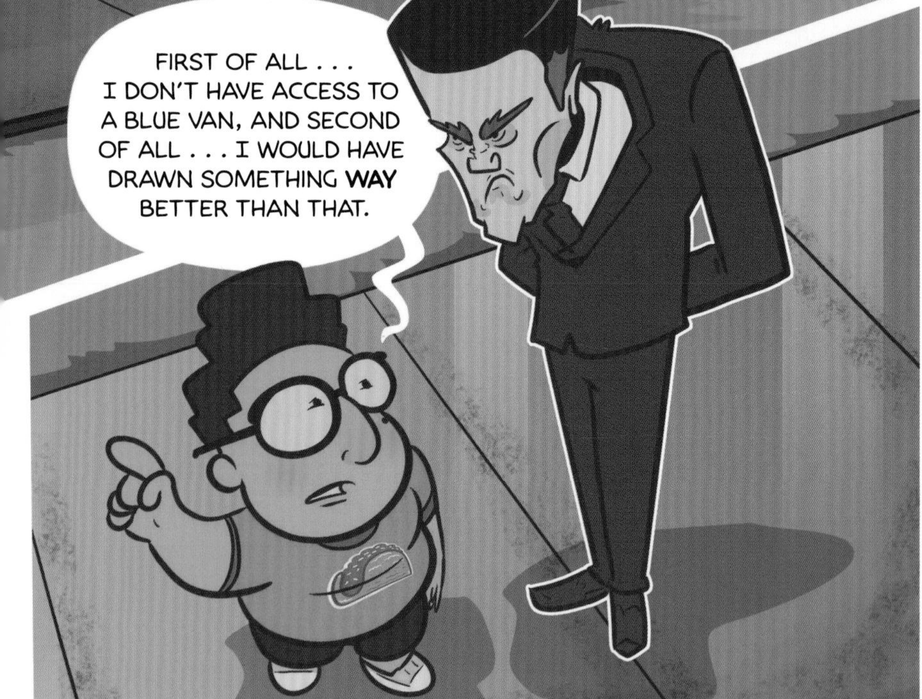
FIRST OF ALL . . . I DON'T HAVE ACCESS TO A BLUE VAN, AND SECOND OF ALL . . . I WOULD HAVE DRAWN SOMETHING **WAY** BETTER THAN THAT.

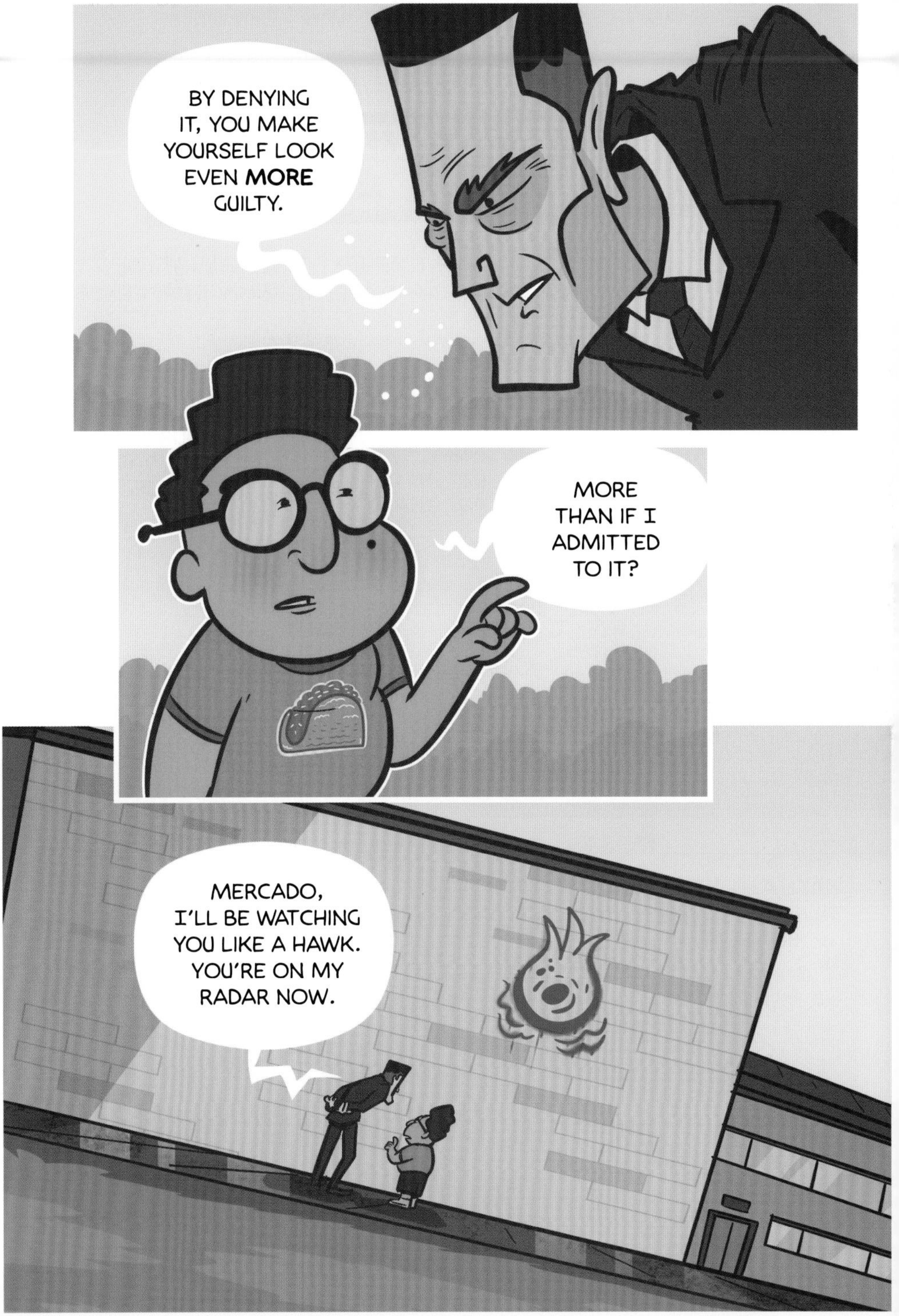
BY DENYING IT, YOU MAKE YOURSELF LOOK EVEN **MORE** GUILTY.
MORE THAN IF I ADMITTED TO IT?
MERCADO, I'LL BE WATCHING YOU LIKE A HAWK. YOU'RE ON MY RADAR NOW.

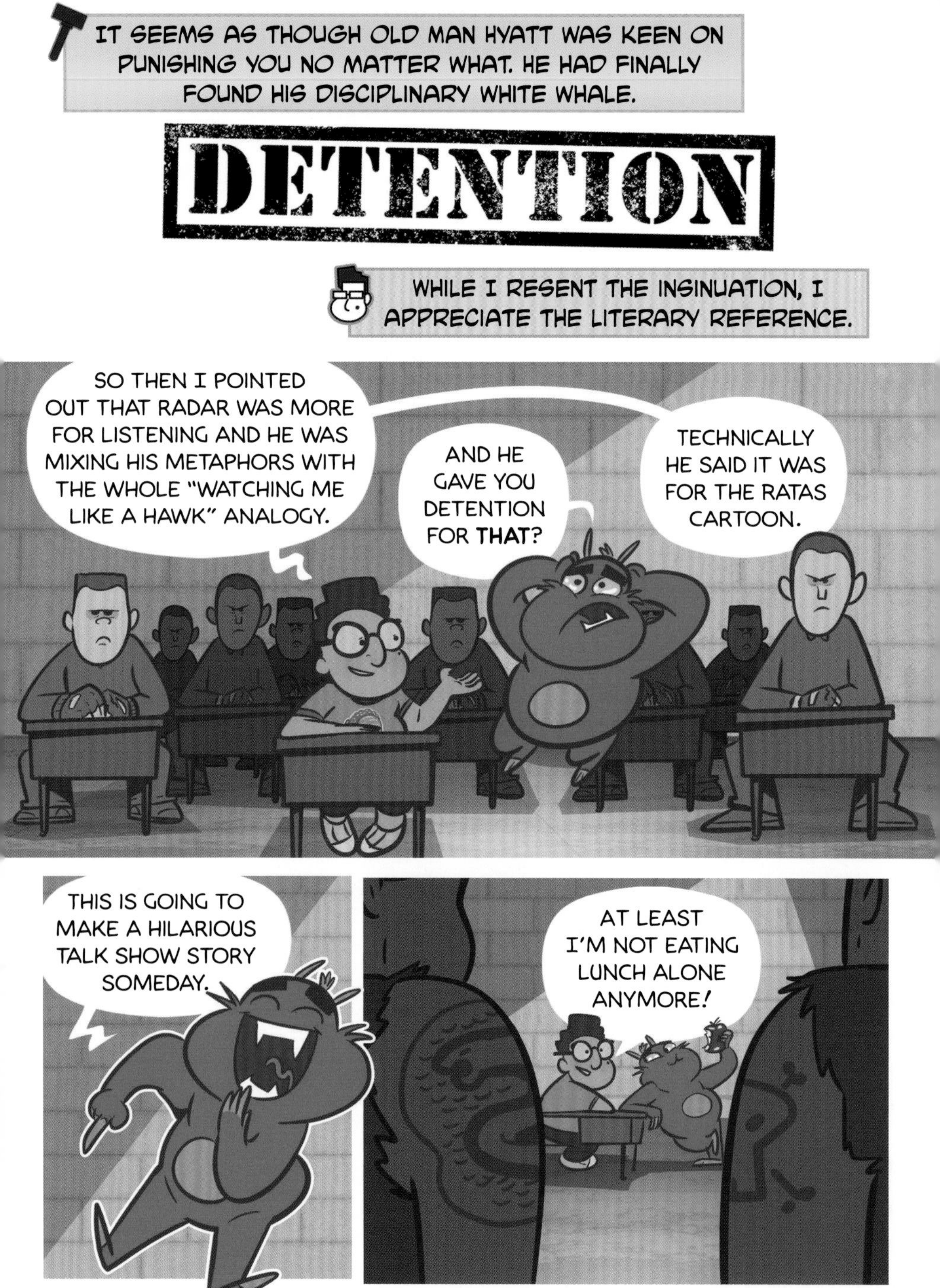
IT SEEMS AS THOUGH OLD MAN HYATT WAS KEEN ON PUNISHING YOU NO MATTER WHAT. HE HAD FINALLY FOUND HIS DISCIPLINARY WHITE WHALE.
DETENTION
WHILE I RESENT THE INSINUATION, I APPRECIATE THE LITERARY REFERENCE.
SO THEN I POINTED OUT THAT RADAR WAS MORE FOR LISTENING AND HE WAS MIXING HIS METAPHORS WITH THE WHOLE "WATCHING ME LIKE A HAWK" ANALOGY.
AND HE GAVE YOU DETENTION FOR **THAT**?
TECHNICALLY HE SAID IT WAS FOR THE RATAS CARTOON.
THIS IS GOING TO MAKE A HILARIOUS TALK SHOW STORY SOMEDAY.
AT LEAST I'M NOT EATING LUNCH ALONE ANYMORE!

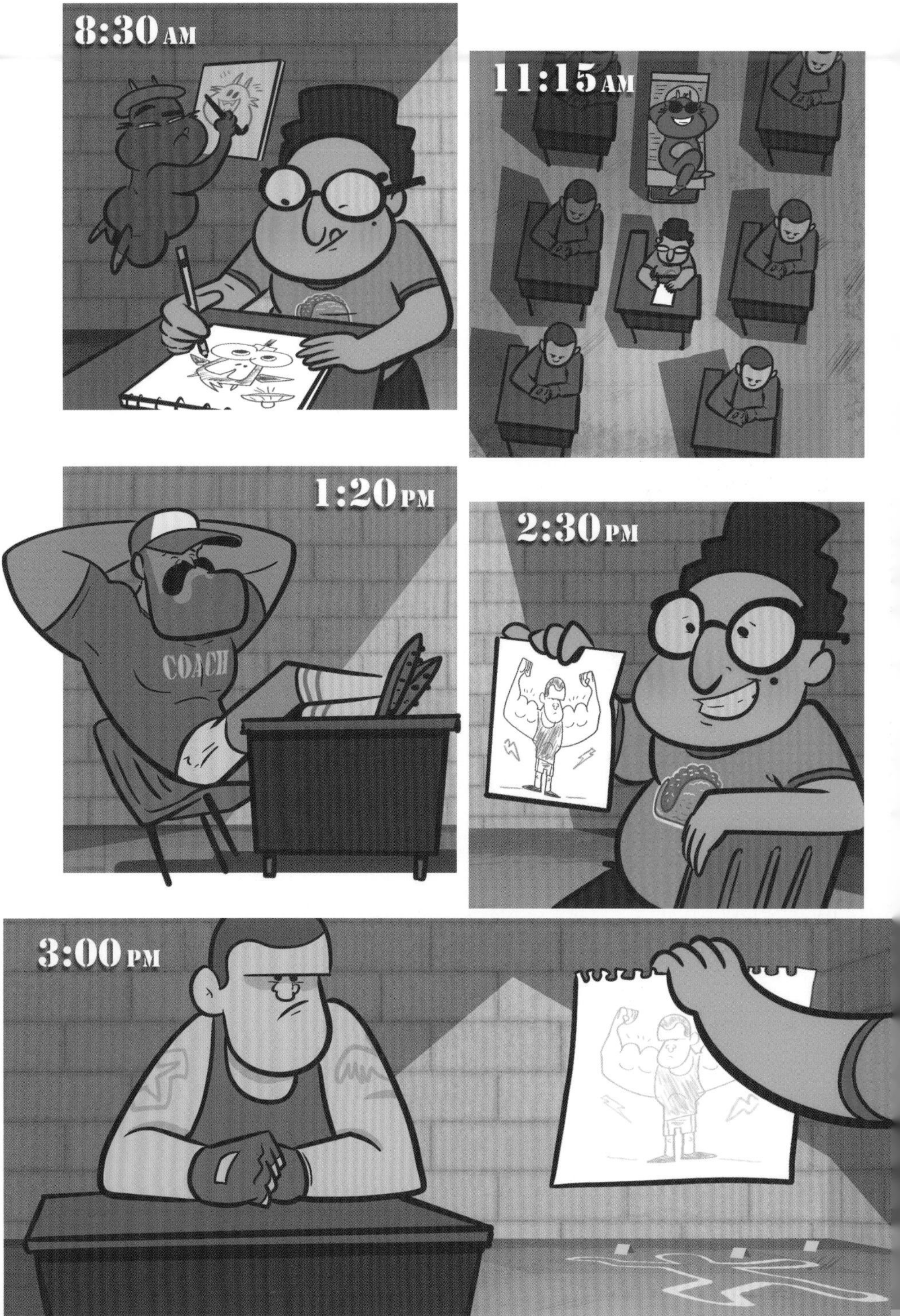
8:30 AM
11:15 AM
1:20 PM
COACH
2:30 PM
3:00 PM

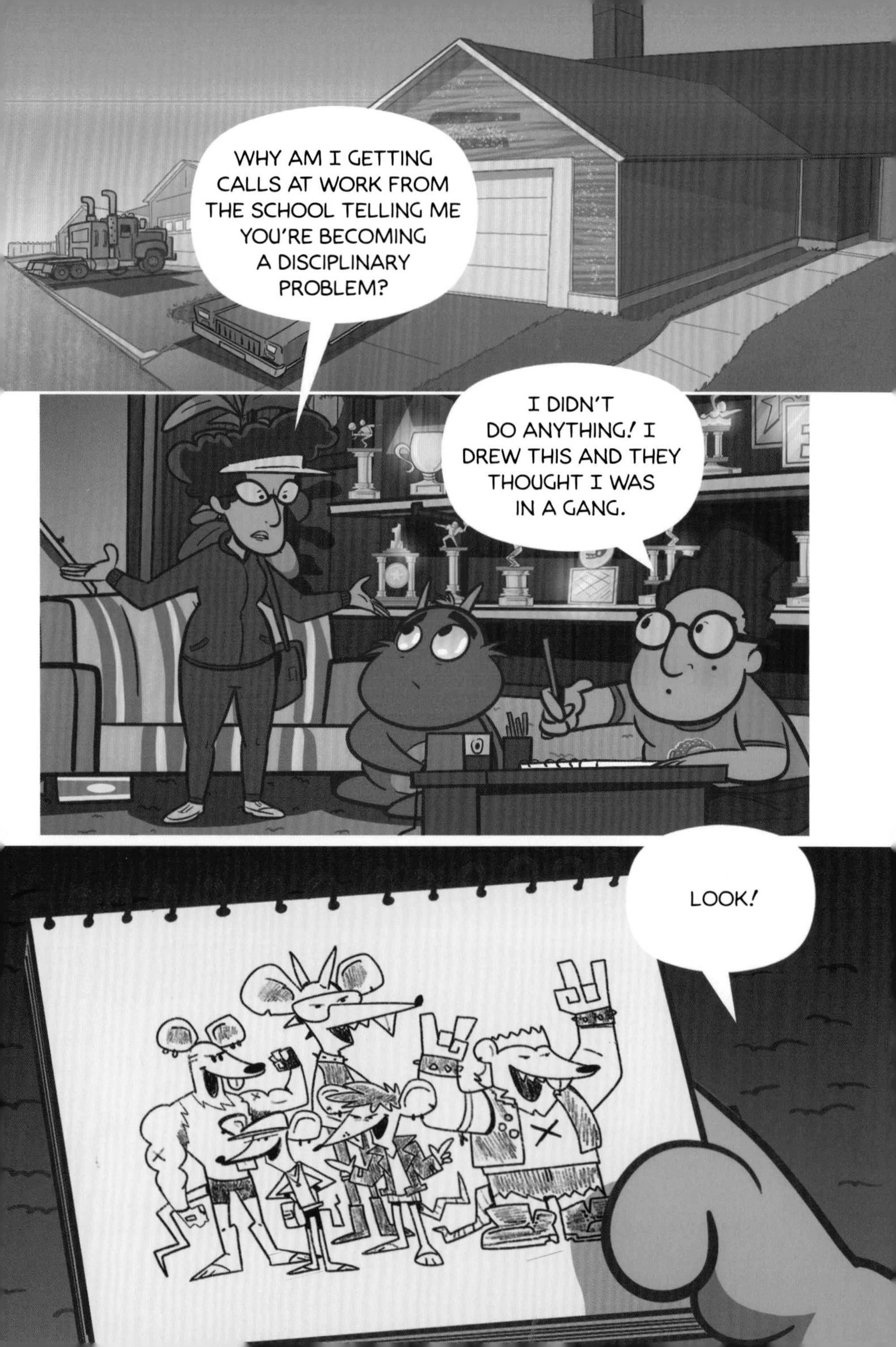
WHY AM I GETTING CALLS AT WORK FROM THE SCHOOL TELLING ME YOU'RE BECOMING A DISCIPLINARY PROBLEM?
I DIDN'T DO ANYTHING! I DREW THIS AND THEY THOUGHT I WAS IN A GANG.
LOOK!

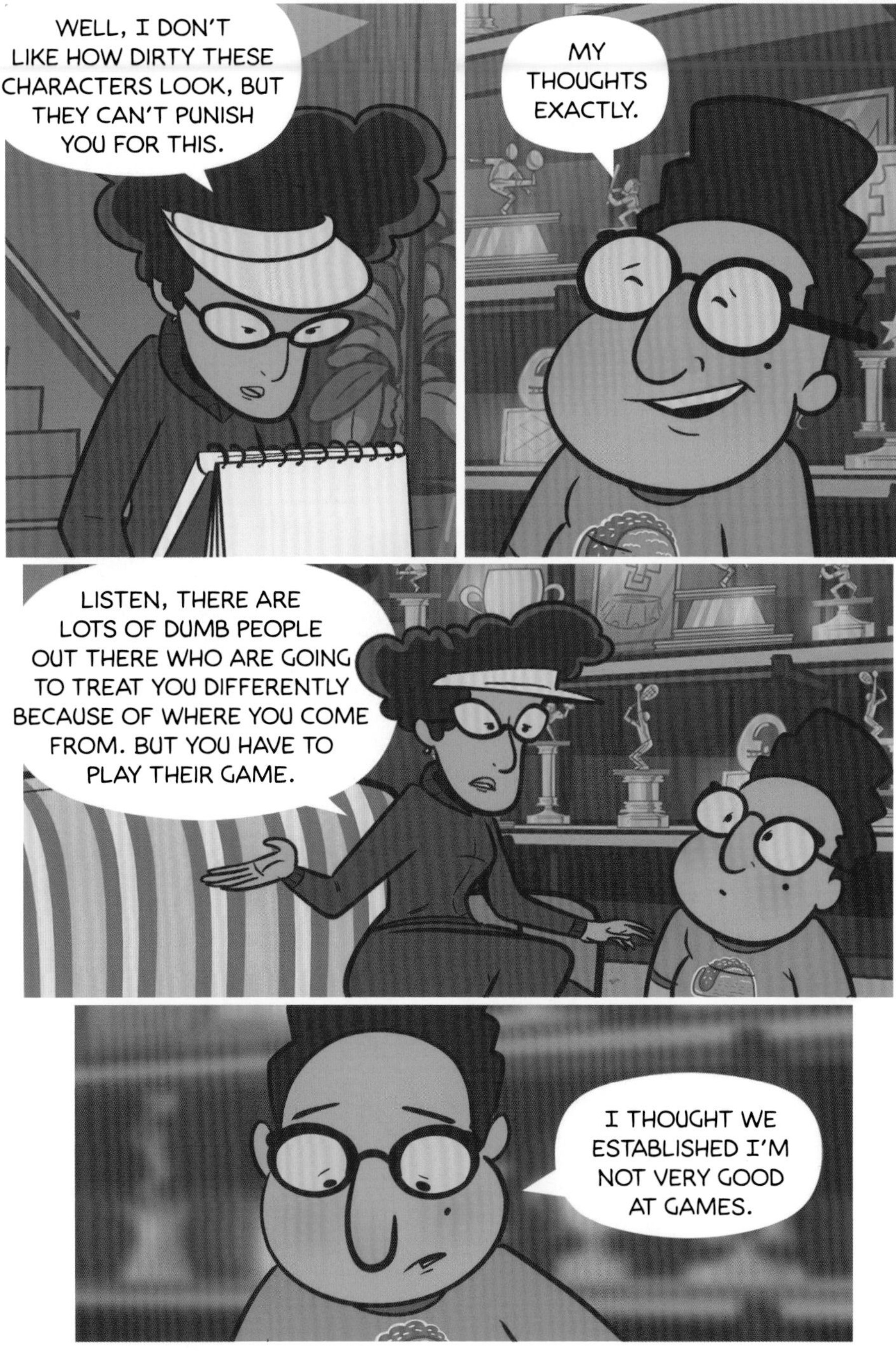
WELL, I DON'T LIKE HOW DIRTY THESE CHARACTERS LOOK, BUT THEY CAN'T PUNISH YOU FOR THIS.
MY THOUGHTS EXACTLY.
LISTEN, THERE ARE LOTS OF DUMB PEOPLE OUT THERE WHO ARE GOING TO TREAT YOU DIFFERENTLY BECAUSE OF WHERE YOU COME FROM. BUT YOU HAVE TO PLAY THEIR GAME.
I THOUGHT WE ESTABLISHED I'M NOT VERY GOOD AT GAMES.

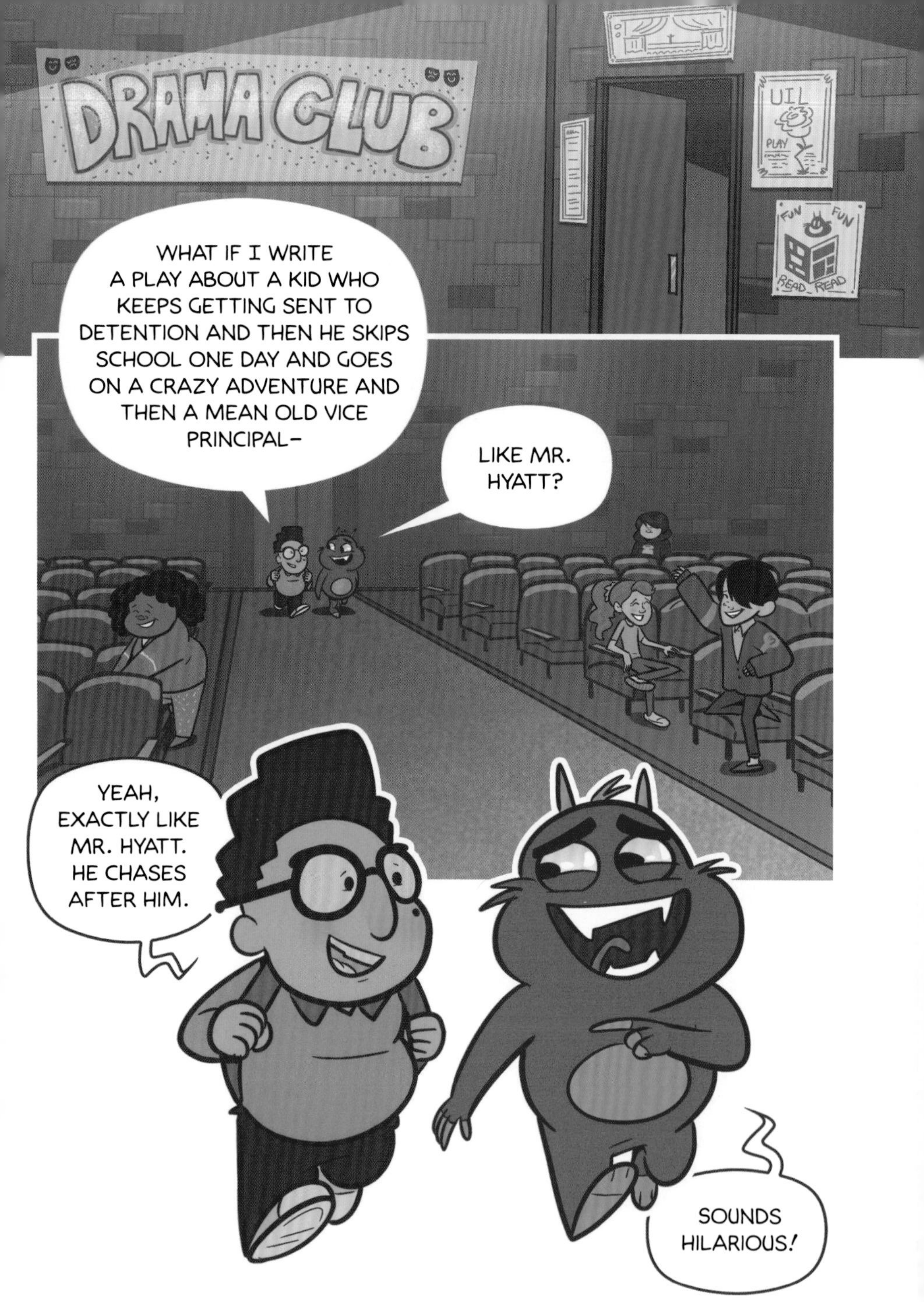
DRAMA CLUB
UIL
PLAY
FUN FUN
READ READ
WHAT IF I WRITE A PLAY ABOUT A KID WHO KEEPS GETTING SENT TO DETENTION AND THEN HE SKIPS SCHOOL ONE DAY AND GOES ON A CRAZY ADVENTURE AND THEN A MEAN OLD VICE PRINCIPAL–
LIKE MR. HYATT?
YEAH, EXACTLY LIKE MR. HYATT. HE CHASES AFTER HIM.
SOUNDS HILARIOUS!

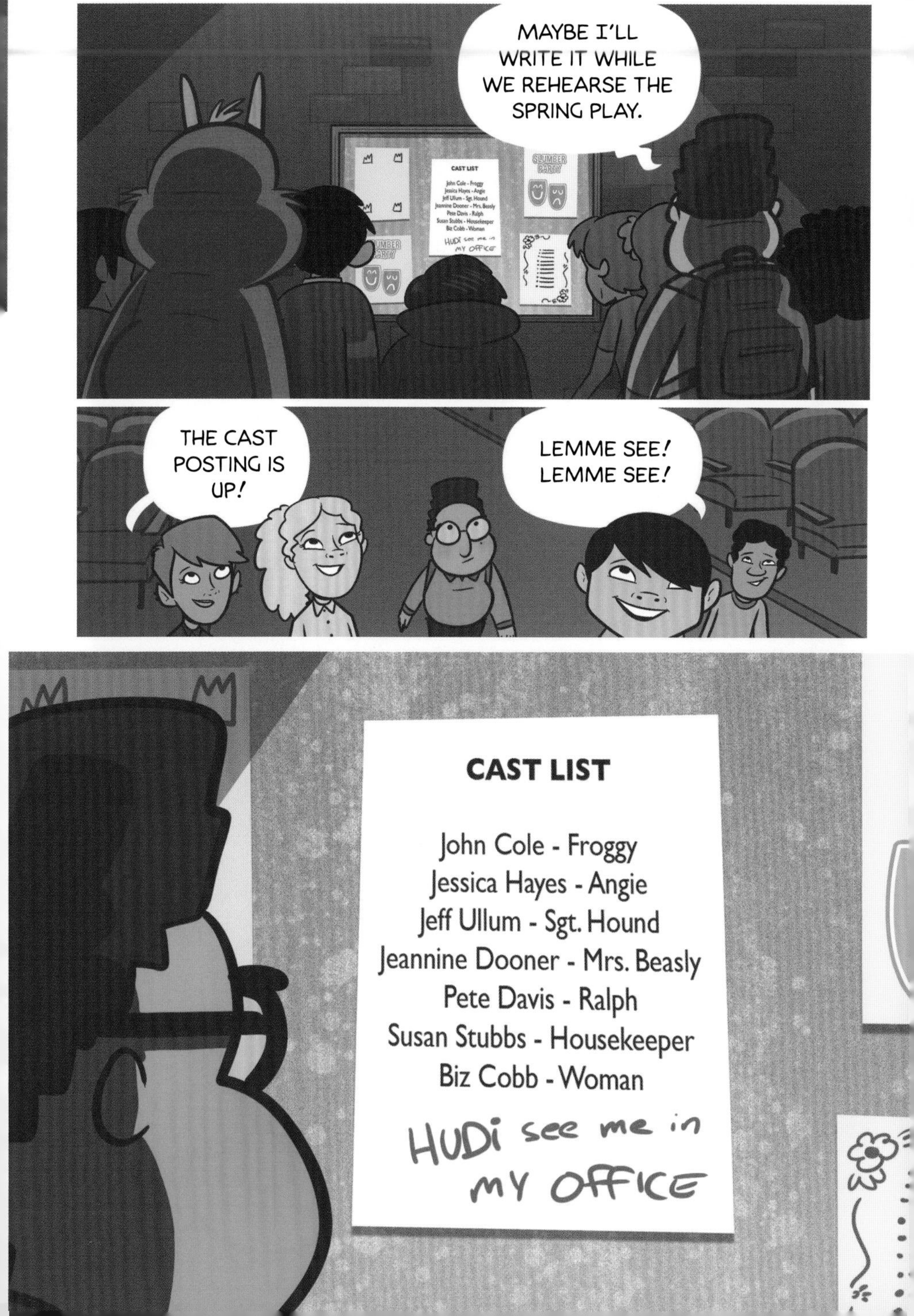
MAYBE I'LL WRITE IT WHILE WE REHEARSE THE SPRING PLAY.
THE CAST POSTING IS UP!
LEMME SEE! LEMME SEE!
CAST LIST
John Cole - Froggy
Jessica Hayes - Angie
Jeff Ullum - Sgt. Hound
Jeannine Dooner - Mrs. Beasly
Pete Davis - Ralph
Susan Stubbs - Housekeeper
Biz Cobb - Woman
HUDi see me in MY OFFICE

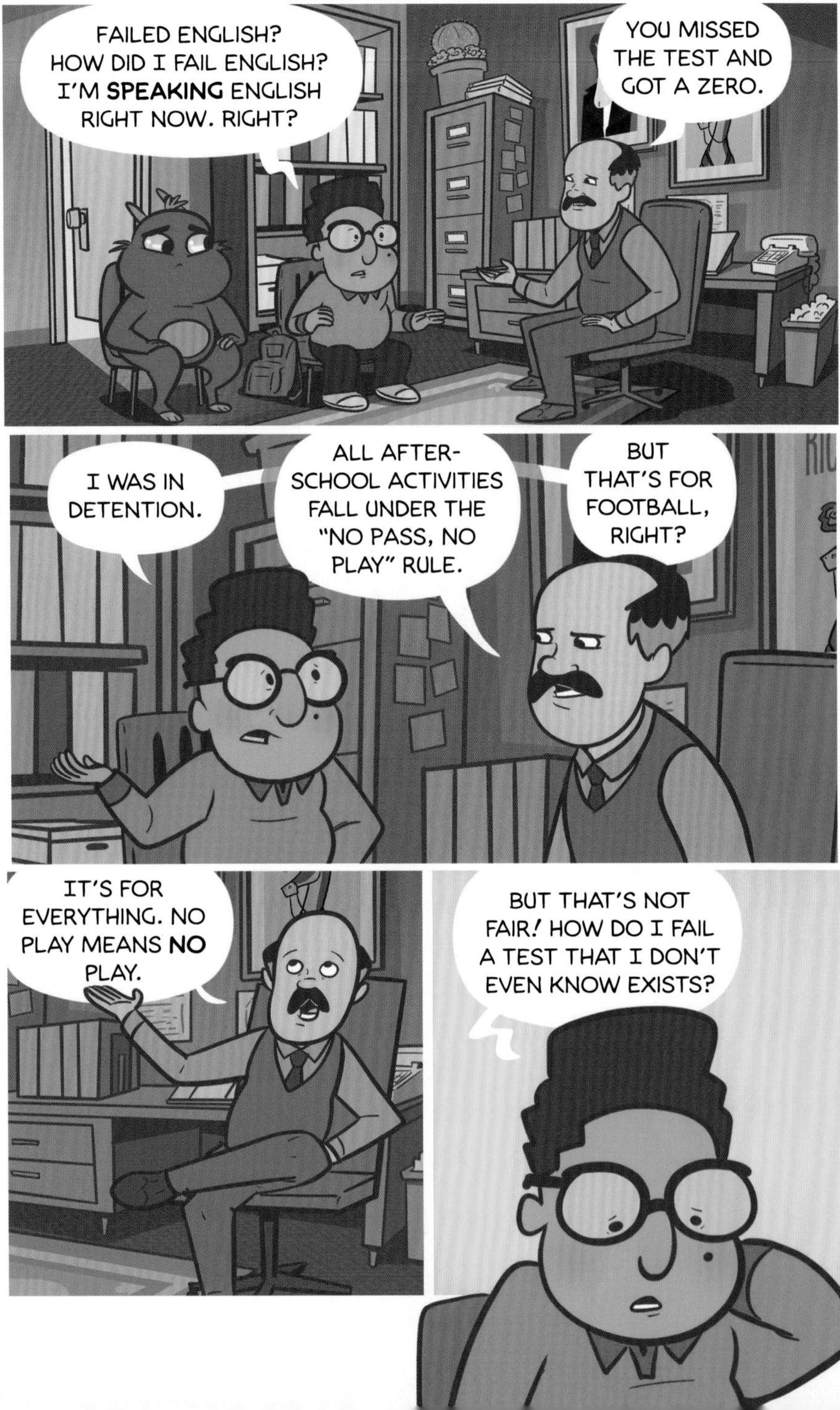
FAILED ENGLISH? HOW DID I FAIL ENGLISH? I'M **SPEAKING** ENGLISH RIGHT NOW. RIGHT?
YOU MISSED THE TEST AND GOT A ZERO.
I WAS IN DETENTION.
ALL AFTER-SCHOOL ACTIVITIES FALL UNDER THE "NO PASS, NO PLAY" RULE.
BUT THAT'S FOR FOOTBALL, RIGHT?
IT'S FOR EVERYTHING. NO PLAY MEANS **NO** PLAY.
BUT THAT'S NOT FAIR! HOW DO I FAIL A TEST THAT I DON'T EVEN KNOW EXISTS?

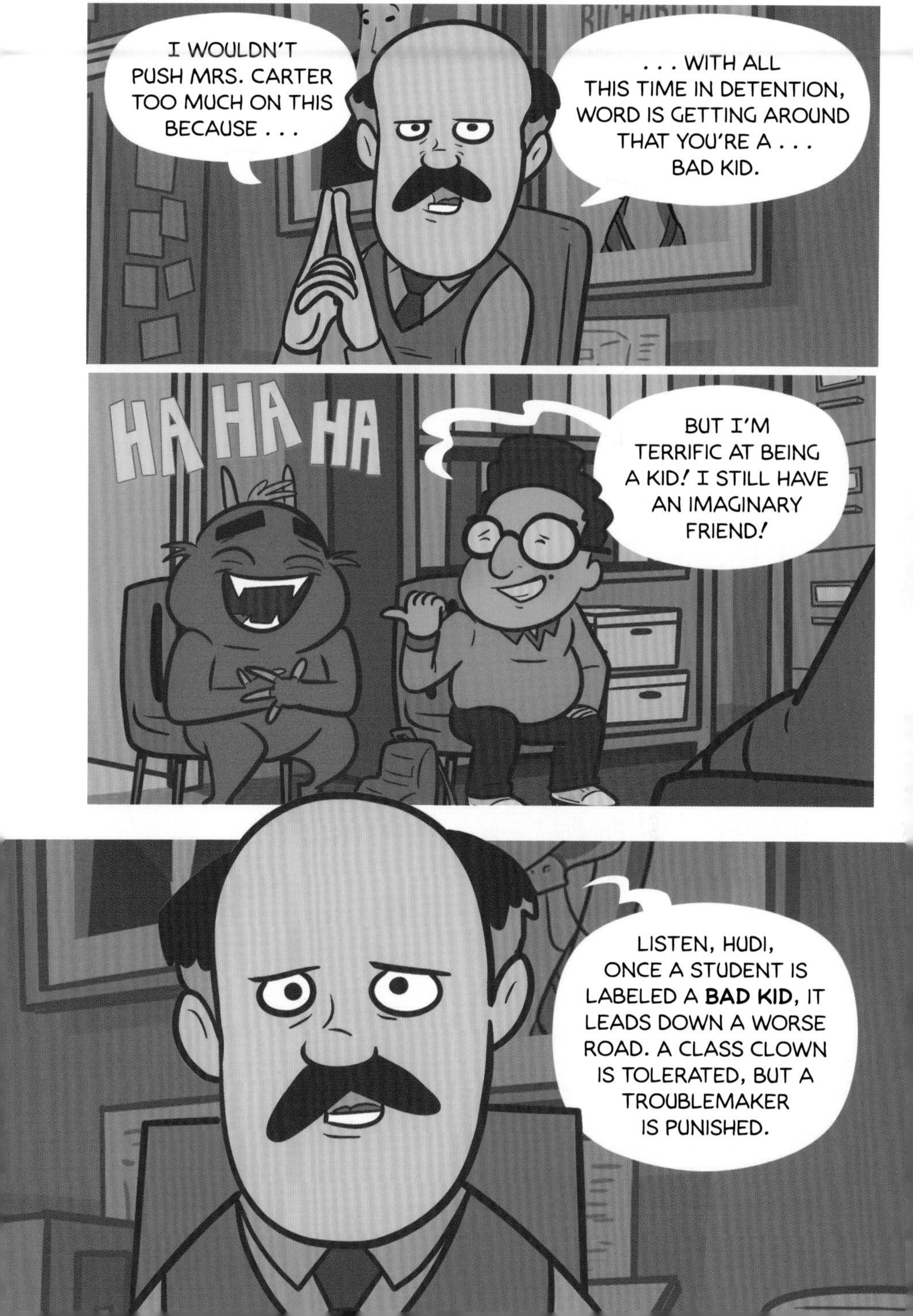
I WOULDN'T PUSH MRS. CARTER TOO MUCH ON THIS BECAUSE . . .
. . . WITH ALL THIS TIME IN DETENTION, WORD IS GETTING AROUND THAT YOU'RE A . . . BAD KID.
HA HA HA
BUT I'M TERRIFIC AT BEING A KID! I STILL HAVE AN IMAGINARY FRIEND!
LISTEN, HUDI, ONCE A STUDENT IS LABELED A **BAD KID**, IT LEADS DOWN A WORSE ROAD. A CLASS CLOWN IS TOLERATED, BUT A TROUBLEMAKER IS PUNISHED.

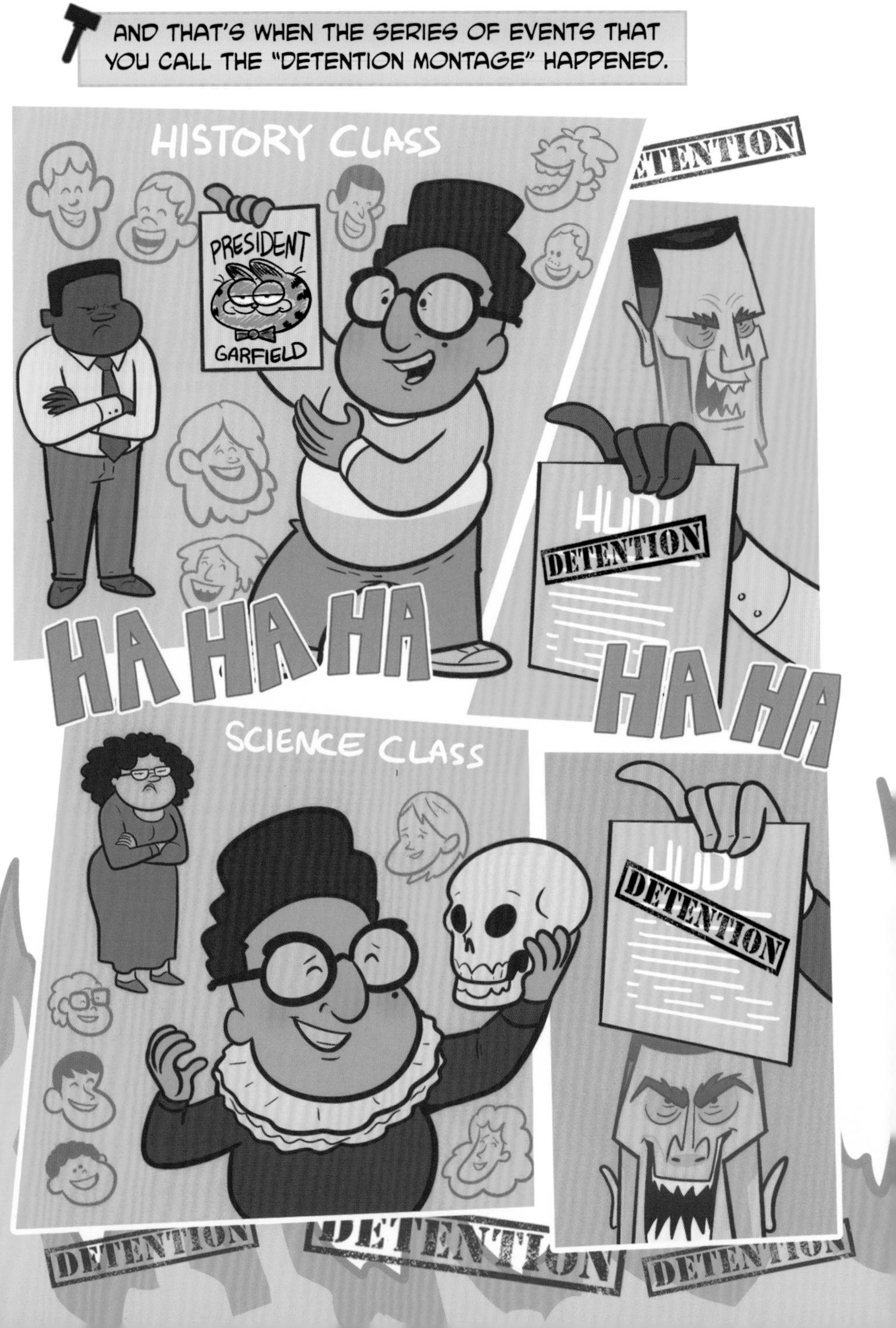
AND THAT'S WHEN THE SERIES OF EVENTS THAT YOU CALL THE "DETENTION MONTAGE" HAPPENED.
HISTORY CLASS
PRESIDENT
GARFIELD
DETENTION
HA HA HA
HA HA
SCIENCE CLASS
DETENTION
DETENTION

THAT'S RIGHT. IMAGINE LISTENING TO "BAD TO THE BONE" BY GEORGE THOROGOOD AND THE DESTROYERS.

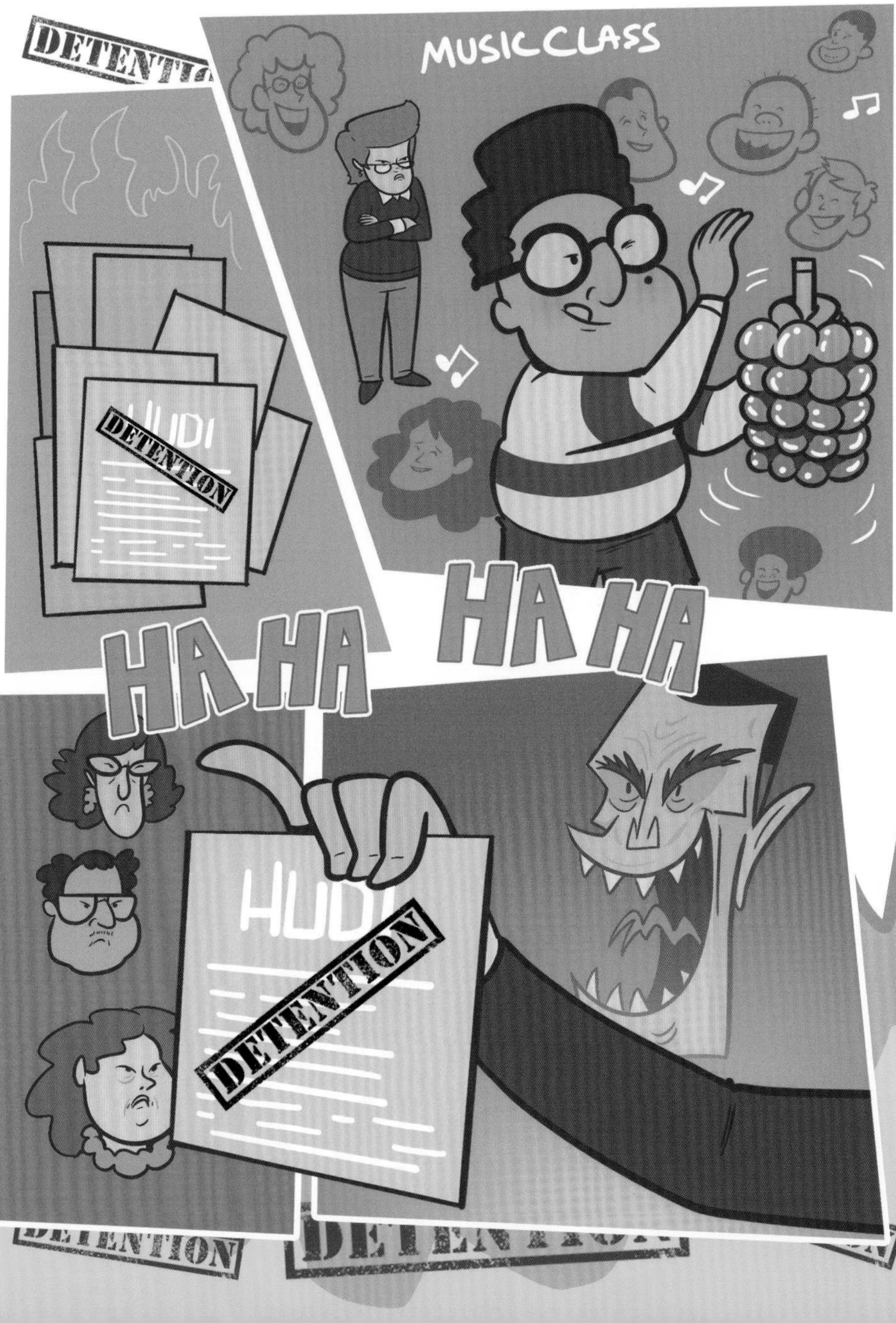
DETENTION
MUSIC CLASS
DETENTION
HA HA
HA HA
DETENTION
DETENTION

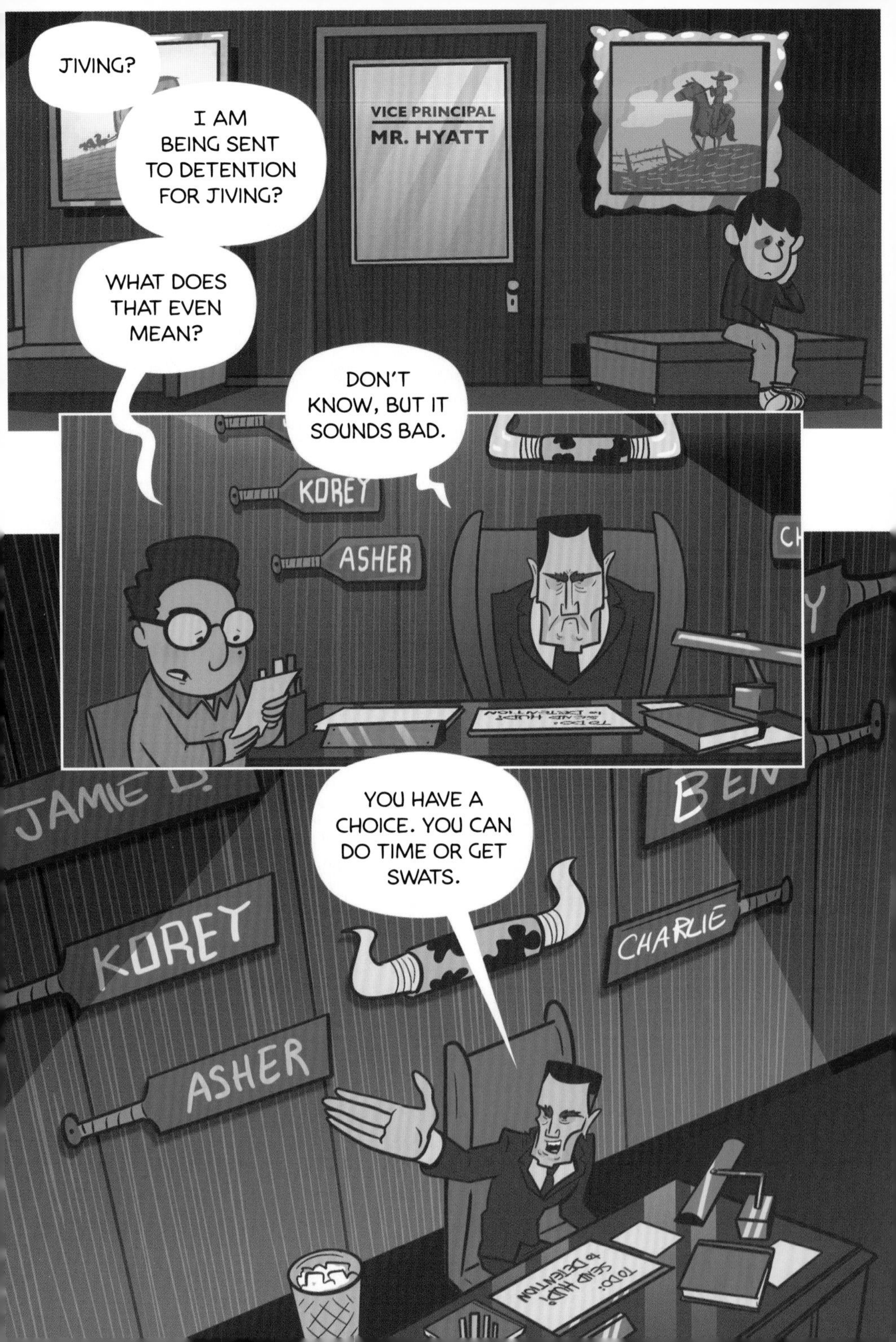
VICE PRINCIPAL
MR. HYATT
JIVING?
I AM BEING SENT TO DETENTION FOR JIVING?
WHAT DOES THAT EVEN MEAN?
DON'T KNOW, BUT IT SOUNDS BAD.
KOREY
ASHER
JAMIE D.
BEN
YOU HAVE A CHOICE. YOU CAN DO TIME OR GET SWATS.
KOREY
CHARLIE
ASHER
TO DO: SEND HUP! to DETENTION

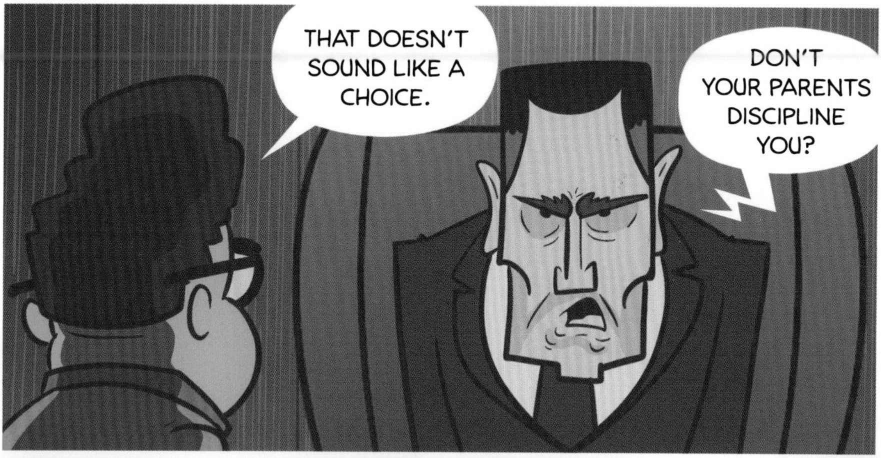
THAT DOESN'T SOUND LIKE A CHOICE.
DON'T YOUR PARENTS DISCIPLINE YOU?

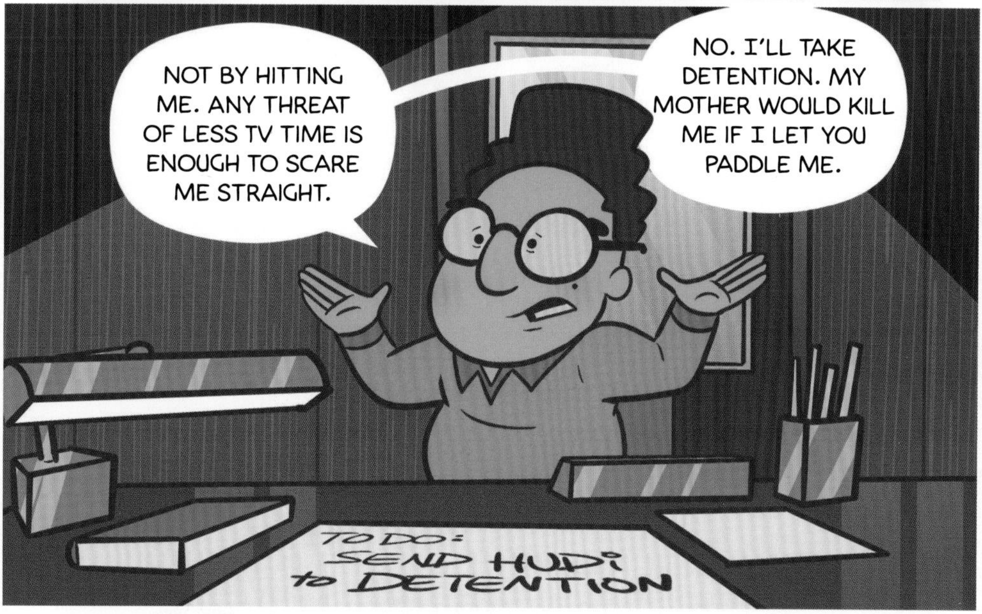
NOT BY HITTING ME. ANY THREAT OF LESS TV TIME IS ENOUGH TO SCARE ME STRAIGHT.
NO. I'LL TAKE DETENTION. MY MOTHER WOULD KILL ME IF I LET YOU PADDLE ME.
TO DO: SEND HUDI to DETENTION

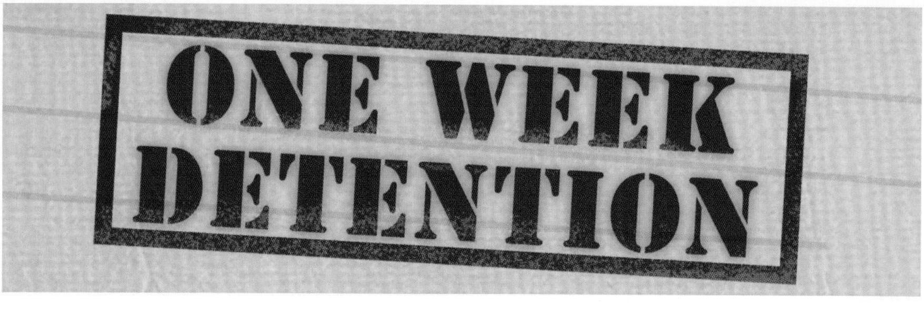
ONE WEEK DETENTION

HUDI on TRIAL

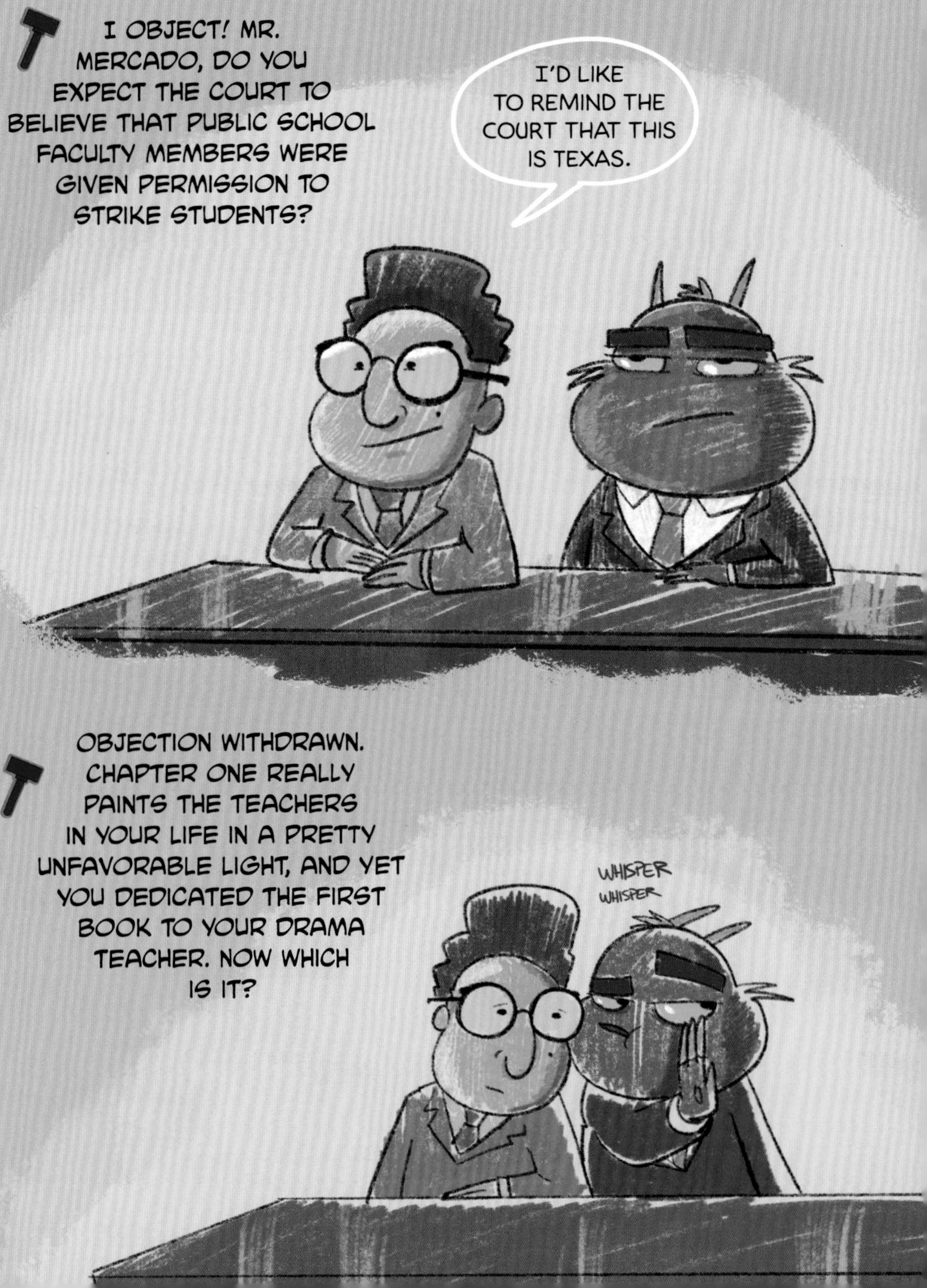
I OBJECT! MR. MERCADO, DO YOU EXPECT THE COURT TO BELIEVE THAT PUBLIC SCHOOL FACULTY MEMBERS WERE GIVEN PERMISSION TO STRIKE STUDENTS?
I'D LIKE TO REMIND THE COURT THAT THIS IS TEXAS.
OBJECTION WITHDRAWN. CHAPTER ONE REALLY PAINTS THE TEACHERS IN YOUR LIFE IN A PRETTY UNFAVORABLE LIGHT, AND YET YOU DEDICATED THE FIRST BOOK TO YOUR DRAMA TEACHER. NOW WHICH IS IT?
WHISPER
WHISPER

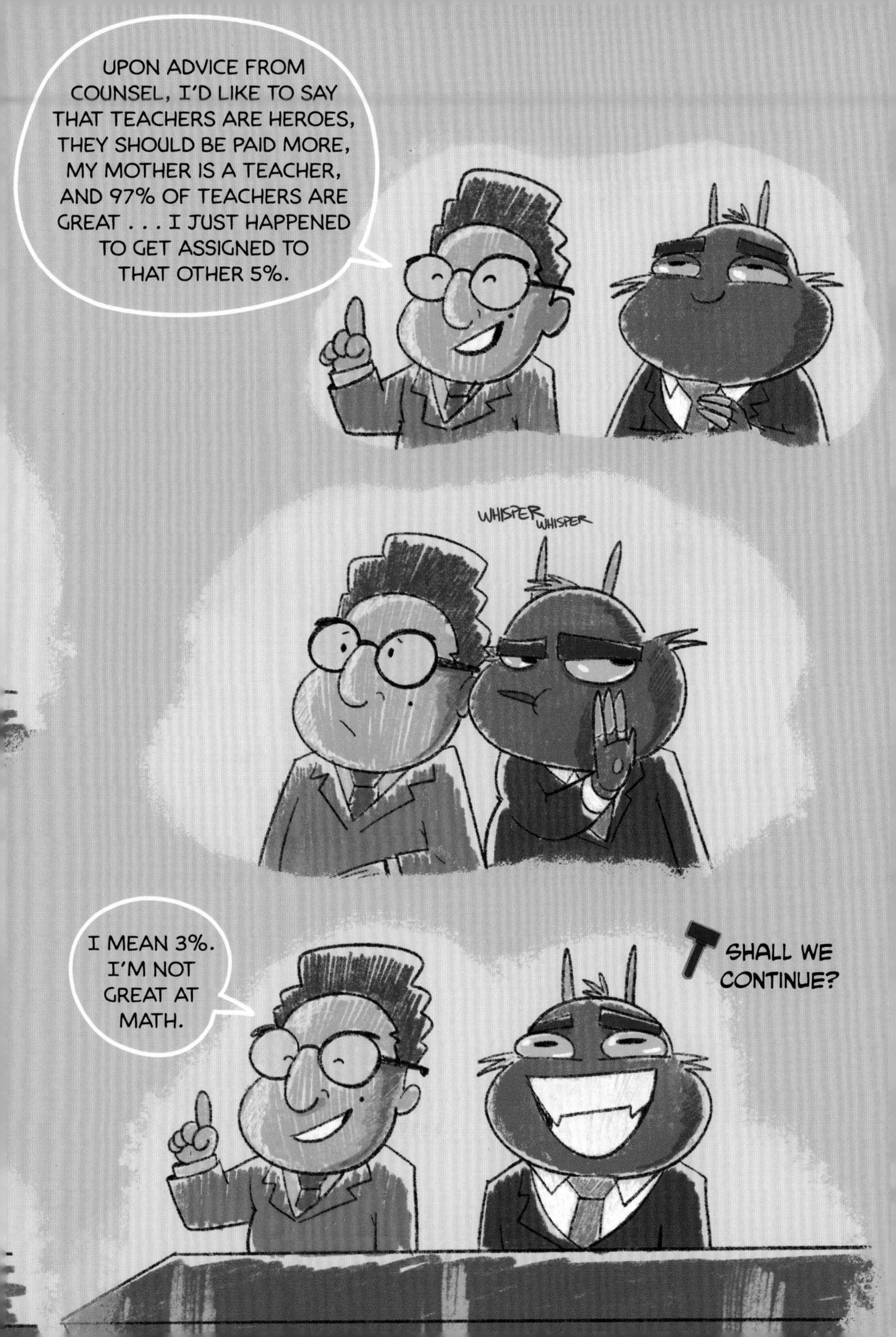
UPON ADVICE FROM COUNSEL, I'D LIKE TO SAY THAT TEACHERS ARE HEROES, THEY SHOULD BE PAID MORE, MY MOTHER IS A TEACHER, AND 97% OF TEACHERS ARE GREAT . . . I JUST HAPPENED TO GET ASSIGNED TO THAT OTHER 5%.
WHISPER WHISPER
I MEAN 3%. I'M NOT GREAT AT MATH.
SHALL WE CONTINUE?

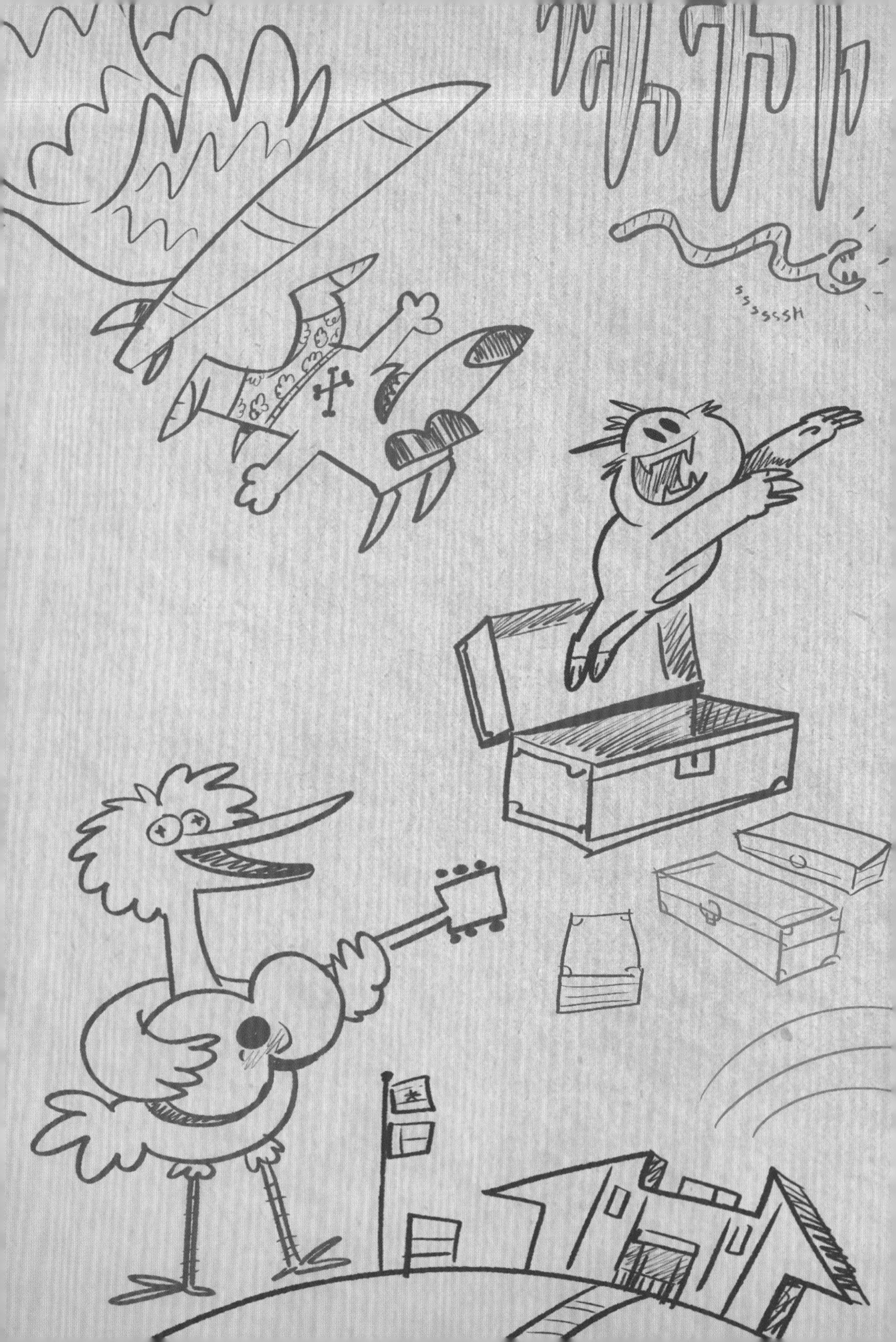
SSSSSSH

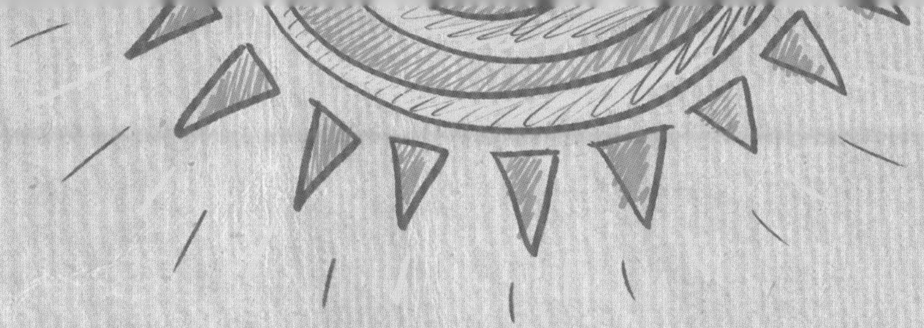

CHAPTER TWO

Goin' to Camp

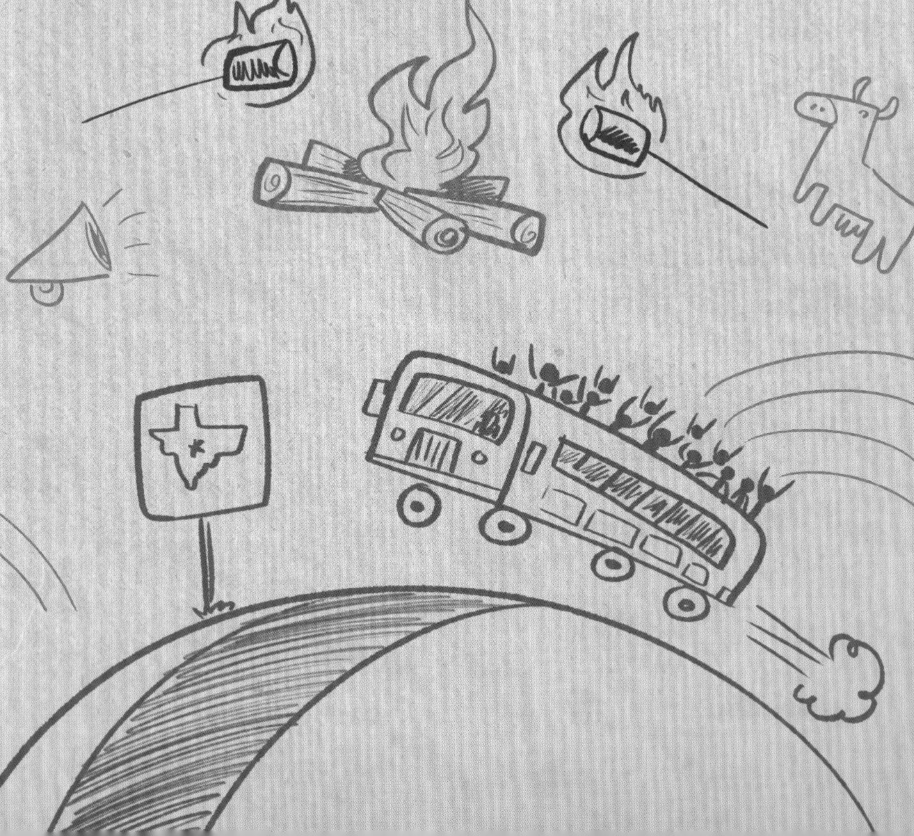

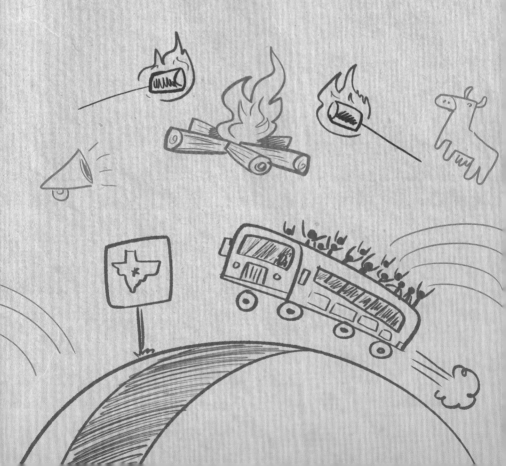

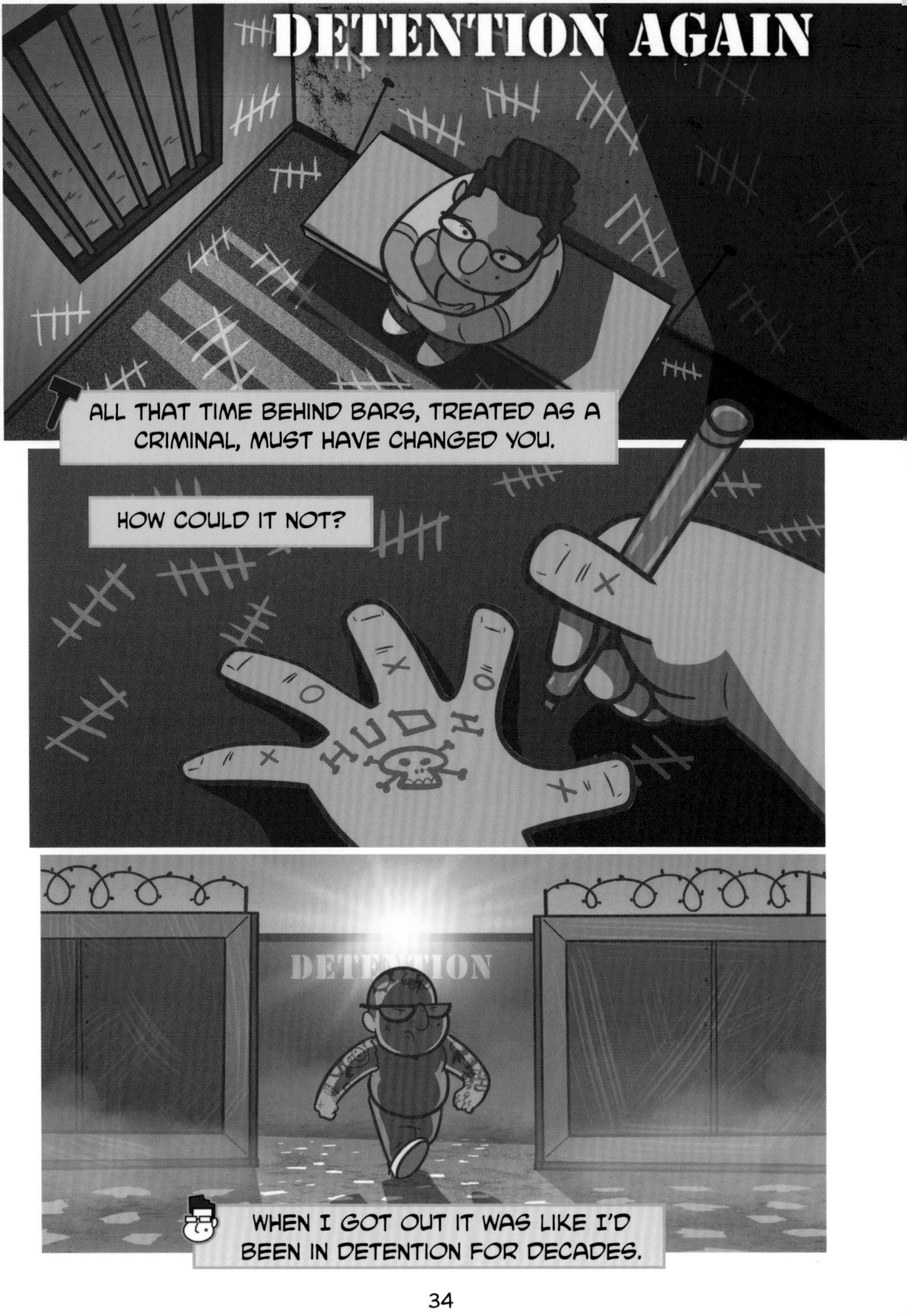
DETENTION AGAIN
ALL THAT TIME BEHIND BARS, TREATED AS A CRIMINAL, MUST HAVE CHANGED YOU.
HOW COULD IT NOT?
WHEN I GOT OUT IT WAS LIKE I'D BEEN IN DETENTION FOR DECADES.

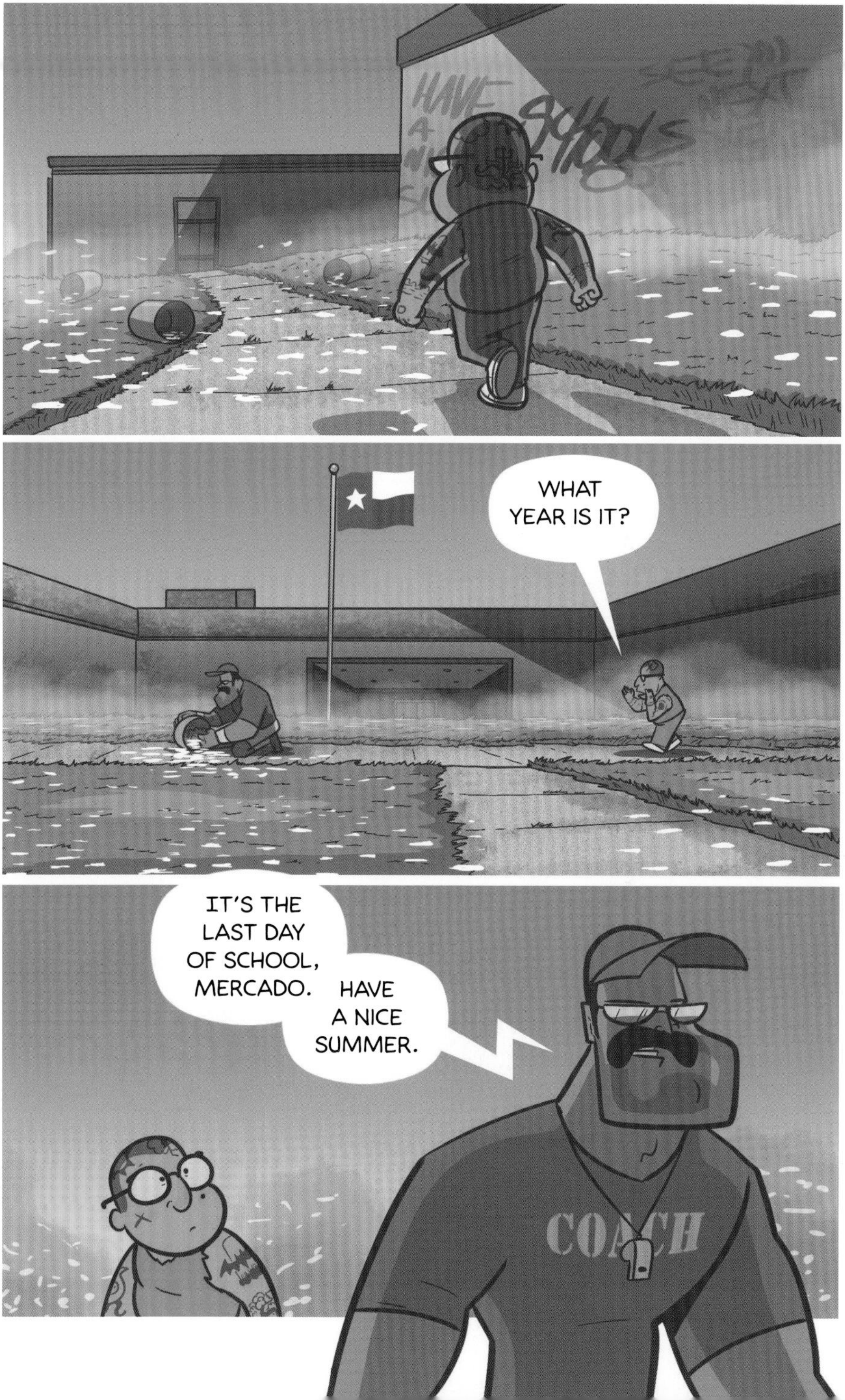
WHAT YEAR IS IT?
IT'S THE LAST DAY OF SCHOOL, MERCADO.
HAVE A NICE SUMMER.
COACH

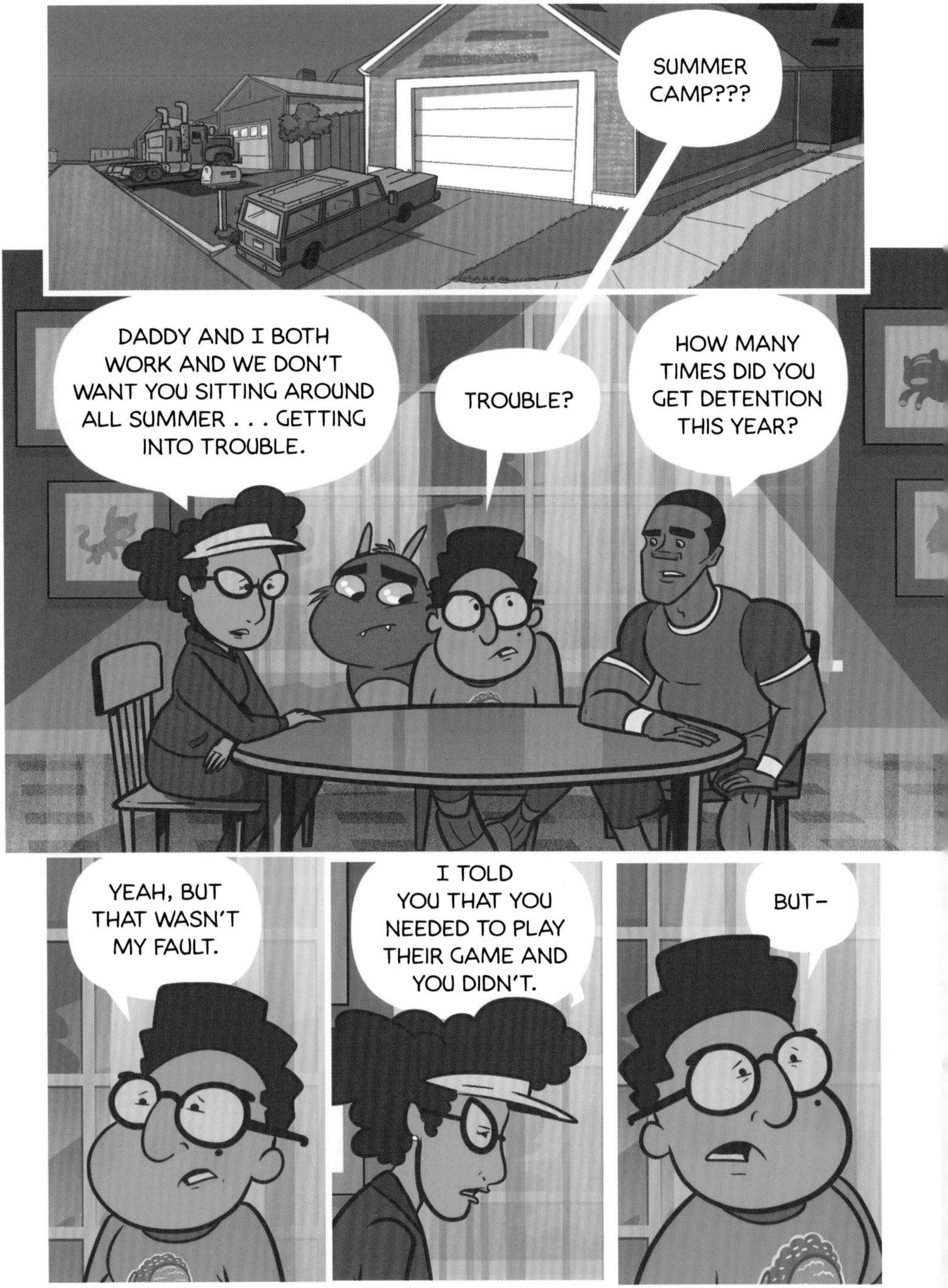
SUMMER CAMP???
DADDY AND I BOTH WORK AND WE DON'T WANT YOU SITTING AROUND ALL SUMMER . . . GETTING INTO TROUBLE.
TROUBLE?
HOW MANY TIMES DID YOU GET DETENTION THIS YEAR?
YEAH, BUT THAT WASN'T MY FAULT.
I TOLD YOU THAT YOU NEEDED TO PLAY THEIR GAME AND YOU DIDN'T.
BUT-

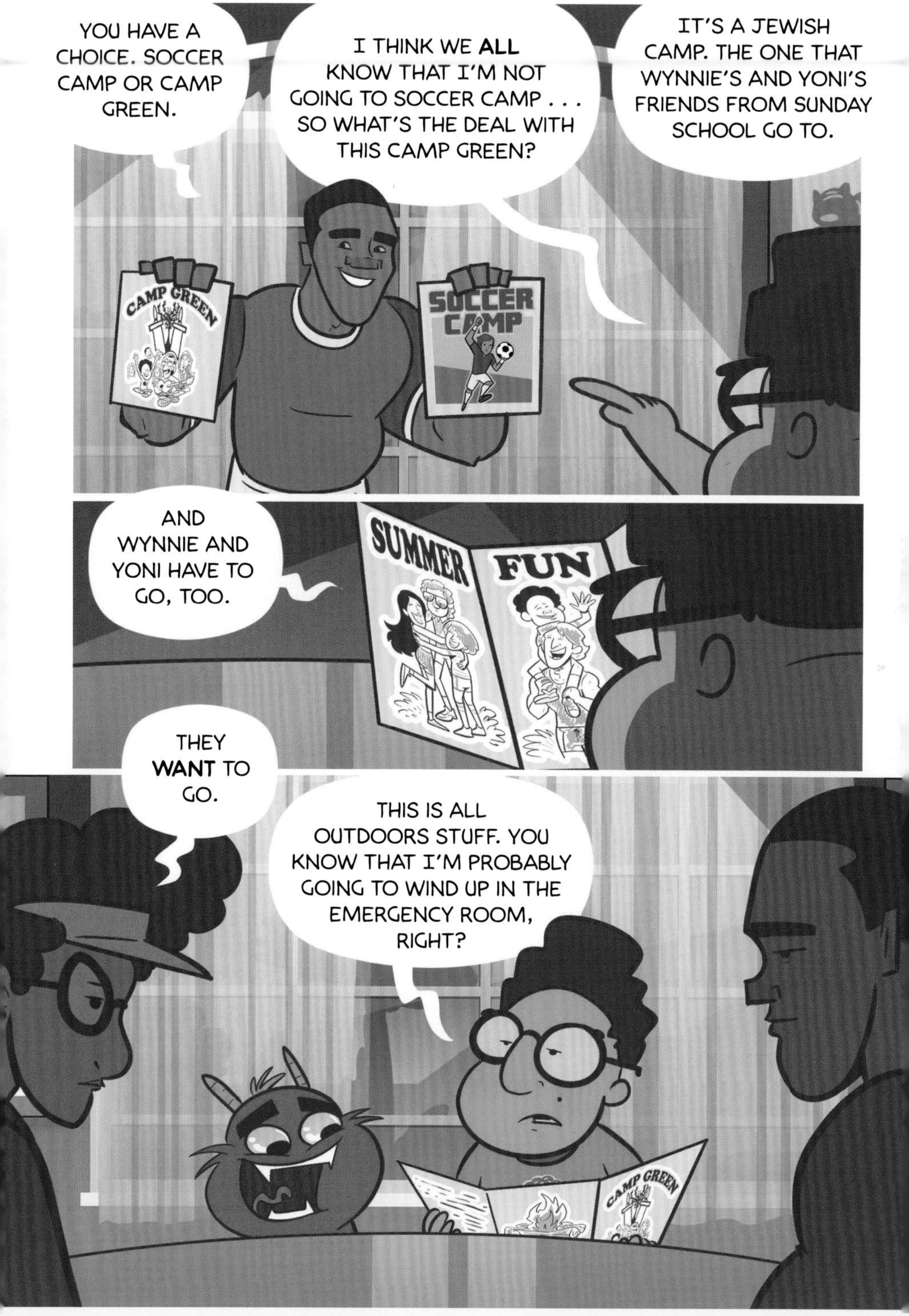
YOU HAVE A CHOICE. SOCCER CAMP OR CAMP GREEN.
I THINK WE **ALL** KNOW THAT I'M NOT GOING TO SOCCER CAMP . . . SO WHAT'S THE DEAL WITH THIS CAMP GREEN?
IT'S A JEWISH CAMP. THE ONE THAT WYNNIE'S AND YONI'S FRIENDS FROM SUNDAY SCHOOL GO TO.
CAMP GREEN
SOCCER CAMP
AND WYNNIE AND YONI HAVE TO GO, TOO.
SUMMER FUN
THEY **WANT** TO GO.
THIS IS ALL OUTDOORS STUFF. YOU KNOW THAT I'M PROBABLY GOING TO WIND UP IN THE EMERGENCY ROOM, RIGHT?
CAMP GREEN

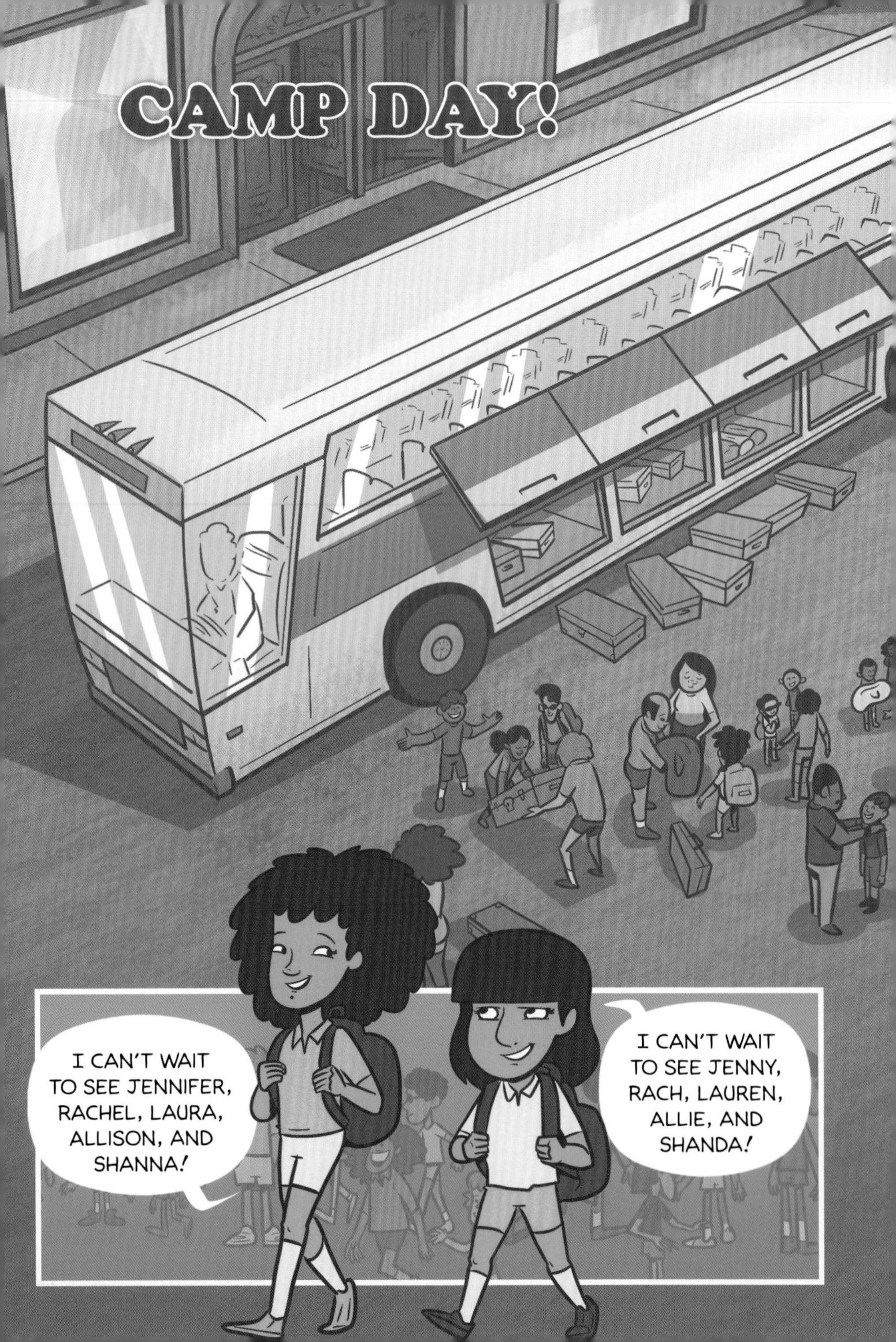
CAMP DAY!
I CAN'T WAIT TO SEE JENNIFER, RACHEL, LAURA, ALLISON, AND SHANNA!
I CAN'T WAIT TO SEE JENNY, RACH, LAUREN, ALLIE, AND SHANDA!

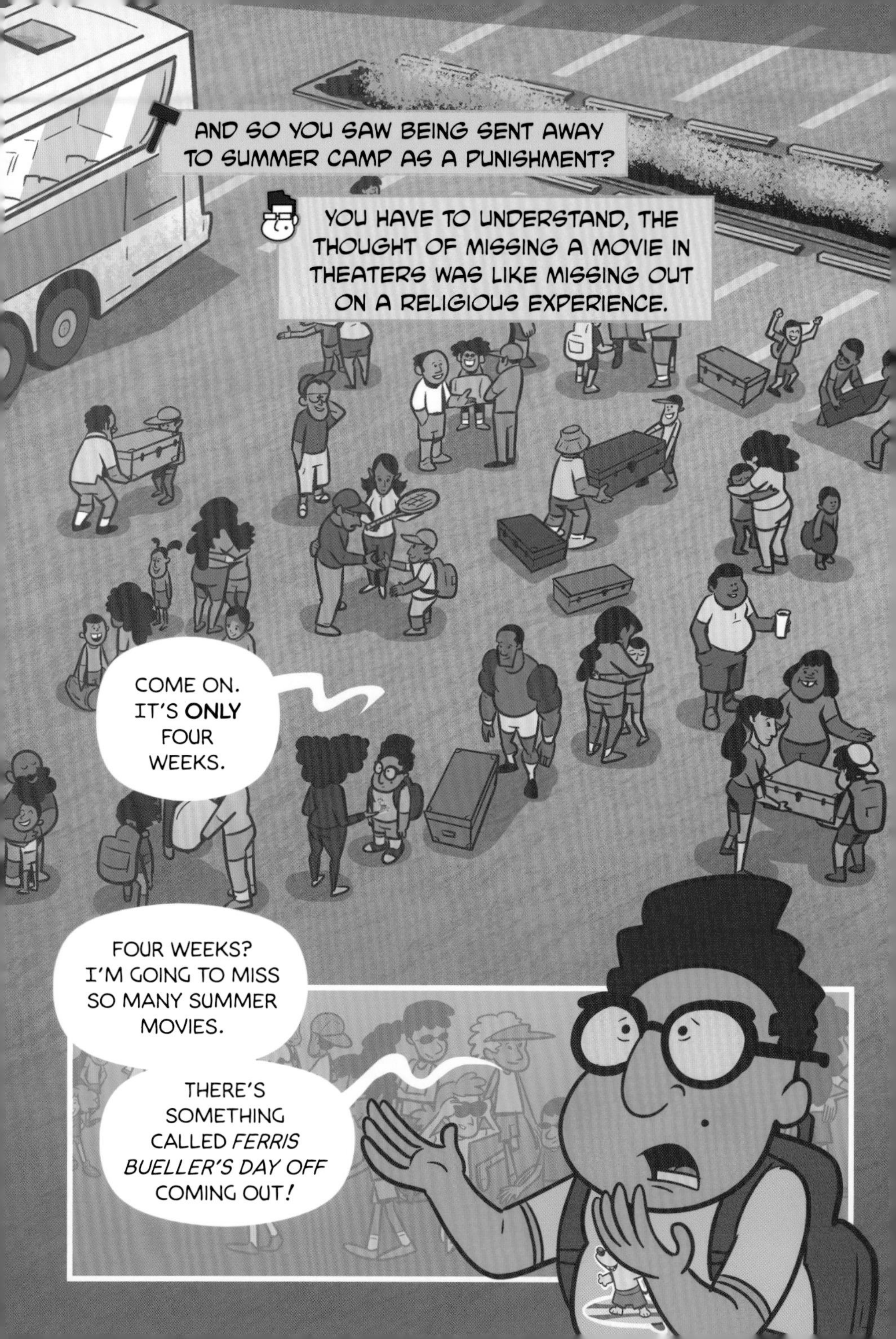
AND SO YOU SAW BEING SENT AWAY TO SUMMER CAMP AS A PUNISHMENT?
YOU HAVE TO UNDERSTAND, THE THOUGHT OF MISSING A MOVIE IN THEATERS WAS LIKE MISSING OUT ON A RELIGIOUS EXPERIENCE.
COME ON. IT'S **ONLY** FOUR WEEKS.
FOUR WEEKS? I'M GOING TO MISS SO MANY SUMMER MOVIES.
THERE'S SOMETHING CALLED *FERRIS BUELLER'S DAY OFF* COMING OUT!

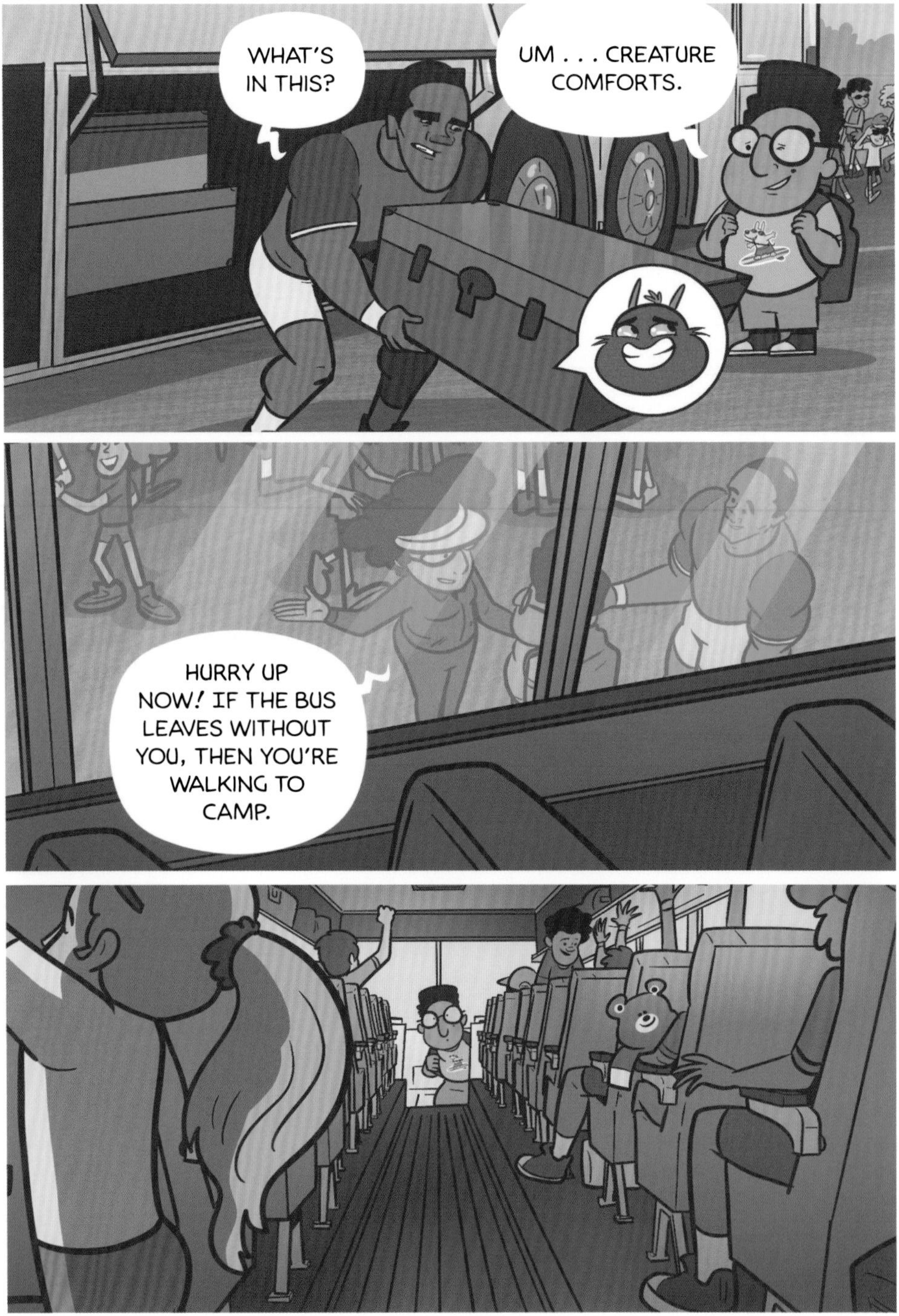
WHAT'S IN THIS?
UM . . . CREATURE COMFORTS.
HURRY UP NOW! IF THE BUS LEAVES WITHOUT YOU, THEN YOU'RE WALKING TO CAMP.

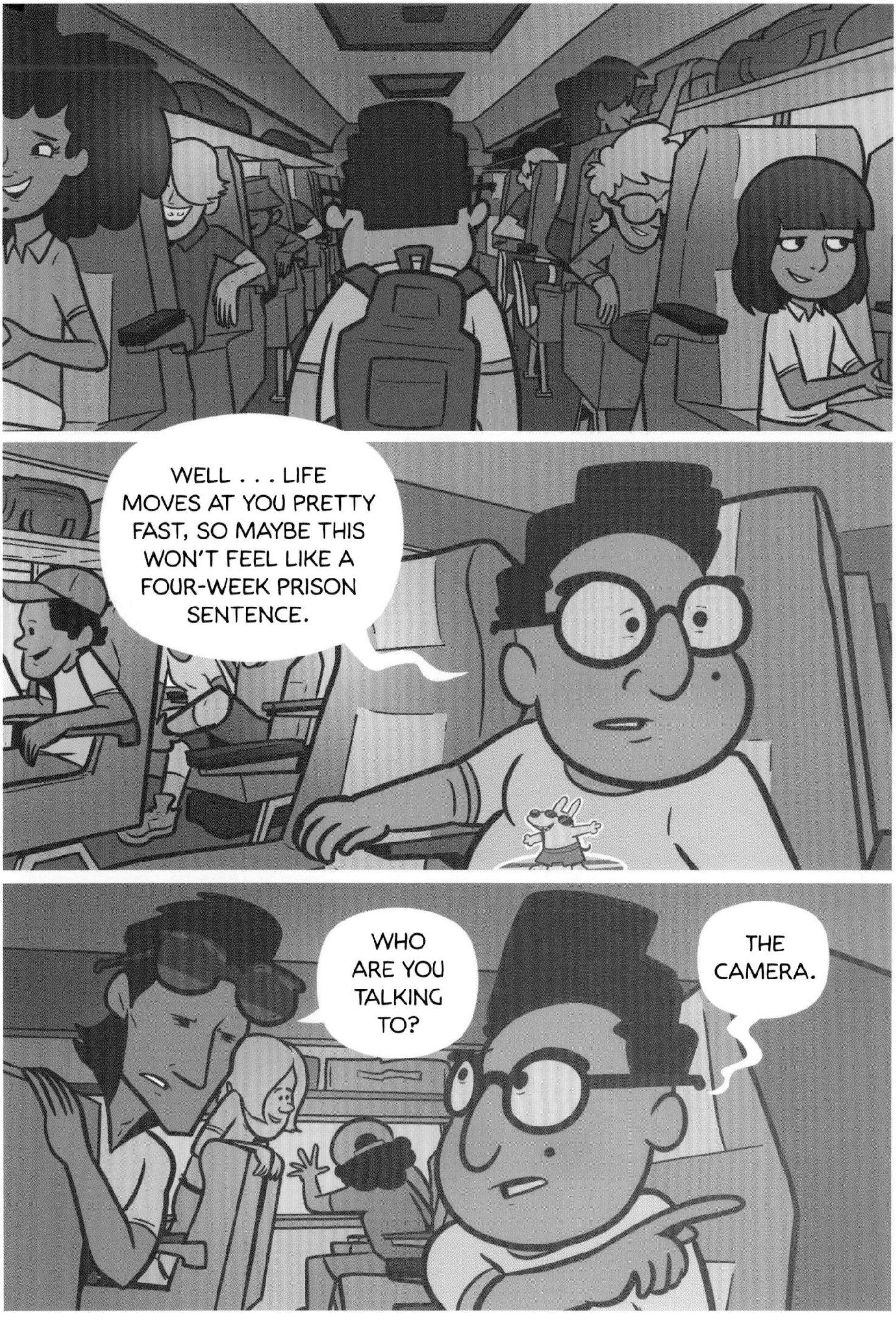
WELL . . . LIFE MOVES AT YOU PRETTY FAST, SO MAYBE THIS WON'T FEEL LIKE A FOUR-WEEK PRISON SENTENCE.
WHO ARE YOU TALKING TO?
THE CAMERA.

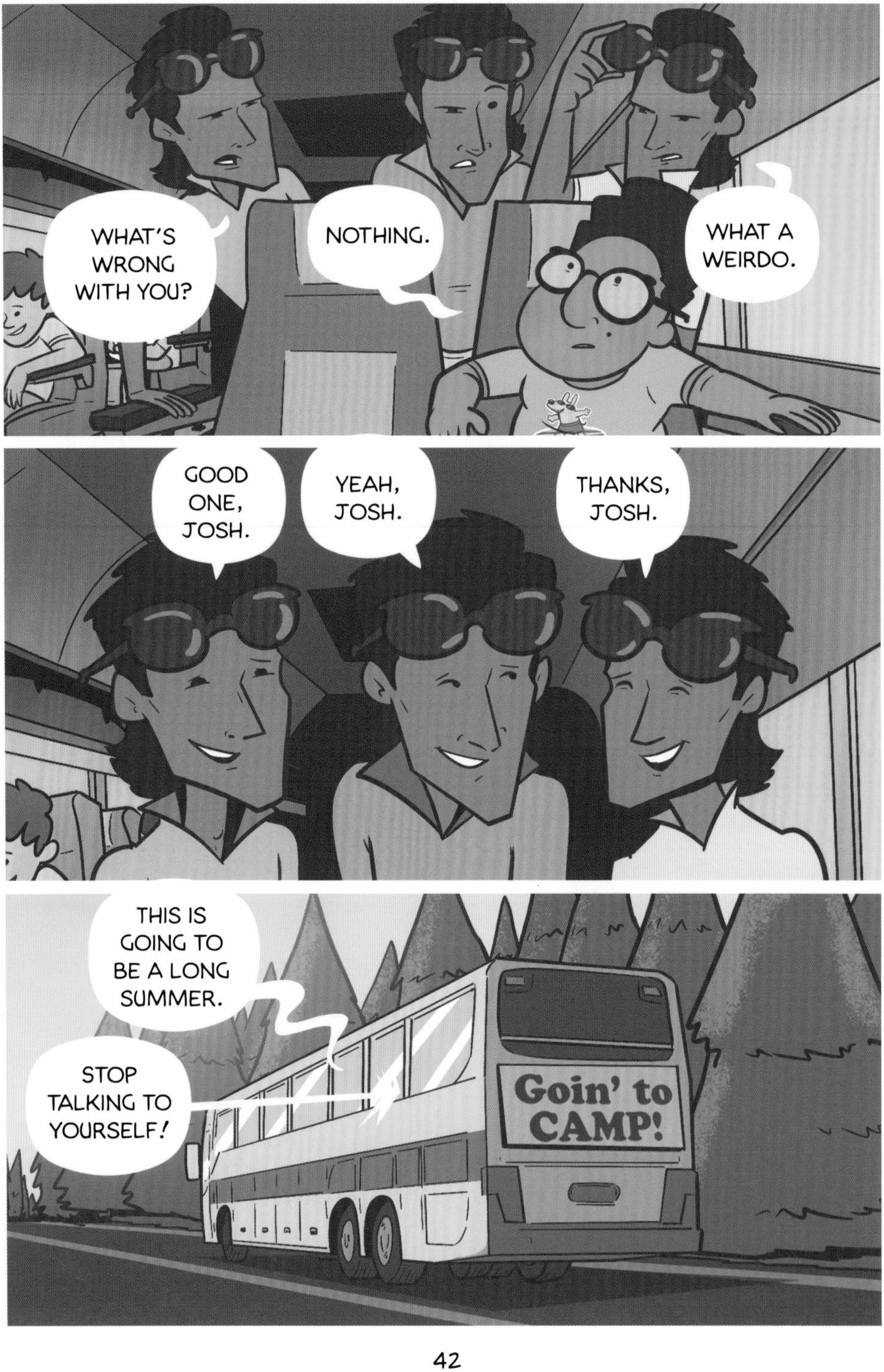
WHAT'S WRONG WITH YOU?
NOTHING.
WHAT A WEIRDO.
GOOD ONE, JOSH.
YEAH, JOSH.
THANKS, JOSH.
THIS IS GOING TO BE A LONG SUMMER.
STOP TALKING TO YOURSELF!
Goin' to CAMP!

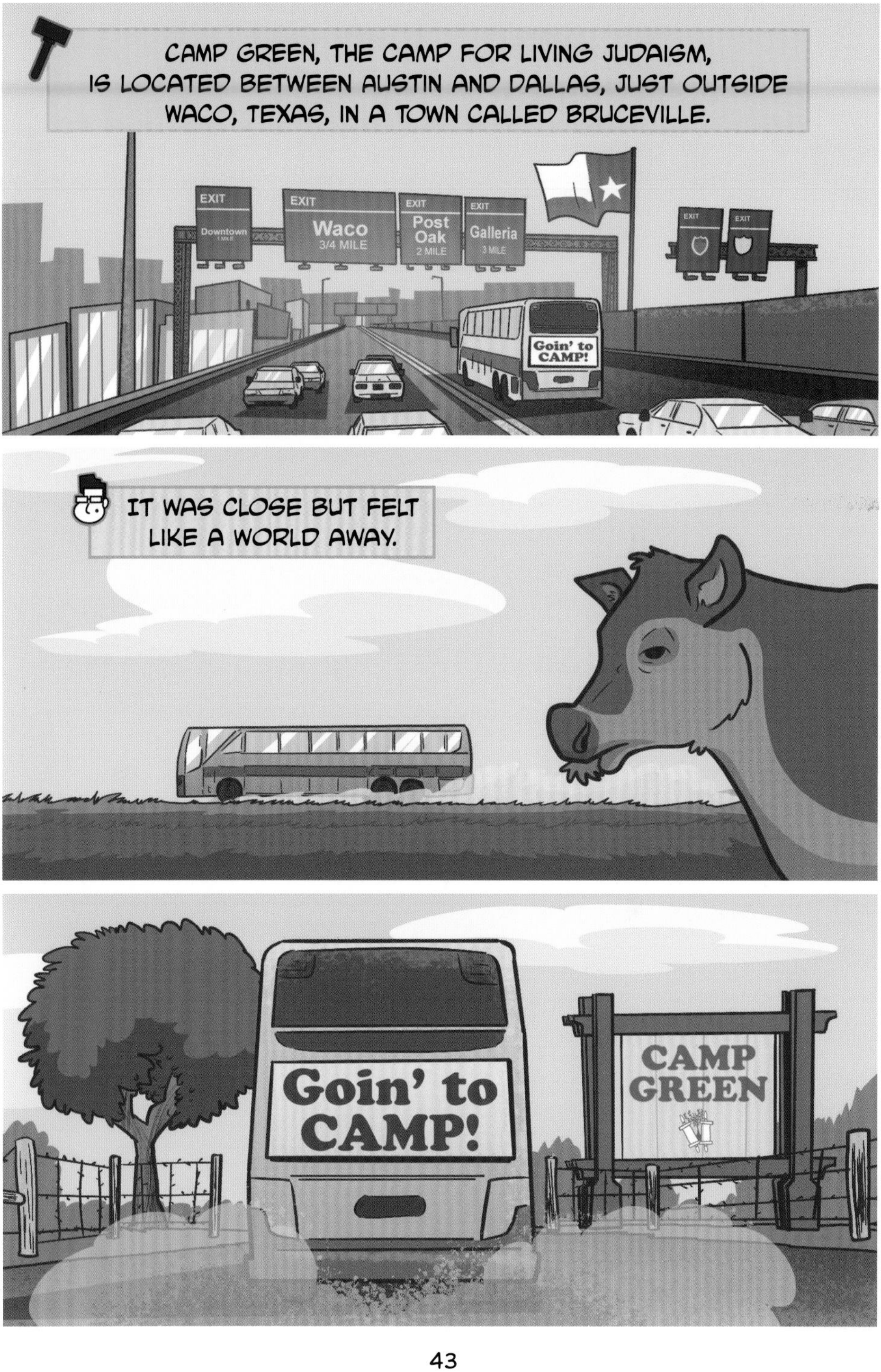
CAMP GREEN, THE CAMP FOR LIVING JUDAISM, IS LOCATED BETWEEN AUSTIN AND DALLAS, JUST OUTSIDE WACO, TEXAS, IN A TOWN CALLED BRUCEVILLE.
EXIT
Downtown
EXIT
Waco
3/4 MILE
EXIT
Post Oak
2 MILE
EXIT
Galleria
3 MILE
EXIT
EXIT
Goin' to CAMP!
IT WAS CLOSE BUT FELT LIKE A WORLD AWAY.
Goin' to CAMP!
CAMP GREEN

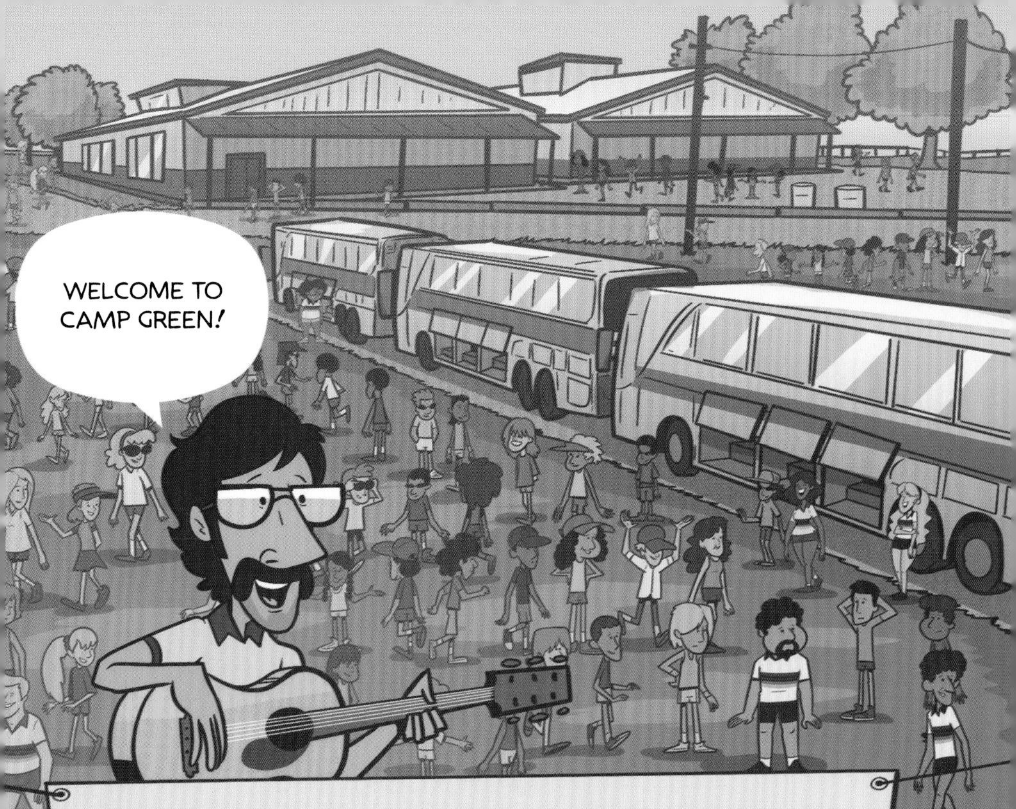
WELCOME TO CAMP GREEN!
SHALOM Y'ALL

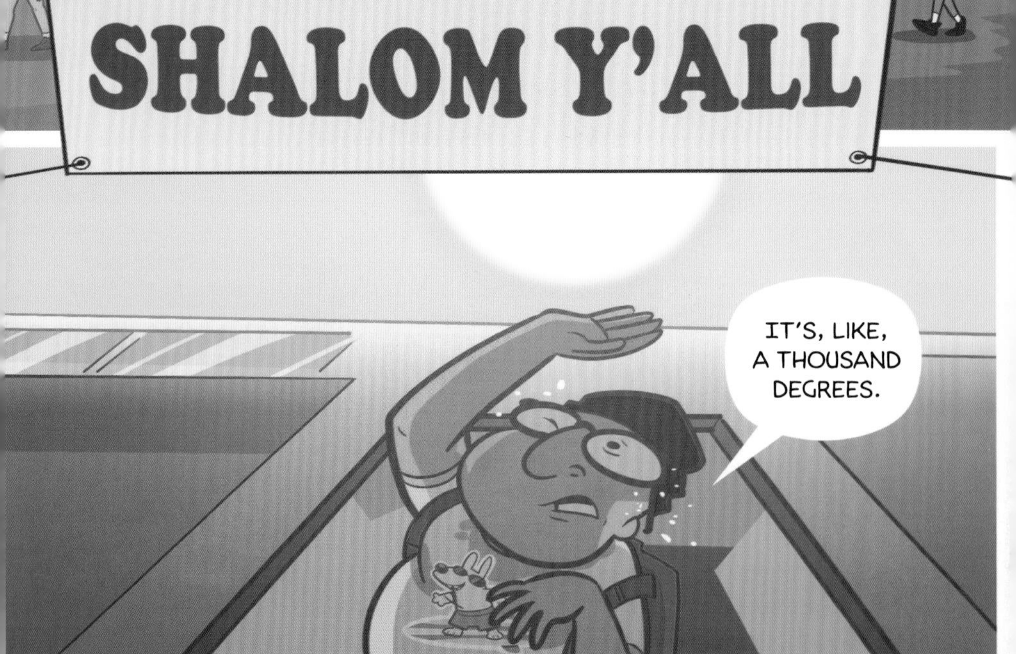
IT'S, LIKE, A THOUSAND DEGREES.

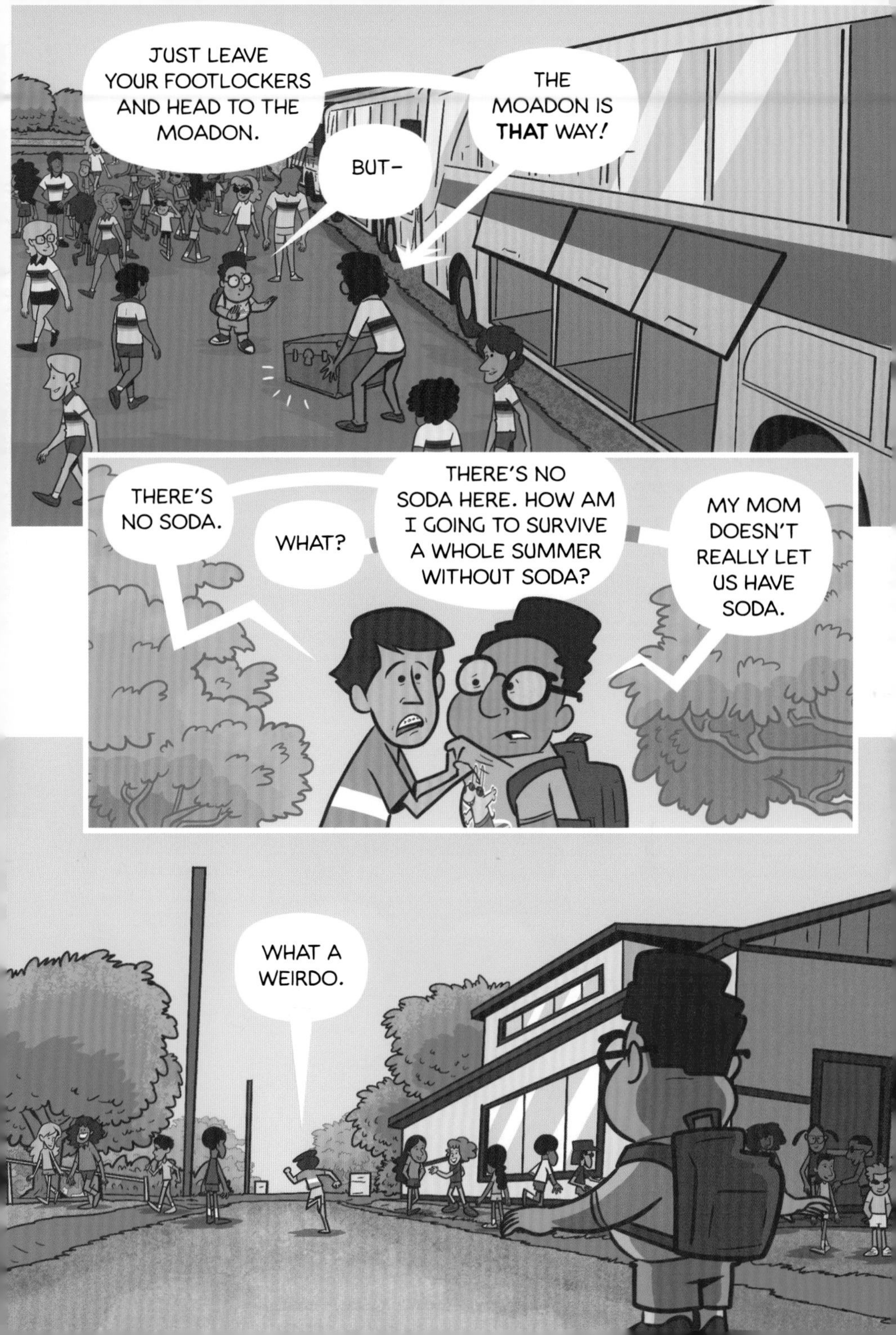
JUST LEAVE YOUR FOOTLOCKERS AND HEAD TO THE MOADON.
BUT-
THE MOADON IS **THAT** WAY!
THERE'S NO SODA.
WHAT?
THERE'S NO SODA HERE. HOW AM I GOING TO SURVIVE A WHOLE SUMMER WITHOUT SODA?
MY MOM DOESN'T REALLY LET US HAVE SODA.
WHAT A WEIRDO.

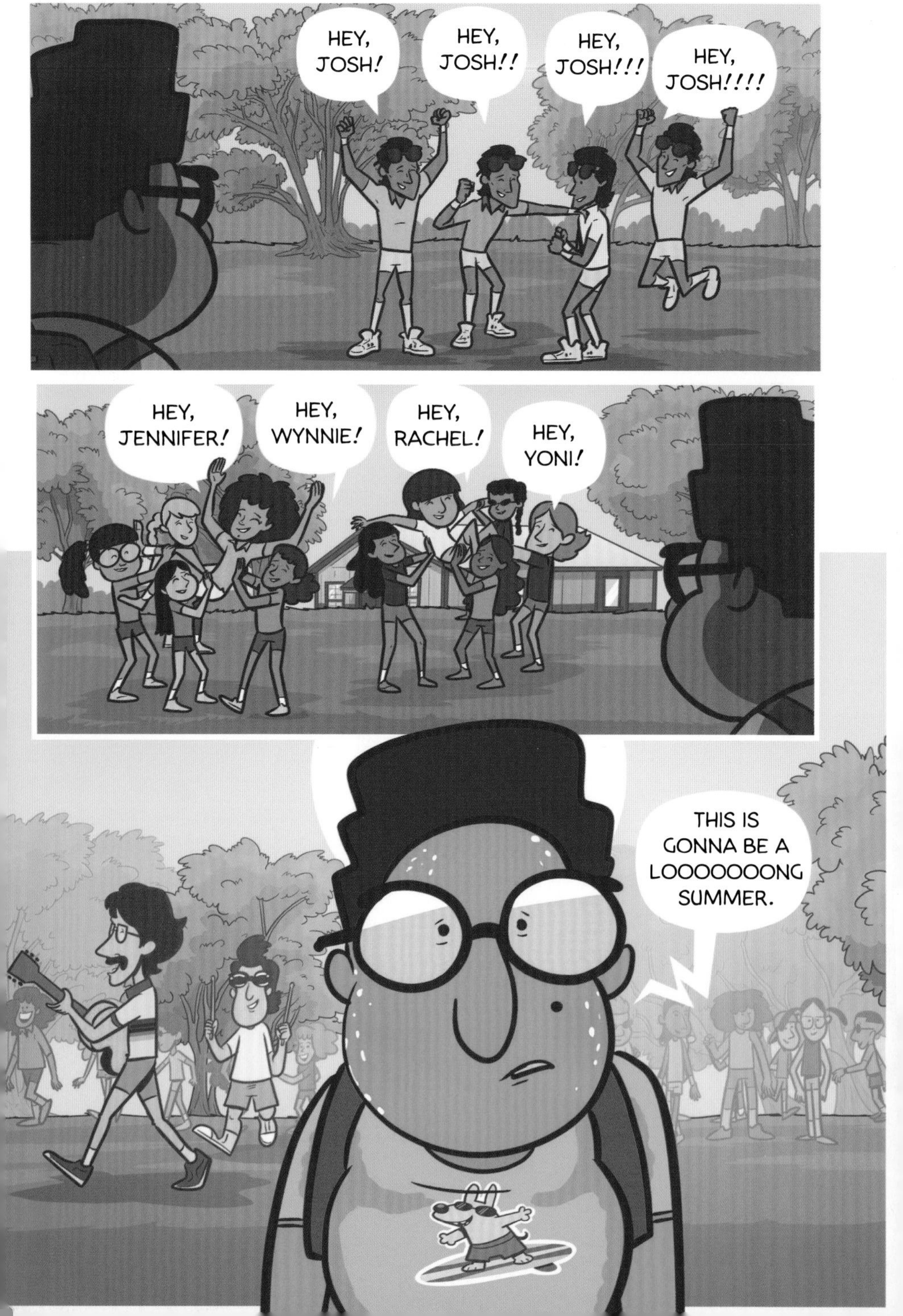
HEY, JOSH!
HEY, JOSH!!
HEY, JOSH!!!
HEY, JOSH!!!!
HEY, JENNIFER!
HEY, WYNNIE!
HEY, RACHEL!
HEY, YONI!
THIS IS GONNA BE A LOOOOOOONG SUMMER.

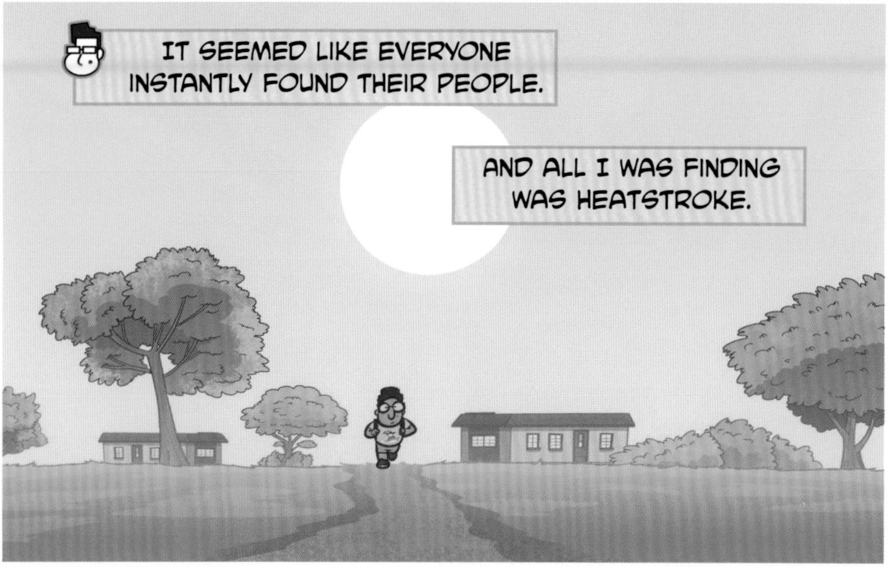
IT SEEMED LIKE EVERYONE INSTANTLY FOUND THEIR PEOPLE.
AND ALL I WAS FINDING WAS HEATSTROKE.

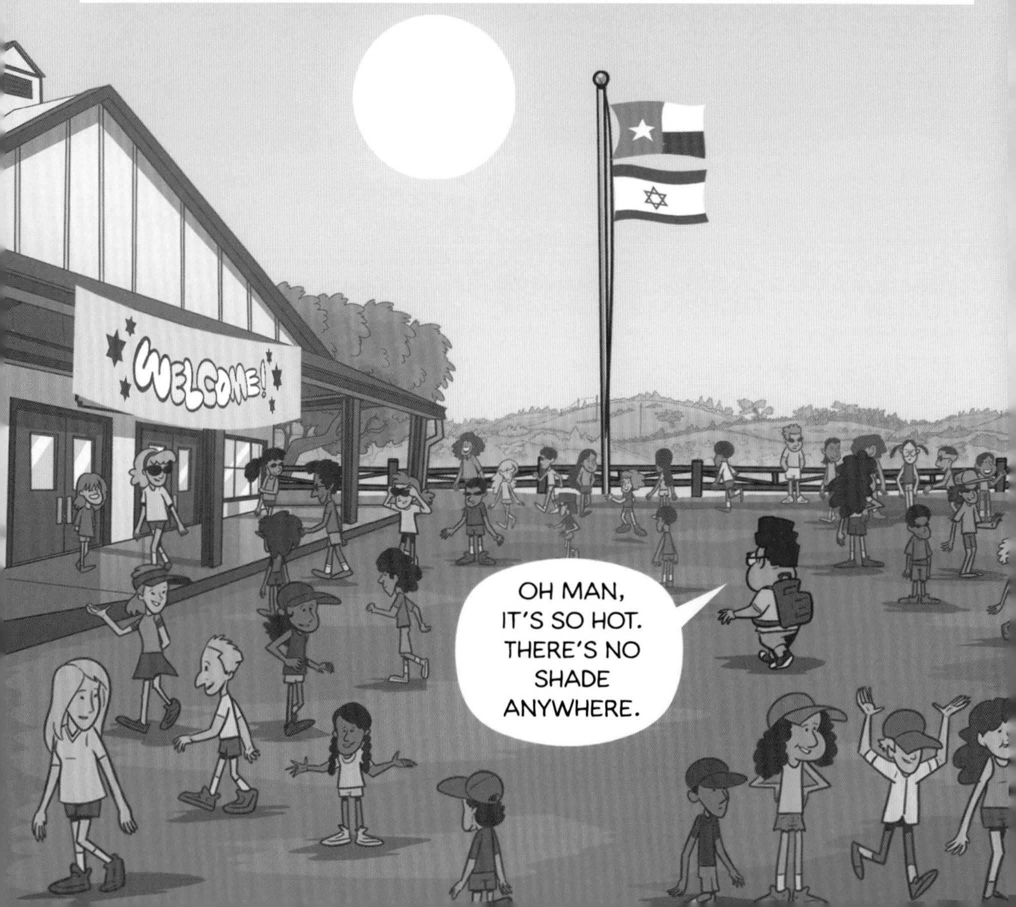
WELCOME!
OH MAN, IT'S SO HOT. THERE'S NO SHADE ANYWHERE.

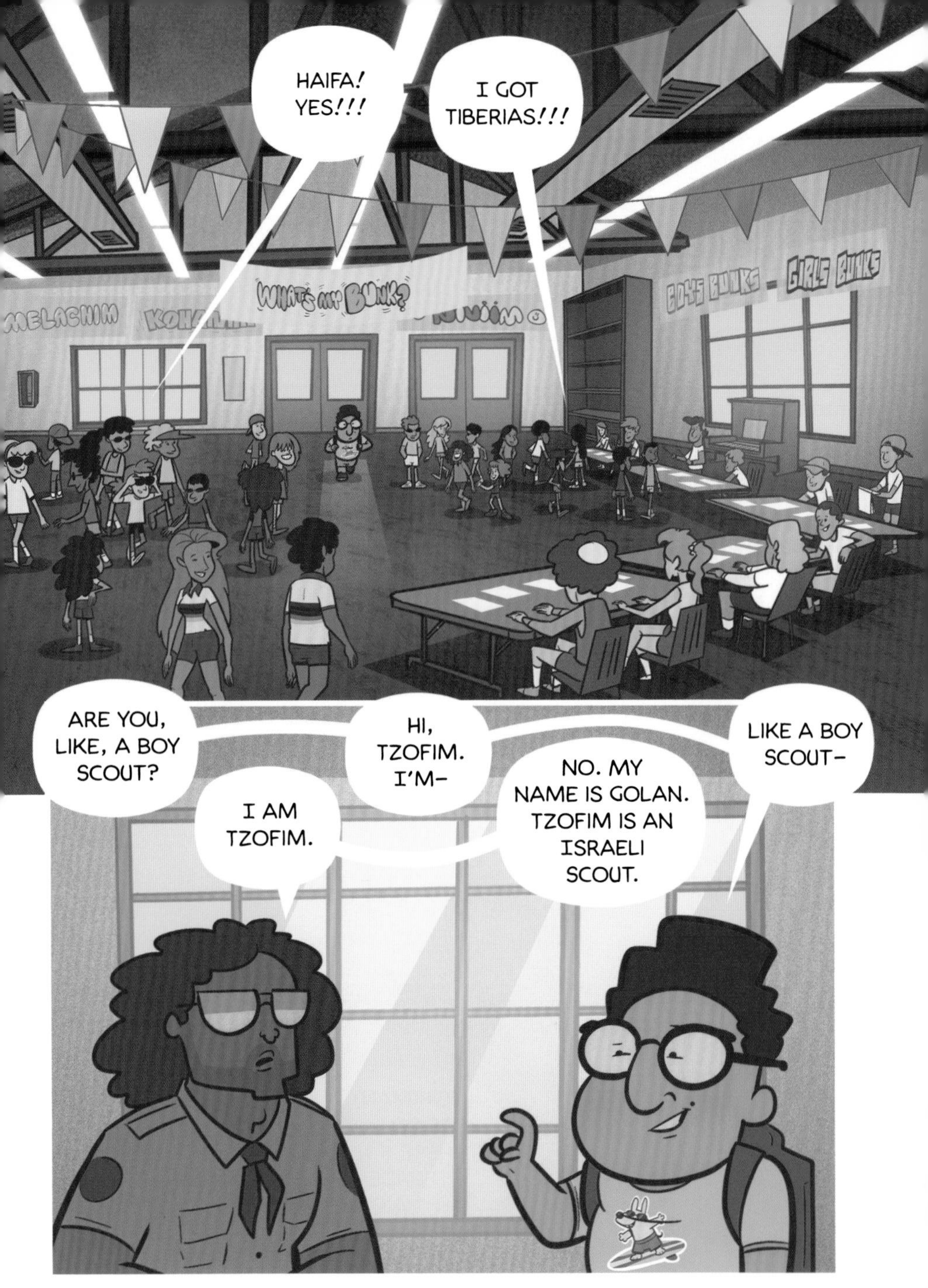
HAIFA! YES!!!
I GOT TIBERIAS!!!
MELACHIM
WHAT'S MY BUNK?
BOYS BUNKS - GIRLS BUNKS
ARE YOU, LIKE, A BOY SCOUT?
I AM TZOFIM.
HI, TZOFIM. I'M–
NO. MY NAME IS GOLAN. TZOFIM IS AN ISRAELI SCOUT.
LIKE A BOY SCOUT–

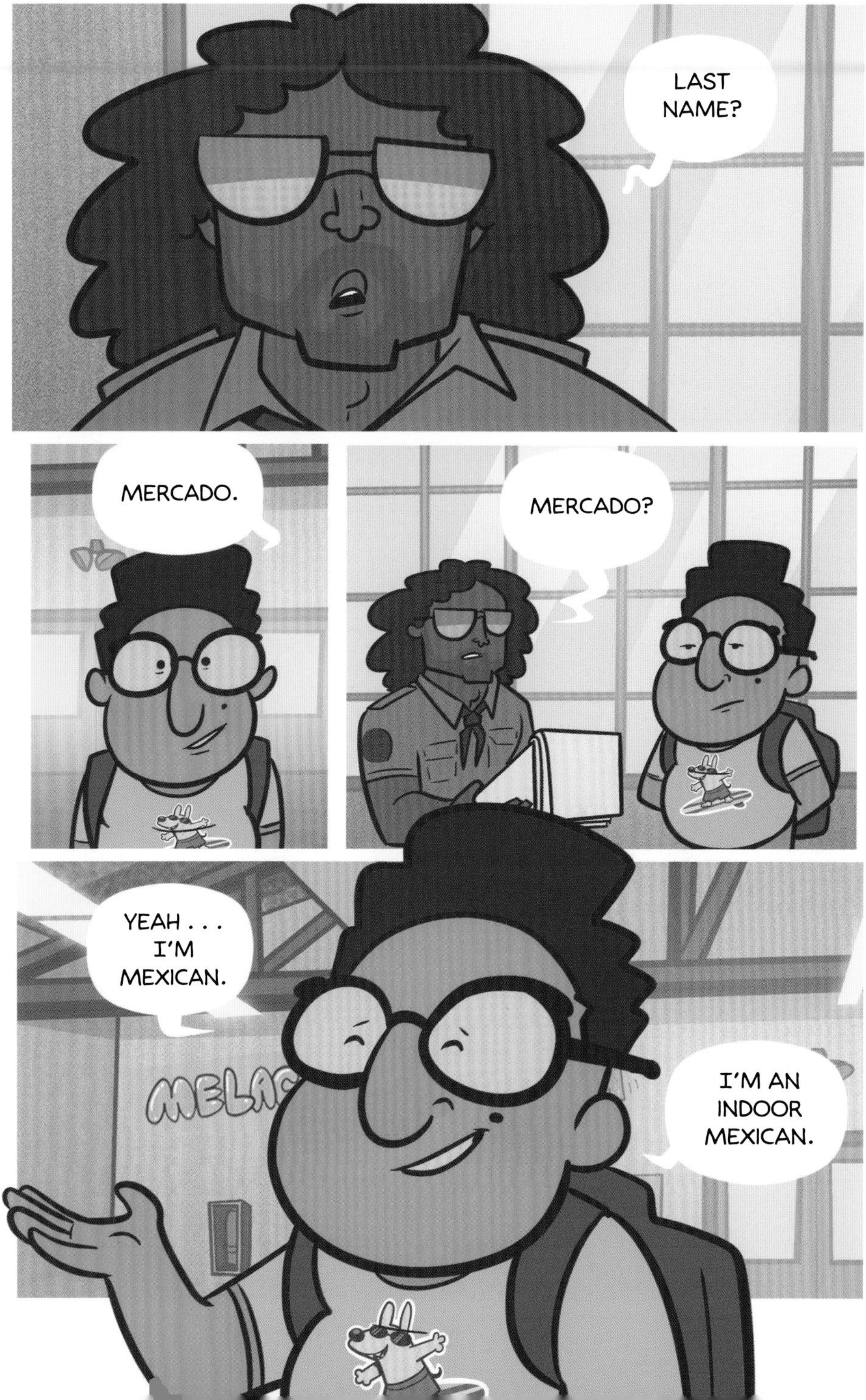
LAST NAME?
MERCADO.
MERCADO?
YEAH . . . I'M MEXICAN.
I'M AN INDOOR MEXICAN.

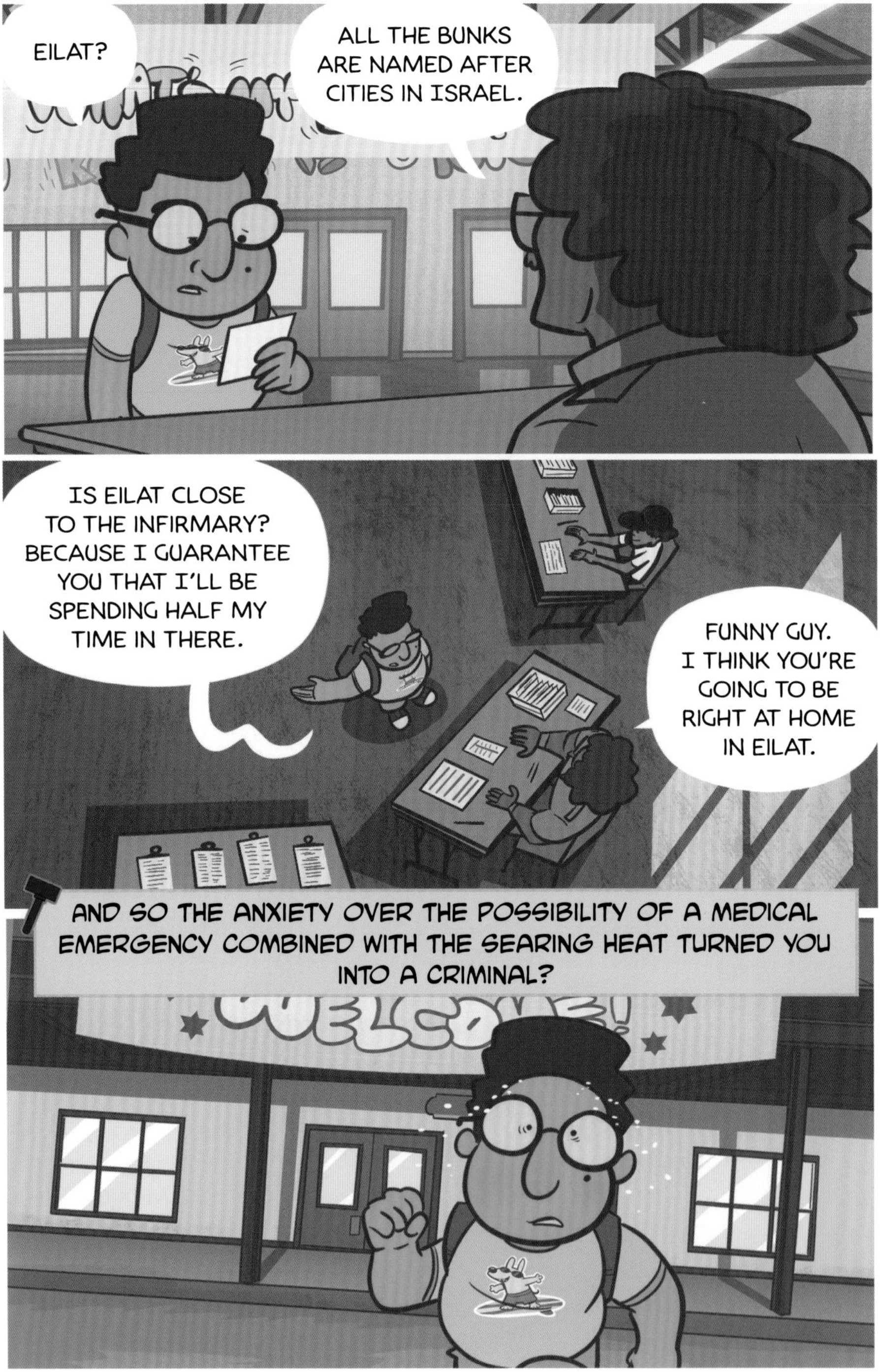
EILAT?
ALL THE BUNKS ARE NAMED AFTER CITIES IN ISRAEL.
IS EILAT CLOSE TO THE INFIRMARY? BECAUSE I GUARANTEE YOU THAT I'LL BE SPENDING HALF MY TIME IN THERE.
FUNNY GUY. I THINK YOU'RE GOING TO BE RIGHT AT HOME IN EILAT.
AND SO THE ANXIETY OVER THE POSSIBILITY OF A MEDICAL EMERGENCY COMBINED WITH THE SEARING HEAT TURNED YOU INTO A CRIMINAL?
WELCOME!

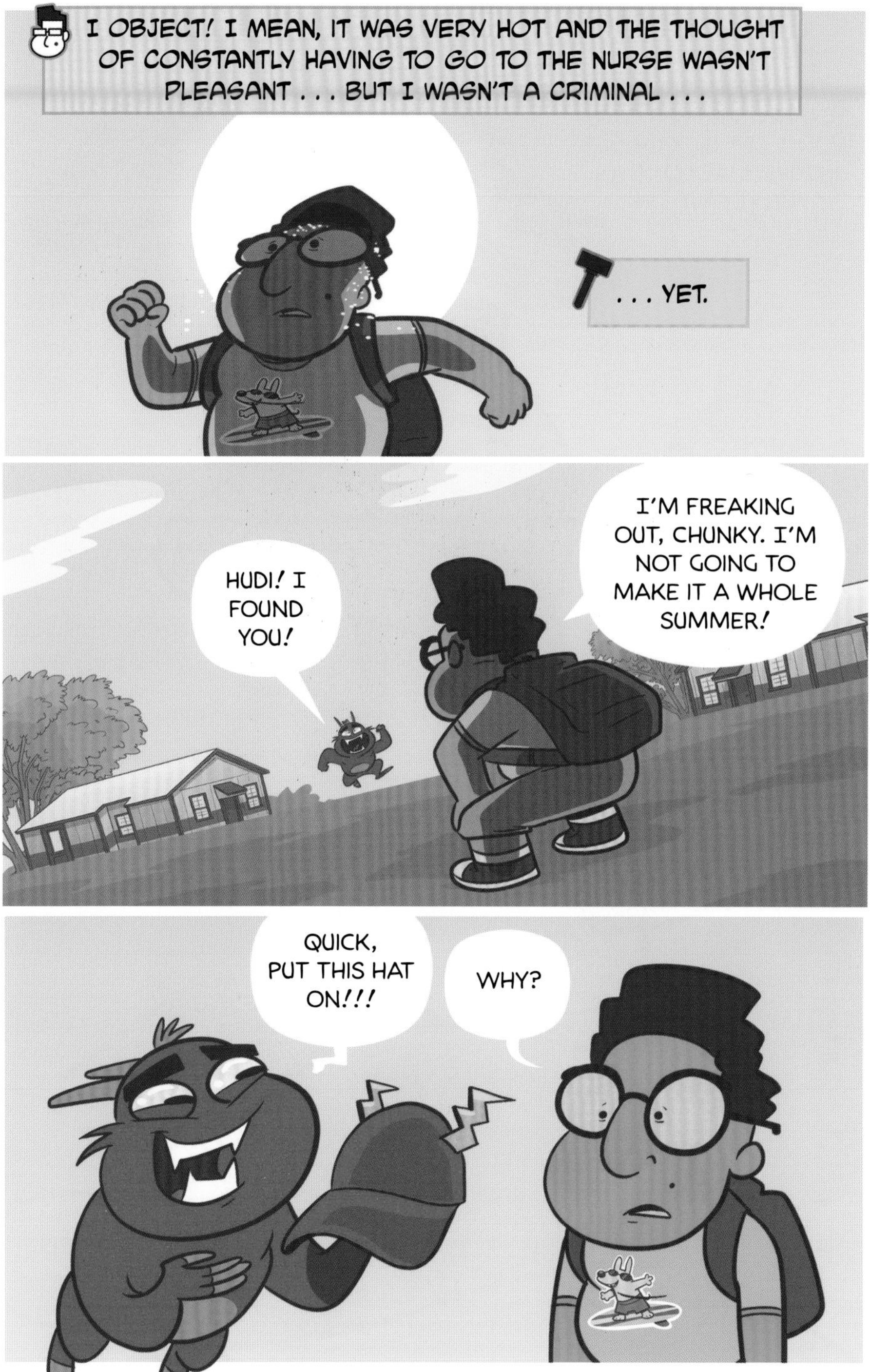
I OBJECT! I MEAN, IT WAS VERY HOT AND THE THOUGHT OF CONSTANTLY HAVING TO GO TO THE NURSE WASN'T PLEASANT . . . BUT I WASN'T A CRIMINAL . . .
. . . YET.
HUDI! I FOUND YOU!
I'M FREAKING OUT, CHUNKY. I'M NOT GOING TO MAKE IT A WHOLE SUMMER!
QUICK, PUT THIS HAT ON!!!
WHY?

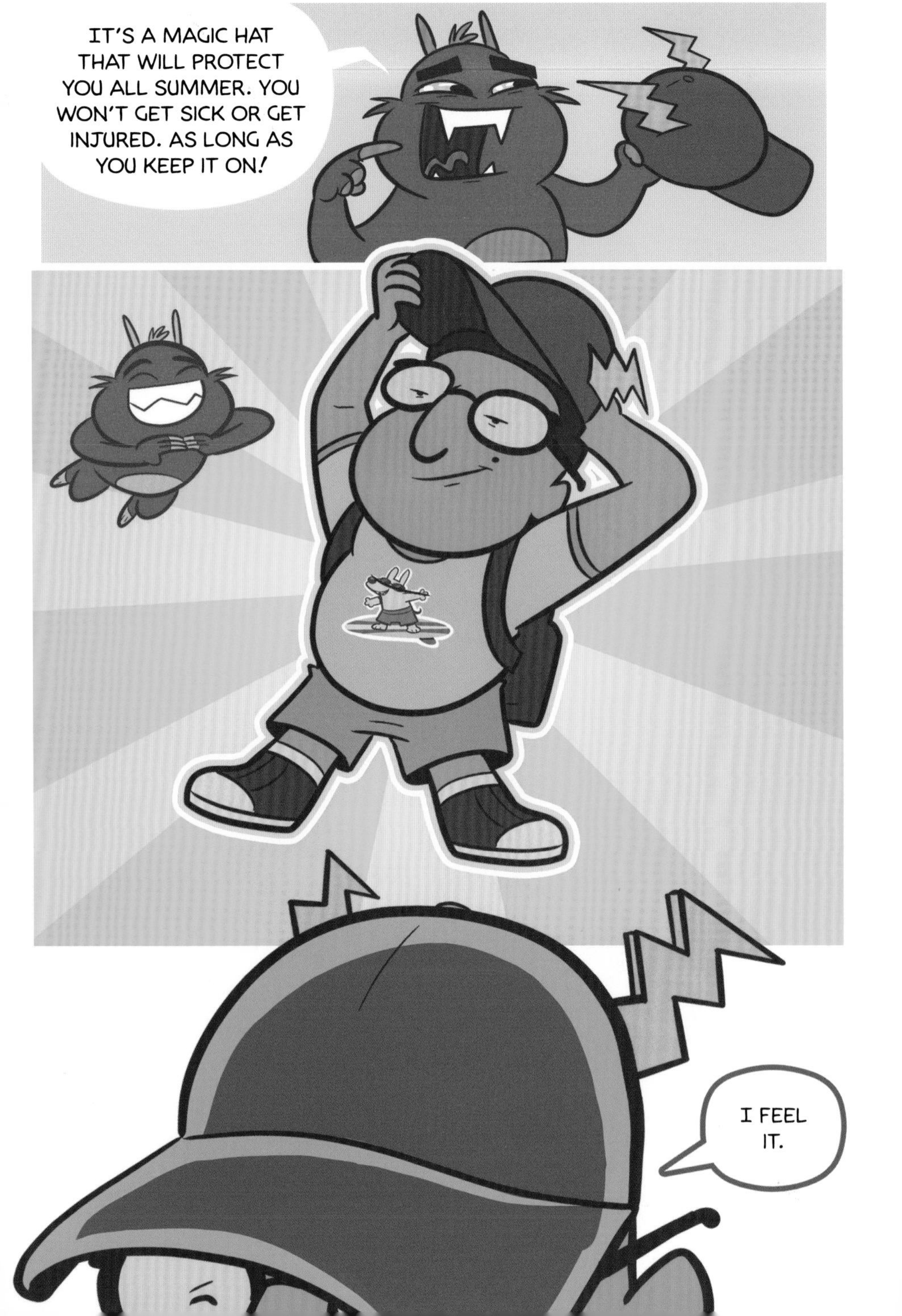
IT'S A MAGIC HAT THAT WILL PROTECT YOU ALL SUMMER. YOU WON'T GET SICK OR GET INJURED. AS LONG AS YOU KEEP IT ON!
I FEEL IT.

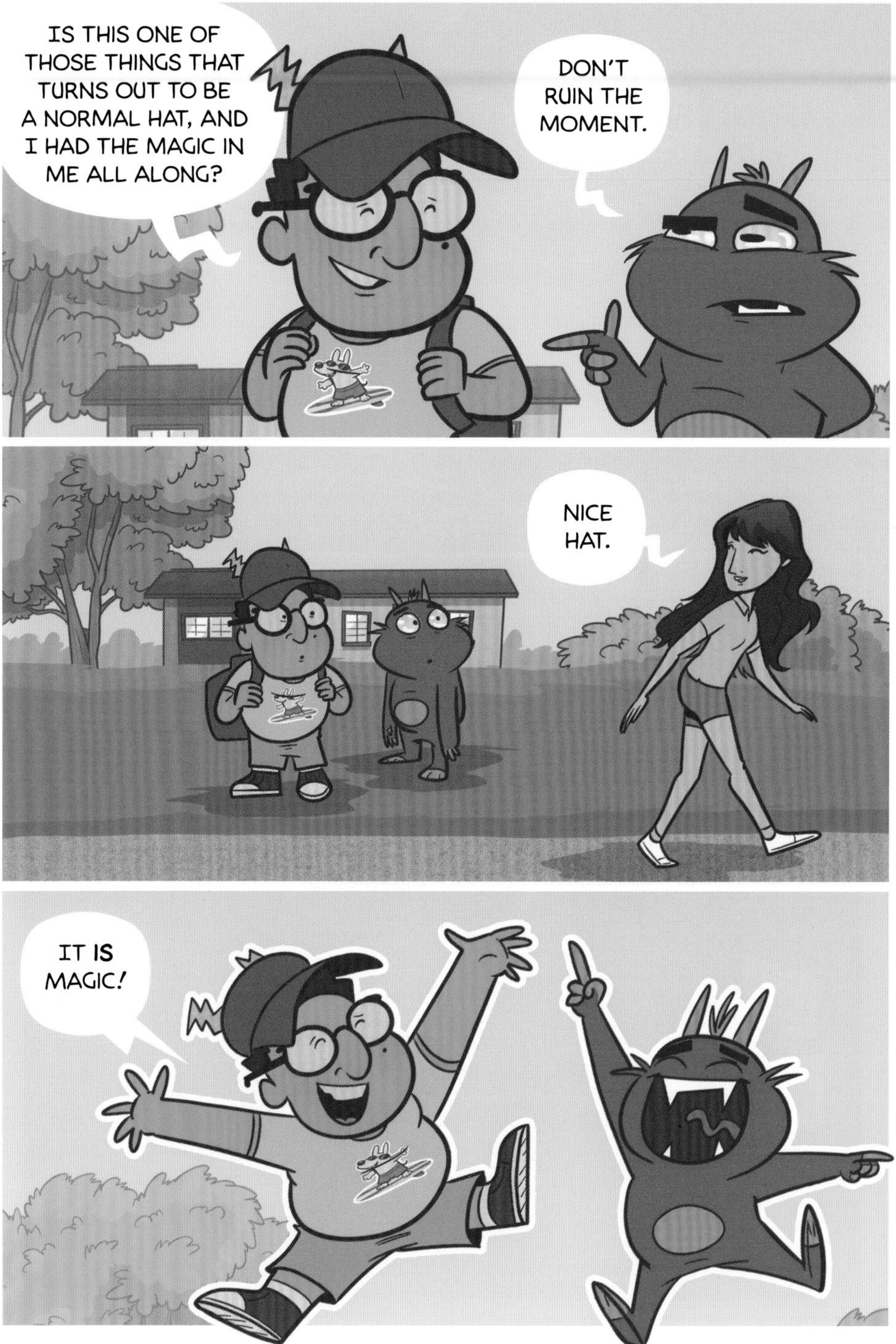
IS THIS ONE OF THOSE THINGS THAT TURNS OUT TO BE A NORMAL HAT, AND I HAD THE MAGIC IN ME ALL ALONG?
DON'T RUIN THE MOMENT.
NICE HAT.
IT **IS** MAGIC!

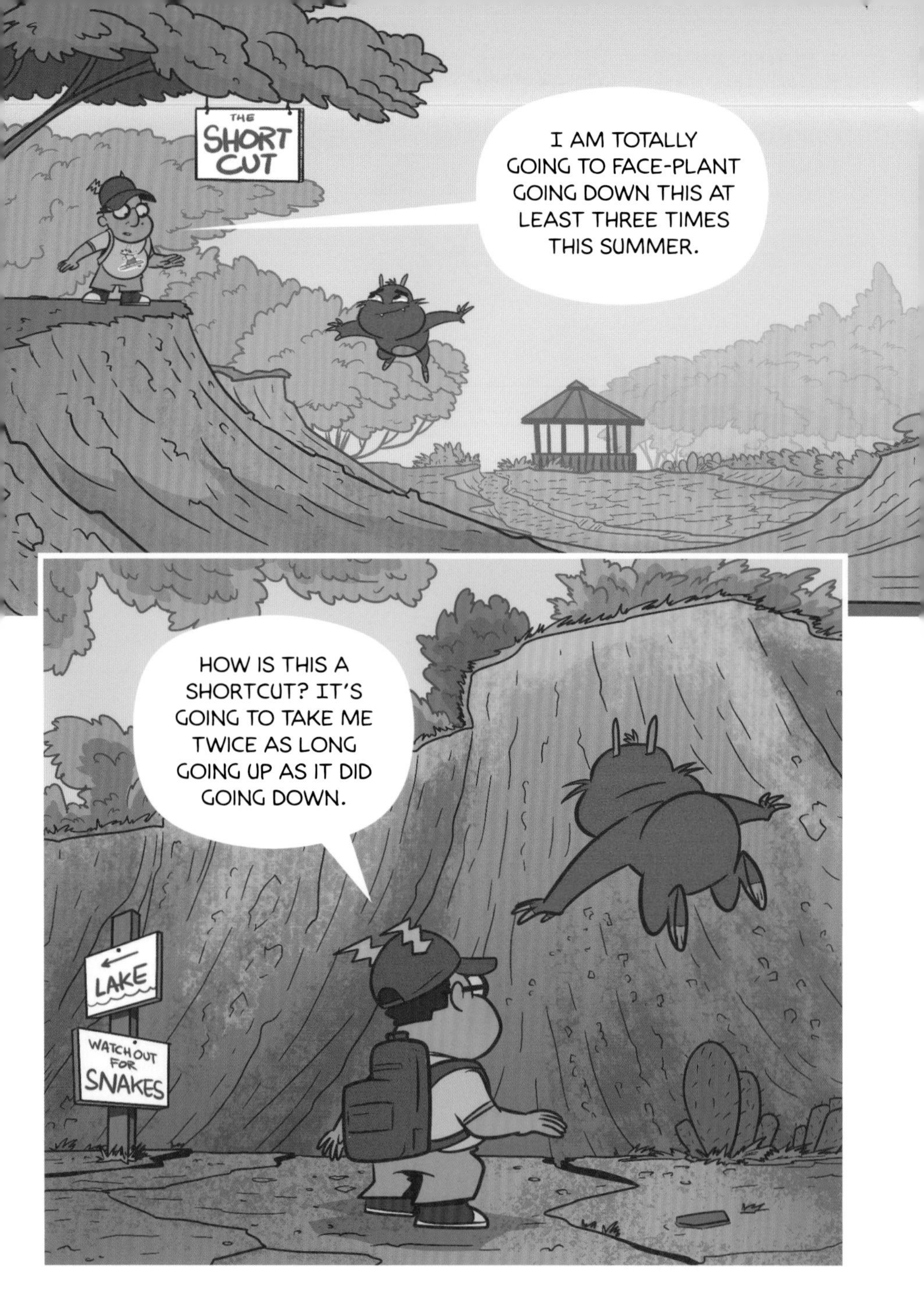
THE SHORT CUT
I AM TOTALLY GOING TO FACE-PLANT GOING DOWN THIS AT LEAST THREE TIMES THIS SUMMER.
HOW IS THIS A SHORTCUT? IT'S GOING TO TAKE ME TWICE AS LONG GOING UP AS IT DID GOING DOWN.
LAKE
WATCH OUT FOR SNAKES

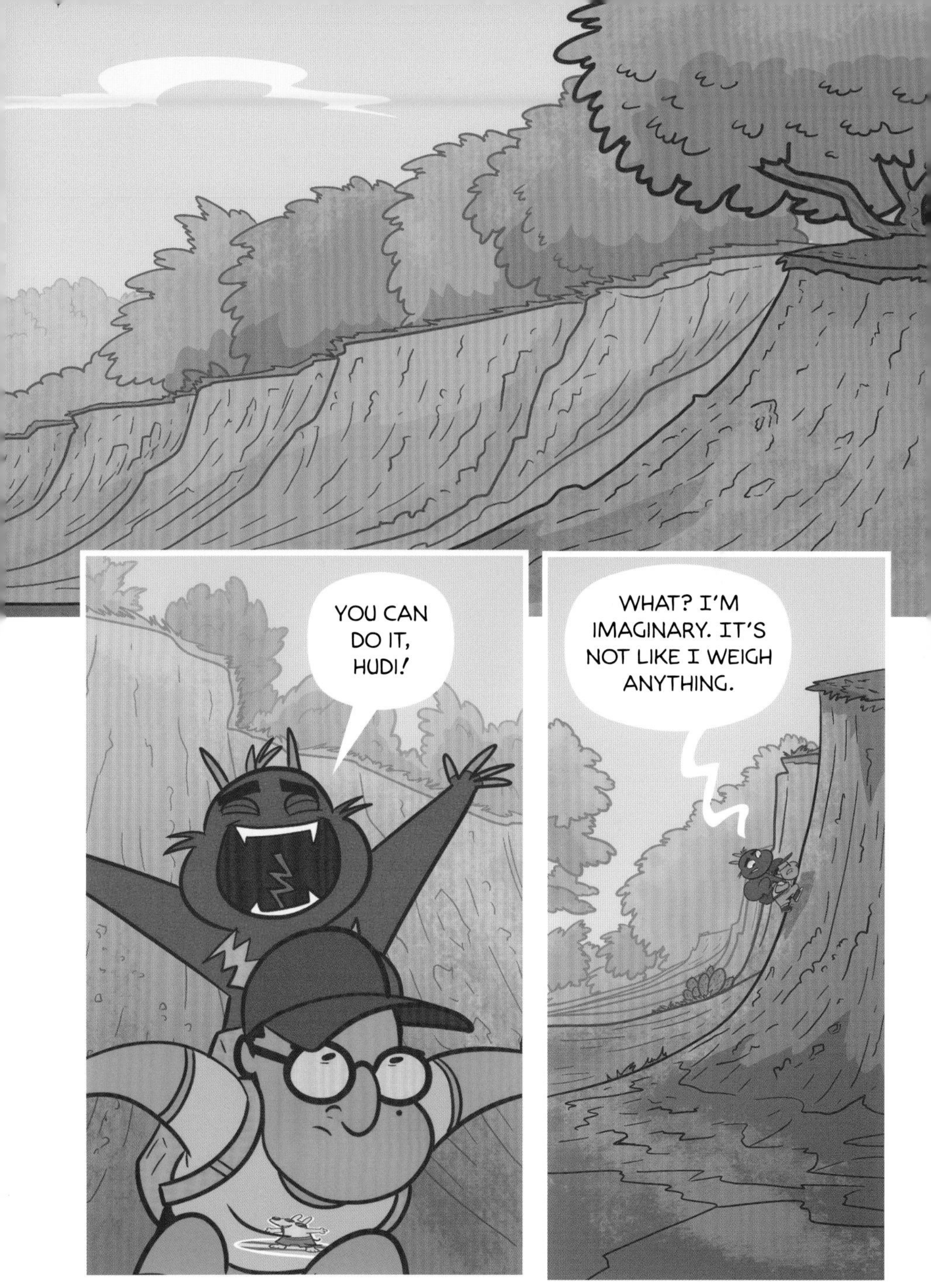
YOU CAN DO IT, HUDI!
WHAT? I'M IMAGINARY. IT'S NOT LIKE I WEIGH ANYTHING.

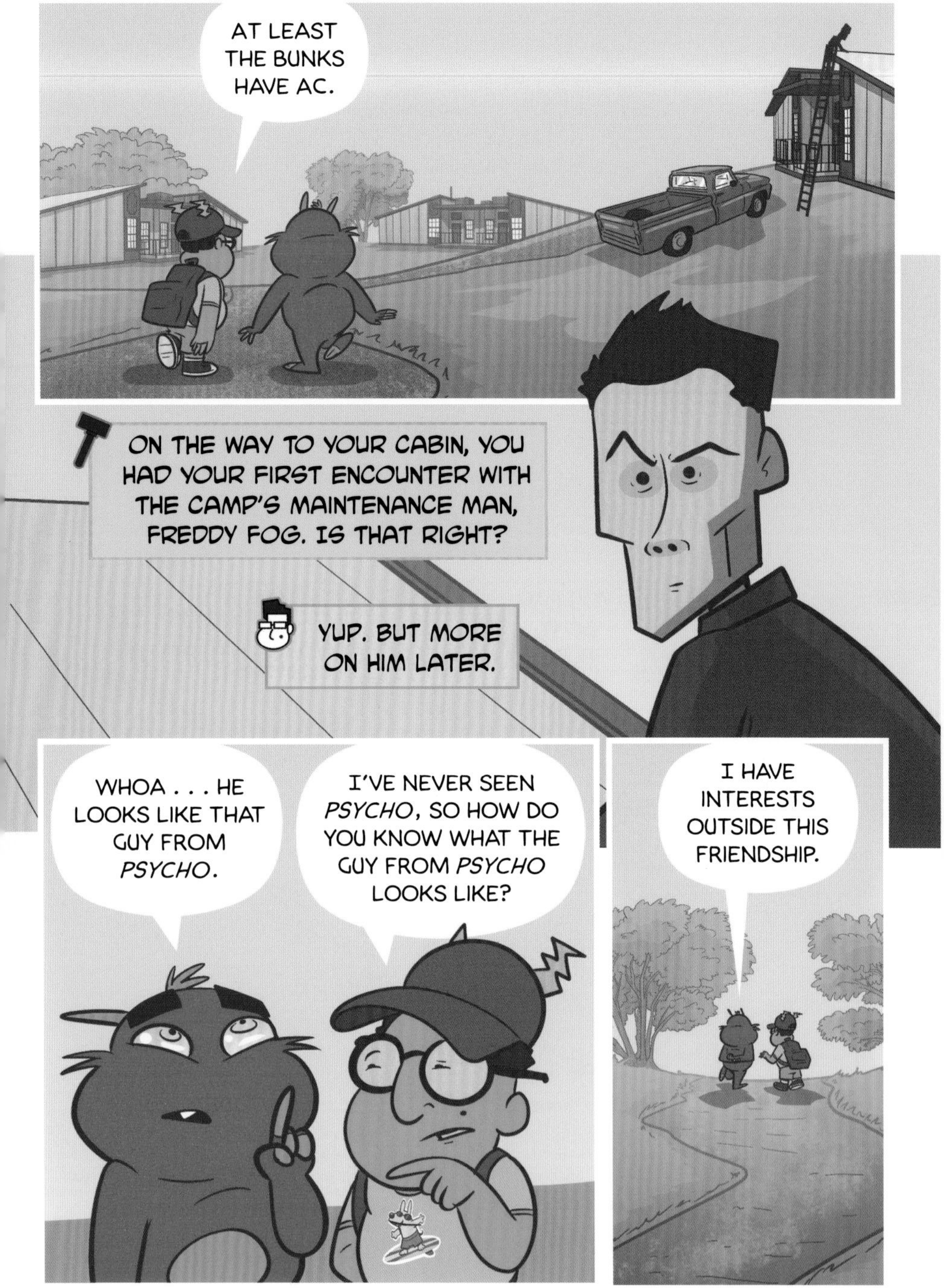
AT LEAST THE BUNKS HAVE AC.
ON THE WAY TO YOUR CABIN, YOU HAD YOUR FIRST ENCOUNTER WITH THE CAMP'S MAINTENANCE MAN, FREDDY FOG. IS THAT RIGHT?
YUP. BUT MORE ON HIM LATER.
WHOA . . . HE LOOKS LIKE THAT GUY FROM *PSYCHO*.
I'VE NEVER SEEN *PSYCHO*, SO HOW DO YOU KNOW WHAT THE GUY FROM *PSYCHO* LOOKS LIKE?
I HAVE INTERESTS OUTSIDE THIS FRIENDSHIP.

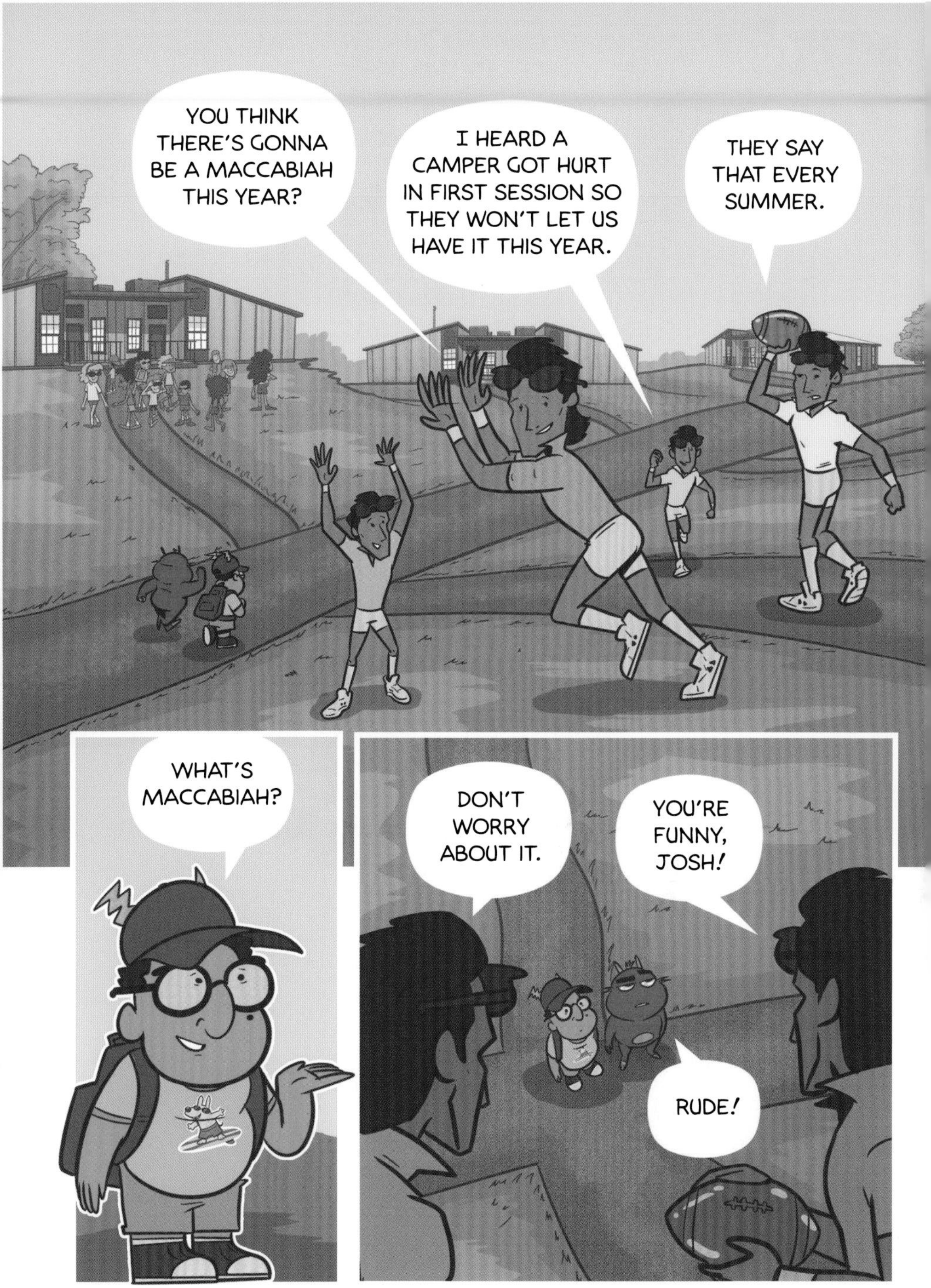
YOU THINK THERE'S GONNA BE A MACCABIAH THIS YEAR?
I HEARD A CAMPER GOT HURT IN FIRST SESSION SO THEY WON'T LET US HAVE IT THIS YEAR.
THEY SAY THAT EVERY SUMMER.
WHAT'S MACCABIAH?
DON'T WORRY ABOUT IT.
YOU'RE FUNNY, JOSH!
RUDE!

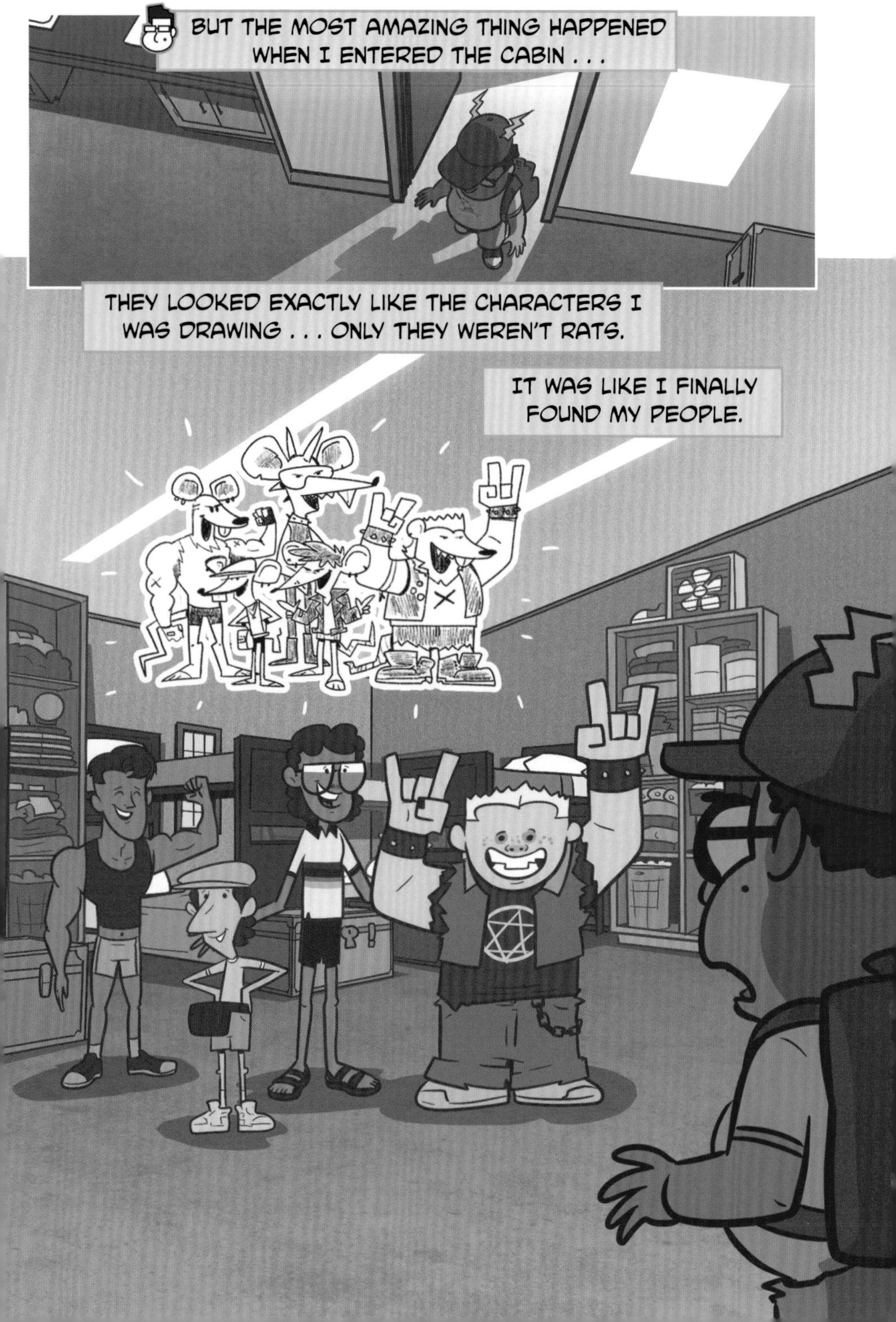
BUT THE MOST AMAZING THING HAPPENED WHEN I ENTERED THE CABIN . . .
THEY LOOKED EXACTLY LIKE THE CHARACTERS I WAS DRAWING . . . ONLY THEY WEREN'T RATS.
IT WAS LIKE I FINALLY FOUND MY PEOPLE.

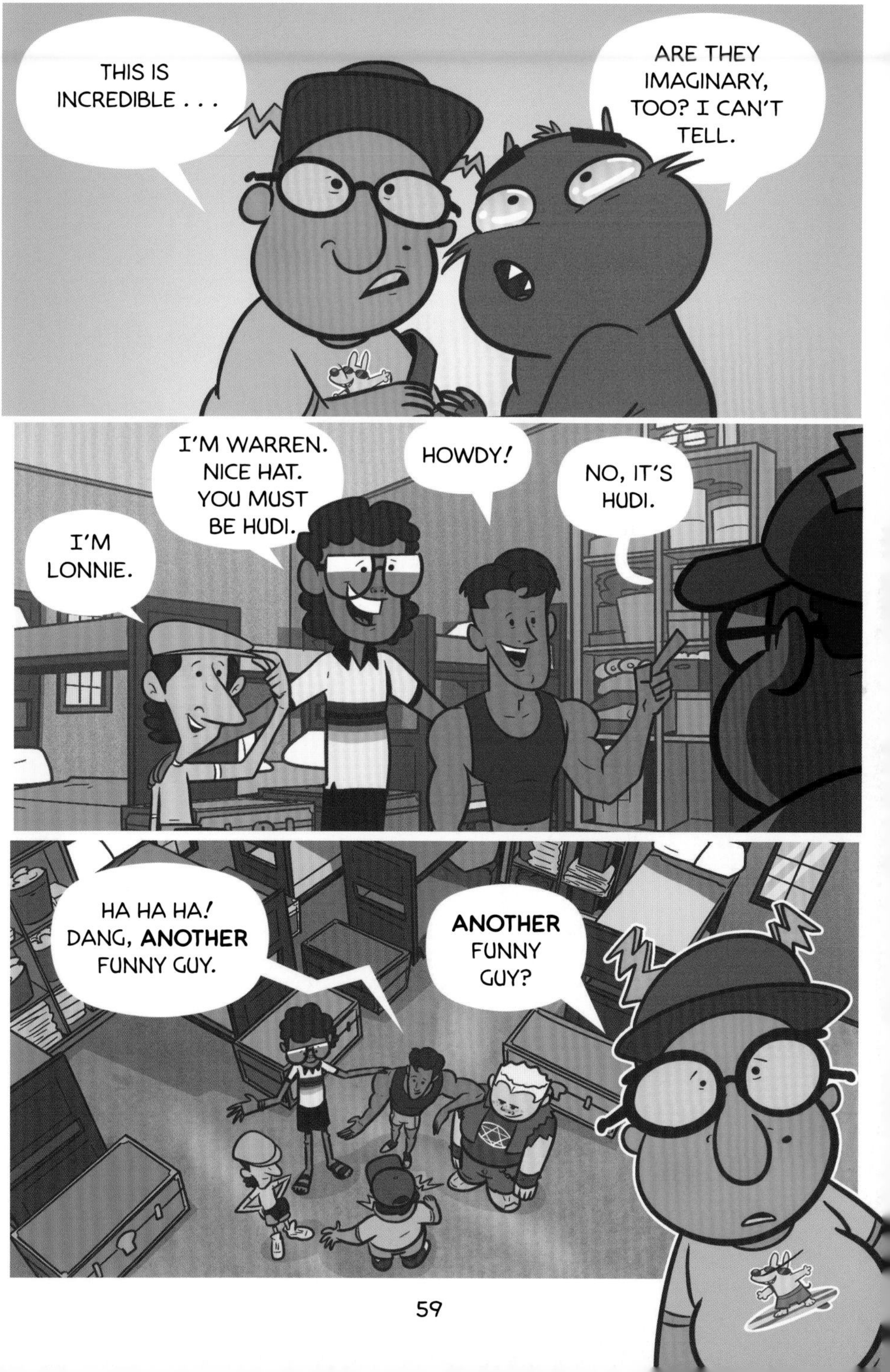
THIS IS INCREDIBLE . . .
ARE THEY IMAGINARY, TOO? I CAN'T TELL.
I'M LONNIE.
I'M WARREN. NICE HAT. YOU MUST BE HUDI.
HOWDY!
NO, IT'S HUDI.
HA HA HA! DANG, **ANOTHER** FUNNY GUY.
ANOTHER FUNNY GUY?

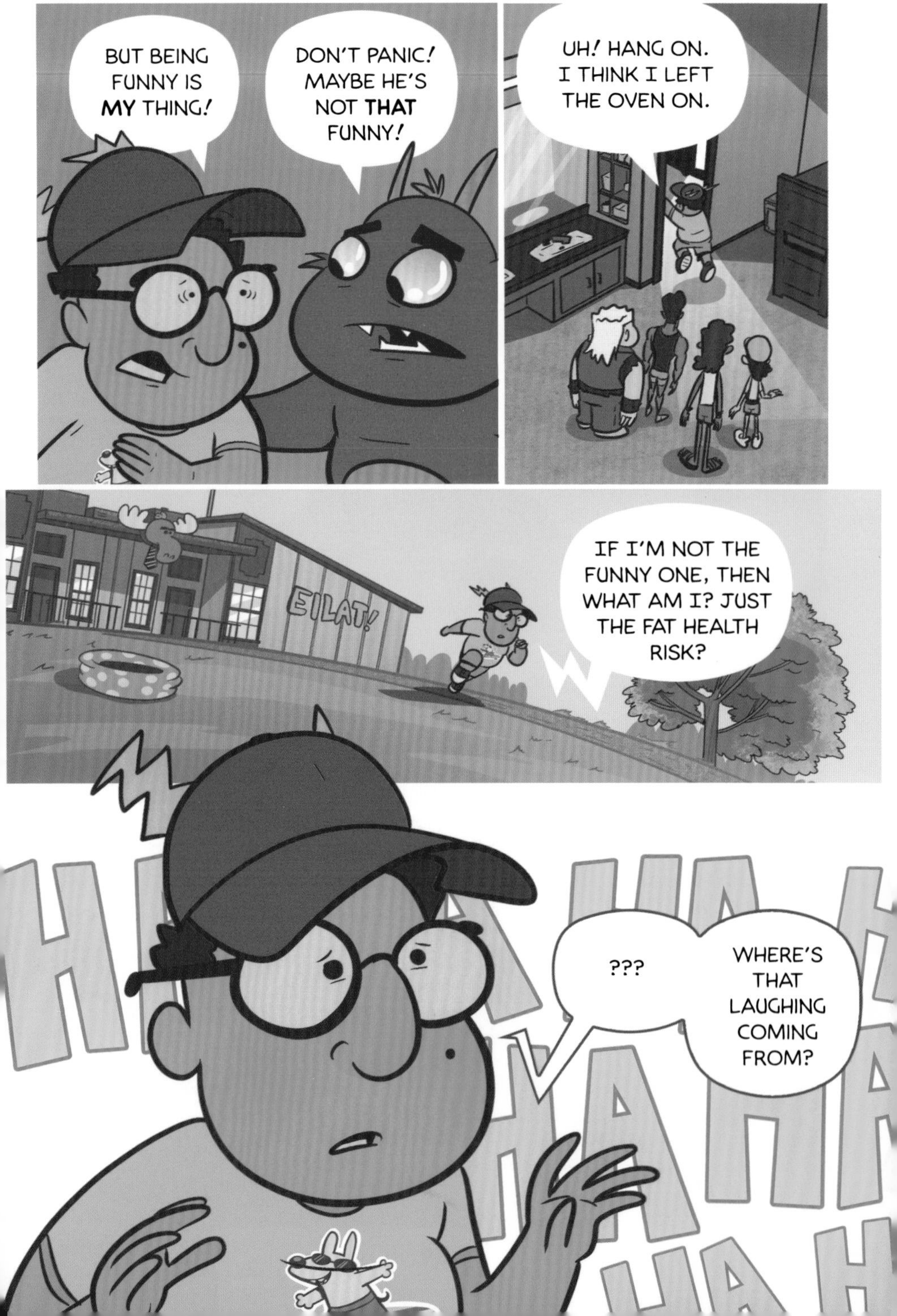
BUT BEING FUNNY IS **MY** THING!
DON'T PANIC! MAYBE HE'S NOT **THAT** FUNNY!
UH! HANG ON. I THINK I LEFT THE OVEN ON.
EILAT!
IF I'M NOT THE FUNNY ONE, THEN WHAT AM I? JUST THE FAT HEALTH RISK?
???
WHERE'S THAT LAUGHING COMING FROM?

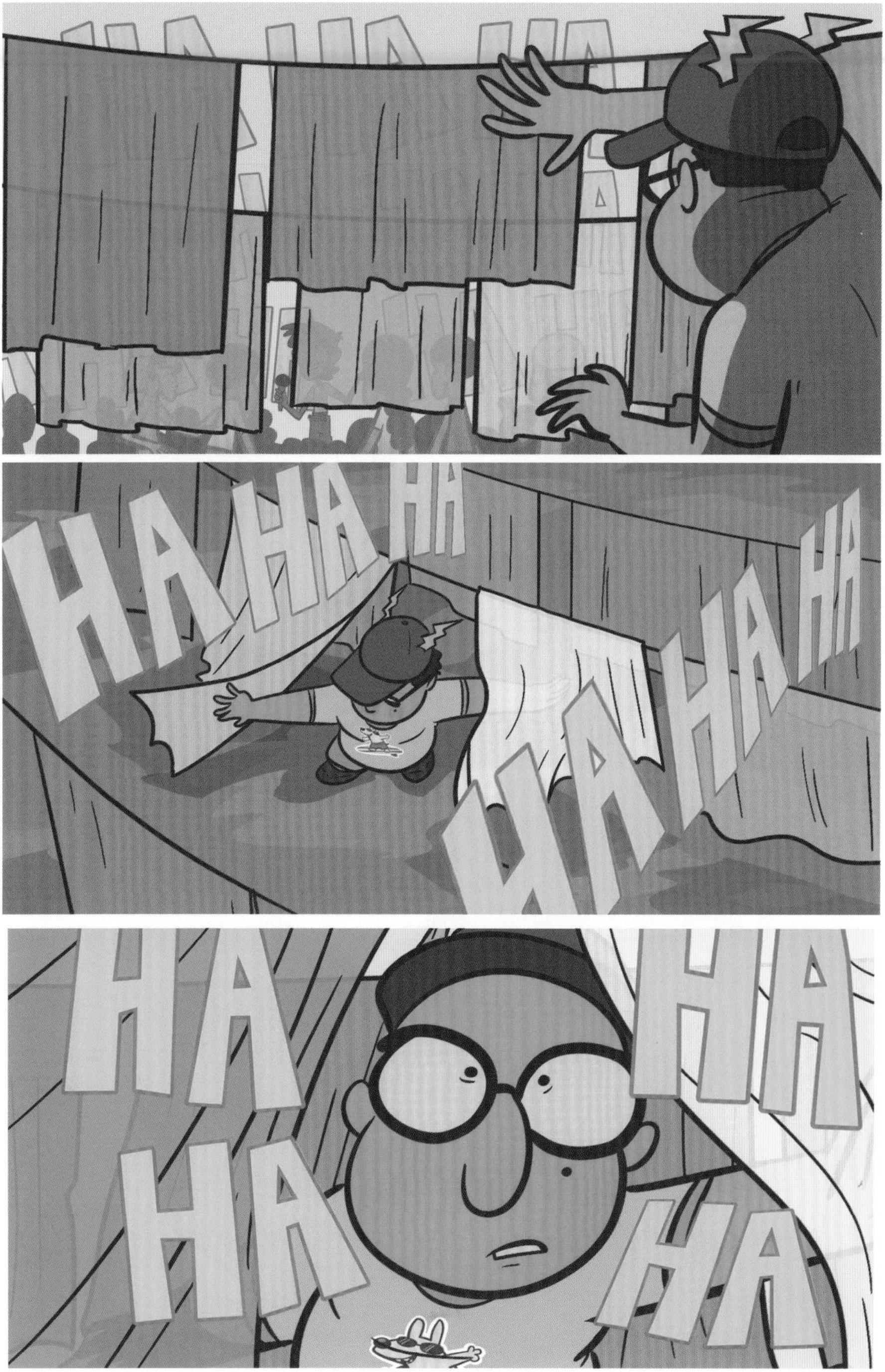
HA HA HA HA
HA HA HA HA
HA
HA HA
HA
HA

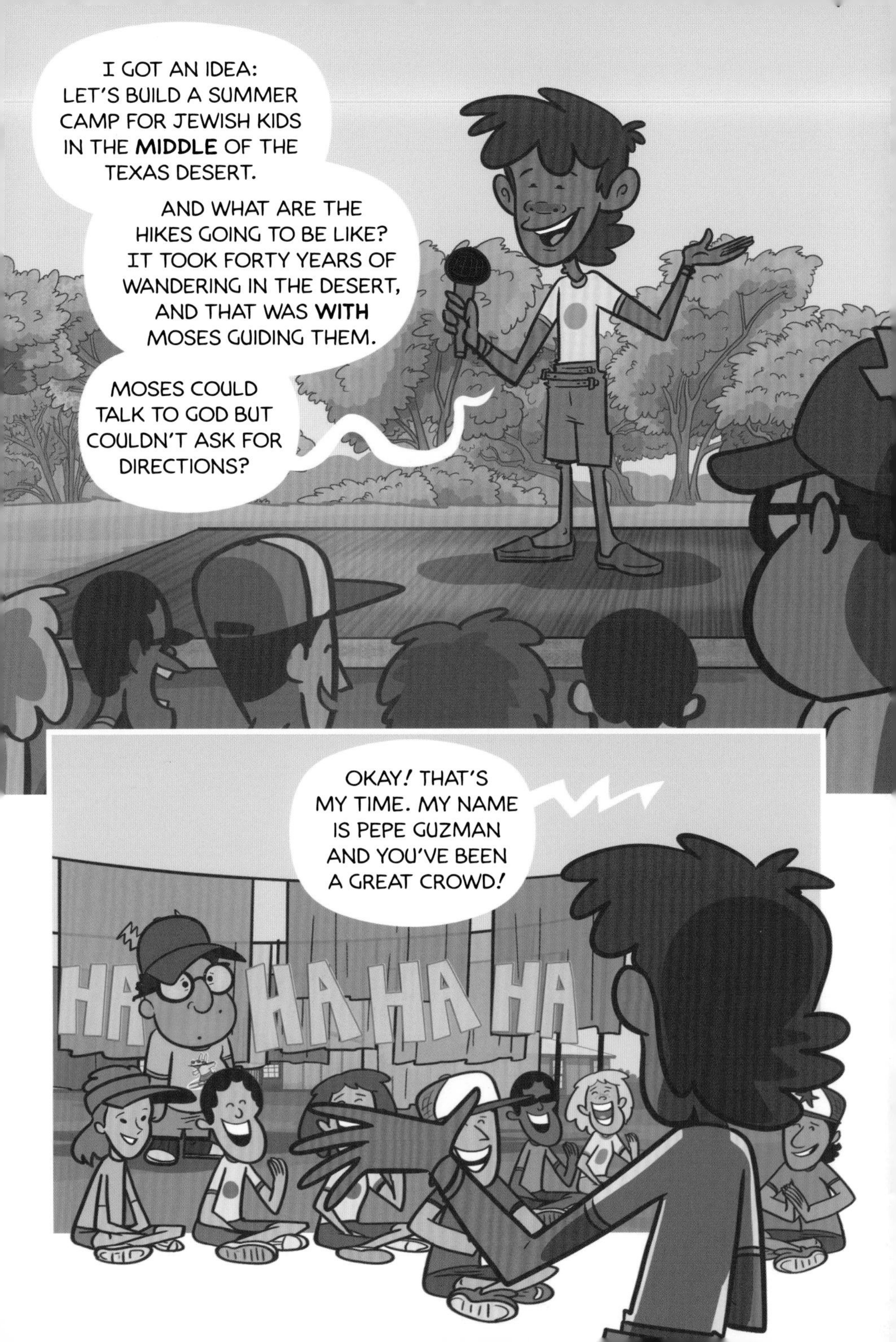
I GOT AN IDEA: LET'S BUILD A SUMMER CAMP FOR JEWISH KIDS IN THE **MIDDLE** OF THE TEXAS DESERT.
AND WHAT ARE THE HIKES GOING TO BE LIKE? IT TOOK FORTY YEARS OF WANDERING IN THE DESERT, AND THAT WAS **WITH** MOSES GUIDING THEM.
MOSES COULD TALK TO GOD BUT COULDN'T ASK FOR DIRECTIONS?
OKAY! THAT'S MY TIME. MY NAME IS PEPE GUZMAN AND YOU'VE BEEN A GREAT CROWD!
HA HA HA HA HA HA

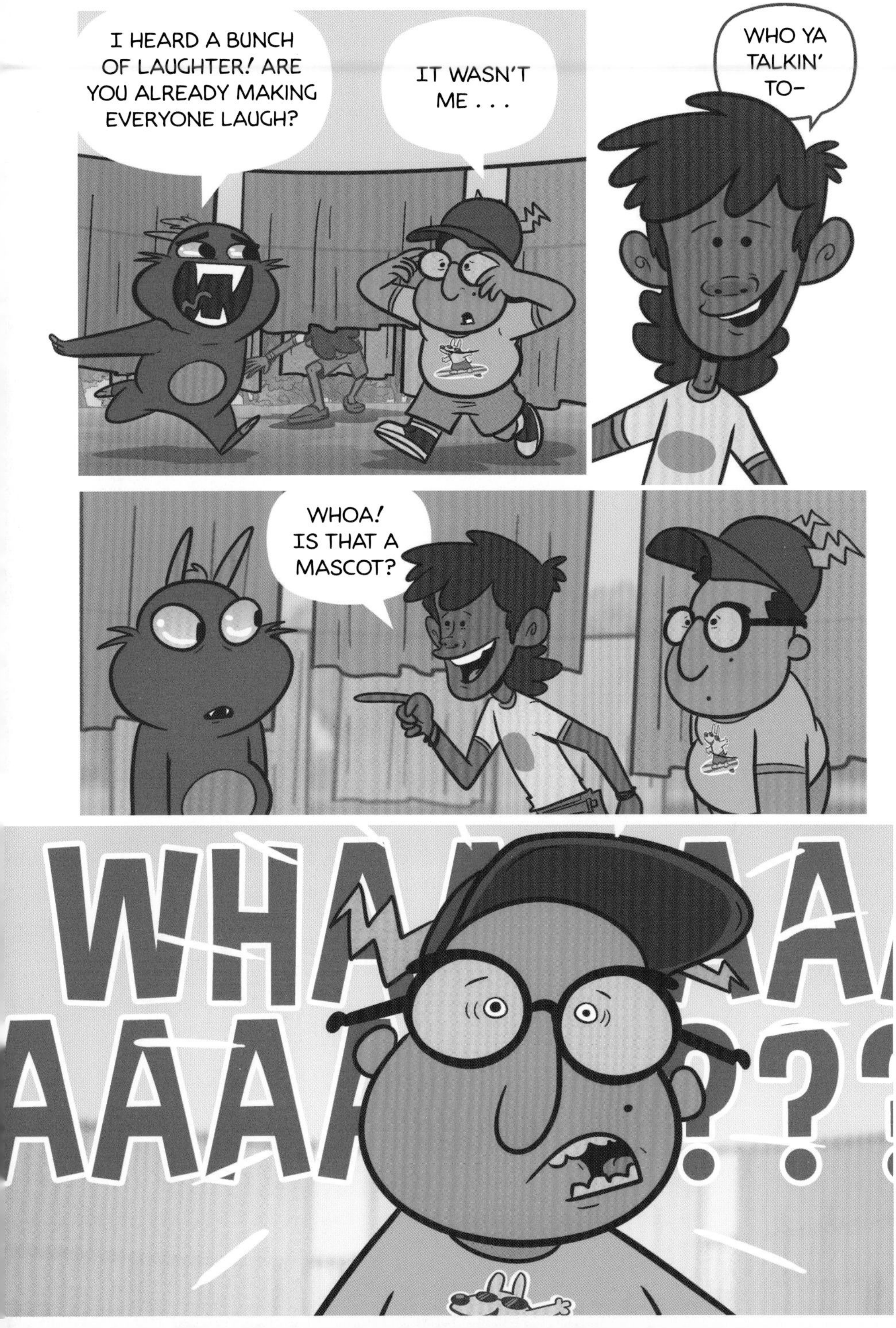
I HEARD A BUNCH OF LAUGHTER! ARE YOU ALREADY MAKING EVERYONE LAUGH?
IT WASN'T ME . . .
WHO YA TALKIN' TO–
WHOA! IS THAT A MASCOT?

HUDI on TRIAL

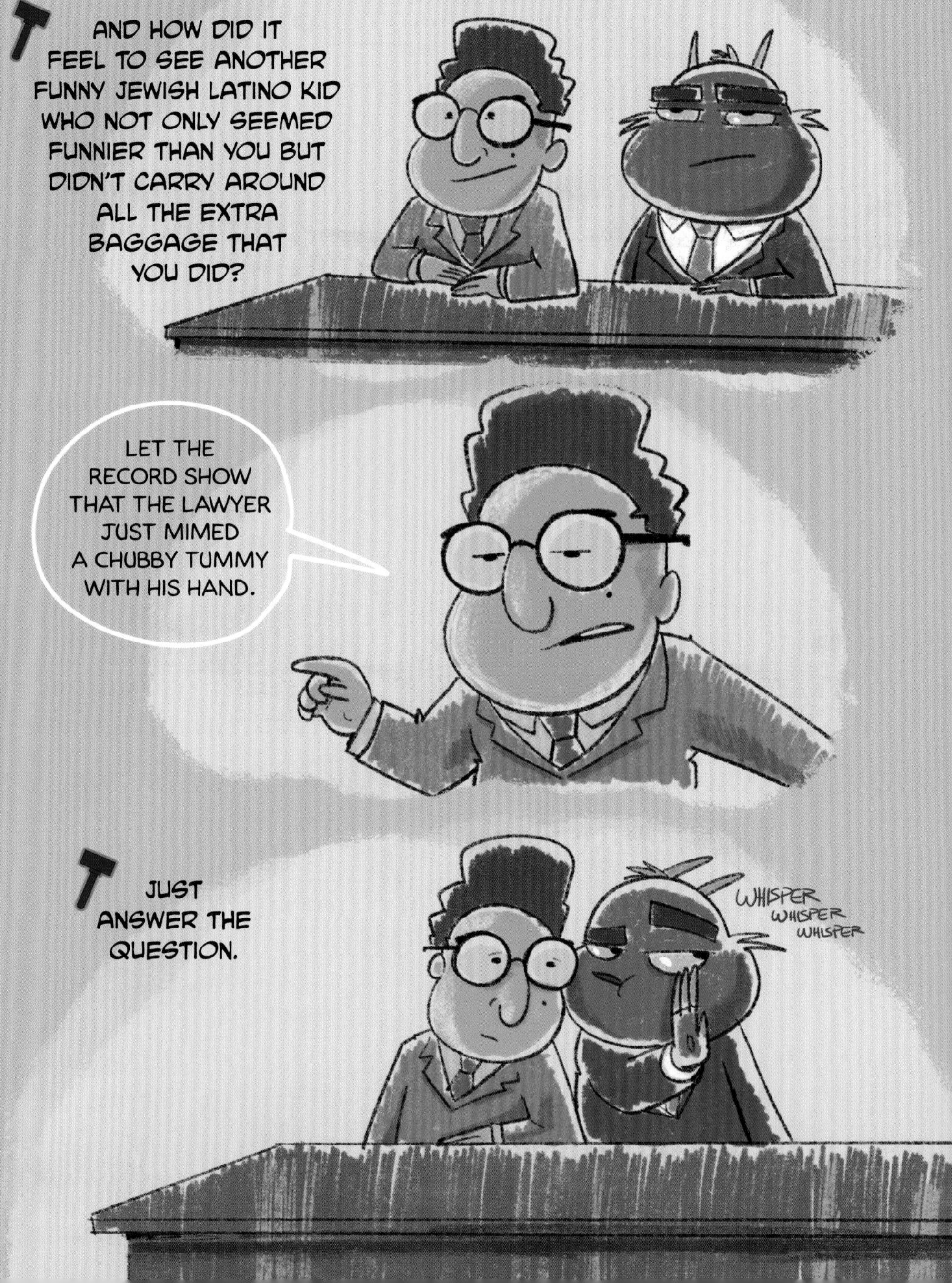
AND HOW DID IT FEEL TO SEE ANOTHER FUNNY JEWISH LATINO KID WHO NOT ONLY SEEMED FUNNIER THAN YOU BUT DIDN'T CARRY AROUND ALL THE EXTRA BAGGAGE THAT YOU DID?
LET THE RECORD SHOW THAT THE LAWYER JUST MIMED A CHUBBY TUMMY WITH HIS HAND.
JUST ANSWER THE QUESTION.
WHISPER
WHISPER
WHISPER

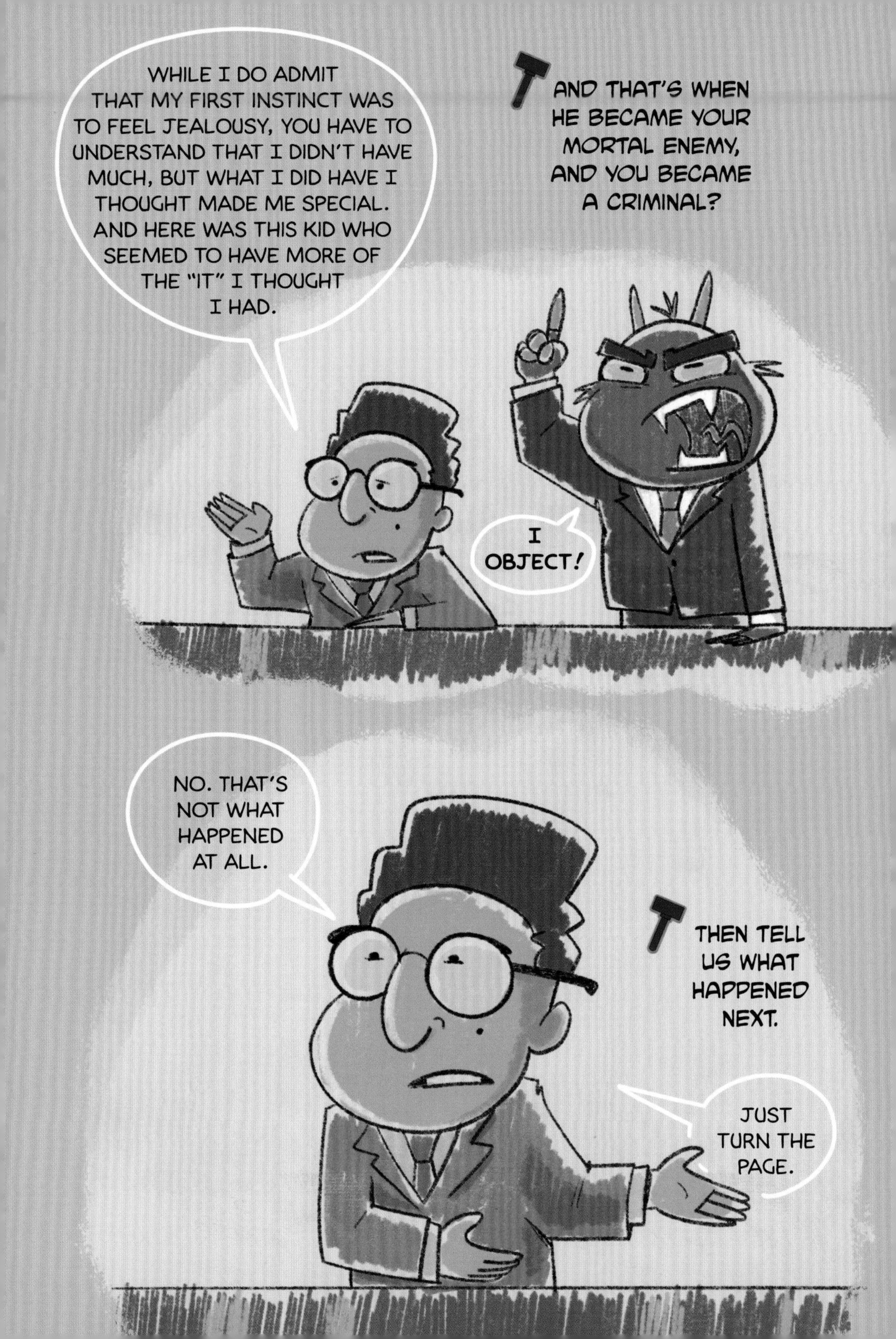
WHILE I DO ADMIT THAT MY FIRST INSTINCT WAS TO FEEL JEALOUSY, YOU HAVE TO UNDERSTAND THAT I DIDN'T HAVE MUCH, BUT WHAT I DID HAVE I THOUGHT MADE ME SPECIAL. AND HERE WAS THIS KID WHO SEEMED TO HAVE MORE OF THE "IT" I THOUGHT I HAD.
AND THAT'S WHEN HE BECAME YOUR MORTAL ENEMY, AND YOU BECAME A CRIMINAL?
I OBJECT!
NO. THAT'S NOT WHAT HAPPENED AT ALL.
THEN TELL US WHAT HAPPENED NEXT.
JUST TURN THE PAGE.

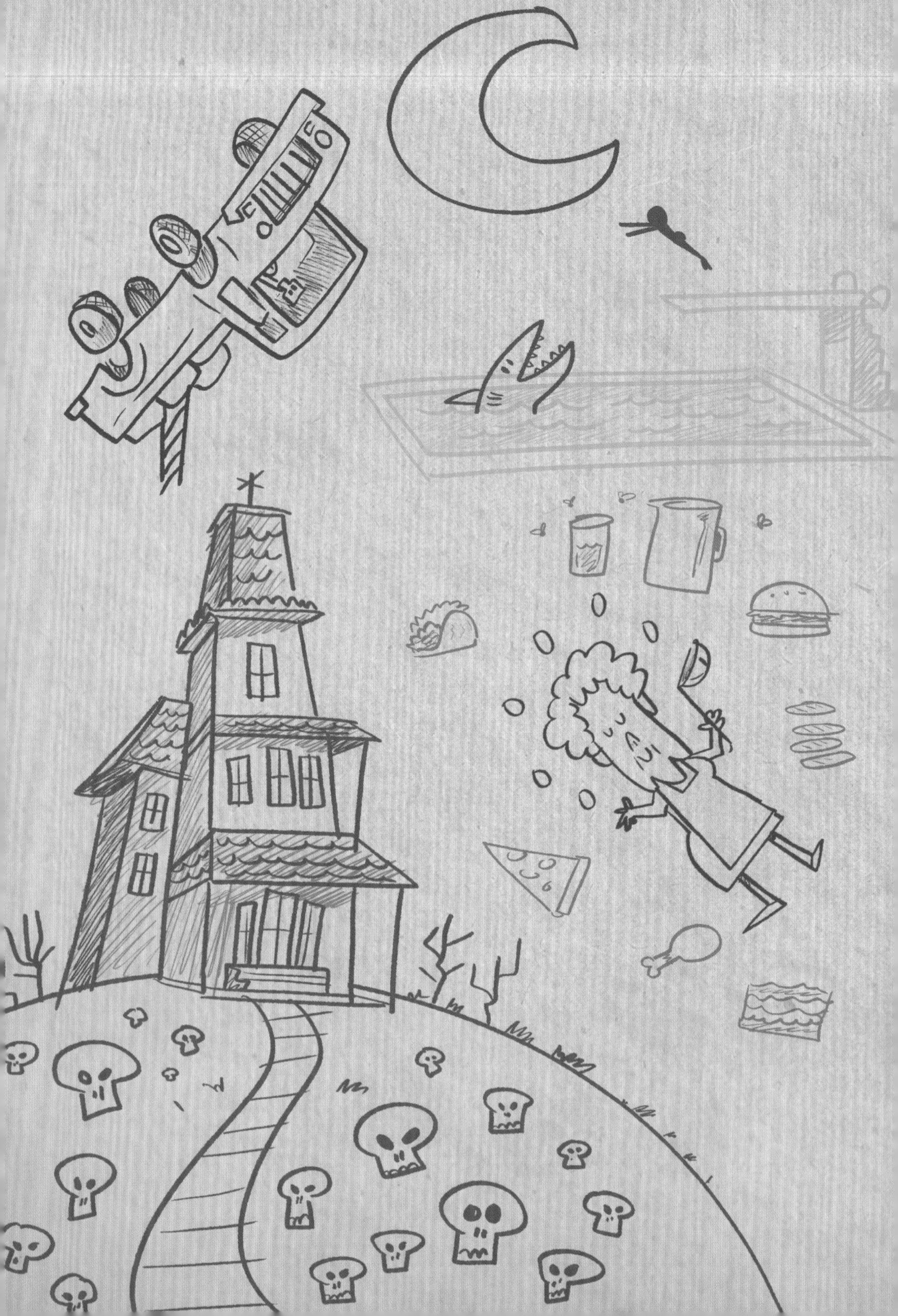

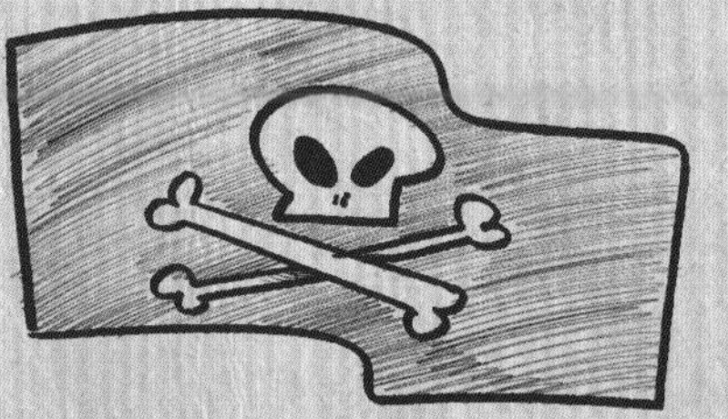

CHAPTER THREE

Meet Pepe

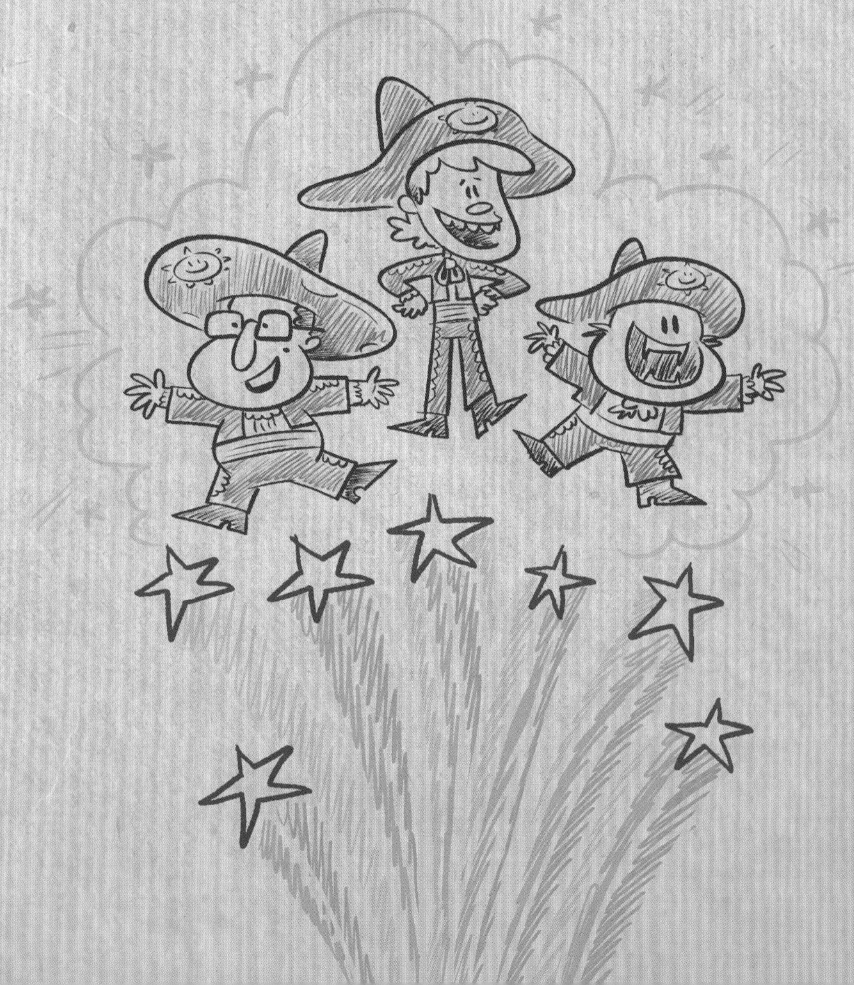

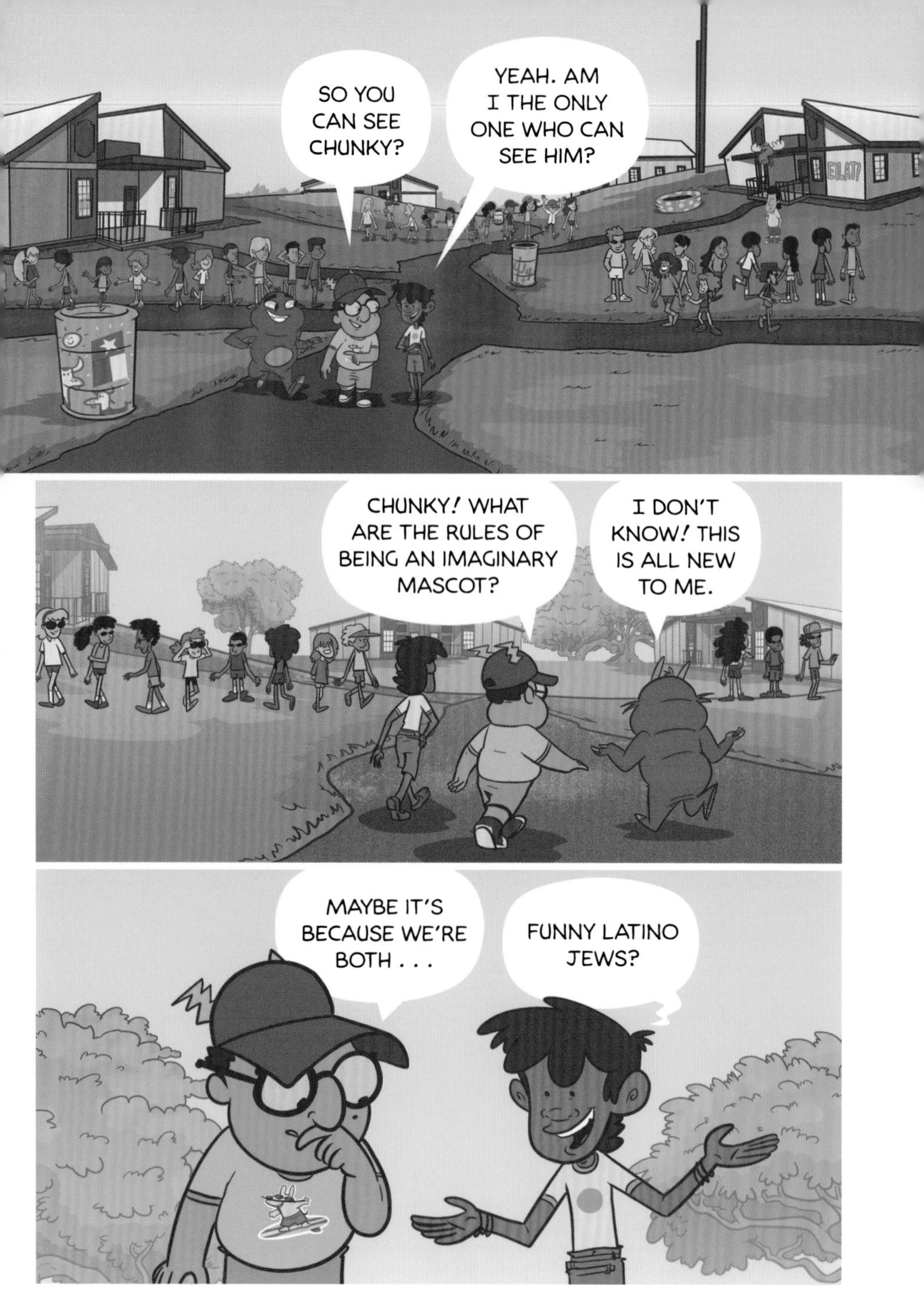
SO YOU CAN SEE CHUNKY?
YEAH. AM I THE ONLY ONE WHO CAN SEE HIM?
EILAT!
CHUNKY! WHAT ARE THE RULES OF BEING AN IMAGINARY MASCOT?
I DON'T KNOW! THIS IS ALL NEW TO ME.
MAYBE IT'S BECAUSE WE'RE BOTH . . .
FUNNY LATINO JEWS?

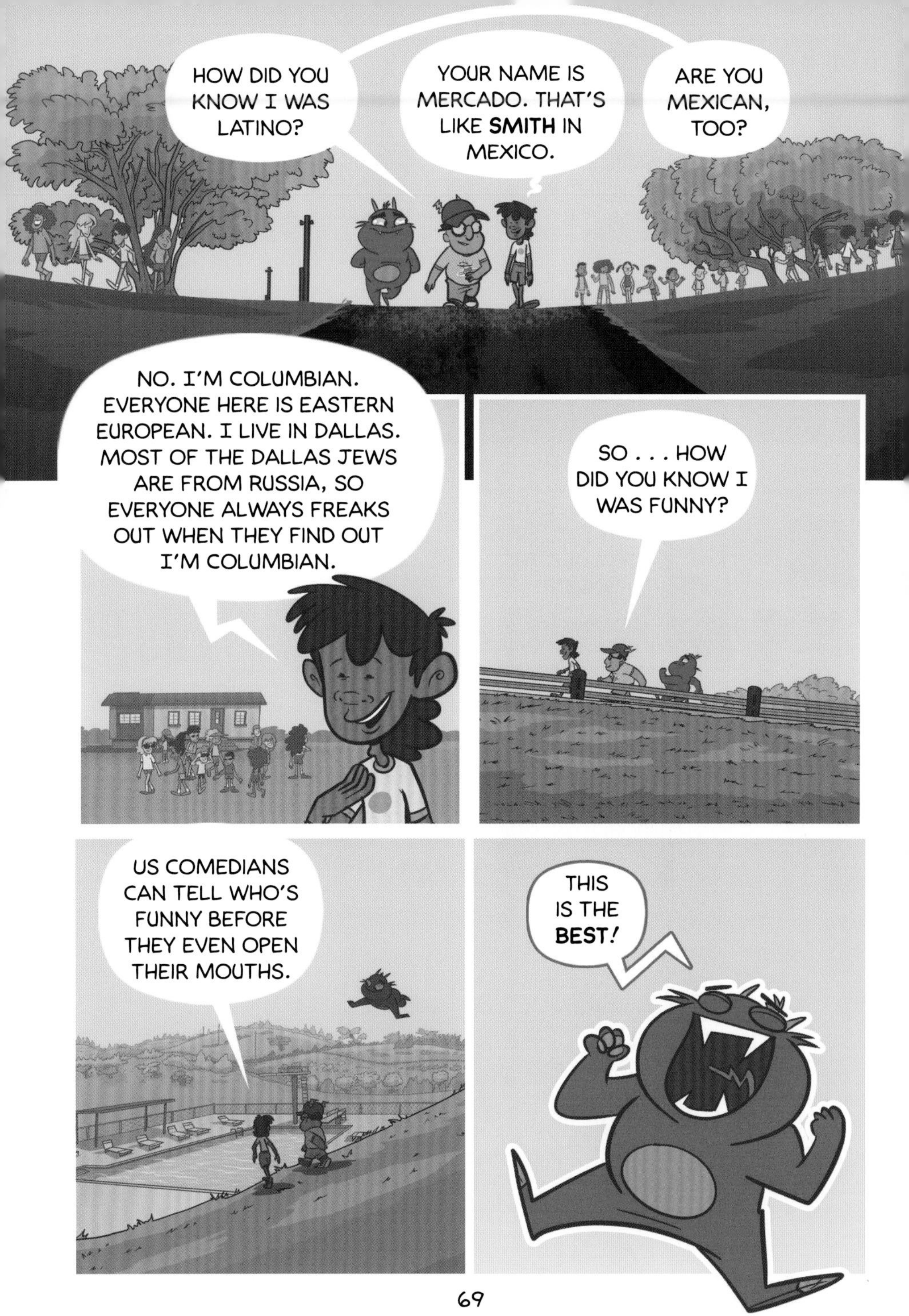
HOW DID YOU KNOW I WAS LATINO?
YOUR NAME IS MERCADO. THAT'S LIKE **SMITH** IN MEXICO.
ARE YOU MEXICAN, TOO?
NO. I'M COLUMBIAN. EVERYONE HERE IS EASTERN EUROPEAN. I LIVE IN DALLAS. MOST OF THE DALLAS JEWS ARE FROM RUSSIA, SO EVERYONE ALWAYS FREAKS OUT WHEN THEY FIND OUT I'M COLUMBIAN.
SO . . . HOW DID YOU KNOW I WAS FUNNY?
US COMEDIANS CAN TELL WHO'S FUNNY BEFORE THEY EVEN OPEN THEIR MOUTHS.
THIS IS THE **BEST**!

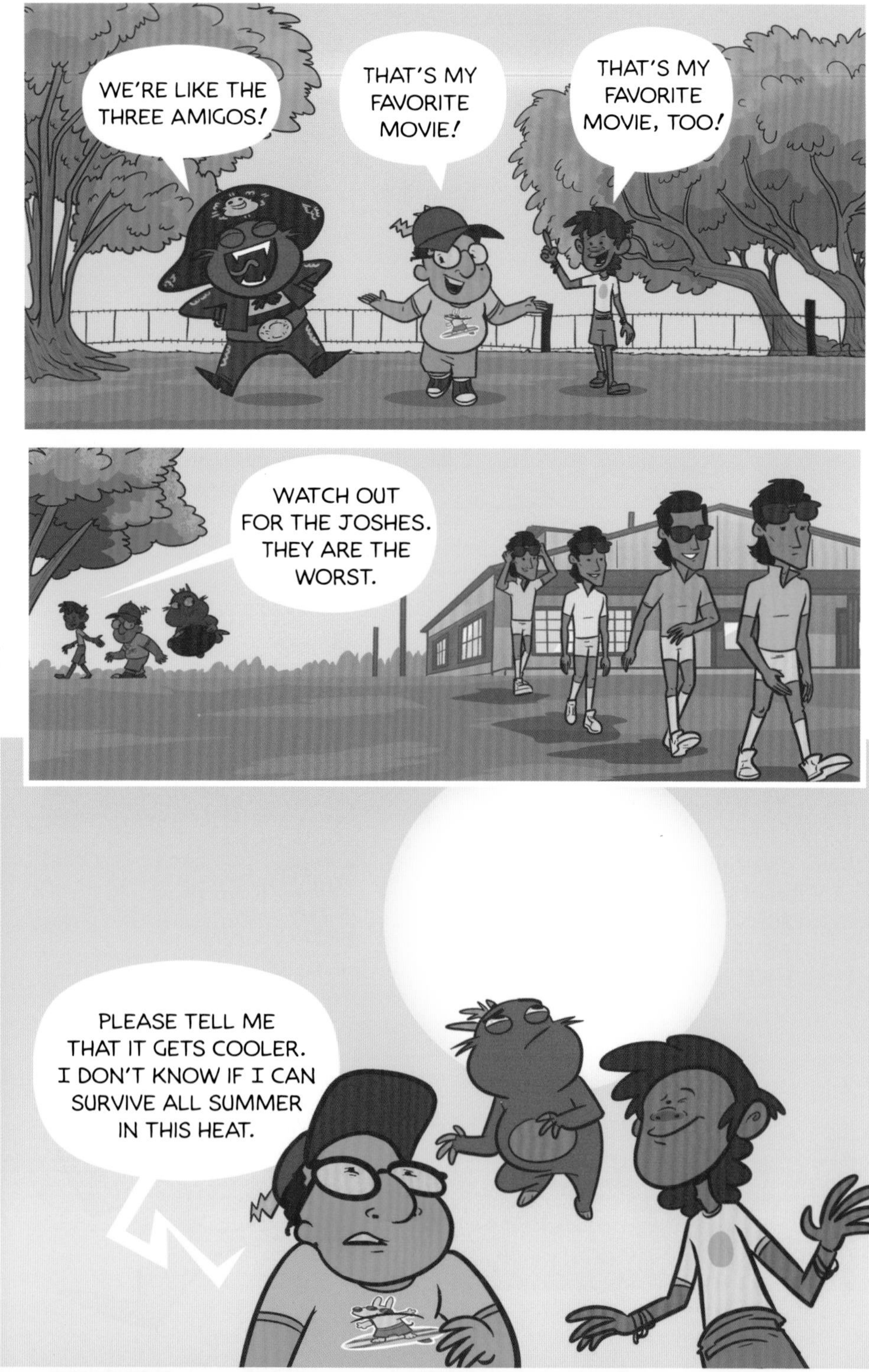
WE'RE LIKE THE THREE AMIGOS!
THAT'S MY FAVORITE MOVIE!
THAT'S MY FAVORITE MOVIE, TOO!
WATCH OUT FOR THE JOSHES. THEY ARE THE WORST.
PLEASE TELL ME THAT IT GETS COOLER. I DON'T KNOW IF I CAN SURVIVE ALL SUMMER IN THIS HEAT.

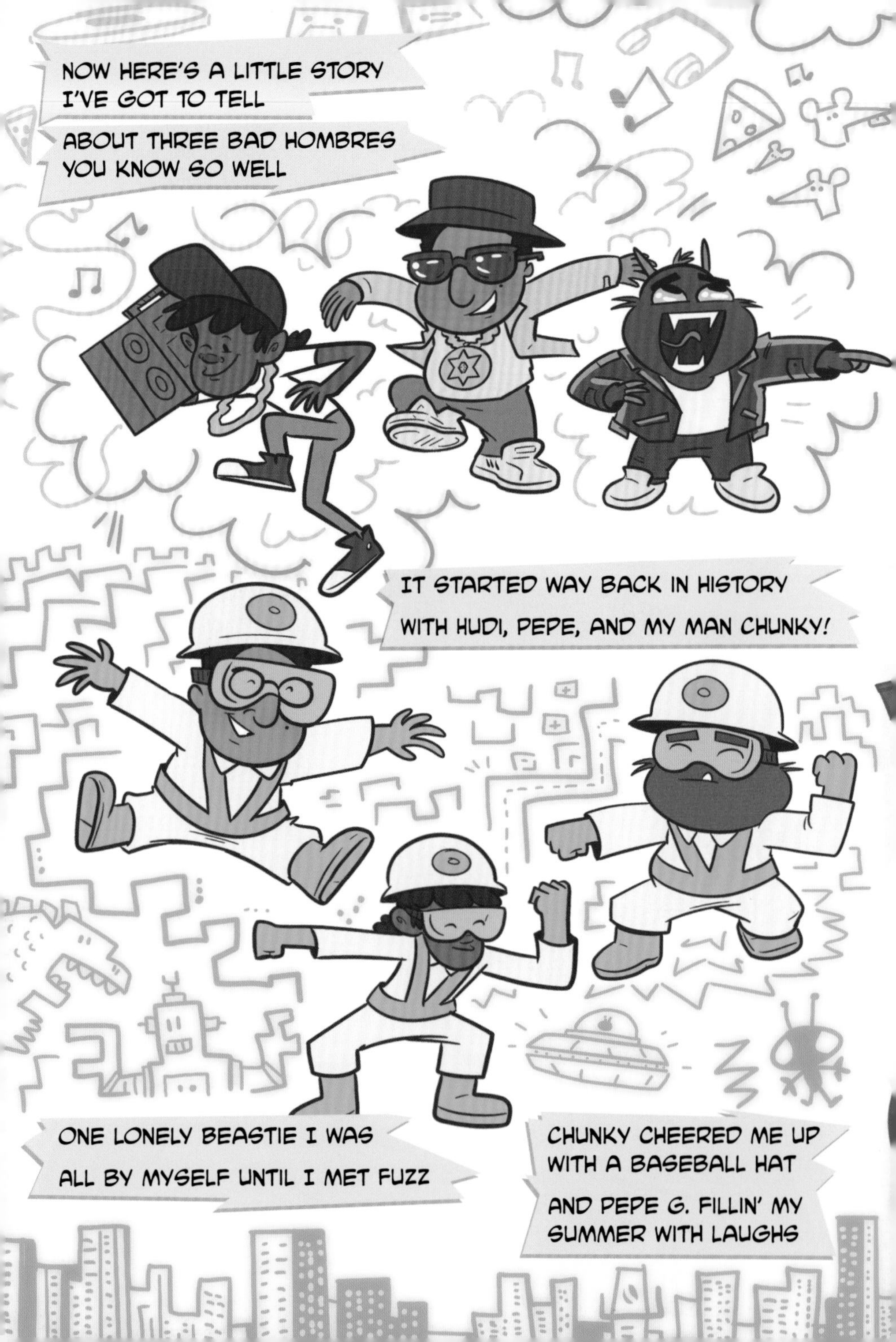
NOW HERE'S A LITTLE STORY I'VE GOT TO TELL
ABOUT THREE BAD HOMBRES YOU KNOW SO WELL
IT STARTED WAY BACK IN HISTORY
WITH HUDI, PEPE, AND MY MAN CHUNKY!
ONE LONELY BEASTIE I WAS
ALL BY MYSELF UNTIL I MET FUZZ
CHUNKY CHEERED ME UP WITH A BASEBALL HAT
AND PEPE G. FILLIN' MY SUMMER WITH LAUGHS

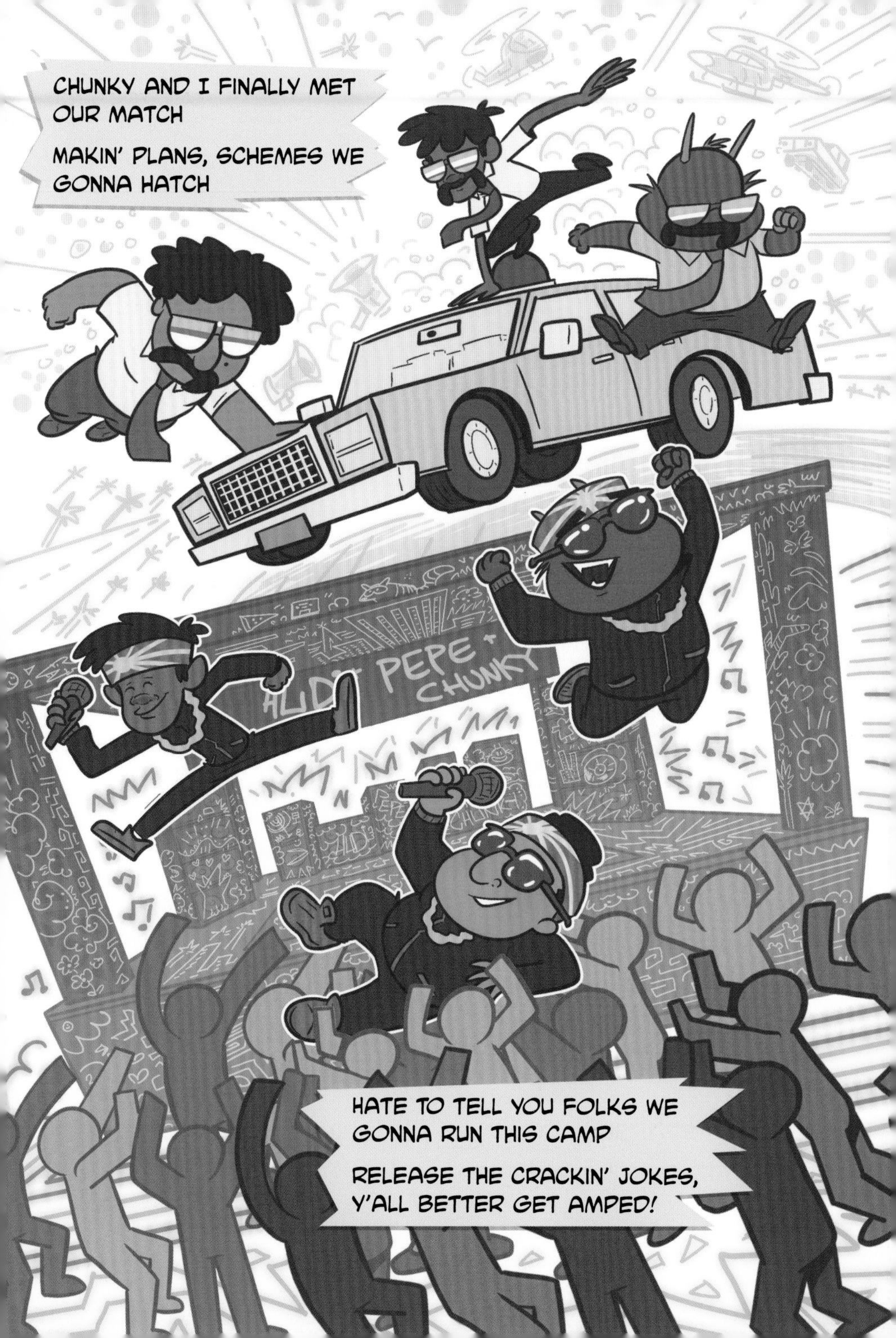
CHUNKY AND I FINALLY MET OUR MATCH
MAKIN' PLANS, SCHEMES WE GONNA HATCH
PEPE
CHUNKY
HATE TO TELL YOU FOLKS WE GONNA RUN THIS CAMP
RELEASE THE CRACKIN' JOKES, Y'ALL BETTER GET AMPED!

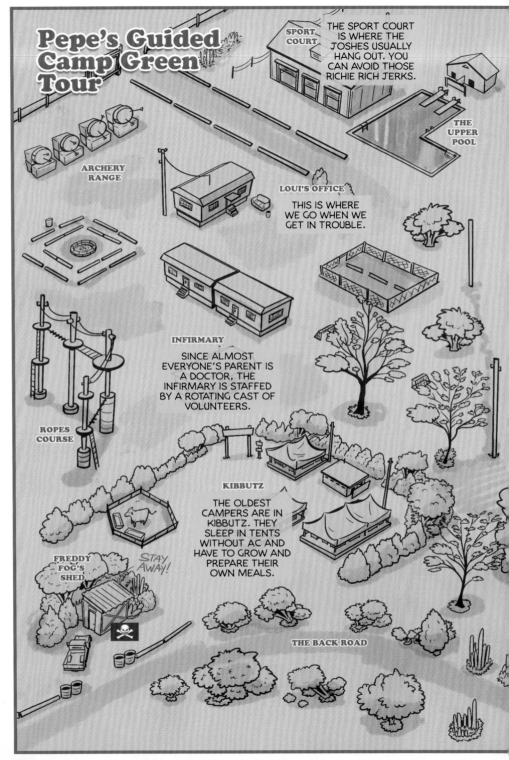

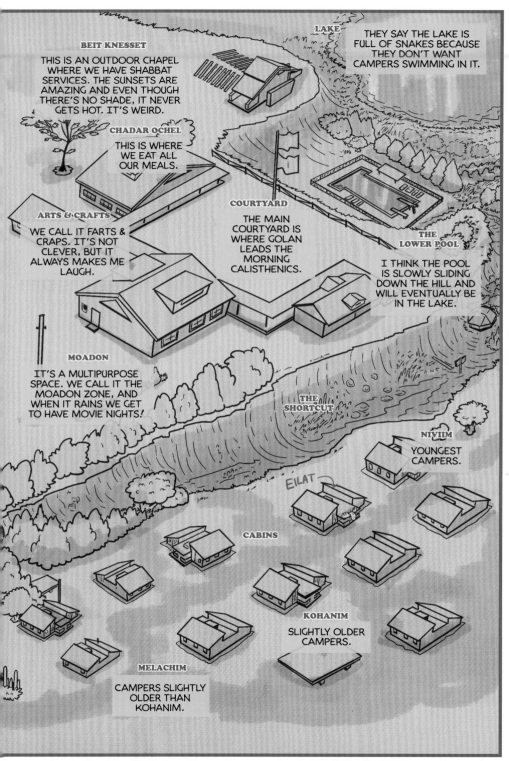

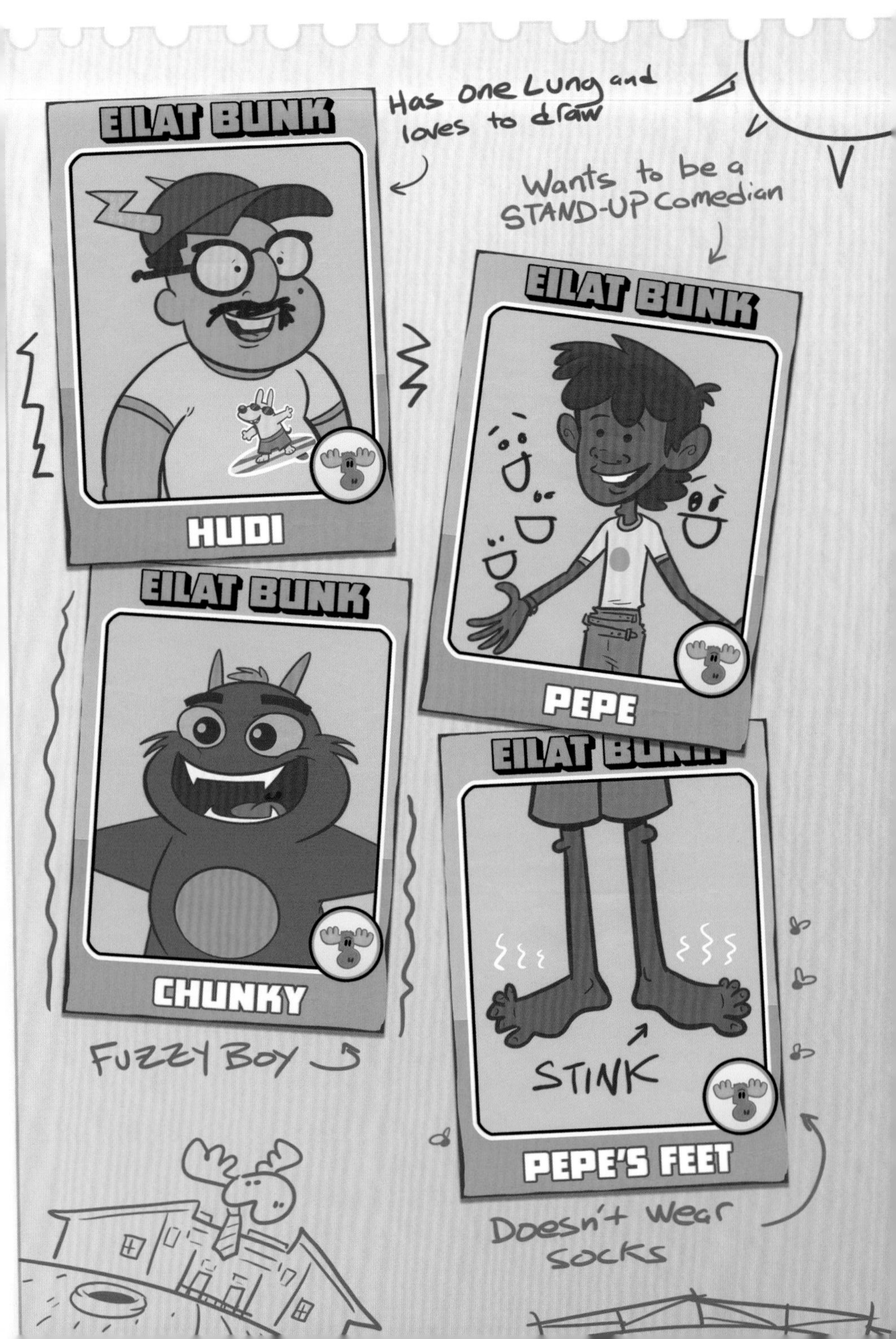

Has one Lung and loves to draw
EILAT BUNK
HUDI
Wants to be a STAND-UP comedian
EILAT BUNK
PEPE
EILAT BUNK
CHUNKY
FUZZY BOY
PEPE'S FEET
STINK
Doesn't wear socks

EILAT BUNK!

EILAT BUNK
LEWIS

LOVES HEAVY METAL & LOVES TO CUSS!

EILAT BUNK
WARREN

The Bunk's Counselor
He used to be a major prankster when he was a camper

Older Camper
Not technically in our Bunk but he's a fellow WEIRDO

~~EILAT~~ BUNK
RICKY

BON-BON

EILAT BUNK
LONNIE

Always wears that Old-Timey NEWSIE CAP

EILAT BUNK
ADAM

HAS the Thickest TEXAS ACCENT I have ever heard

~~EILAT~~ BUNK
GOLAN

In charge of the BONFIRES. He might burn the whole camp down.

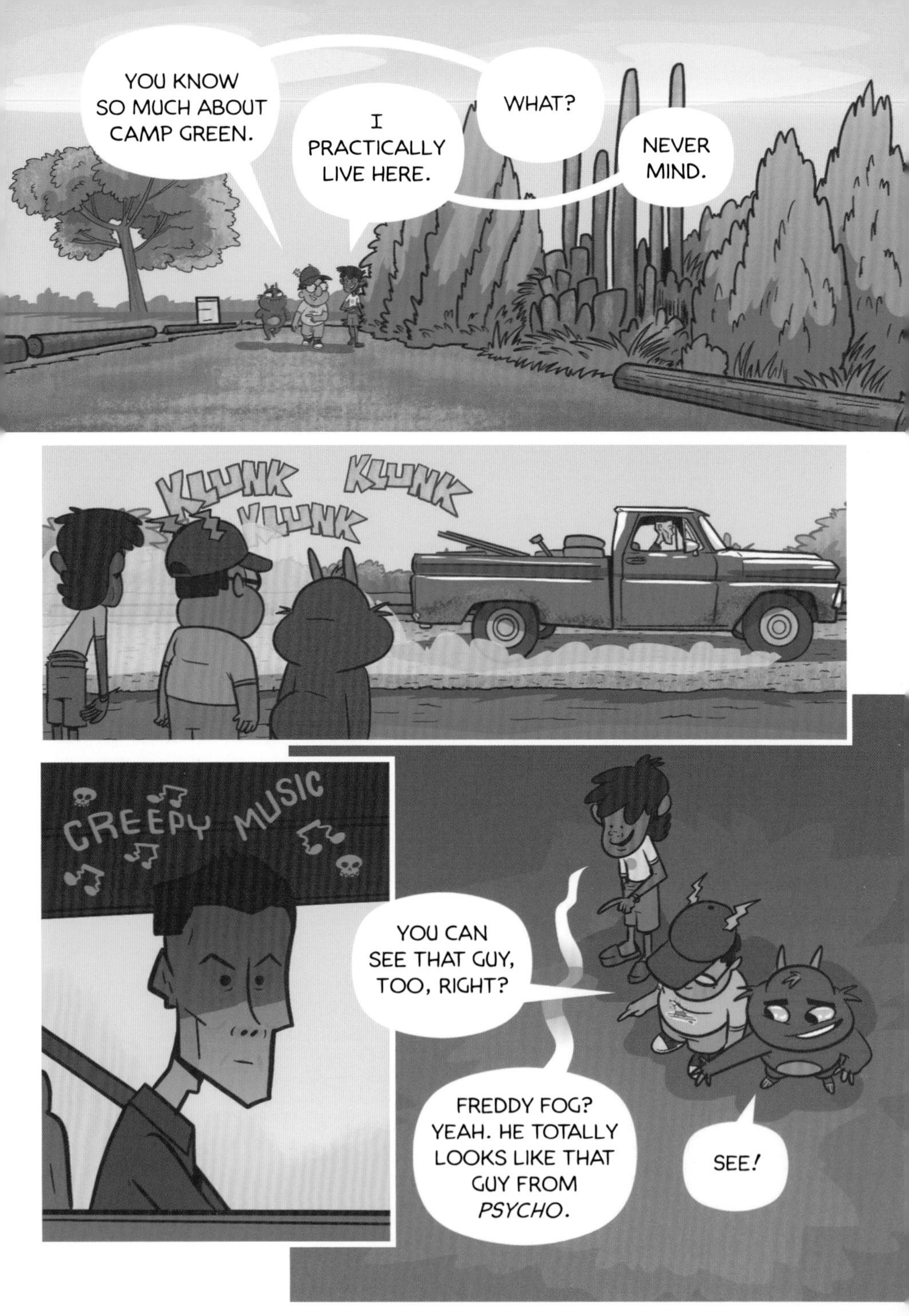
YOU KNOW SO MUCH ABOUT CAMP GREEN.
I PRACTICALLY LIVE HERE.
WHAT?
NEVER MIND.
KLUNK
KLUNK
KLUNK
CREEPY MUSIC
YOU CAN SEE THAT GUY, TOO, RIGHT?
FREDDY FOG? YEAH. HE TOTALLY LOOKS LIKE THAT GUY FROM *PSYCHO*.
SEE!

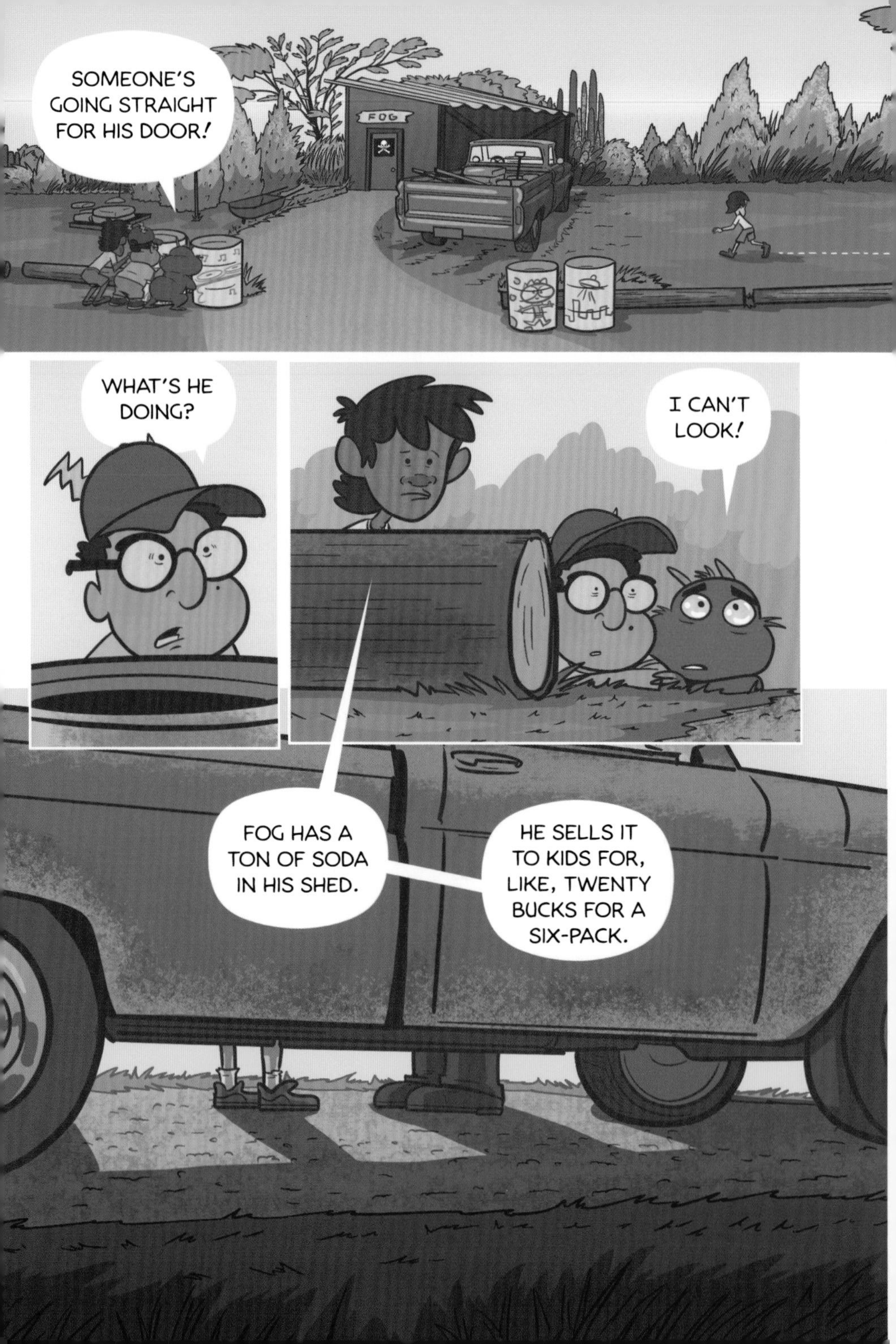
SOMEONE'S GOING STRAIGHT FOR HIS DOOR!
FOG
WHAT'S HE DOING?
I CAN'T LOOK!
FOG HAS A TON OF SODA IN HIS SHED.
HE SELLS IT TO KIDS FOR, LIKE, TWENTY BUCKS FOR A SIX-PACK.

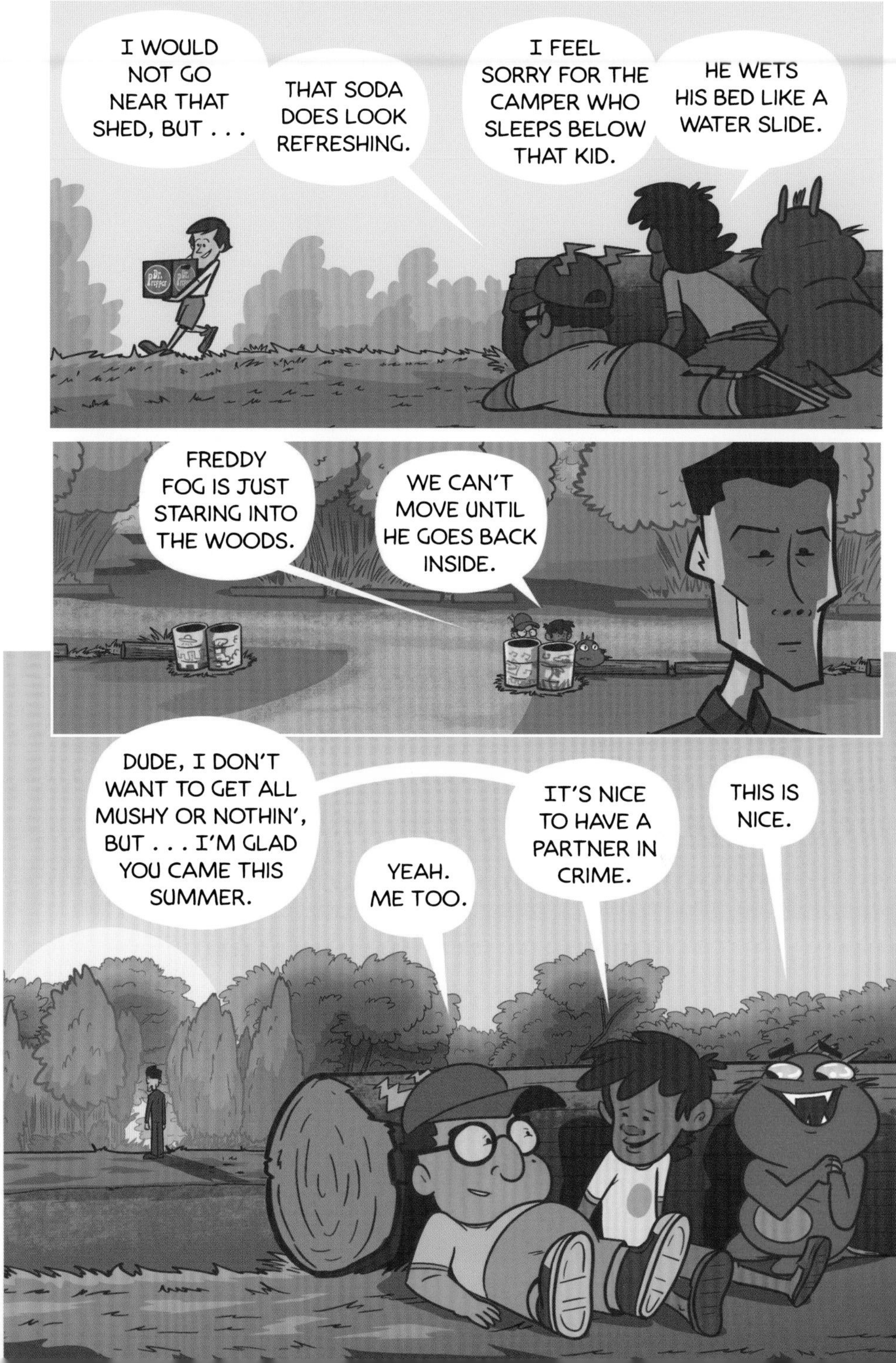
I WOULD NOT GO NEAR THAT SHED, BUT . . .
THAT SODA DOES LOOK REFRESHING.
I FEEL SORRY FOR THE CAMPER WHO SLEEPS BELOW THAT KID.
HE WETS HIS BED LIKE A WATER SLIDE.
FREDDY FOG IS JUST STARING INTO THE WOODS.
WE CAN'T MOVE UNTIL HE GOES BACK INSIDE.
DUDE, I DON'T WANT TO GET ALL MUSHY OR NOTHIN', BUT . . . I'M GLAD YOU CAME THIS SUMMER.
YEAH. ME TOO.
IT'S NICE TO HAVE A PARTNER IN CRIME.
THIS IS NICE.

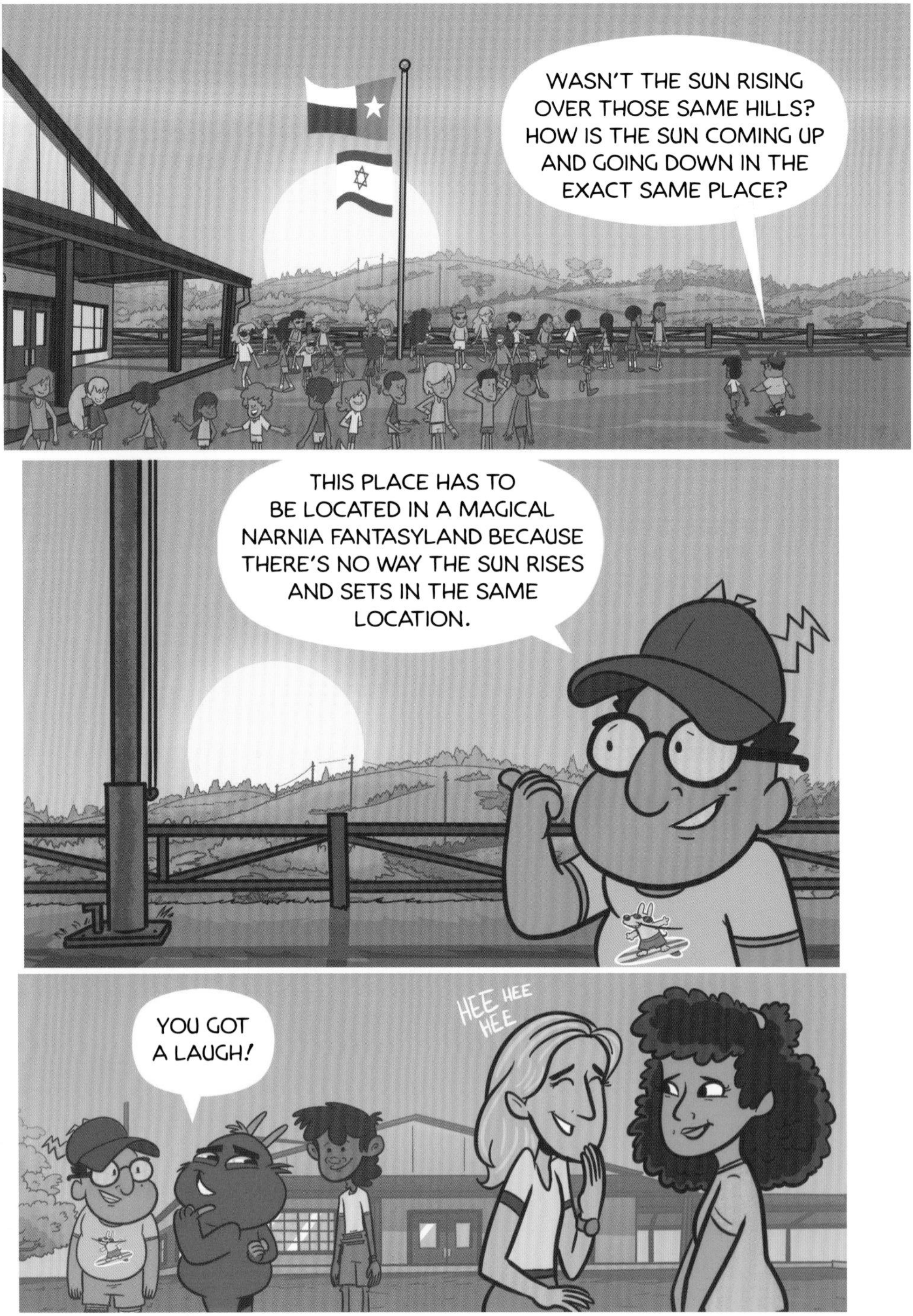
WASN'T THE SUN RISING OVER THOSE SAME HILLS? HOW IS THE SUN COMING UP AND GOING DOWN IN THE EXACT SAME PLACE?
THIS PLACE HAS TO BE LOCATED IN A MAGICAL NARNIA FANTASYLAND BECAUSE THERE'S NO WAY THE SUN RISES AND SETS IN THE SAME LOCATION.
YOU GOT A LAUGH!
HEE HEE HEE

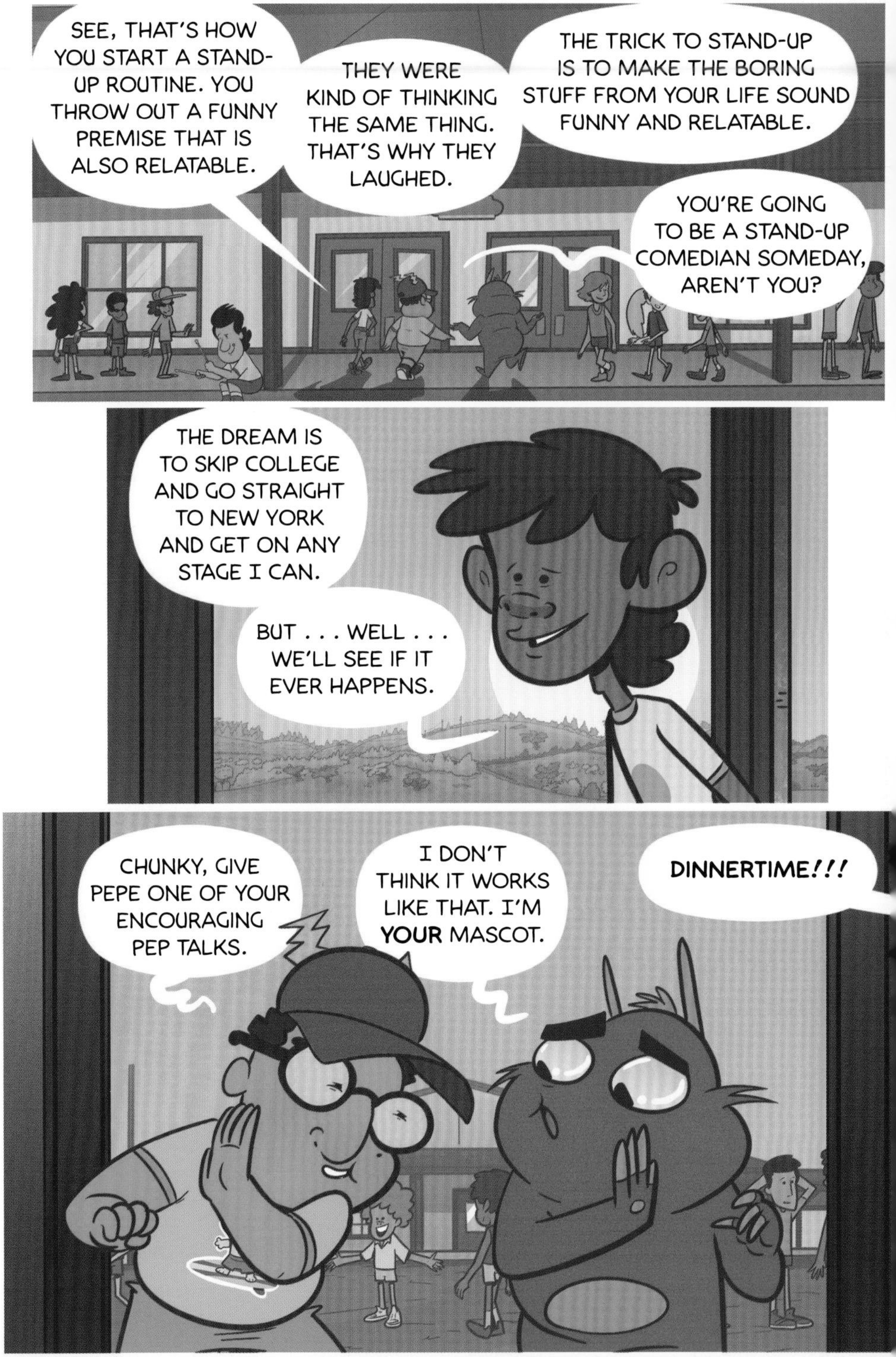
SEE, THAT'S HOW YOU START A STAND-UP ROUTINE. YOU THROW OUT A FUNNY PREMISE THAT IS ALSO RELATABLE.
THEY WERE KIND OF THINKING THE SAME THING. THAT'S WHY THEY LAUGHED.
THE TRICK TO STAND-UP IS TO MAKE THE BORING STUFF FROM YOUR LIFE SOUND FUNNY AND RELATABLE.
YOU'RE GOING TO BE A STAND-UP COMEDIAN SOMEDAY, AREN'T YOU?
THE DREAM IS TO SKIP COLLEGE AND GO STRAIGHT TO NEW YORK AND GET ON ANY STAGE I CAN.
BUT . . . WELL . . . WE'LL SEE IF IT EVER HAPPENS.
CHUNKY, GIVE PEPE ONE OF YOUR ENCOURAGING PEP TALKS.
I DON'T THINK IT WORKS LIKE THAT. I'M **YOUR** MASCOT.
DINNERTIME!!!

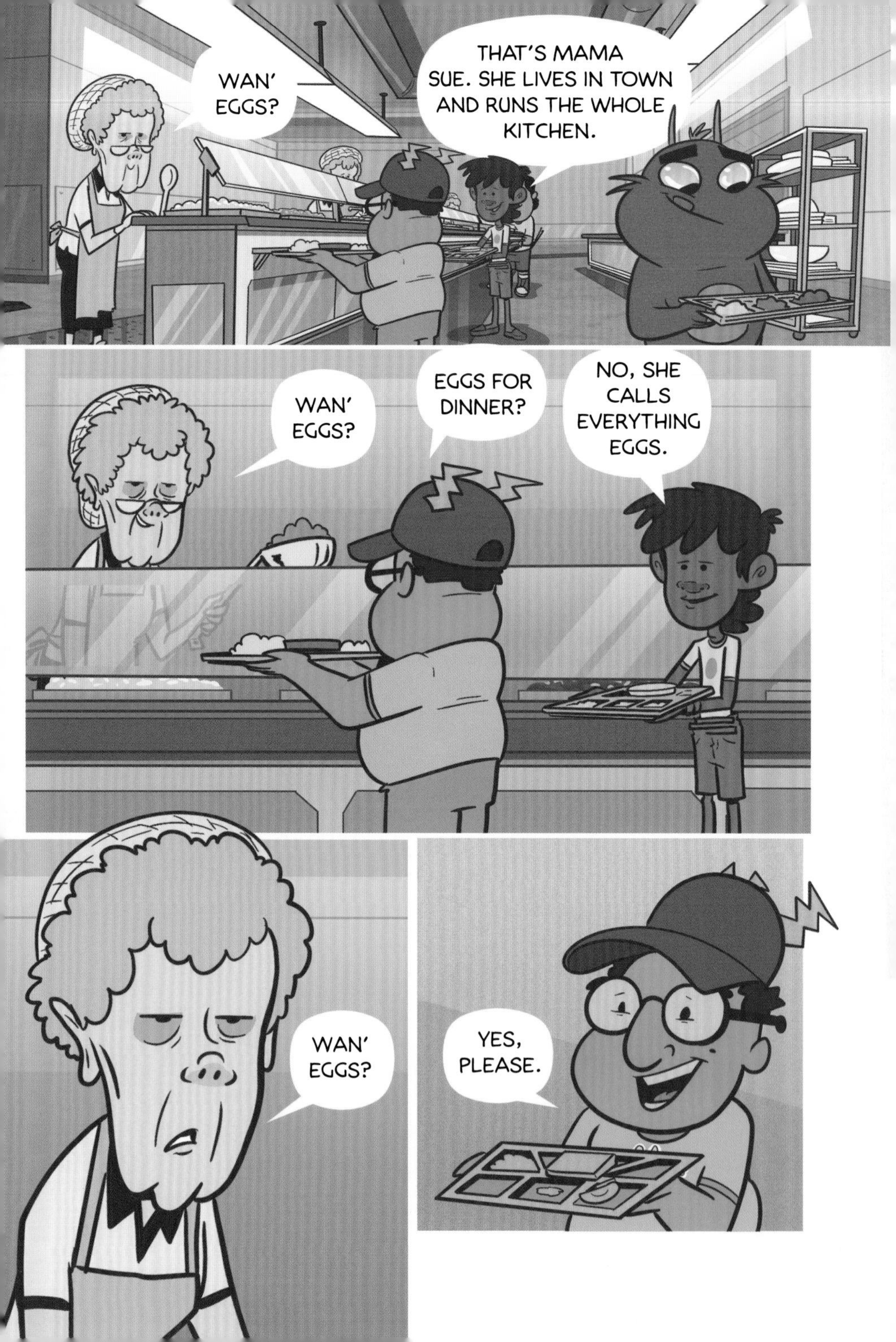
WAN' EGGS?
THAT'S MAMA SUE. SHE LIVES IN TOWN AND RUNS THE WHOLE KITCHEN.
WAN' EGGS?
EGGS FOR DINNER?
NO, SHE CALLS EVERYTHING EGGS.
WAN' EGGS?
YES, PLEASE.

85

88

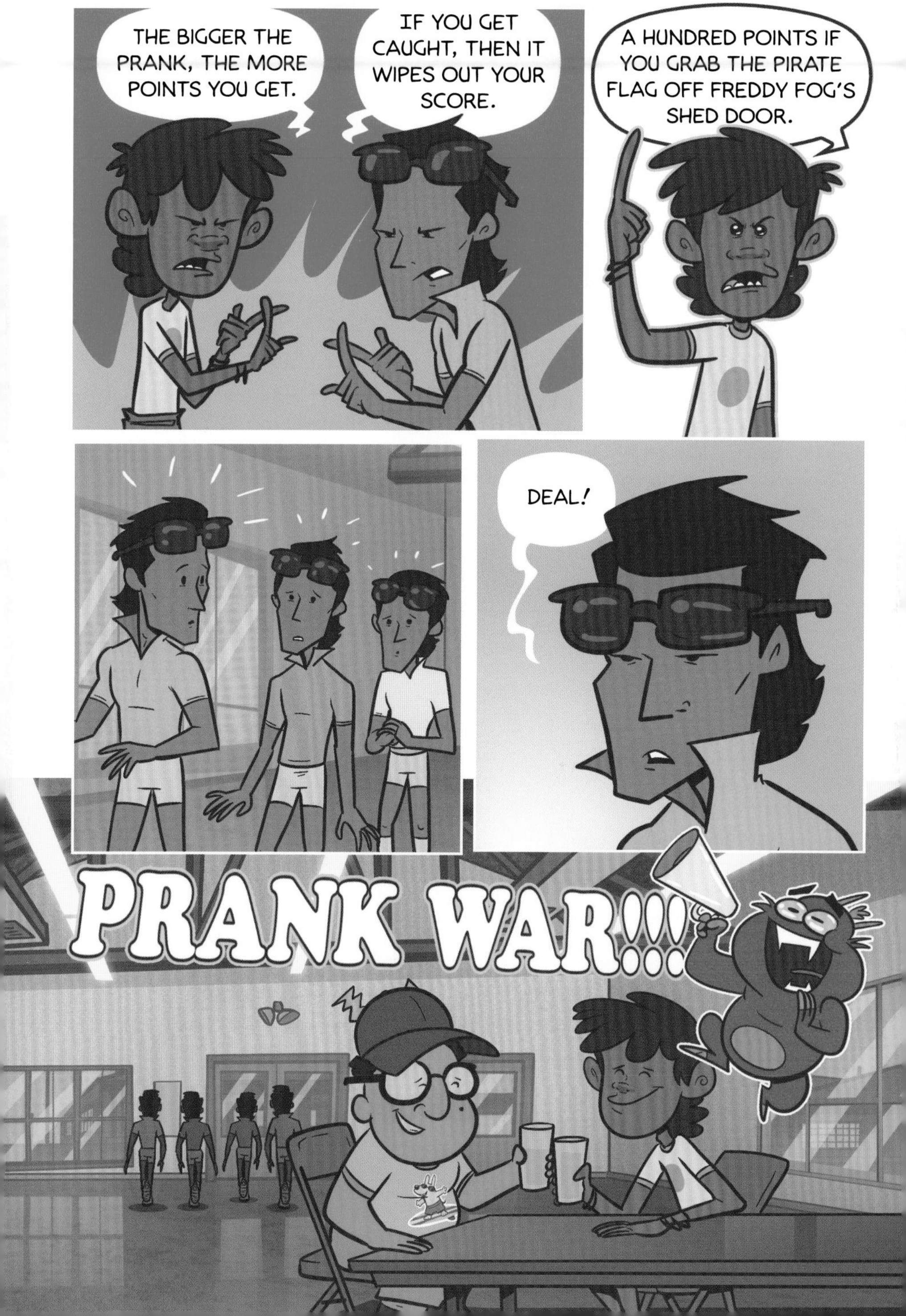
THE BIGGER THE PRANK, THE MORE POINTS YOU GET.
IF YOU GET CAUGHT, THEN IT WIPES OUT YOUR SCORE.
A HUNDRED POINTS IF YOU GRAB THE PIRATE FLAG OFF FREDDY FOG'S SHED DOOR.
DEAL!
PRANK WAR!!!

HUDI on TRIAL

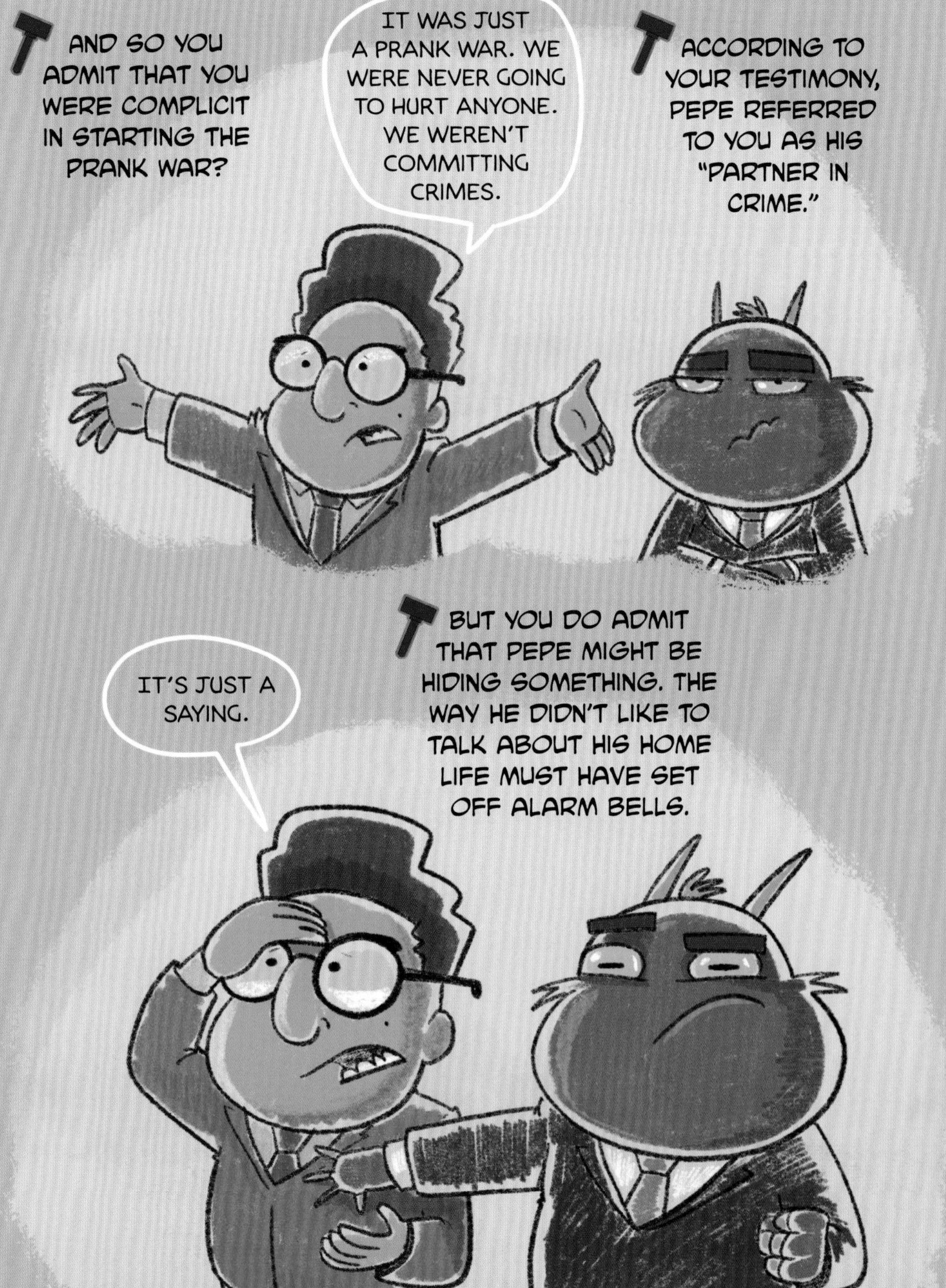

AND SO YOU ADMIT THAT YOU WERE COMPLICIT IN STARTING THE PRANK WAR?
IT WAS JUST A PRANK WAR. WE WERE NEVER GOING TO HURT ANYONE. WE WEREN'T COMMITTING CRIMES.
ACCORDING TO YOUR TESTIMONY, PEPE REFERRED TO YOU AS HIS "PARTNER IN CRIME."
IT'S JUST A SAYING.
BUT YOU DO ADMIT THAT PEPE MIGHT BE HIDING SOMETHING. THE WAY HE DIDN'T LIKE TO TALK ABOUT HIS HOME LIFE MUST HAVE SET OFF ALARM BELLS.

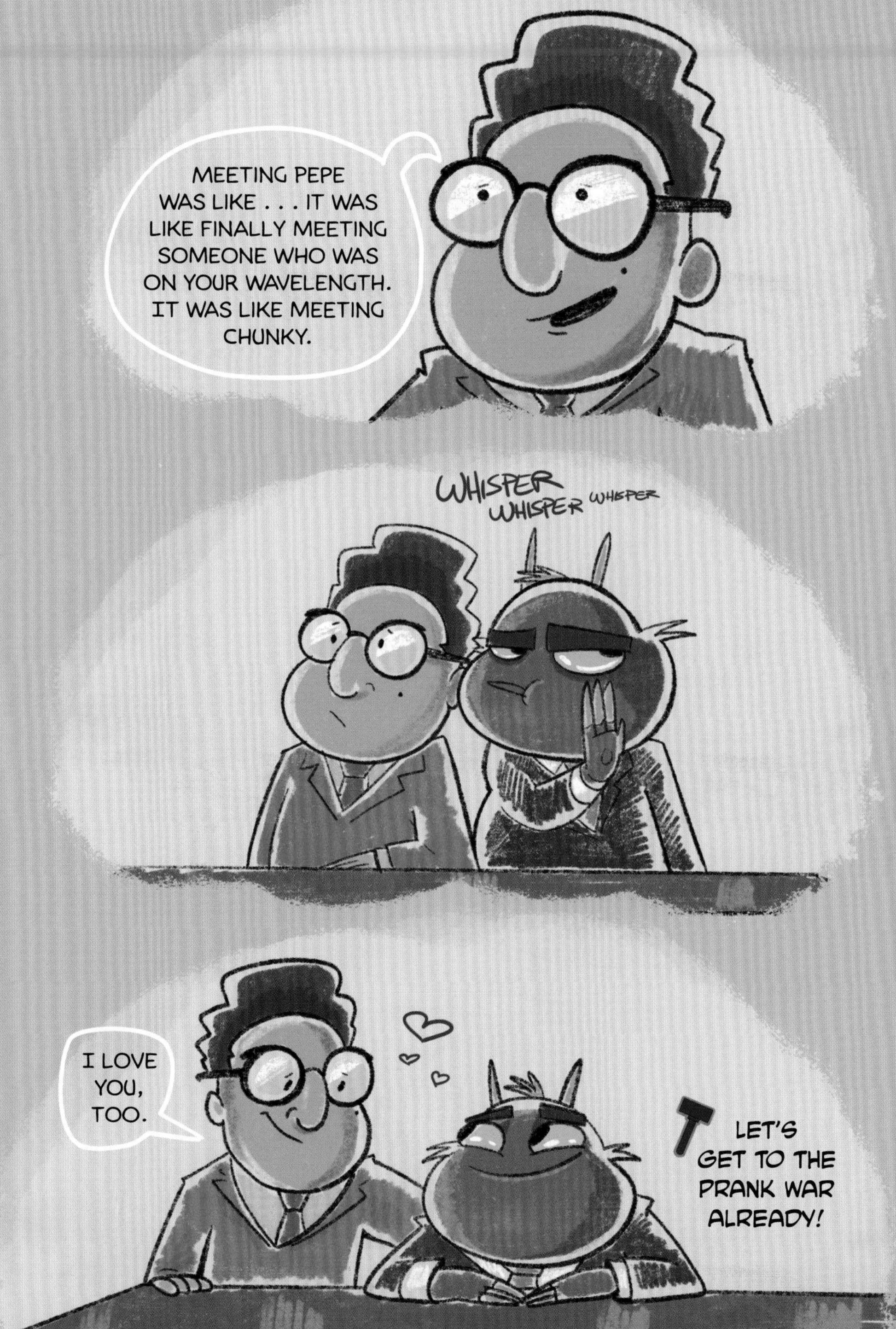
MEETING PEPE WAS LIKE . . . IT WAS LIKE FINALLY MEETING SOMEONE WHO WAS ON YOUR WAVELENGTH. IT WAS LIKE MEETING CHUNKY.
WHISPER WHISPER WHISPER
I LOVE YOU, TOO.
LET'S GET TO THE PRANK WAR ALREADY!

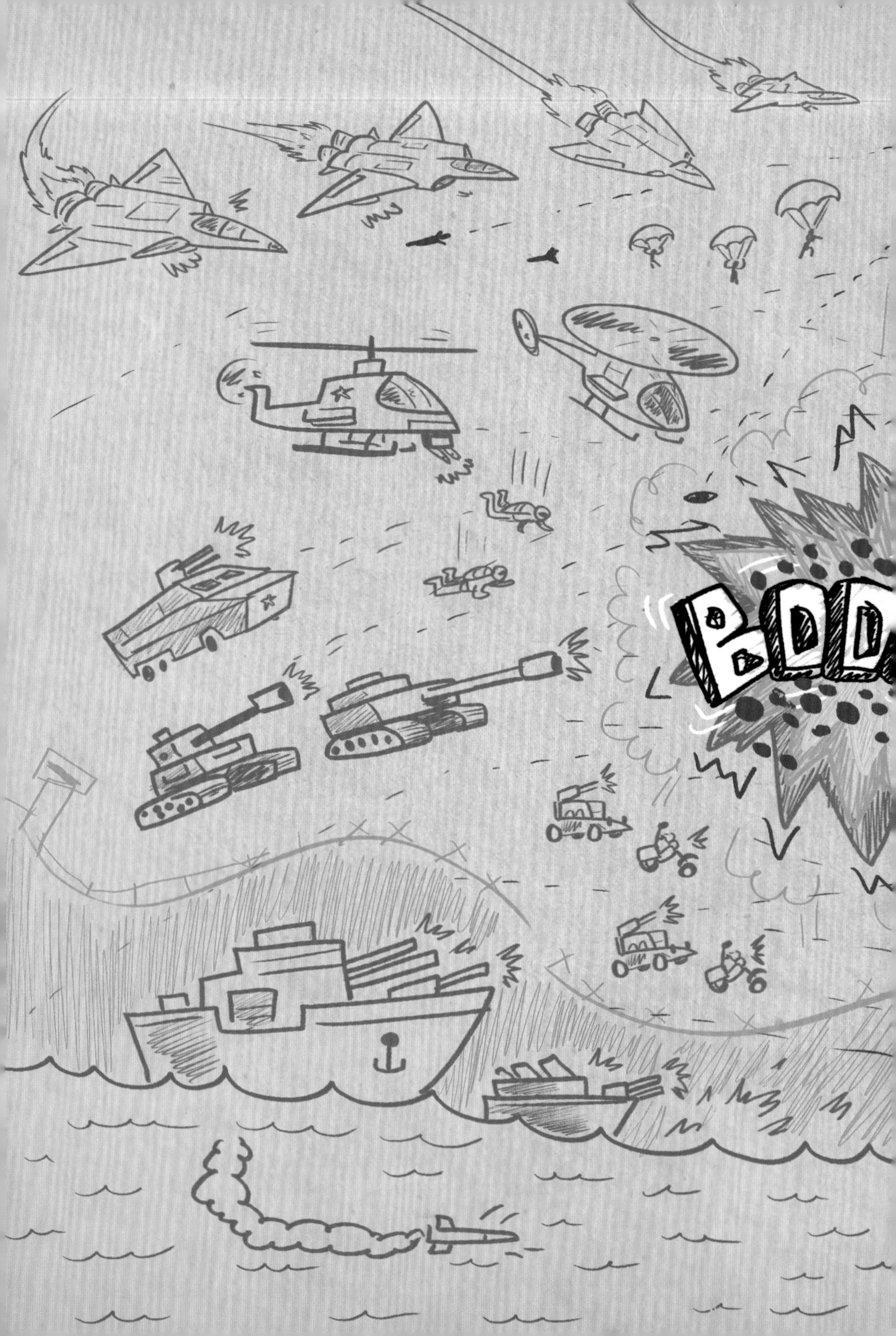
BOO

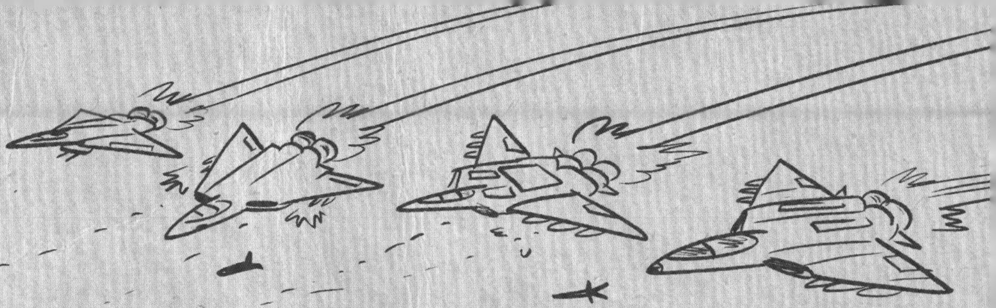

CHAPTER FOUR

PRANK WAR

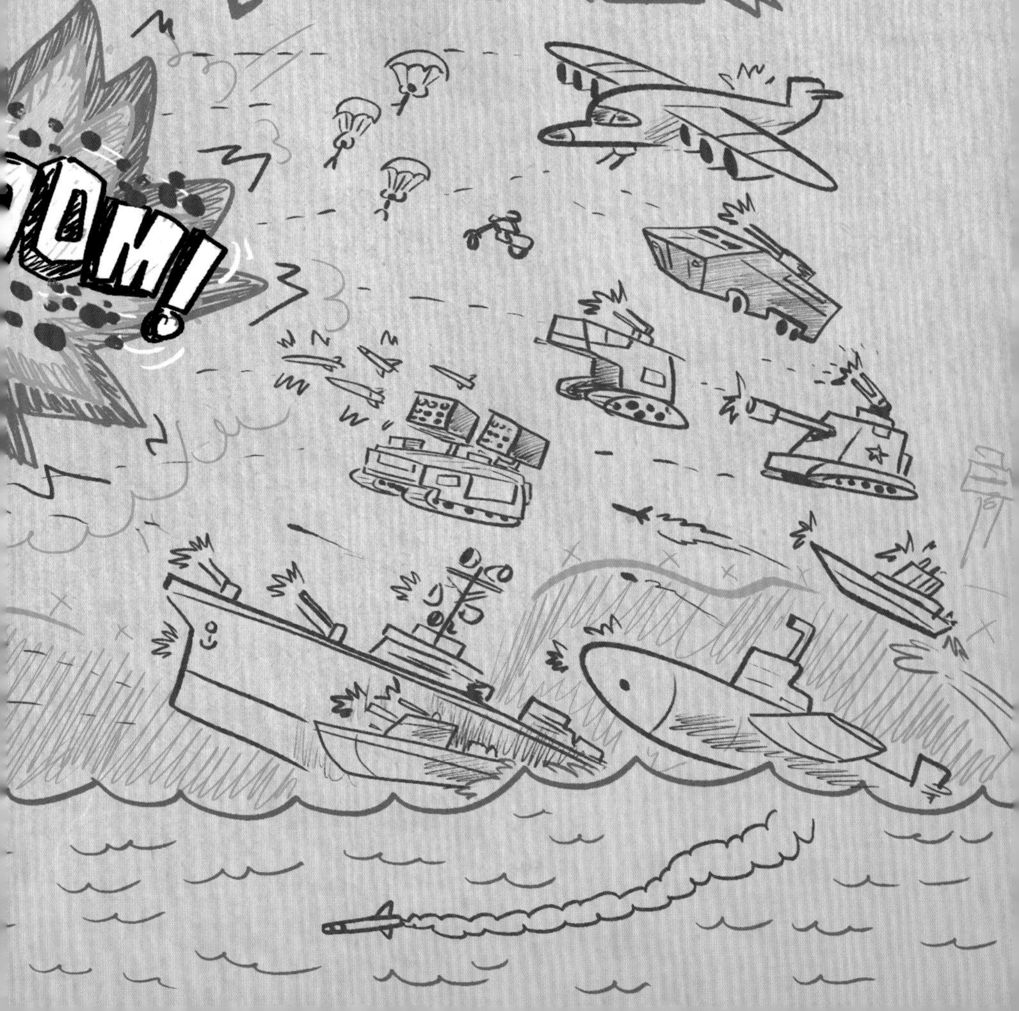

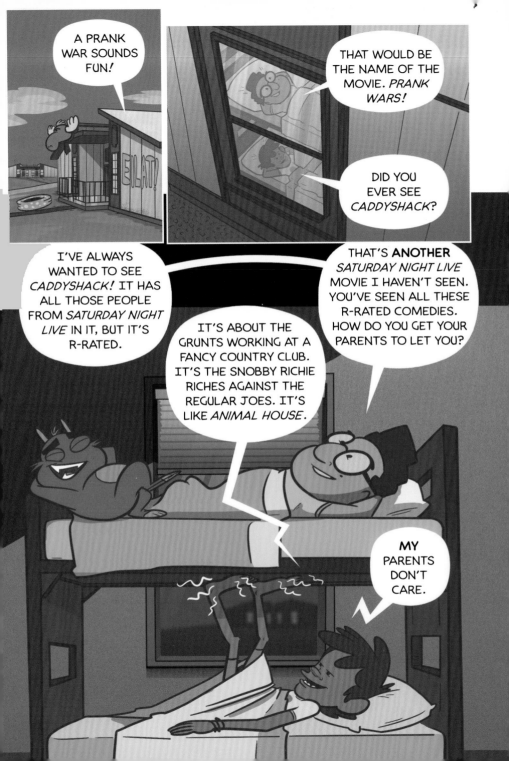

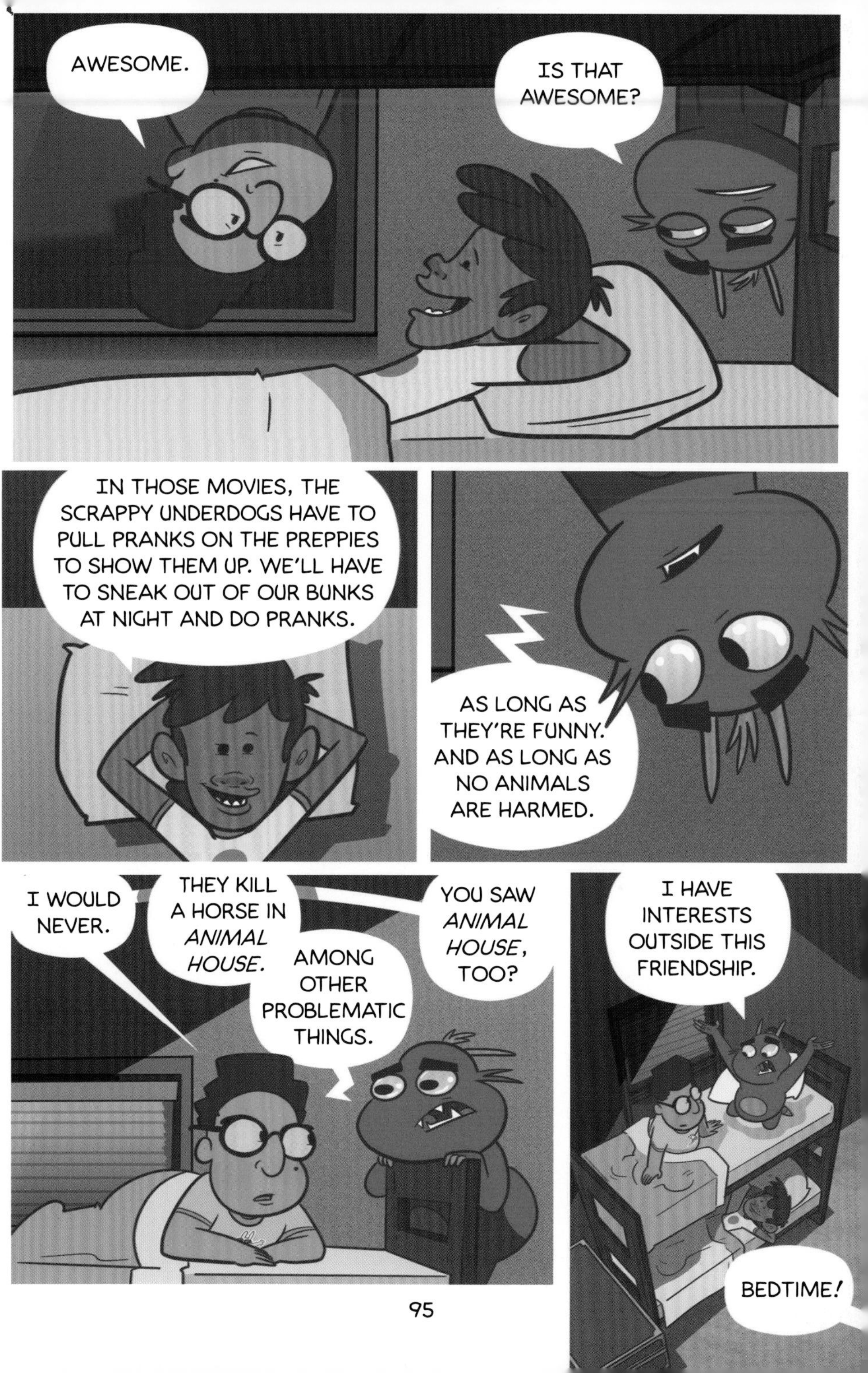
AWESOME.
IS THAT AWESOME?
IN THOSE MOVIES, THE SCRAPPY UNDERDOGS HAVE TO PULL PRANKS ON THE PREPPIES TO SHOW THEM UP. WE'LL HAVE TO SNEAK OUT OF OUR BUNKS AT NIGHT AND DO PRANKS.
AS LONG AS THEY'RE FUNNY. AND AS LONG AS NO ANIMALS ARE HARMED.
I WOULD NEVER.
THEY KILL A HORSE IN *ANIMAL HOUSE*.
AMONG OTHER PROBLEMATIC THINGS.
YOU SAW *ANIMAL HOUSE*, TOO?
I HAVE INTERESTS OUTSIDE THIS FRIENDSHIP.
BEDTIME!

PRANK WAR

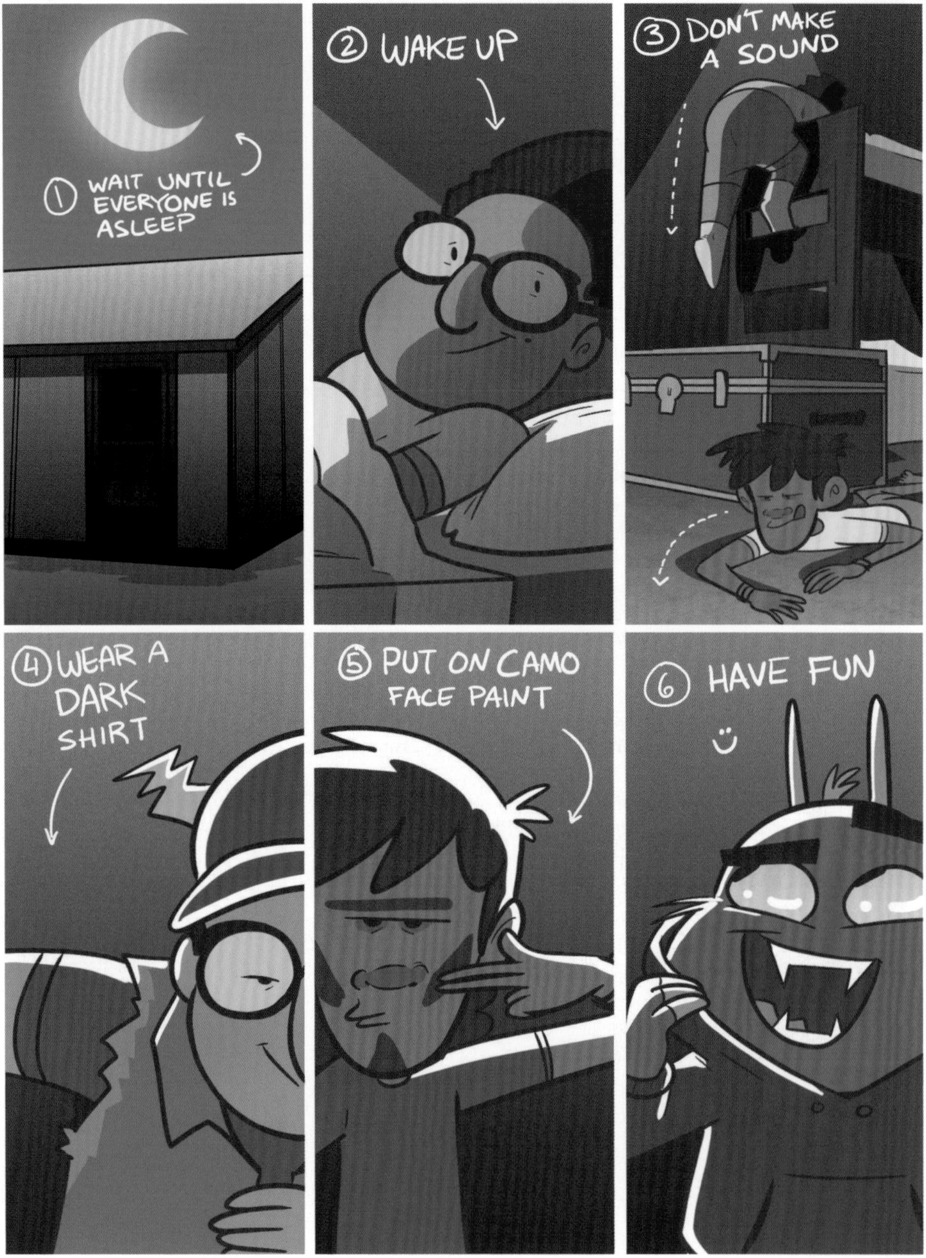

① WAIT UNTIL EVERYONE IS ASLEEP
② WAKE UP
③ DON'T MAKE A SOUND
④ WEAR A DARK SHIRT
⑤ PUT ON CAMO FACE PAINT
⑥ HAVE FUN

NIGHT ONE

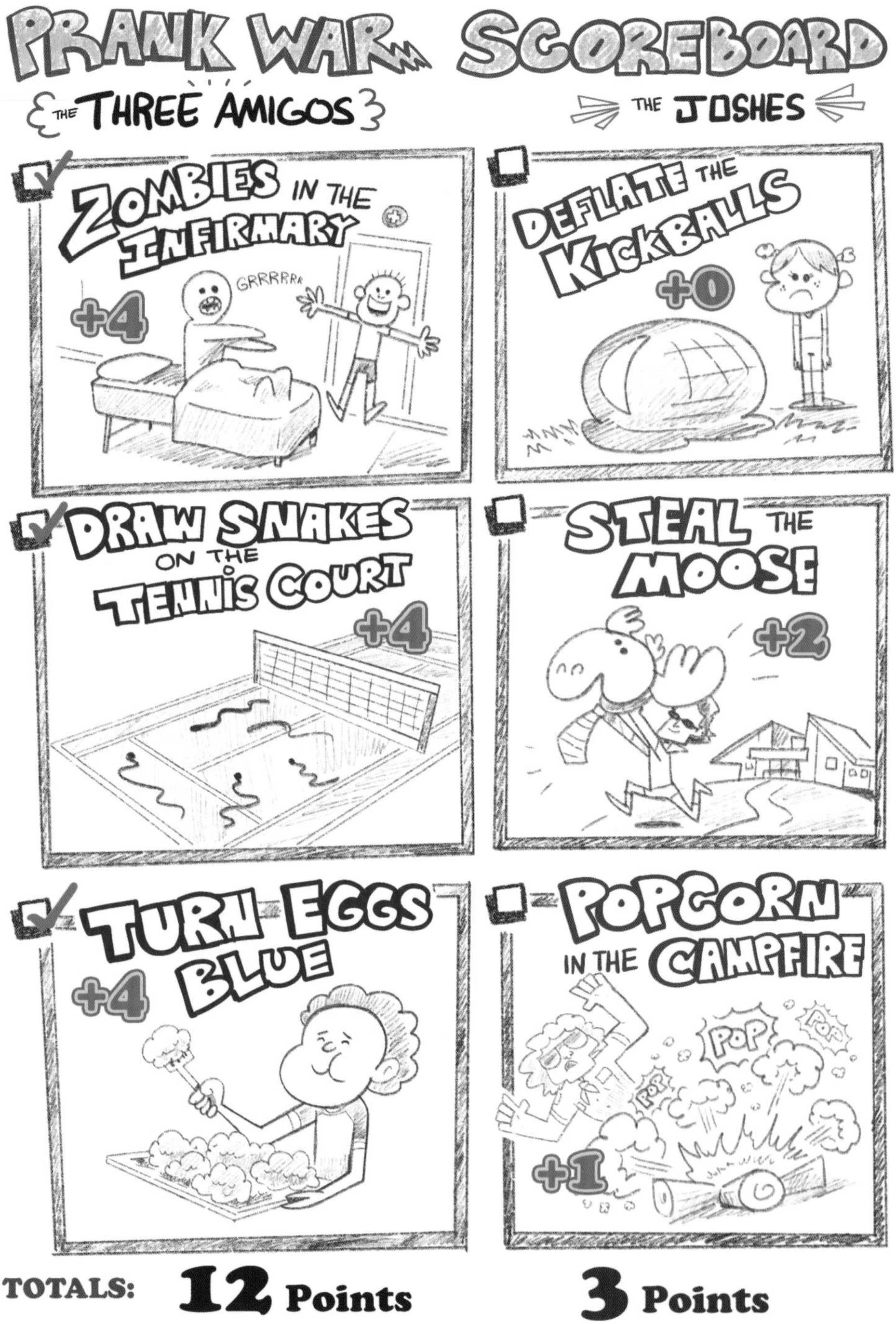
PRANK WAR SCOREBOARD
THE THREE AMIGOS
THE JOSHES
ZOMBIES IN THE INFIRMARY
GRRRRRR
+4
DEFLATE THE KICKBALLS
+0
DRAW SNAKES ON THE TENNIS COURT
+4
STEAL THE MOOSE
+2
TURN EGGS BLUE
+4
POPCORN IN THE CAMPFIRE
POP
POP
POP
+1

TOTALS: 12 Points 3 Points

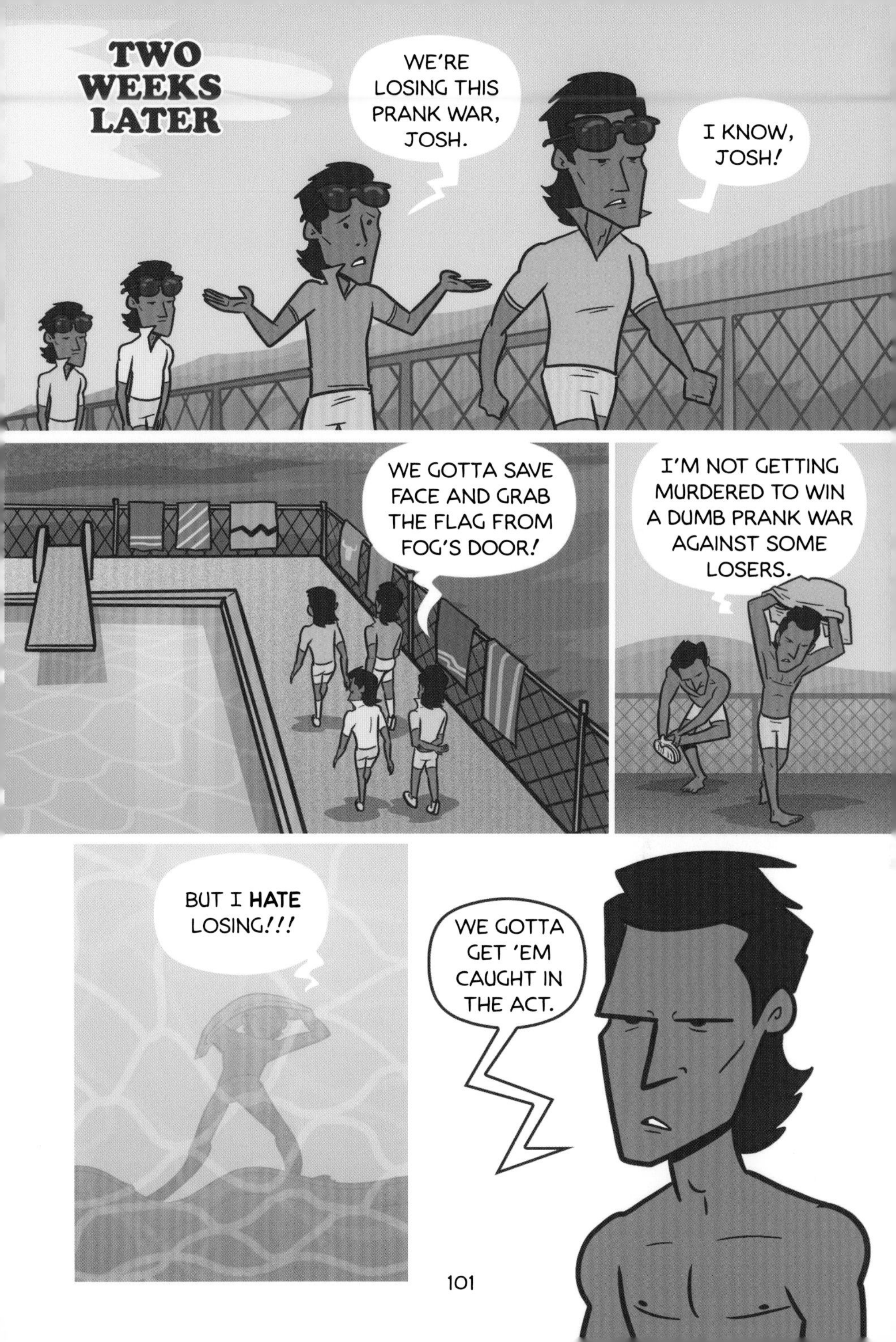
TWO WEEKS LATER
WE'RE LOSING THIS PRANK WAR, JOSH.
I KNOW, JOSH!
WE GOTTA SAVE FACE AND GRAB THE FLAG FROM FOG'S DOOR!
I'M NOT GETTING MURDERED TO WIN A DUMB PRANK WAR AGAINST SOME LOSERS.
BUT I **HATE** LOSING!!!
WE GOTTA GET 'EM CAUGHT IN THE ACT.

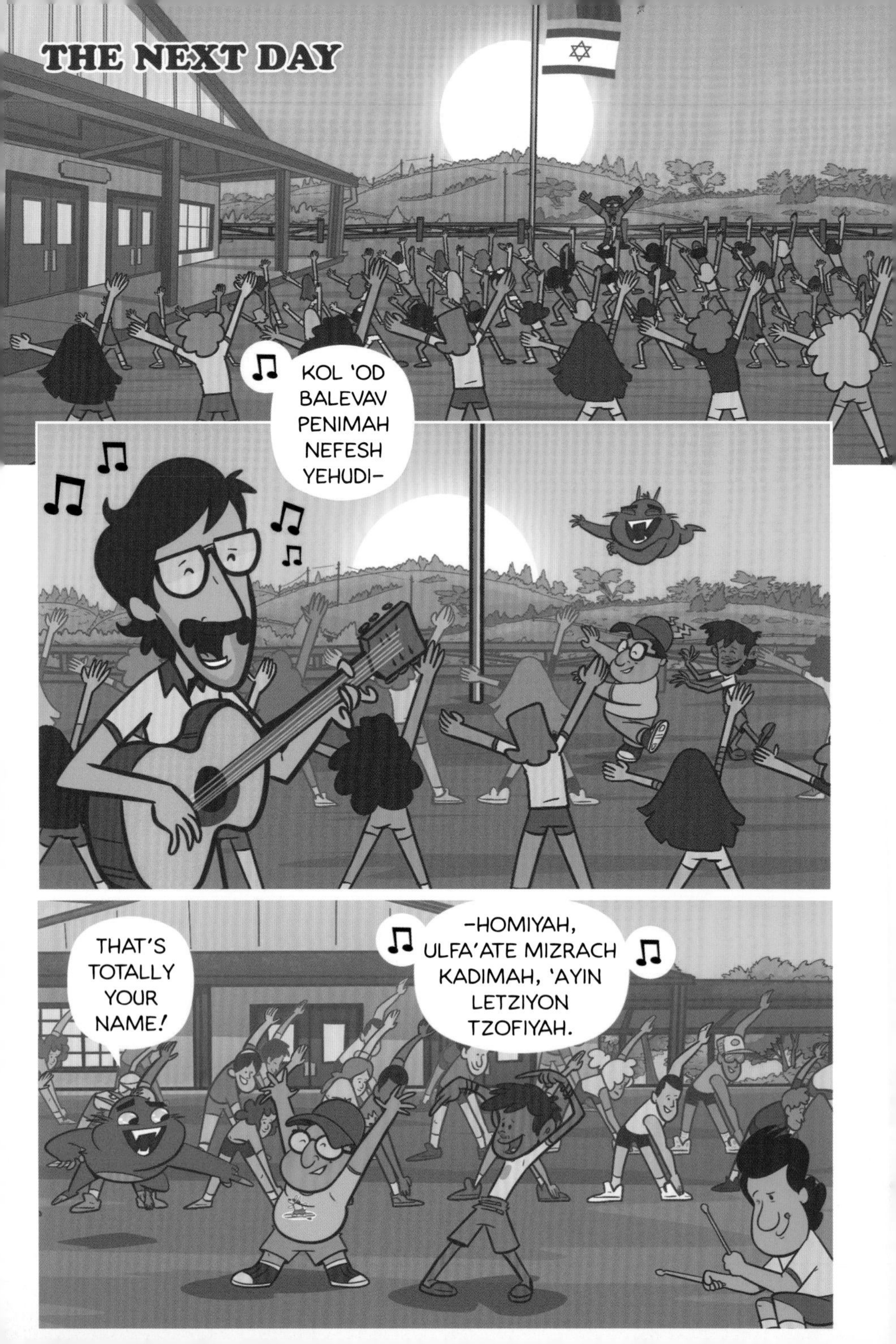
THE NEXT DAY
KOL 'OD BALEVAV PENIMAH NEFESH YEHUDI–
THAT'S TOTALLY YOUR NAME!
–HOMIYAH, ULFA'ATE MIZRACH KADIMAH, 'AYIN LETZIYON TZOFIYAH.

HEY! IT'S HUDI AND PEPE, RIGHT?

OH NO. AM I IN TROUBLE?

NO, NOT AT ALL. YOU TWO LOOK LIKE YOU MIGHT BE COMFORTABLE ON A STAGE.

PEPE'S A STAND-UP COMEDIAN.

WE'RE HAVING A VERY SPECIAL FRIDAY NIGHT SHABBAT SERVICE FOR THE CAMP COMMITTEE THIS FRIDAY, AND I'D LIKE YOU TWO TO SAY A LITTLE SOMETHING ABOUT CAMP AND LIGHT THE CANDLES.

COUNT US IN!

THANKS, LOUI!

YEAH!

GREAT. I'LL TELL WARREN, AND I'LL GET YOU MORE INFORMATION LATER.

THEN YOU AND PEPE WENT TO THE BEIT KNESSET TO WRITE WHAT YOU WERE GOING TO SAY IN FRONT OF THE ENTIRE CAMP?

WE WERE SPENDING SO MUCH TIME PLANNING PRANKS THAT WE FORGOT TO WRITE OUR SHABBAT SPEECH.

SO WE THOUGHT THAT WE COULD GET A BETTER IDEA IF WE WROTE IN THE PLACE WHERE WE WERE GOING TO GIVE THE SPEECH.

108

STOP SHAKING THE TABLE!

IT WAS KNOWN AS THE STARS AND CLOUDS INCIDENT.

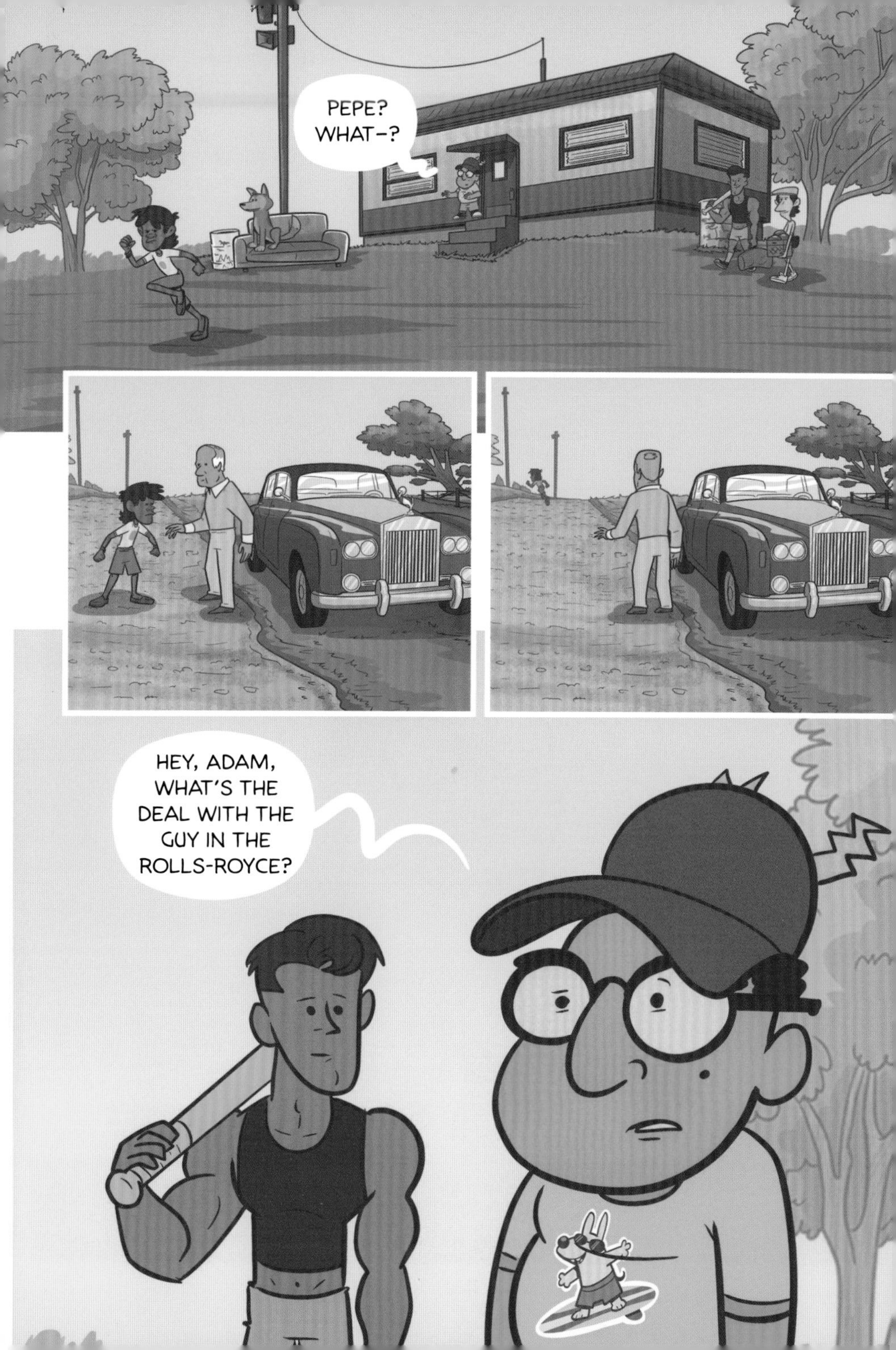
PEPE? WHAT–?
HEY, ADAM, WHAT'S THE DEAL WITH THE GUY IN THE ROLLS-ROYCE?

116

PEPE SAID HE HAD TO GO GRAB STUFF FROM THE ARTS AND CRAFTS ROOM FOR TONIGHT.

SO I RUSHED FOR NOTHING!

HEY . . . SO . . . I DON'T THINK WE SHOULD DO THE PRANK TONIGHT.

PEPE REALLY THINKS WE SHOULD.

SOMETHING IS UP WITH HIM. IT'S ALMOST LIKE HE'S MORE INTERESTED IN ACTING OUT THAN BEING FUNNY.

BUT PEOPLE THINK THE PRANKS **ARE** FUNNY.

I JUST DON'T WANT THEM TO GO TOO FAR.

WELL, WE'RE THE THREE AMIGOS, AND SURE, THE ONE AMIGO DIDN'T WANT US TO MEET HIS FATHER FOR SOME REASON AND LIED ABOUT BEING REALLY RICH . . . BUT HE NEEDS US.

MAYBE I SHOULD TRY TO TALK TO HIM.

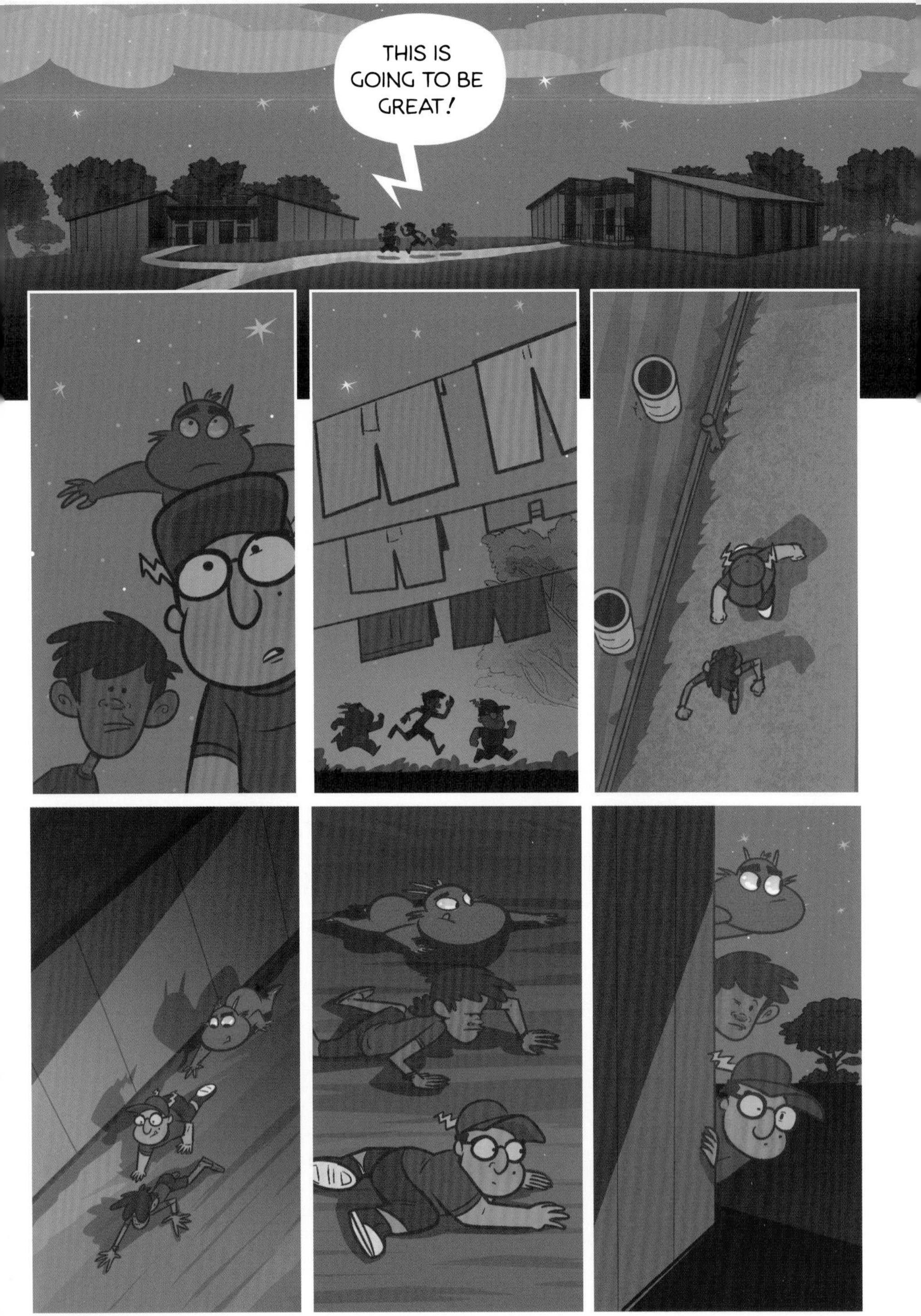
THIS IS GOING TO BE GREAT!

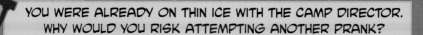
YOU WERE ALREADY ON THIN ICE WITH THE CAMP DIRECTOR. WHY WOULD YOU RISK ATTEMPTING ANOTHER PRANK?

THE FIRST CASUALTY OF PRANK WARS . . . IS COMMON SENSE.

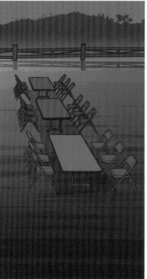

IT'S FUNNY HOW A CHORE ISN'T SO BAD WHEN IT'S A PRANK. LIKE, IF MY PARENTS ASKED ME TO MOVE AND ASSEMBLE AN ENTIRE MESS HALL, I WOULD HAVE THOUGHT IT WAS A PUNISHMENT.

HUDI on TRIAL

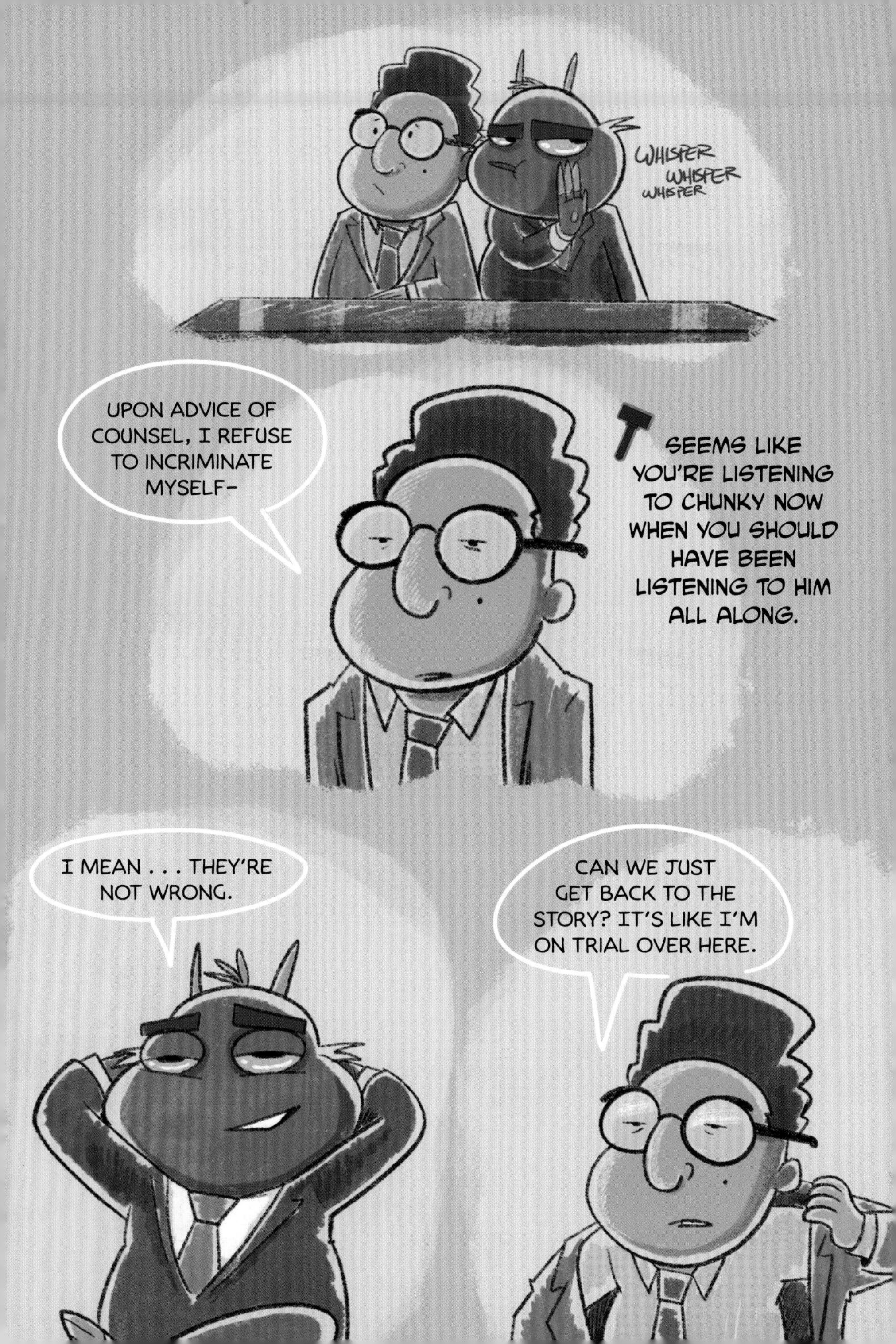
WHISPER
WHISPER
WHISPER
UPON ADVICE OF COUNSEL, I REFUSE TO INCRIMINATE MYSELF–
SEEMS LIKE YOU'RE LISTENING TO CHUNKY NOW WHEN YOU SHOULD HAVE BEEN LISTENING TO HIM ALL ALONG.
I MEAN . . . THEY'RE NOT WRONG.
CAN WE JUST GET BACK TO THE STORY? IT'S LIKE I'M ON TRIAL OVER HERE.

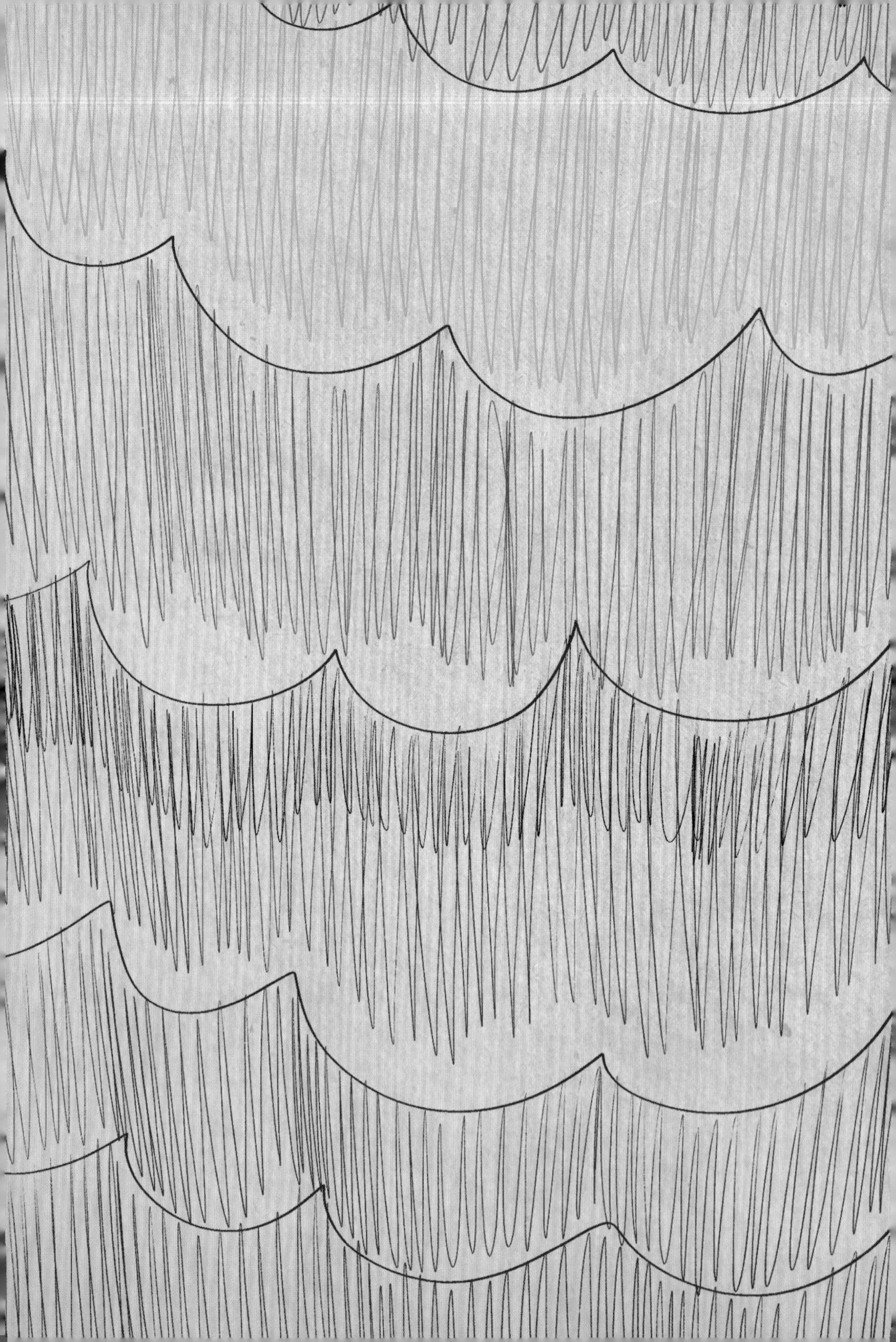

CHAPTER FIVE

STORM CLOUDS

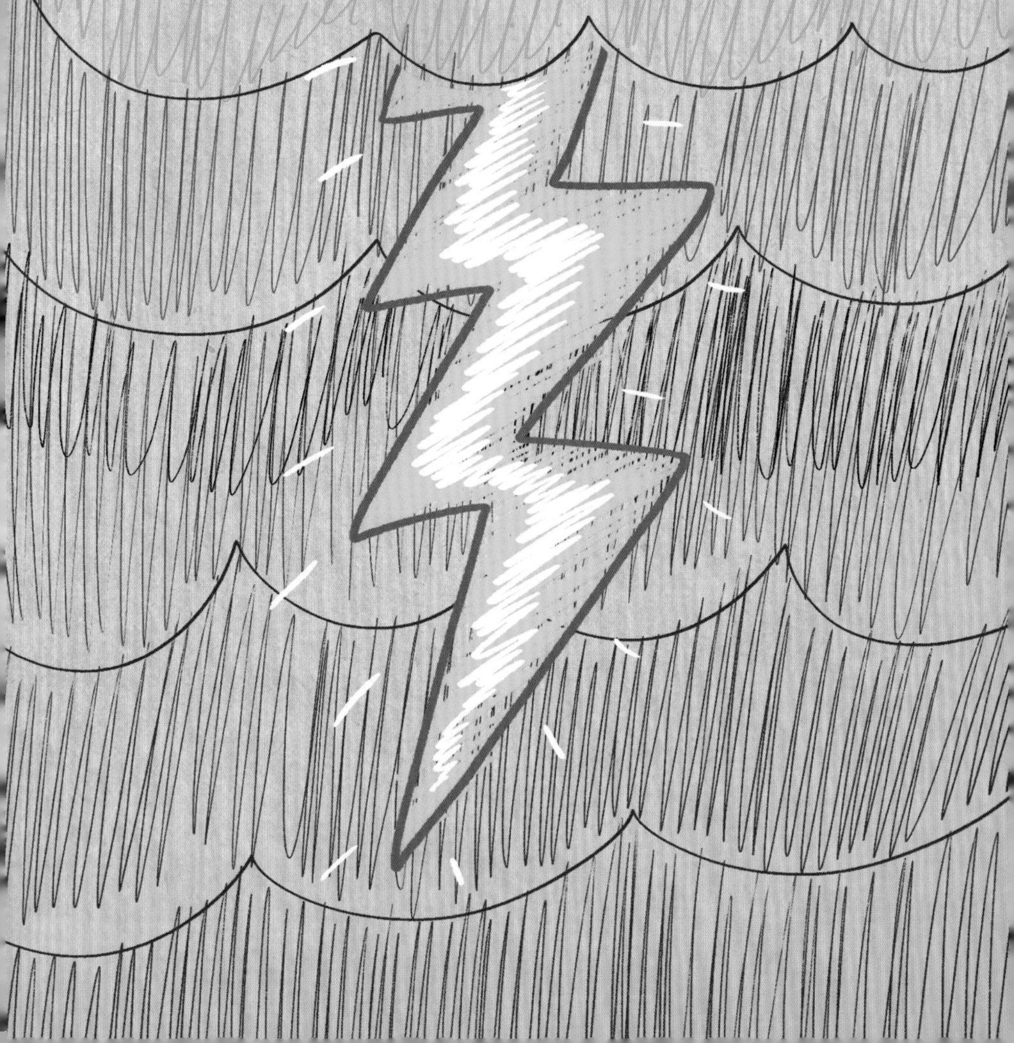

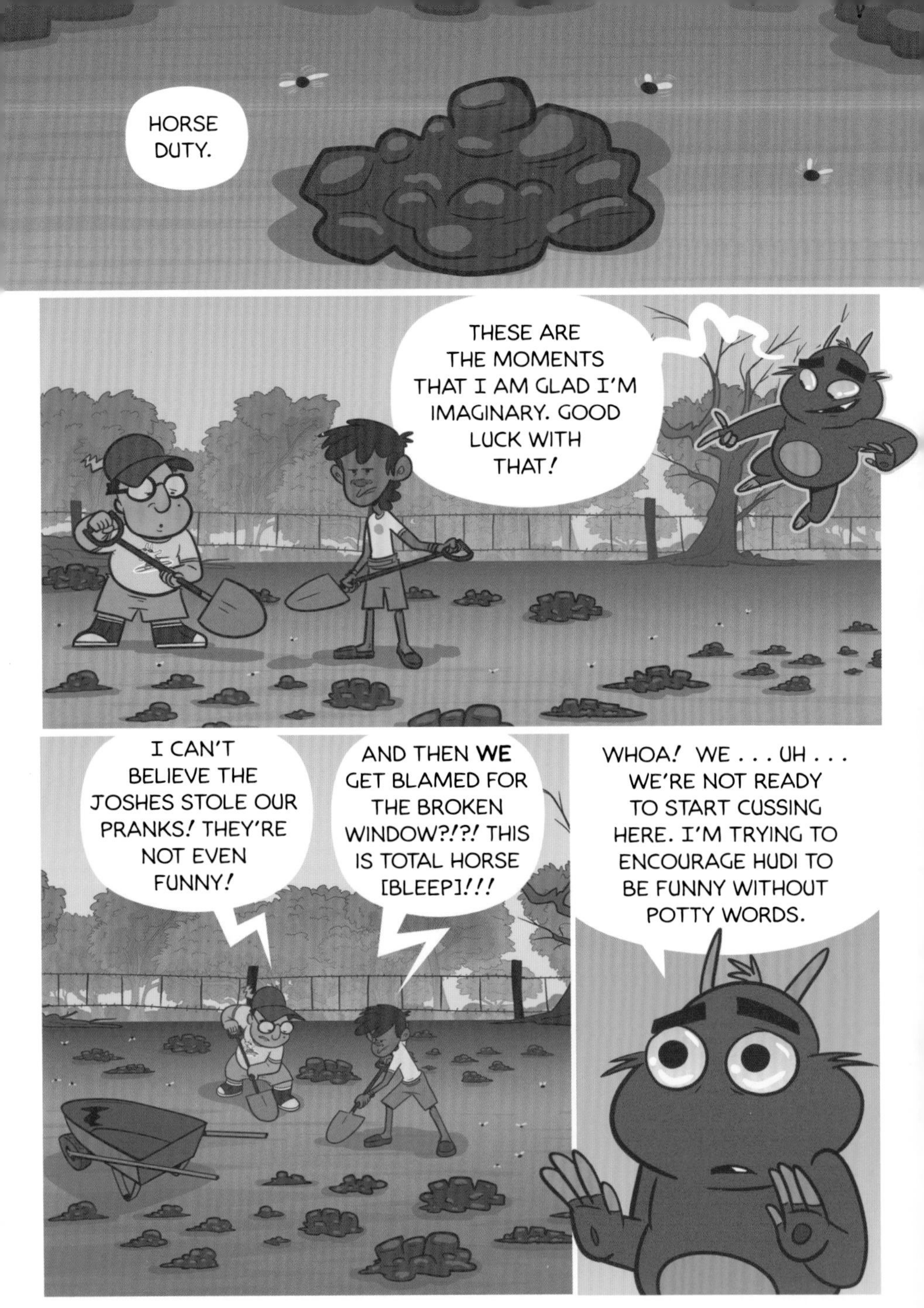
HORSE DUTY.
THESE ARE THE MOMENTS THAT I AM GLAD I'M IMAGINARY. GOOD LUCK WITH THAT!
I CAN'T BELIEVE THE JOSHES STOLE OUR PRANKS! THEY'RE NOT EVEN FUNNY!
AND THEN **WE** GET BLAMED FOR THE BROKEN WINDOW?!?! THIS IS TOTAL HORSE [BLEEP]!!!
WHOA! WE . . . UH . . . WE'RE NOT READY TO START CUSSING HERE. I'M TRYING TO ENCOURAGE HUDI TO BE FUNNY WITHOUT POTTY WORDS.

137

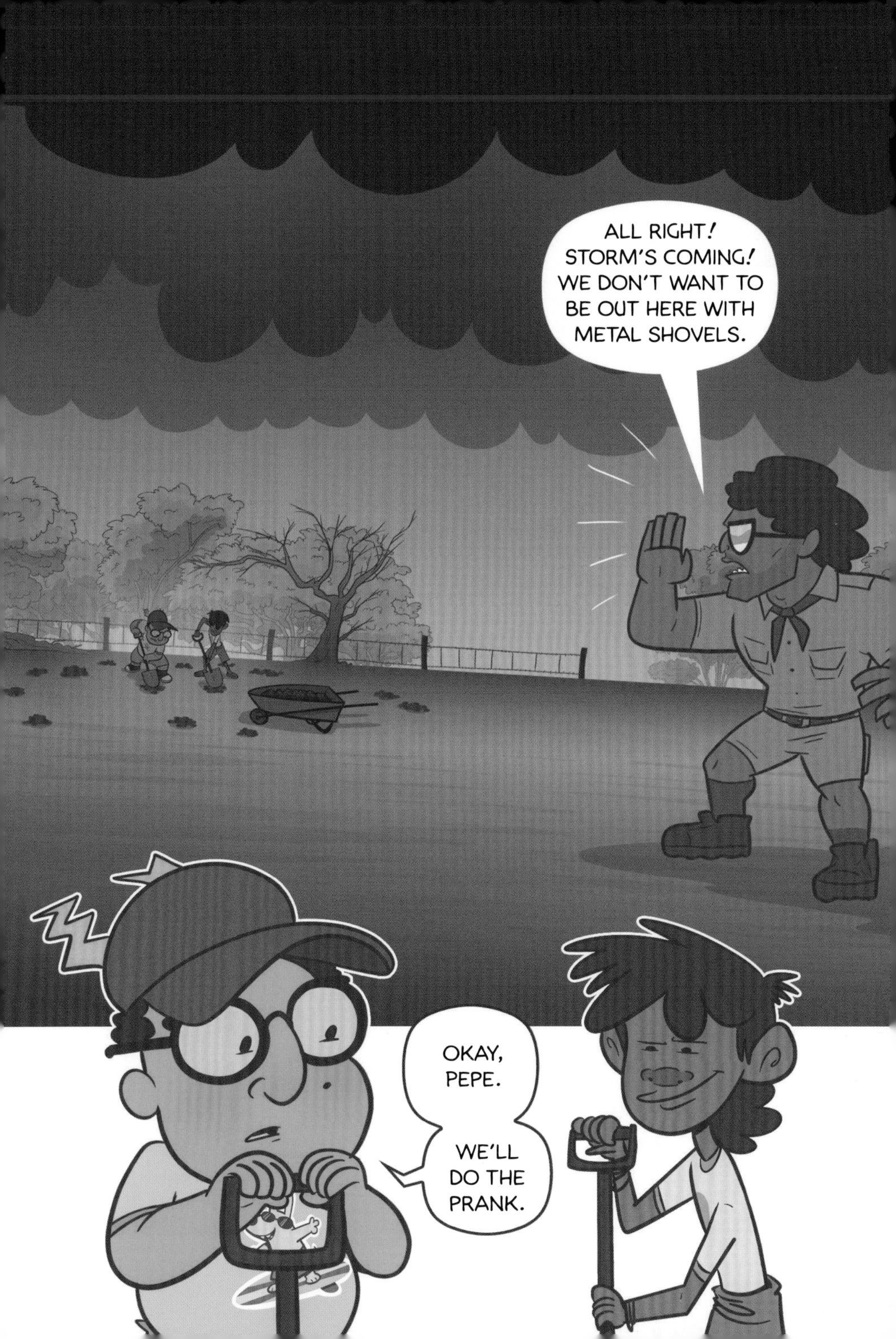
ALL RIGHT! STORM'S COMING! WE DON'T WANT TO BE OUT HERE WITH METAL SHOVELS.
OKAY, PEPE.
WE'LL DO THE PRANK.

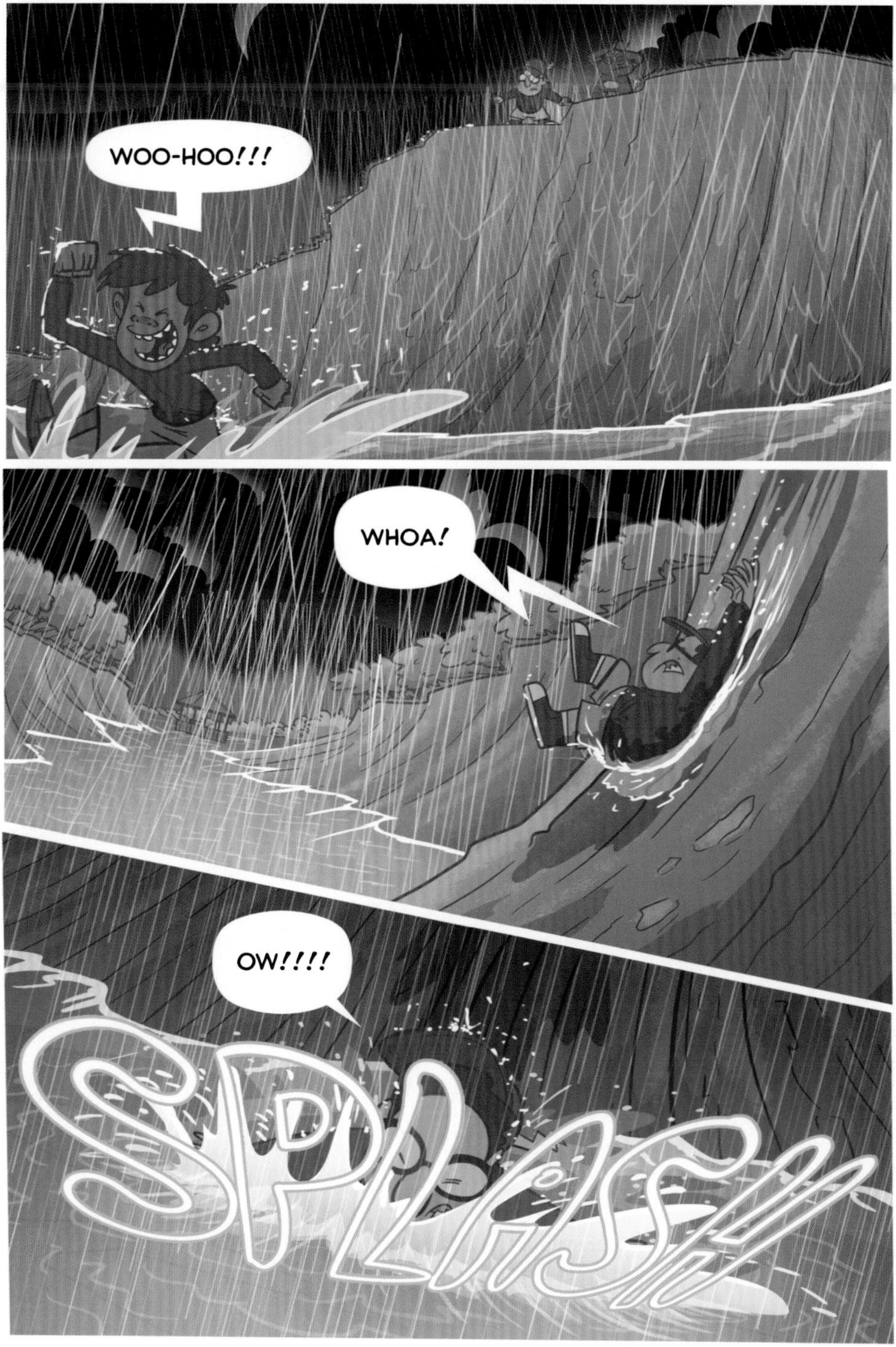
WOO-HOO!!!
WHOA!
OW!!!!
SPLASH

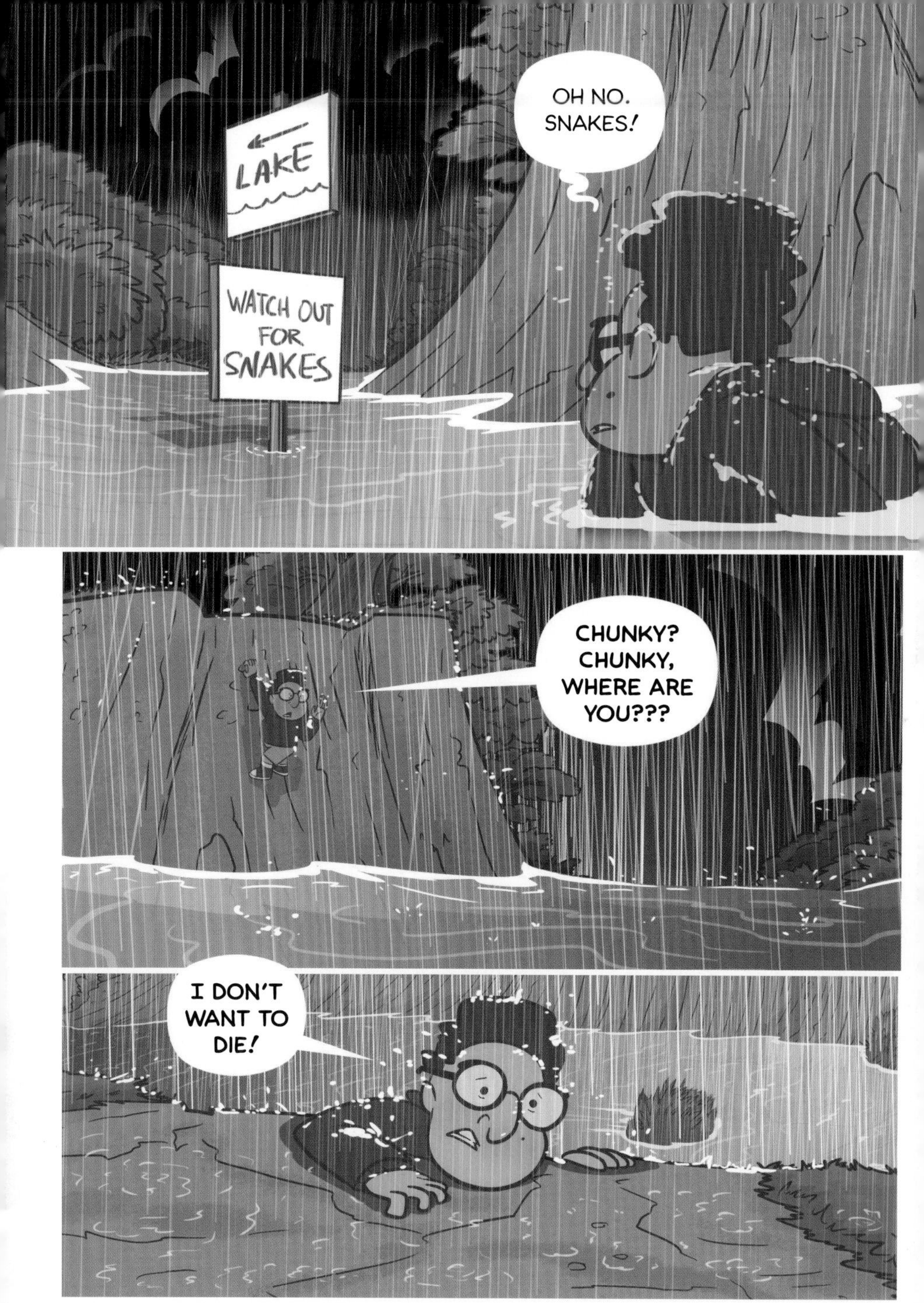
LAKE
WATCH OUT FOR SNAKES
OH NO. SNAKES!
CHUNKY? CHUNKY, WHERE ARE YOU???
I DON'T WANT TO DIE!

153

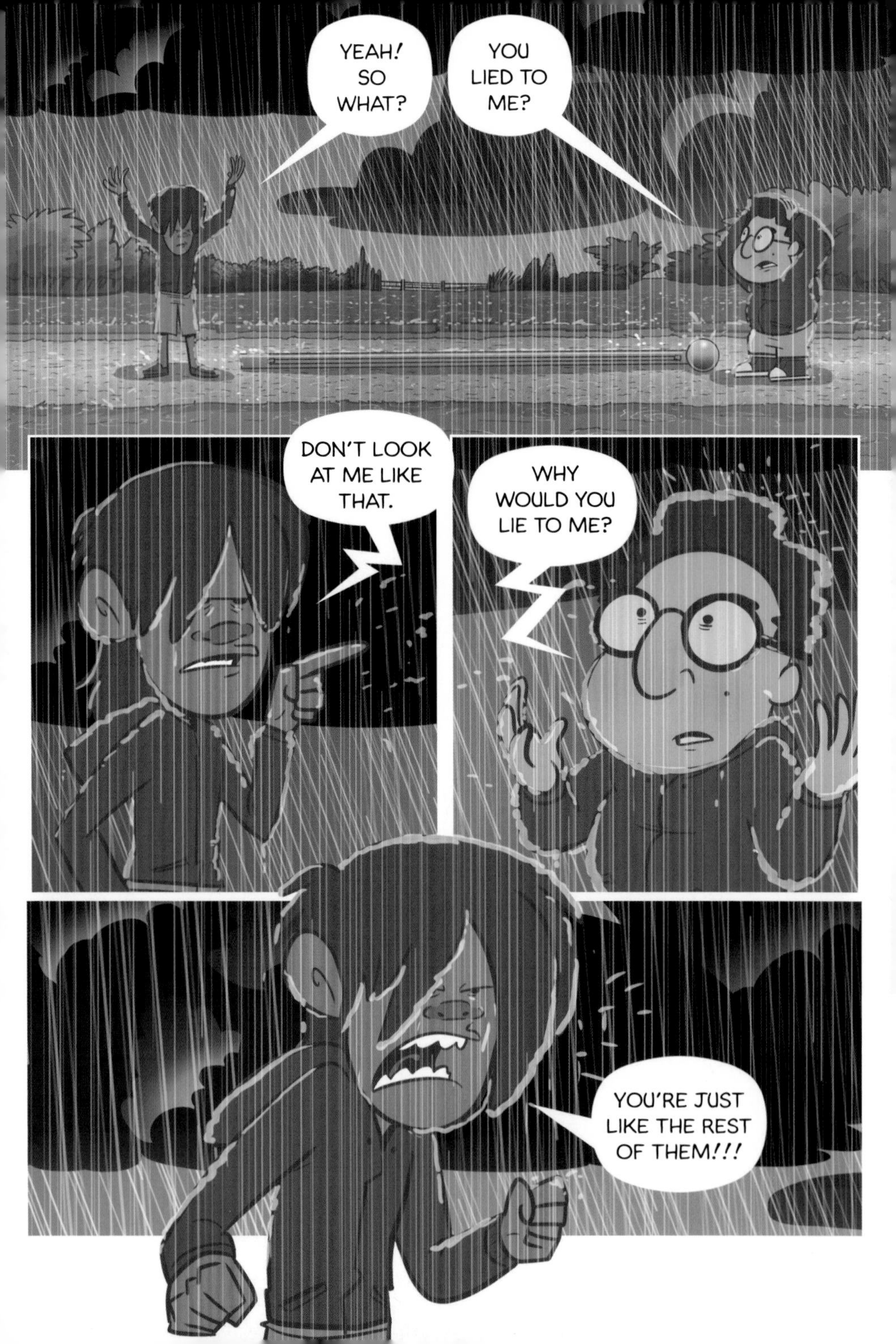
YEAH! SO WHAT?
YOU LIED TO ME?
DON'T LOOK AT ME LIKE THAT.
WHY WOULD YOU LIE TO ME?
YOU'RE JUST LIKE THE REST OF THEM!!!

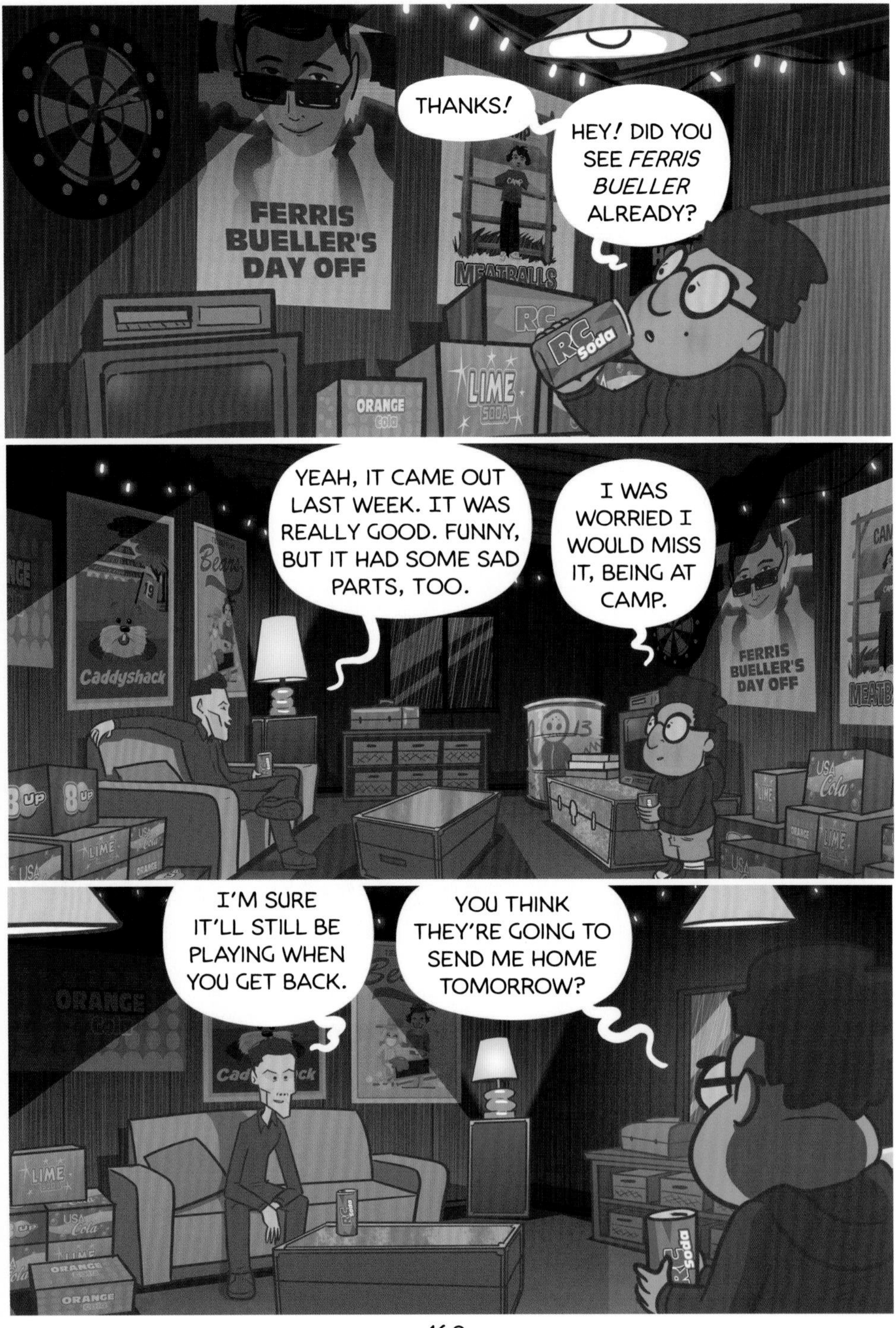
THANKS!
HEY! DID YOU SEE *FERRIS BUELLER* ALREADY?
FERRIS BUELLER'S DAY OFF
ORANGE Cola
LIME SODA
RC Soda
YEAH, IT CAME OUT LAST WEEK. IT WAS REALLY GOOD. FUNNY, BUT IT HAD SOME SAD PARTS, TOO.
I WAS WORRIED I WOULD MISS IT, BEING AT CAMP.
Caddyshack
FERRIS BUELLER'S DAY OFF
I'M SURE IT'LL STILL BE PLAYING WHEN YOU GET BACK.
YOU THINK THEY'RE GOING TO SEND ME HOME TOMORROW?

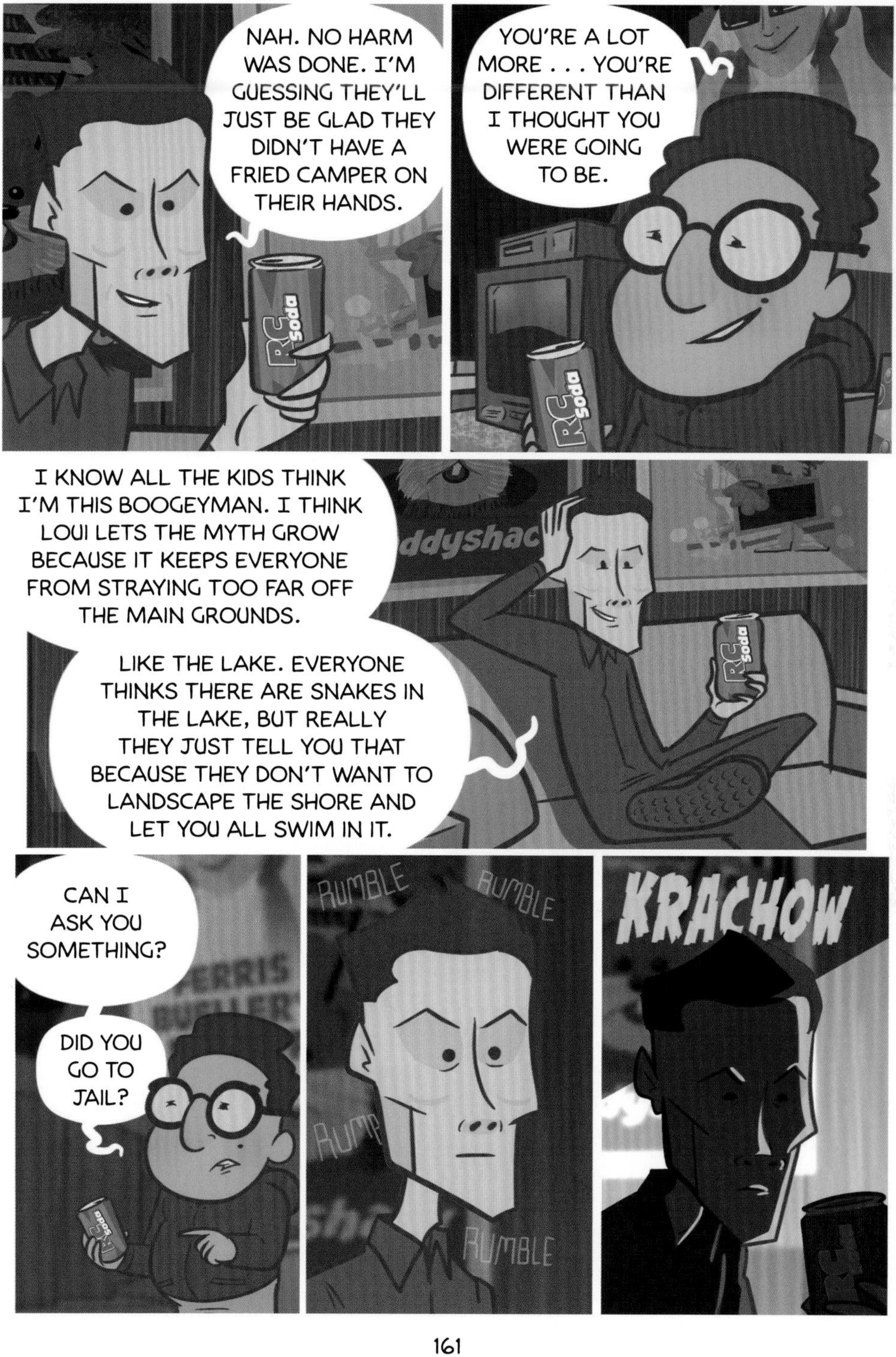
NAH. NO HARM WAS DONE. I'M GUESSING THEY'LL JUST BE GLAD THEY DIDN'T HAVE A FRIED CAMPER ON THEIR HANDS.
RC Soda
YOU'RE A LOT MORE . . . YOU'RE DIFFERENT THAN I THOUGHT YOU WERE GOING TO BE.
RC Soda
I KNOW ALL THE KIDS THINK I'M THIS BOOGEYMAN. I THINK LOUI LETS THE MYTH GROW BECAUSE IT KEEPS EVERYONE FROM STRAYING TOO FAR OFF THE MAIN GROUNDS.
LIKE THE LAKE. EVERYONE THINKS THERE ARE SNAKES IN THE LAKE, BUT REALLY THEY JUST TELL YOU THAT BECAUSE THEY DON'T WANT TO LANDSCAPE THE SHORE AND LET YOU ALL SWIM IN IT.
ddyshac
RC Soda
CAN I ASK YOU SOMETHING?
DID YOU GO TO JAIL?
FERRIS
RC Soda
RUMBLE
RUMBLE
RUMBLE
KRACHOW

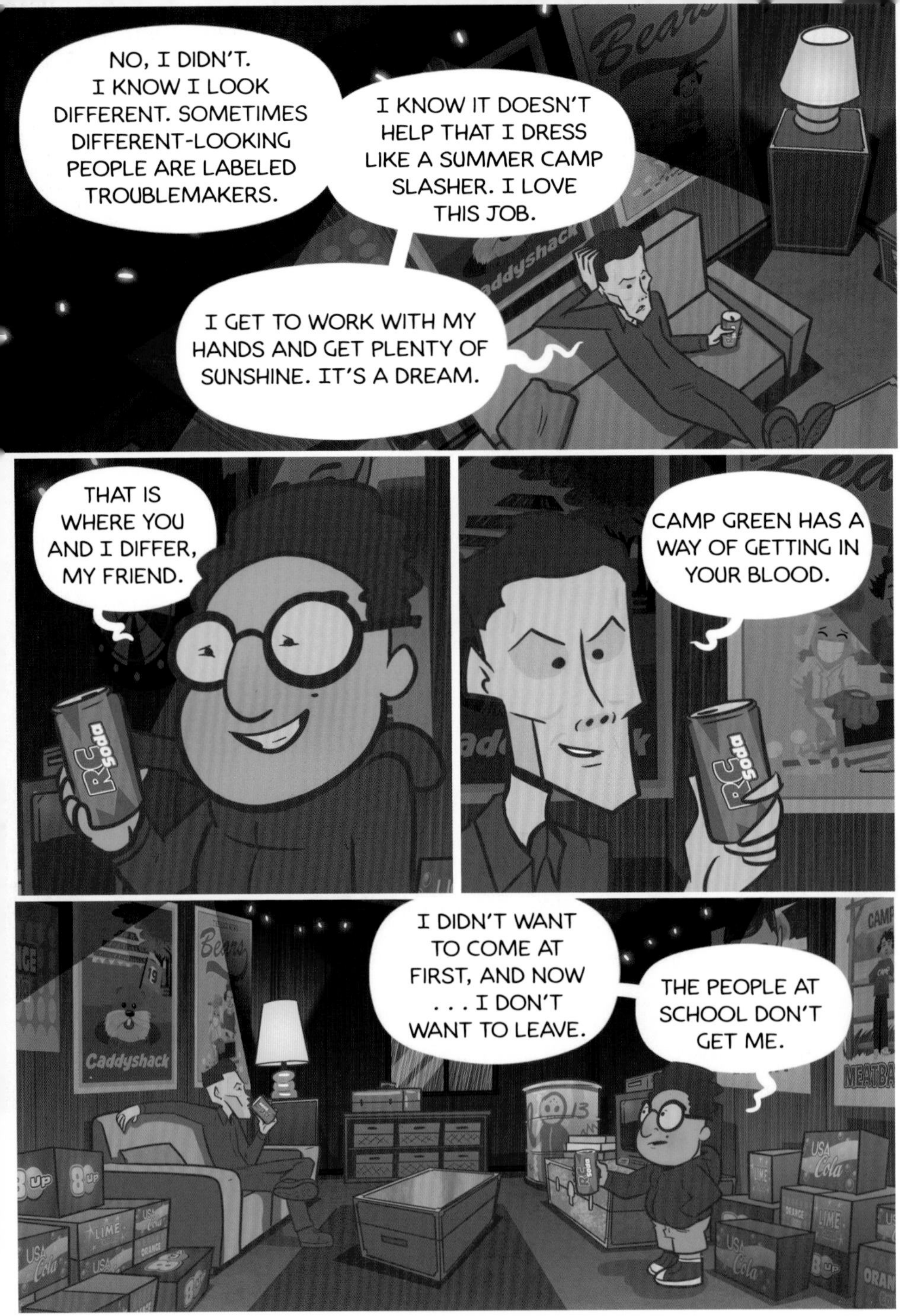
NO, I DIDN'T. I KNOW I LOOK DIFFERENT. SOMETIMES DIFFERENT-LOOKING PEOPLE ARE LABELED TROUBLEMAKERS.
I KNOW IT DOESN'T HELP THAT I DRESS LIKE A SUMMER CAMP SLASHER. I LOVE THIS JOB.
I GET TO WORK WITH MY HANDS AND GET PLENTY OF SUNSHINE. IT'S A DREAM.
THAT IS WHERE YOU AND I DIFFER, MY FRIEND.
CAMP GREEN HAS A WAY OF GETTING IN YOUR BLOOD.
I DIDN'T WANT TO COME AT FIRST, AND NOW . . . I DON'T WANT TO LEAVE.
THE PEOPLE AT SCHOOL DON'T GET ME.

HUDI on TRIAL

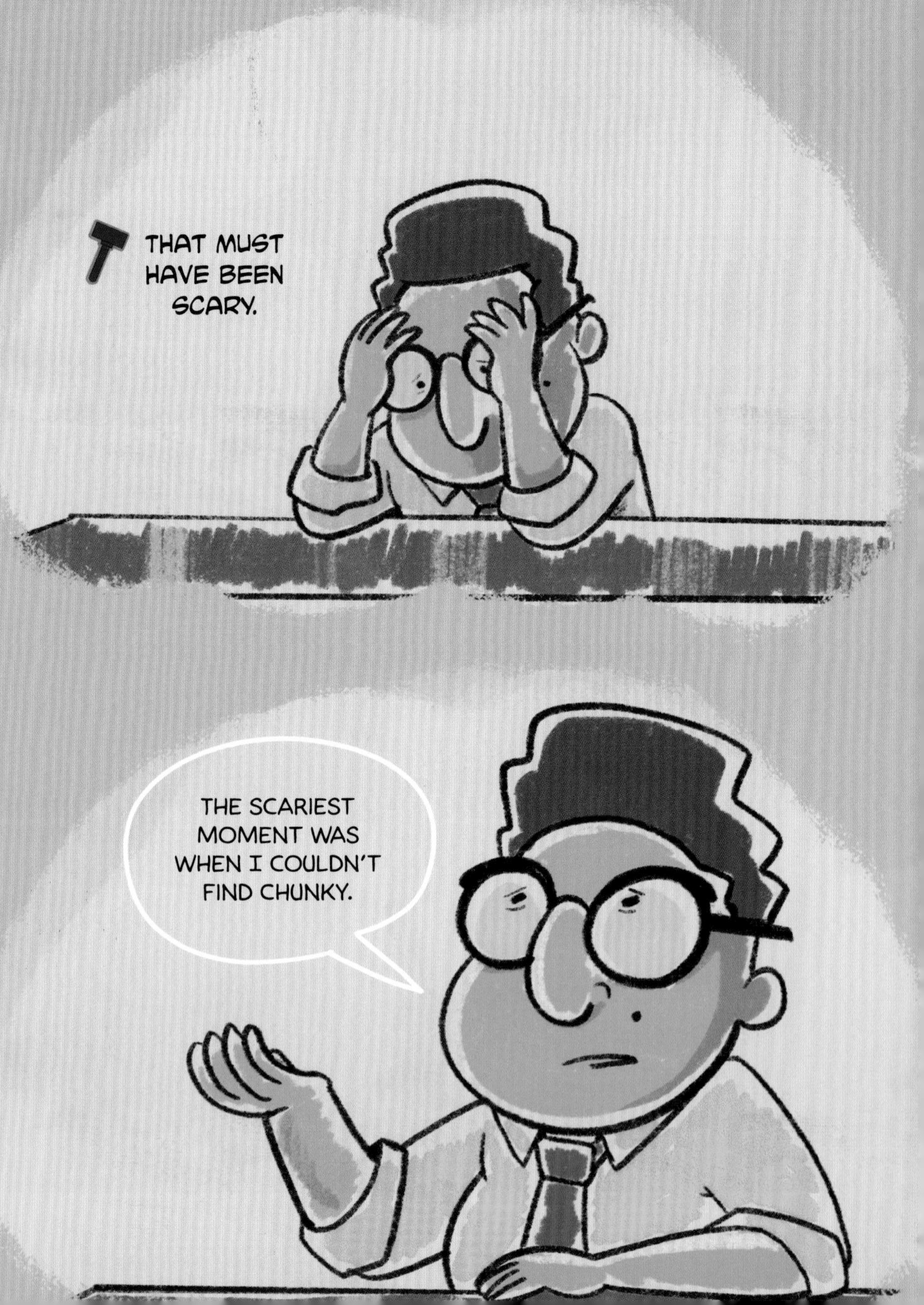
THAT MUST HAVE BEEN SCARY.
THE SCARIEST MOMENT WAS WHEN I COULDN'T FIND CHUNKY.

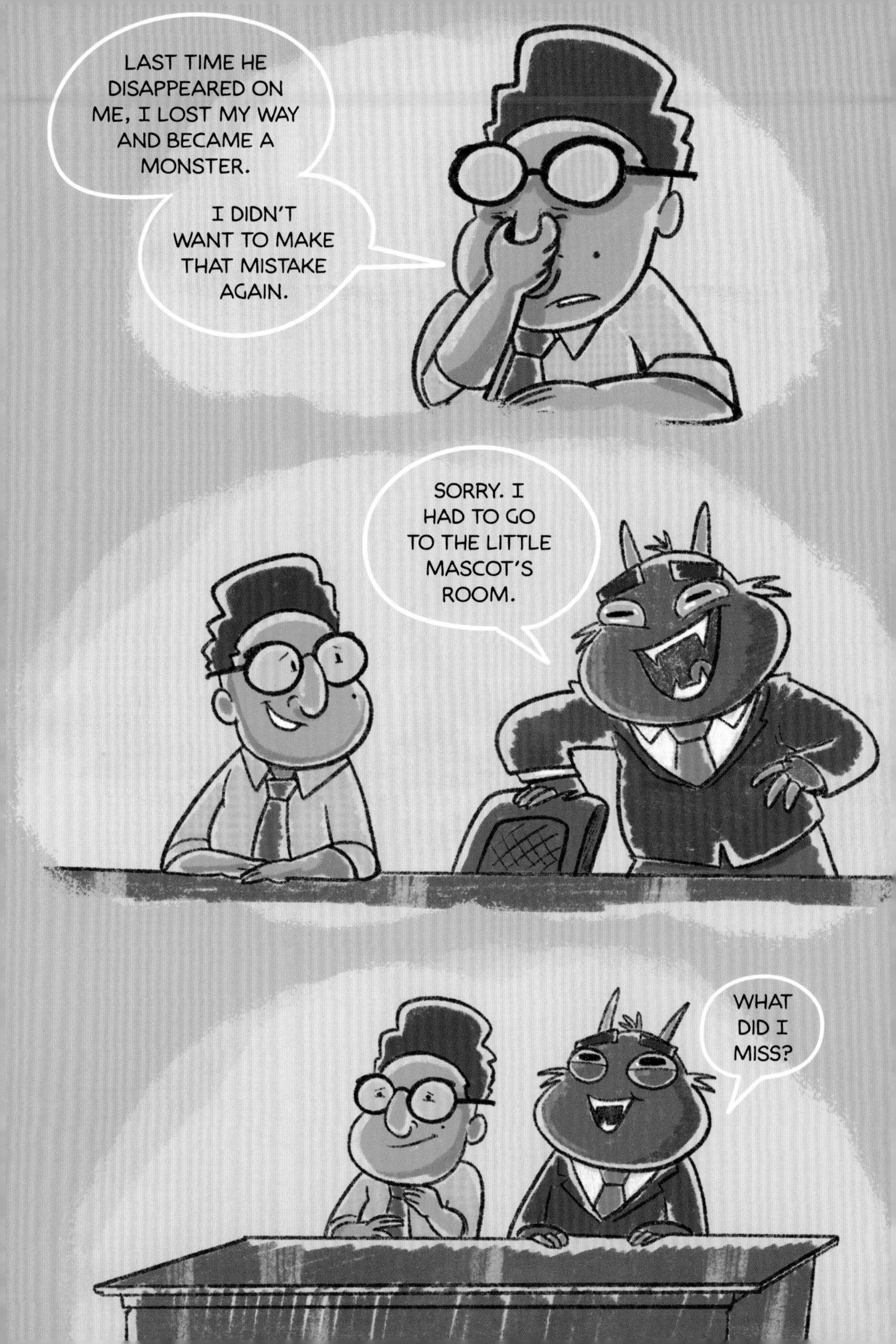
LAST TIME HE DISAPPEARED ON ME, I LOST MY WAY AND BECAME A MONSTER.
I DIDN'T WANT TO MAKE THAT MISTAKE AGAIN.
SORRY. I HAD TO GO TO THE LITTLE MASCOT'S ROOM.
WHAT DID I MISS?

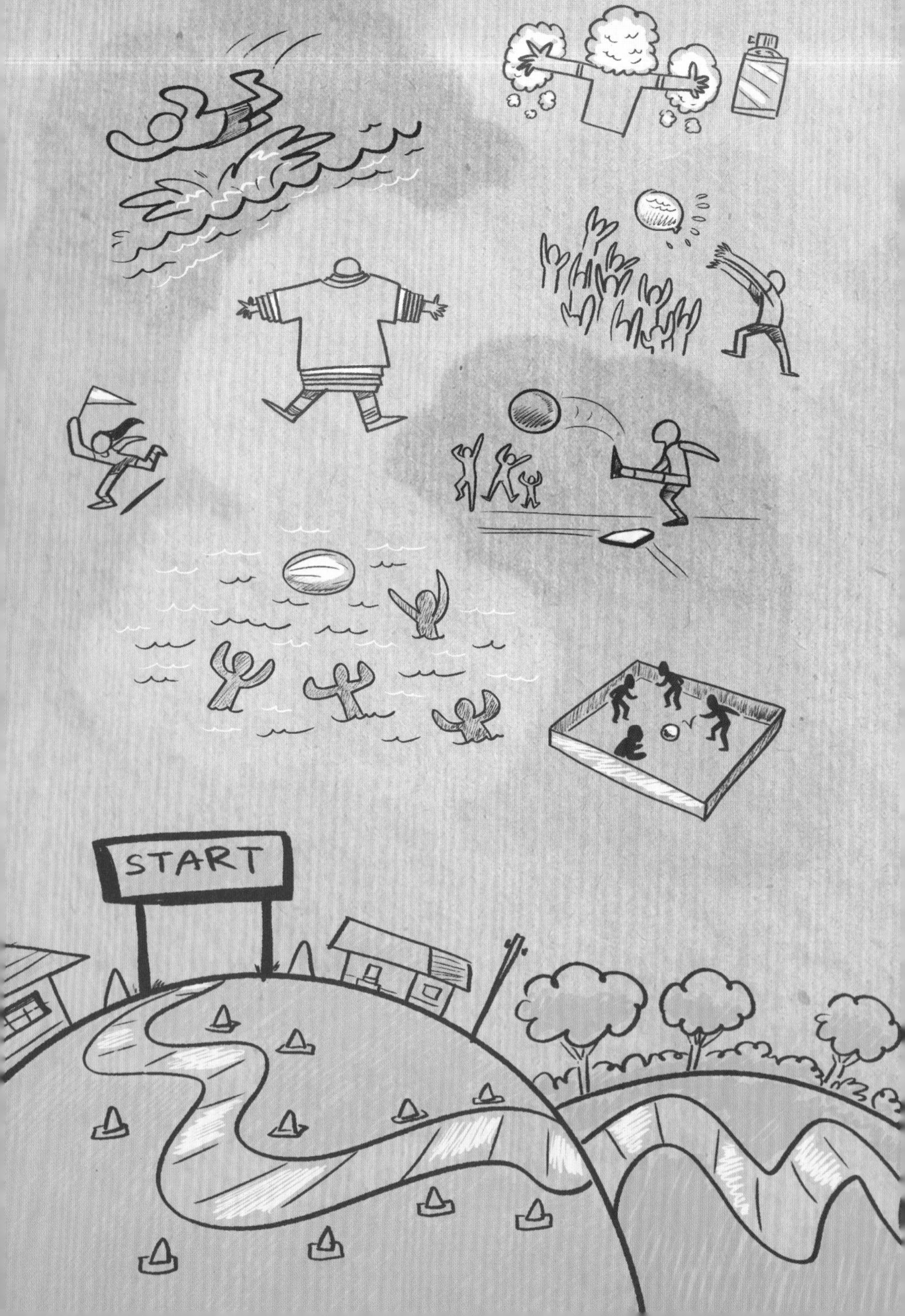
START

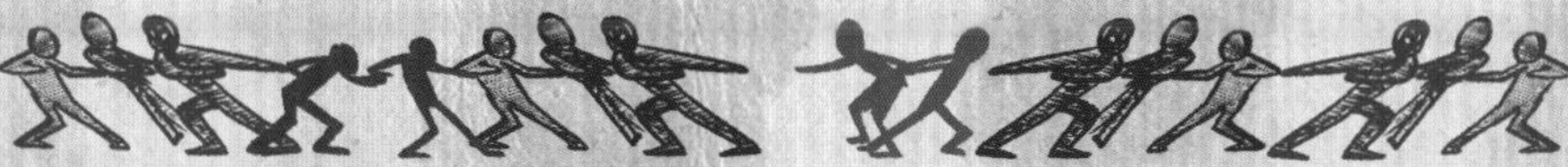

CHAPTER SIX
MACCABIAH

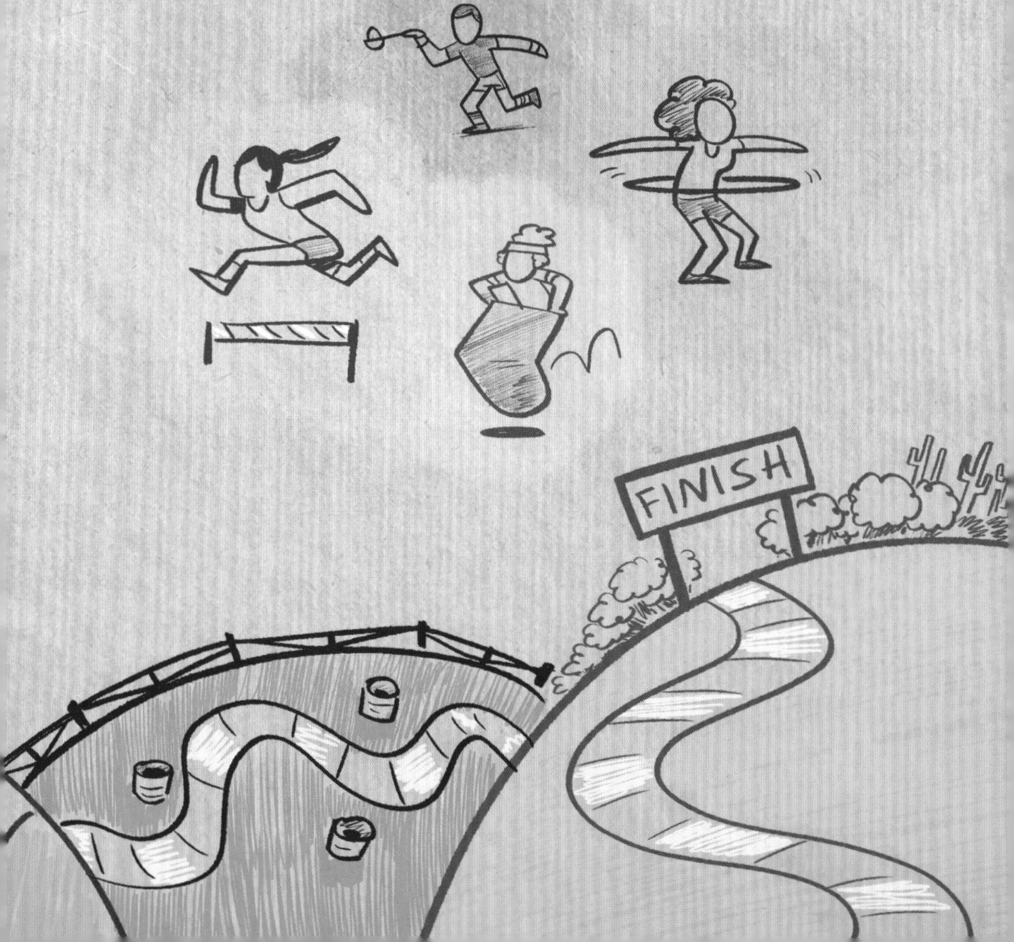
FINISH

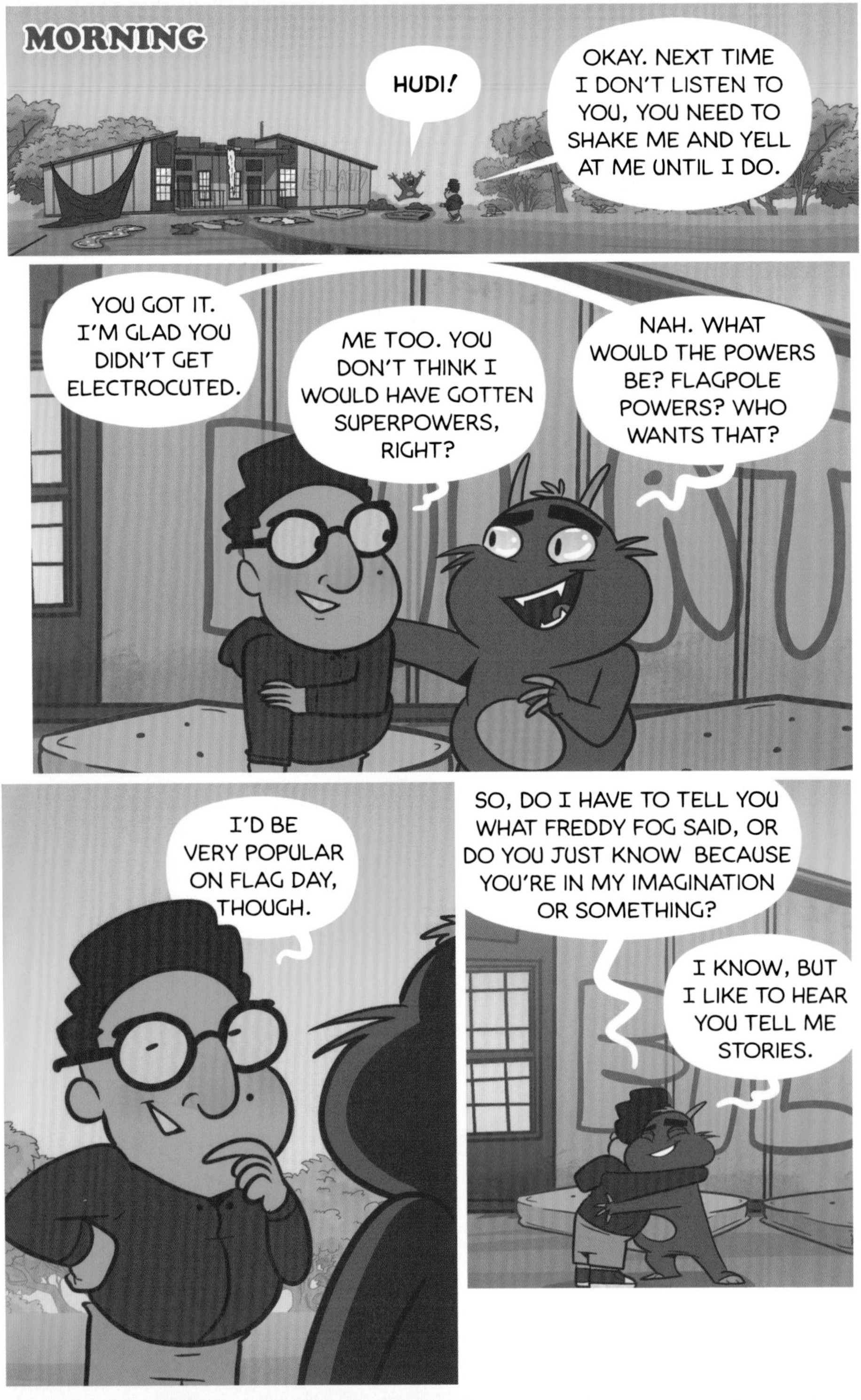
MORNING
HUDI!
OKAY. NEXT TIME I DON'T LISTEN TO YOU, YOU NEED TO SHAKE ME AND YELL AT ME UNTIL I DO.
YOU GOT IT. I'M GLAD YOU DIDN'T GET ELECTROCUTED.
ME TOO. YOU DON'T THINK I WOULD HAVE GOTTEN SUPERPOWERS, RIGHT?
NAH. WHAT WOULD THE POWERS BE? FLAGPOLE POWERS? WHO WANTS THAT?
I'D BE VERY POPULAR ON FLAG DAY, THOUGH.
SO, DO I HAVE TO TELL YOU WHAT FREDDY FOG SAID, OR DO YOU JUST KNOW BECAUSE YOU'RE IN MY IMAGINATION OR SOMETHING?
I KNOW, BUT I LIKE TO HEAR YOU TELL ME STORIES.

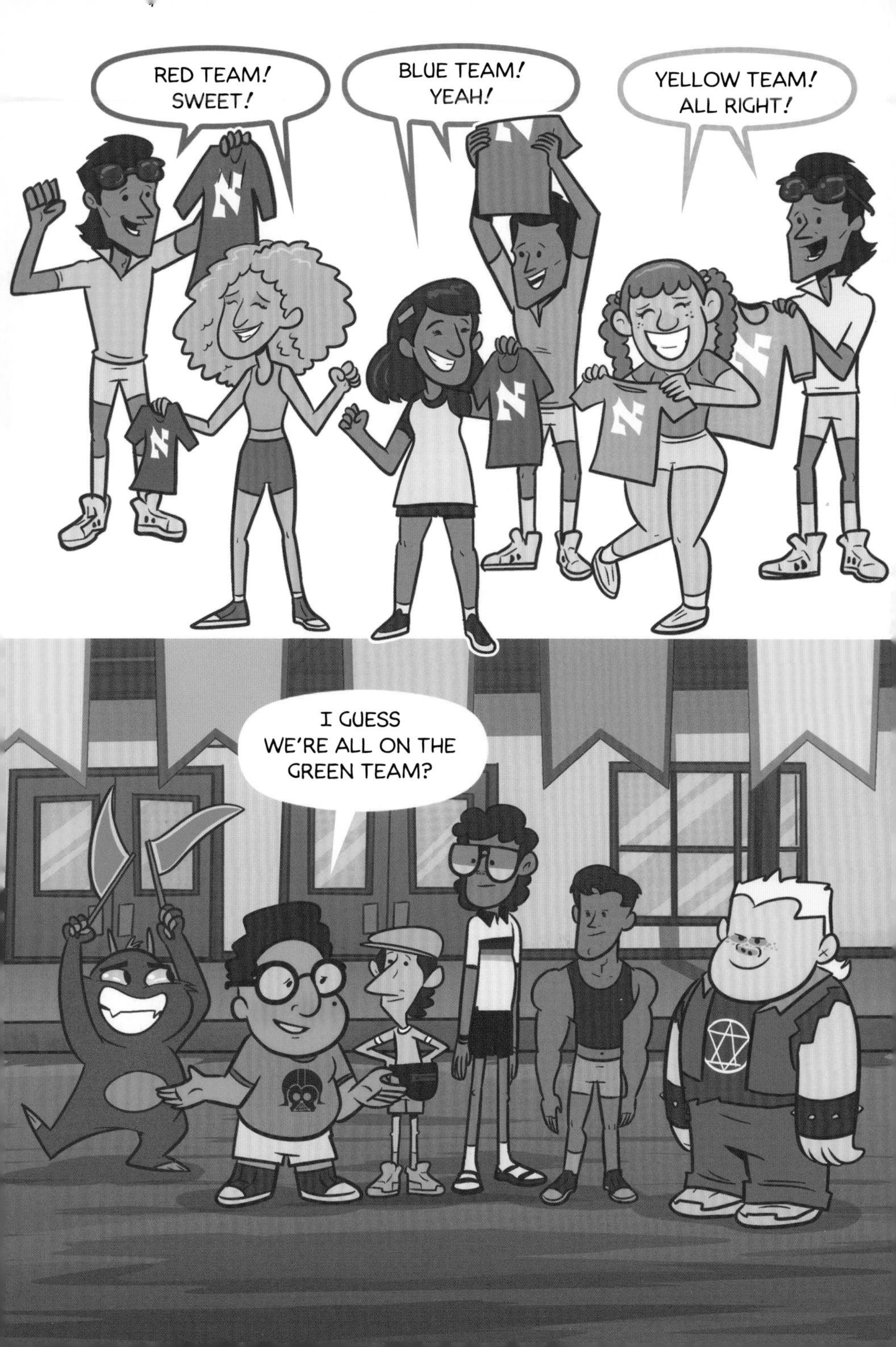
RED TEAM! SWEET!
BLUE TEAM! YEAH!
YELLOW TEAM! ALL RIGHT!
I GUESS WE'RE ALL ON THE GREEN TEAM?

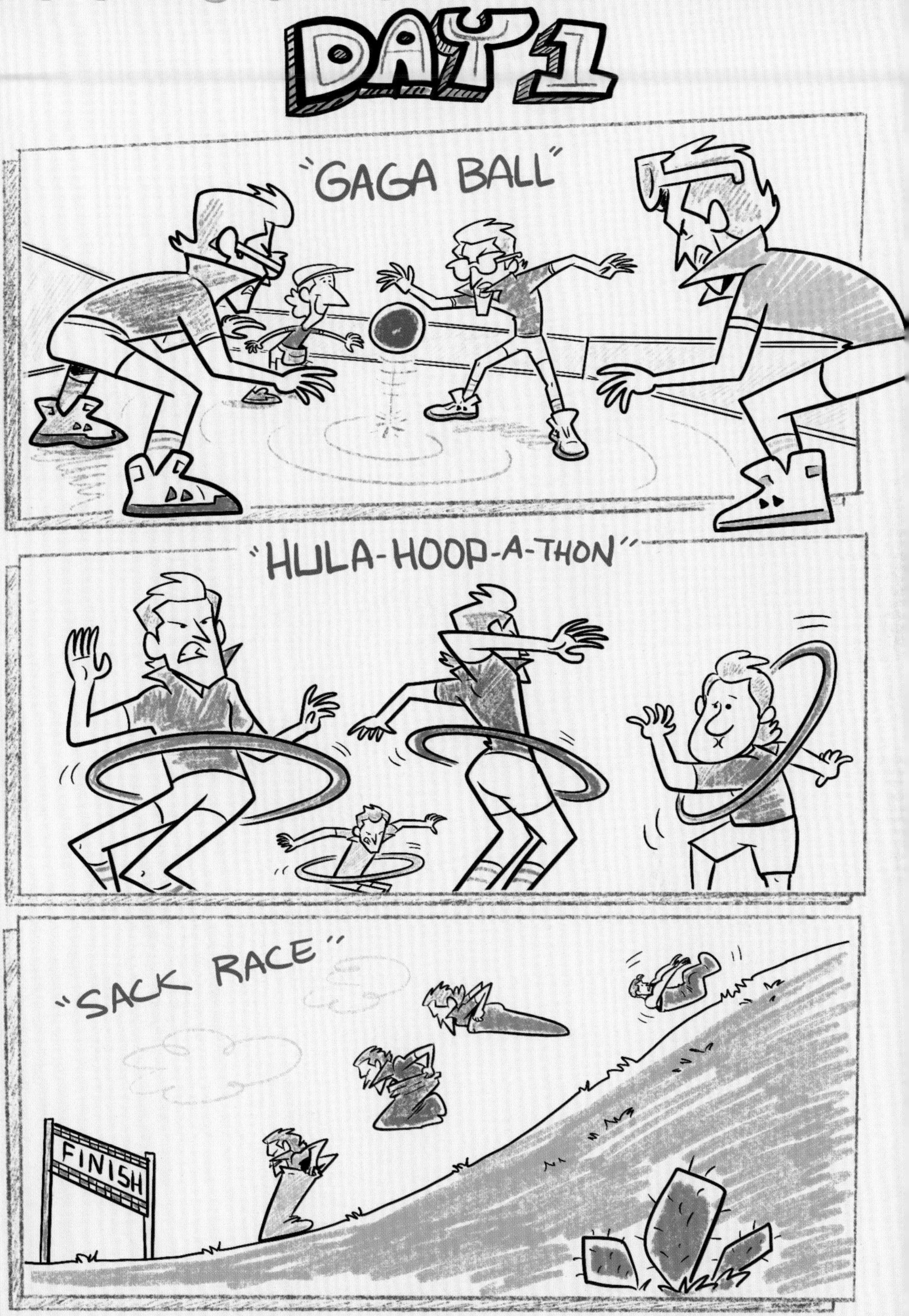
DAY 1
"GAGA BALL"
"HULA-HOOP-A-THON"
"SACK RACE"
FINISH

DAY 2

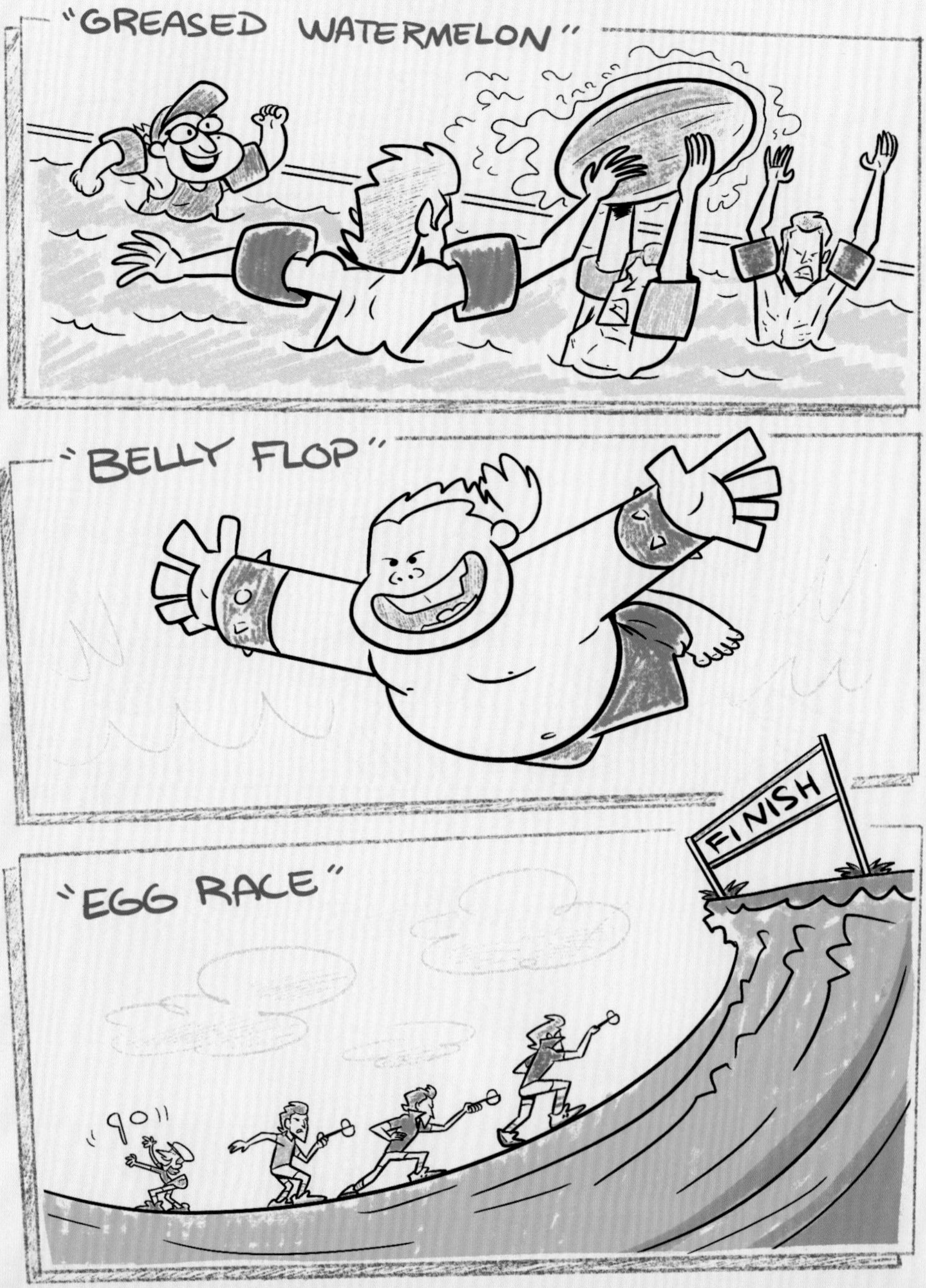
"GREASED WATERMELON"
"BELLY FLOP"
"EGG RACE"
FINISH
"GO!!"

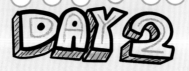

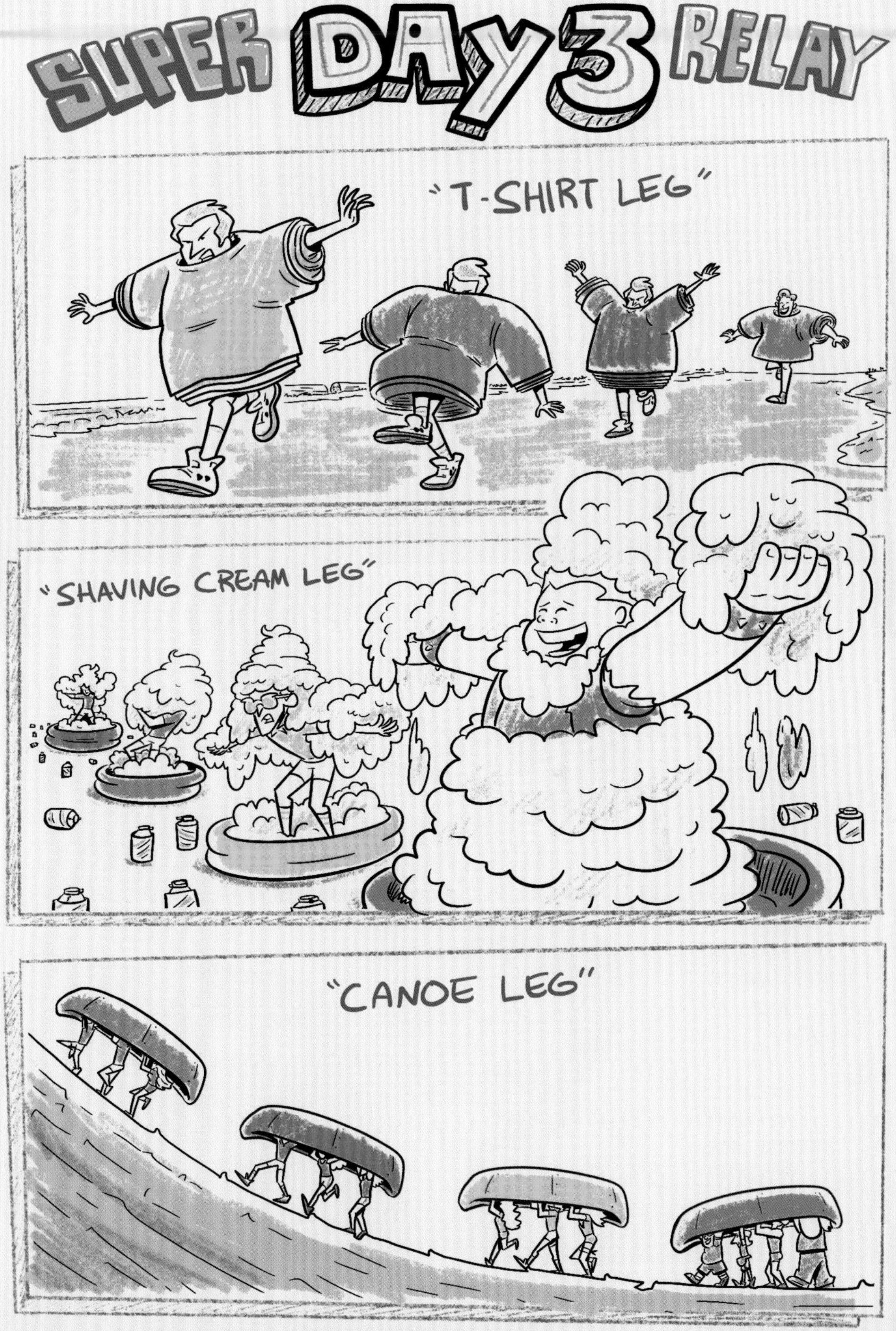
SUPER DAY 3 RELAY
"T-SHIRT LEG"
"SHAVING CREAM LEG"
"CANOE LEG"

180

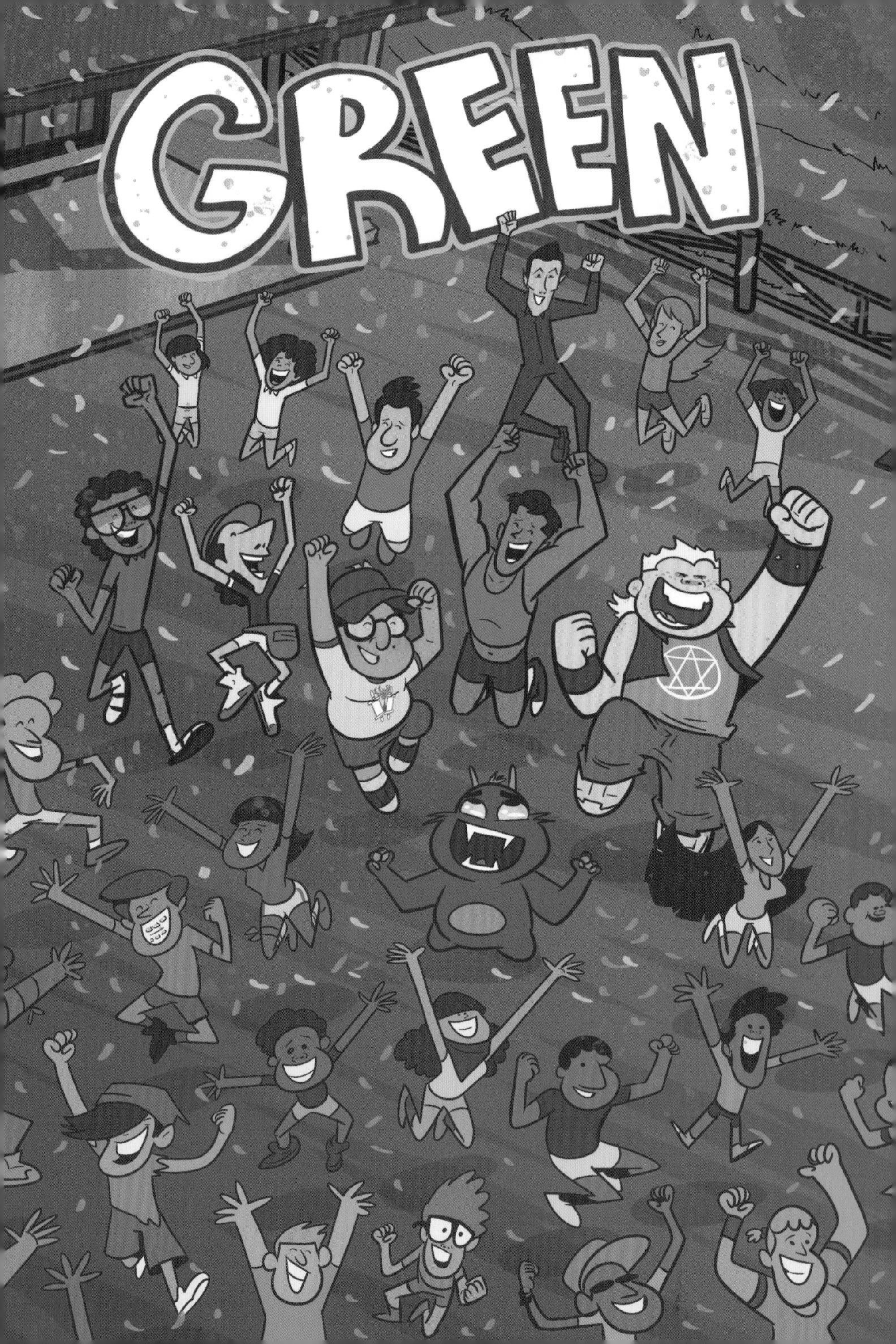
GREEN

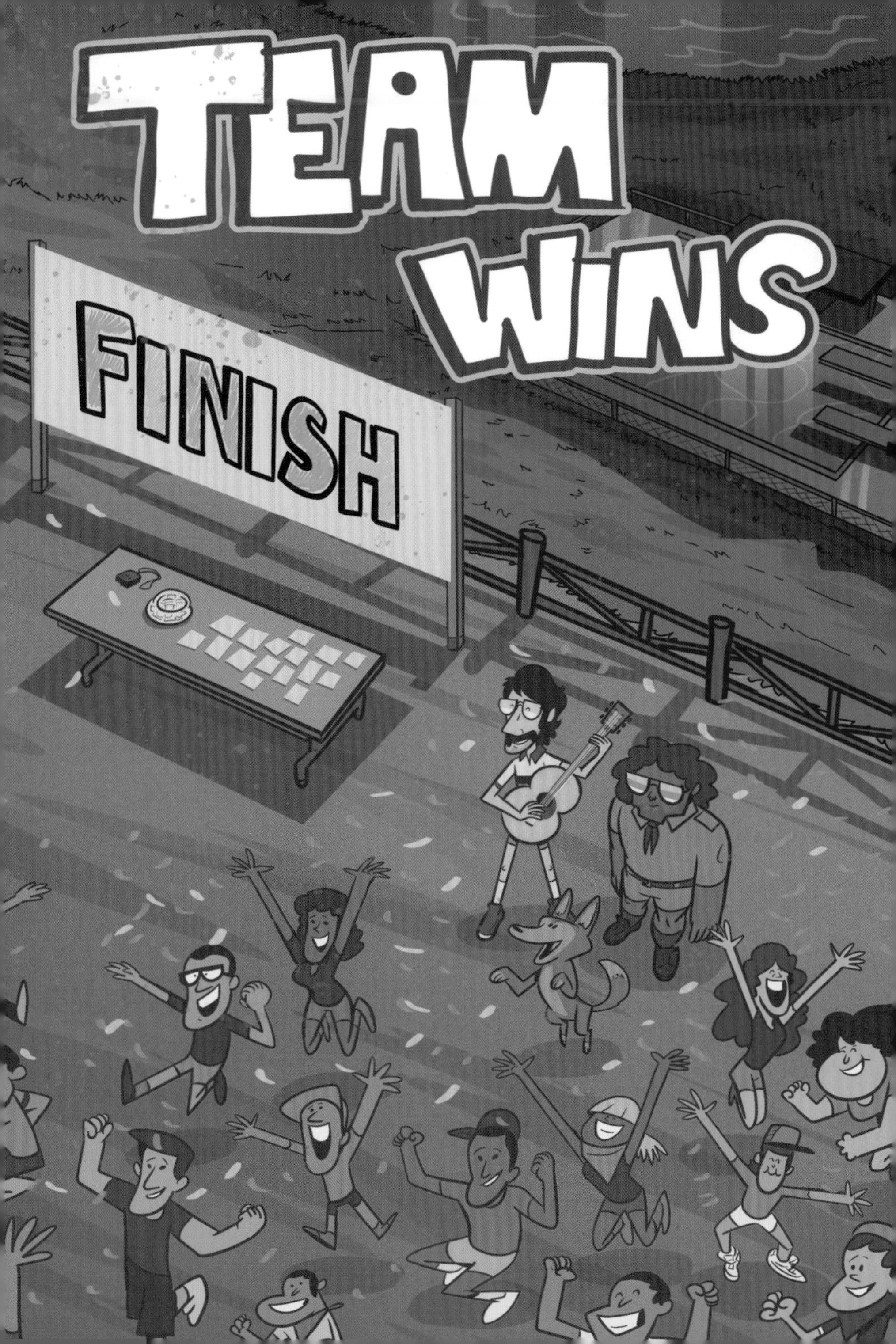
TEAM
WINS
FINISH

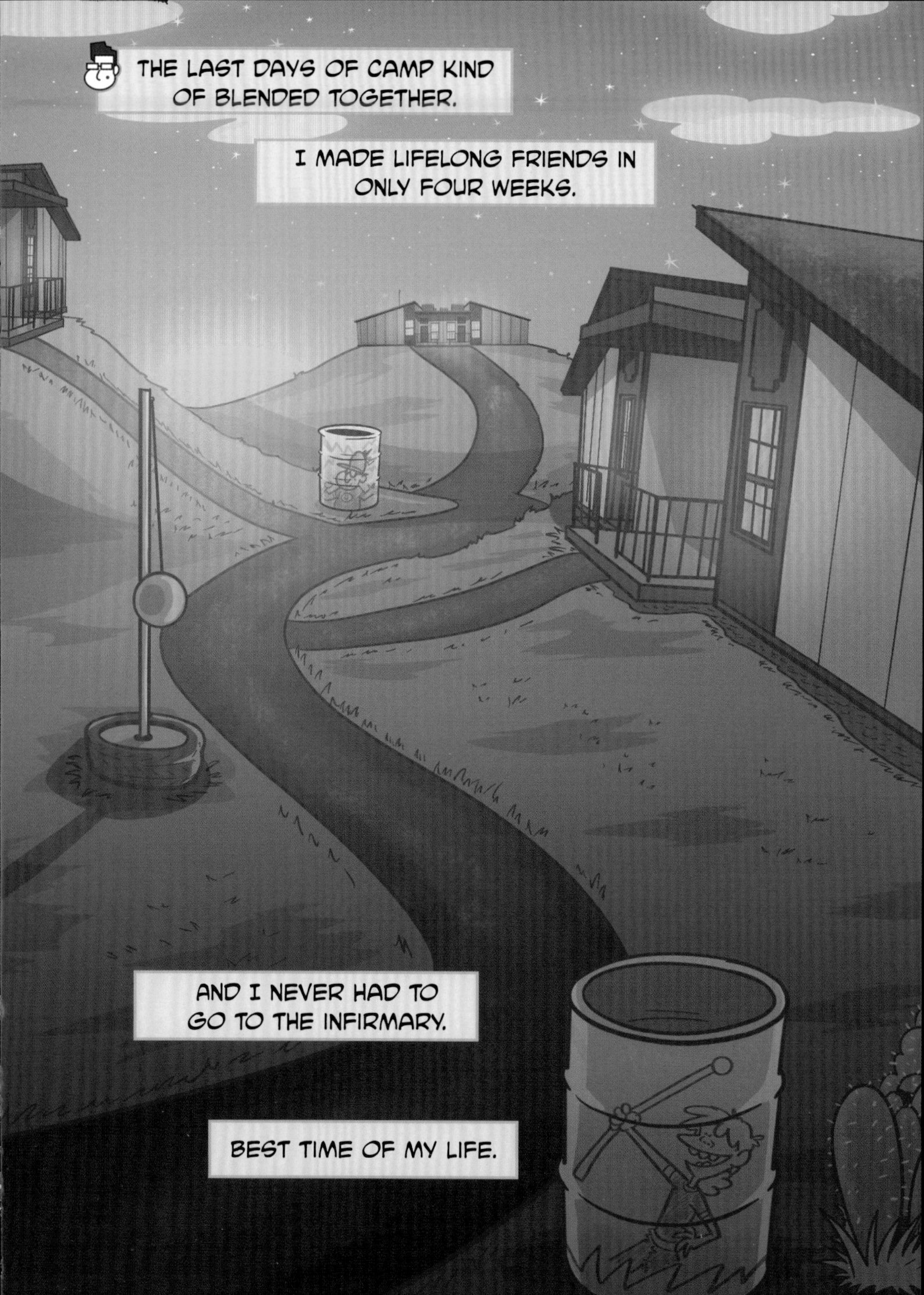
THE LAST DAYS OF CAMP KIND OF BLENDED TOGETHER.
I MADE LIFELONG FRIENDS IN ONLY FOUR WEEKS.
AND I NEVER HAD TO GO TO THE INFIRMARY.
BEST TIME OF MY LIFE.

HUDI on TRIAL

ARENT YOU LEAVING SOMETHING OUT?

I MENTIONED GETTING MY HAT BACK.

NO. ACCORDING TO TESTIMONY FROM OTHER CAMPERS, THE PIRATE FLAG ON FREDDY FOG'S SHED DOOR WAS MISSING AT SUMMER'S END. SO WHO TOOK THE FLAG? WHO WON THE PRANK WAR?

ALL I KNOW IS THAT I DIDN'T TAKE IT. BUT AT THE END OF THE DAY, IT DIDN'T MATTER WHO WON THE PRANK WAR.

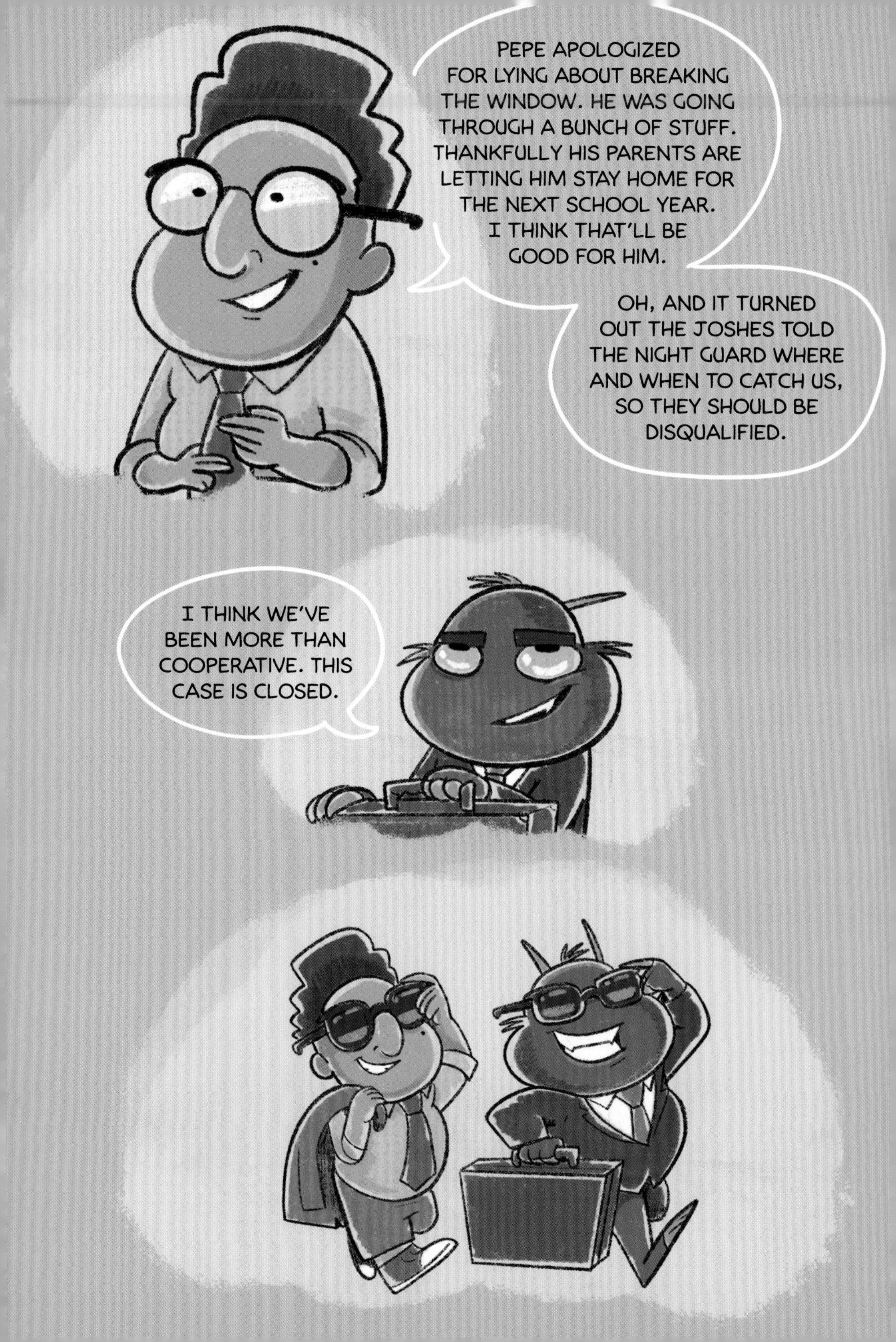
PEPE APOLOGIZED FOR LYING ABOUT BREAKING THE WINDOW. HE WAS GOING THROUGH A BUNCH OF STUFF. THANKFULLY HIS PARENTS ARE LETTING HIM STAY HOME FOR THE NEXT SCHOOL YEAR. I THINK THAT'LL BE GOOD FOR HIM.
OH, AND IT TURNED OUT THE JOSHES TOLD THE NIGHT GUARD WHERE AND WHEN TO CATCH US, SO THEY SHOULD BE DISQUALIFIED.
I THINK WE'VE BEEN MORE THAN COOPERATIVE. THIS CASE IS CLOSED.

CHAPTER SEVEN
BACK TO SCHOOL

A NOTE FROM PEPE GUZMAN

I am so honored to play such a prominent role in this highly entertaining book. As this story contains many true events, I just wish to point out that my bad behavior was all my own and not due to any indifference by my parents. I am one of those lucky people who knew that my parents loved me dearly.

I would also like to point out that if you asked a hundred of our fellow campers who was funnier, me or Yehudi, all of them would have said Yehudi. The part where people lined up to have Yehudi make fun of them happened daily. Never did someone speak to Yehudi and not smile. To put it simply, he brightened everyone's day with laughter and is the most popular person I have ever met. To be Robin to his Batman was the absolute pinnacle of camp life for me and something I treasure to this day.

This book and its predecessor (and all Yehudi's books!) not only show his great talent and humor but also his gift of making one smile, laugh, and just feel good.

–Pepe Guzman

A NOTE FROM YEHUDI

The real-life Chunky in my camp experience was my lifelong friend Lonnie Levitan. He was actually the third amigo and was the one on the shabbat stage with Pepe and me during the infamous Stars and Clouds Incident. It's still our inside joke that cracks us up to this day. While we did carry a flagpole during a lightning storm, I invented the scene in Freddy Fog's shed. There was a real-life groundskeeper for the camp, and I did buy a six-pack of RC Cola from him for twenty dollars, but his persona and his backstory were fictionalized for this book. To me he represents the misunderstood boogeyman, which ties into the way I felt I was treated in school.

If *Chunky* was about my journey as a middle grader finding my funny, then *Chunky Goes to Camp* is about finding my people. Meeting Pepe Guzman at the Jewish summer camp was like meeting an imaginary friend in real life. It's a miracle to meet someone and instantly be on the same wavelength, especially when it comes to comedy. Being a funny kid was great, but it also put a target on my back when it came to teachers who didn't get me.

For some reason I spent a lot of time in detention as a kid. I was not a bad kid, but the faculty of my school seemed to want to convince me I was. In fact, I was sent to detention for "jiving," and I was given the choice of being paddled by my vice principal or given more detention. I'm pretty sure they don't paddle kids anymore in public school, and it seemed barbaric at the time. I do have to say that I did have a handful of teachers who did get me and appreciated my humor.

Greene Family Camp was such a formative time in my life. My fellow bunkmates were all such oddballs, just like me. We were all weirdos. We didn't feel like we fit in with the other bunks, and I loved that about us. If any of you reading this book feel like you don't belong, I promise that you have a special tribe of people waiting for you somewhere, ready to cheer you on. Find your Chunky.

Special thanks to:

Ben Rosenthal
Amy Ryan
Laura Mock
Caitlin Lonning
Kristen Eckhardt
Alexandra Rakaczki
Charlie Olsen
Loui Dobin
Ludmilla and Gerardo
The Hoodis family
The Warfields
The Pueblitz Boys
Raina Telgemeier
Dave, Scoot & Brandon
Colby Sharp

Pepe Guzman and Yehudi Mercado

Wynnie, Yehudi, Gerardo (father), and Yoni Mercado